CONROY © 29.

CATTLE BRANDS

Ironclad Signatures

CATTLE BRANDS

Ironclad Signatures

By Jane Pattie

Foreword by Elmer Kelton

Introduction by Cheri Wolfe

BRIGHT SKY PRESS

Albany, Texas

bright sky press

Albany, Texas

10   9   8   7   6   5   4   3   2

Library of Congress Cataloging-in-Publication Data

Pattie, Jane, 1935–
    Cattle brands : ironclad signatures / by Jane Pattie.
        p. cm.
    Includes bibliographical references (p. 154).
    ISBN 0-9709987-7-5 / 978-0-9709987-7-4 (alk. paper)
1. Cattle brands—Texas—History. 2. Stiles, Leonard, 1920–2001.
3. Detectives—Texas—Biography. 4. Cattle stealing—Texas—Prevention—History. I. Title.

SF103.4.T4 P38 2002
636.2'0812'09764—dc21

2002018261

Photographs from the Cattle Raisers Museum, Texas and Southwestern Cattle Raisers Foundation, pp. ii, vi, xi–xii, xiv–xv, xix–xx, xxiv, xxviii, 6, 8, 14, 18, 20, 25, 32, 36, 38, 40, 43–45
Cover photograph by Geno Loro Jr.
Photographs by Watt M. Casey Jr., pp. 2, 10, 48
Photographs by Jane Pattie, pp. xvi, xxiii, 17
Photographs courtesy King Ranch Archives, King Ranch, Inc., pp. 26, 28, 31
Photograph courtesy Hartung Photo Collection, p. xxv
Photograph courtesy Stiles Collection, p. viii

Book and cover design with brand illustrations by Isabel Lasater Hernandez

Printed in China

This book is dedicated to Mary Stiles—
as Leonard would have liked.

From the Cattle Raisers Museum Permanent Collection

CONTENTS

Leonard Stiles (1920–2001)

Foreword

Historian J. Evetts Haley called cattle brands "the heraldry of the range." The brand has come to mean more than simply a sign of ownership. It is like a flag, an icon, a symbol of the owner or of the ranch it represents.

Jane Pattie, who long ago won her spurs as a historian of the cattle and horse industries, has fashioned this book around the best collection of branding irons anywhere—the Leonard Stiles Collection at the Cattle Raisers Museum of the Texas and Southwestern Cattle Raisers Foundation in Fort Worth, Texas. The late Leonard Stiles, an outstanding cowman and horseman, gathered them over most of his adult life. The history of these brands is, in a very strong sense, the history of the Southwestern cattle industry.

Each of us sees these brands in the light of our own individual experiences. When I was a boy, growing up on the McElroy Ranch near Crane, Texas, most of the ranches were referred to by the brands they used more than by the name or names of their owners. And usually the brand's name was stated in plural form. The McElroy was known as the Jigger Ys. In the same general area were such ranches as the K Bars and the Cs. My grandfather branded the Hackamore N, which included a bar across the nose. When it haired over the hair stood up and curled over, making the cattle look as if they bore a hackamore.

In an earlier time the Jigger Ys also used a "butt bar," a line branded across the rump. The explanation was that the cattle were so wild you usually got just a glimpse of their south end as they stampeded northward into the brush. You rarely saw the brand on side or hip unless you were ready for a fast, hard ride.

Every ranch town of any consequence had a blacksmith shop which, among other things, made branding irons. Midland was the ranching headquarters town in our area. The blacksmith shop was operated by Czech immigrant John Pliska, a man of diverse mechanical and artistic talents. In his younger days, inspired by the Wright brothers, he had built an airplane. He flew his little plane around Midland, taking up sightseers, until a bad crash convinced his wife to put her foot down. For as long as the blacksmith shop stood, that old plane hung from the smoky rafters for all to see. It has since been restored and is on permanent display at the Midland airport.

But what fascinated most of us youngsters more than the plane was the vast number of brands burned on the inner walls of that shop. When Pliska fashioned an iron, he would test it before he let it go. His walls were like an encyclopedia of brands from ranches all over the Midland-Odessa country and west into New Mexico. When the shop was demolished, the doors with their dozens of brands were salvaged and placed in a local museum.

From the ornate brands of the early Spanish cowmen to the simpler and more utilitarian irons used today, each has a story worth telling. Each reminds us of an open-handed way of life that seems to be slipping from our grasp. It is a way of life that still has much to teach us about individual freedom and the entrepreneurial spirit exemplified by those enterprising cattlemen who were our forebears.

It is a legacy we should not let go.

Elmer Kelton

San Angelo, Texas

For well over a century, cowboys have put in many a long day during the spring work on the Pitchfork Ranch in West Texas, ca. 1983.

School children gather at an exhibit in the Cattle Raisers Museum as they learn the history of the cattle industry as illustrated by the Leonard Stiles branding iron collection.

Introduction

For 125 years, the Texas and Southwestern Cattle Raisers Association (TSCRA) has been catching and convicting cattle thieves. Founded during the era of the great trail drives by a group of ranchers determined to put a stop to cattle rustling, TSCRA today employs thirty-one Field Inspectors—Special Texas and Oklahoma Rangers who investigate ranch theft and protect those involved in the cattle business—and eighty livestock market inspectors. We are unique in that regard.

It is no coincidence that Leonard Stiles started collecting branding irons just two years after he went to work as a TSCRA Field Inspector in 1950. His interest in irons, Leonard said simply back then, "is just part of my job. Brand identification is what I do—I'm at it 24 hours a day." But few Field Inspectors, even those as dedicated as TSCRA's own Special Rangers, took the time to stop every time they saw an unfamiliar brand and to investigate whose it was. Leonard always did.

An outstanding Field Inspector, Leonard made many friends in the cattle business. During the eleven years he worked for TSCRA, Leonard collected the majority of his irons. All were gifts. He was proud of the fact that he never bought or bartered for an iron. In most cases, it was the original owner or a descendant who donated it. Leonard believed that ranchers' respect for TSCRA made it easier for him to gather the branding irons.

Leonard's great gift of 1,096 irons first came to the Cattle Raisers Museum in 1988. But forty years earlier, he had begun sharing what would be his life's work with TSCRA by mounting a branding iron display at our annual convention. Even after Leonard left the Association's employ in 1961, he never missed a convention if he could help it. His rope was tied hard and fast—and for that we are grateful.

Leonard's involvement and dedication was evident in the meticulous documentation that accompanied his collection. Once he acquired a brand, whenever he happened across anything relating to the piece—personal stories or stories about the ranch—Leonard added the information to his growing files. Only someone with a lifelong involvement with western history and culture, we felt, should be entrusted with the monumental task of sorting through Leonard's folders and gleaning the material for this book. Better still, award winning author Jane Pattie is a personal friend of the Stiles family. We are delighted that Jane undertook this project and that Bright Sky Press, with its own brand and historic ranching connections, is the publisher. Many of the historic photographs we added from our own W. T. Waggoner Memorial Library.

Leonard Stiles considered his branding irons to be gifts from the ranchers he served. Donating his collection to the Cattle Raisers Museum was, he felt, "a life's dream come true." That's the kind of man he was. With *Cattle Brands: Ironclad Signatures*, the Texas and Southwestern Cattle Raisers Foundation shares these gifts, greater still because they passed through the hands of Leonard Stiles.

Cheri Wolfe, Ph.D.

Museum & Library Director

Fort Worth, Texas

The sign on the fence identifies the ranch owner as a member of Texas & Southwestern Cattle Raisers Association and notifies would-be thieves that this ranch property is protected by the Association's Field Inspectors.

John A. Stryker photo from the Cattle Raisers Museum Permanent Collection
Cowboys brand calves at the SMS Ranch near Stamford, Texas. Derived from the initials of Svante Magnus
Swenson, the SMS brand is one of the earliest registered in West Texas (brand number 682), ca. 1940.

Cowboys on the 6666 Ranch catch a colt during the annual colt branding at ranch headquarters in King County, Texas. The ranch's horse brand is an **L** on the left shoulder, the dam's number on the left jaw, and the year foaled on the left butt, ca. 1962.

Acknowledgments
Much Obliged

How do you say "much obliged" to an industry? That is what it would take to say thank you to every rancher who shared his history and every writer who recorded his stories, so I'll just give them all a tip of the hat and say thanks individually to those immediately responsible for making this book possible.

The first two on the list are, of course, Leonard Stiles, and his best friend and wife of sixty years, Mary. Only a man as respected by his peers as Leonard Stiles could have gained the friendship and confidence of ranchers, large and small, throughout the country and the world. Every iron in his collection was important to him.

I first met Leonard in the 1960s when I was on a trip to South Texas with my good friends, Connie and Louis "Tex" Fields, owner of Western Feeders in Fort Worth. We stopped by the King Ranch to say hello to Tex's friend, Leonard Stiles, and found him shipping heifers at Plomo Pens. That was the beginning of my long friendship with a man I came to admire very much, as did everyone who knew him—everyone, that is, except cattle thieves. It was through Leonard that I first met the legendary TSCRA inspector and rancher, Graves Peeler, a man as unique as the Texas that spawned him—a man who recognized a kindred soul in the trustworthy Stiles.

Leonard's knowledge of brands was vast and his enthusiasm was catching, so we often looked at his collection, and I wrote articles about it and about Leonard. Recently, when Cattle Raisers Museum Director, Dr. Cheri Wolfe, asked if I'd be interested in writing a book on the Stiles collection that was at the museum, I said, "Of course!"

It is only natural that the publisher should be Bright Sky Press of Albany, Texas, and New York. The highly respected cowman, Watt Matthews, died after living almost a century on the Lambshead Ranch. Ardon Judd, Watt's nephew and husband of Bright Sky CEO, Rue Judd, is now the managing partner of Lambshead Ranch, and with members of the Matthews family, strives to continue the legacy. Rue divides her time between New York and Texas, and her Bright Sky Press brand, ꝏ, is recorded with the county clerk in Shackelford County.

Many thanks to my friend and editor, Fran Vick of Dallas, who patiently looked at cattle brands; to my daughter, Elise Reed, who worked her computer magic on the index; and to Cattle Raisers Museum docent Reece Coppenger whose interview with Leonard added new insights to the story.

My special thanks go to my longtime friend and inspiration, the highly respected author and Westerner, Elmer Kelton, for his contribution to this book. My thanks also to Carol Williams of Fort Worth, longtime educational director of the Cattle Raisers Museum who was there when the Stiles Collection came to the museum. She has been generous with her time and knowledge, and with the information on the collection that she had carefully stored in her computer, some of which is repeated here.

Last but not least, my thanks to Leonard and Mary Stiles and their family for furnishing the information that makes this book possible.

It is through the interest and efforts of Cattle Raisers Museum Director Dr. Cheri Wolfe that this book is being published by Bright Sky Press. The shipping date is at hand, and with the Bright Sky brand on the book, we're hoping to make delivery during the Texas & Southwestern Cattle Raisers Association's Convention in Fort Worth, Texas, in March of 2002, celebrating the Association's 125th anniversary.

Jane Pattie

Aledo, Texas

These ranch women handle the annual branding chores. Janet Halchett Baird (center) was the twenty-ninth Rodeo Queen at the Big Springs, Texas, rodeo, ca. 1935.

TSCRA Inspector Leonard Stiles explains the art of branding to visitors from San German, Puerto Rico, at an exhibit of his branding iron collection at the 1960 Texas State Fair.

Preface

Webster's definition of a brand is "a mark made on cattle with a hot iron to show ownership." It is a cowman's ironclad signature, and there is no question to whom that animal belongs. Since Cortés brought the first horses to this continent and ran cattle branded with his **Three Crosses**, billions of animals have carried millions of variations of these marks of ownership throughout Texas and the West. For fifty years, Texan Leonard Stiles studied cattle brands as part of his business and for his enjoyment. And the two began at almost the same time.

Stiles was hired by the Texas & Southwestern Cattle Raisers Association (TSCRA) in 1950 as a "field inspector"—a cattle detective or brand inspector, if you like, and he worked in that capacity for eleven years. It was during this time that he became interested in brands and their history. Each mark has a story that represents a cattleman's life. When Stiles showed an interest in a rancher's brand, the man often told him its history and gave him an iron.

Stiles's district covered six counties southwest of Houston. When he was checking cattle shipments or theft cases or counting cattle for estate settlements, he'd often find an old branding iron hanging in a tree or see one that had been discarded and left at the working pens or standing forgotten and dusty in an old barn. The owner would give it to him, and Leonard would write down its story. When he returned to his home in Sweeny, he tagged the iron and carefully filed away the information.

He was given his first branding iron, the **Fleur de Lis L**, in 1952, and his collection grew to 1,096 irons. He never bought an iron, sold one, or traded one. This unique collection represents the history of the cattle business. It began as irons mainly from the coastal area and South Texas, since that was Stiles's country, but there are also branding irons from other parts of Texas and other states and countries. Portions of the collection have been exhibited throughout the United States and Europe, and they always draw a crowd, because they represent the legendary cowman. In 1965 during September alone, 100 irons from Stiles's collection were on exhibit at Texas Tech University in Lubbock, Texas; 101 in Belgium, Germany, and Spain; 176 were displayed at Six Flags Over Texas; and the balance were at Texas A&I University in Kingsville, Texas.

In 1988, Stiles and his wife, Mary, donated their entire collection to the Texas and Southwestern Cattle Raisers Foundation at the TSCRA headquarters in Fort Worth, Texas. The majority of these irons and their stories represent the history of members of the Association. Since they were given to Leonard and are very personal and important to their owners, the Stileses felt that they belonged in the Cattle Raisers Museum as part of the history of the cattle industry in Texas and the Southwest.

One thing that is unique about a Texas brand is that it is recorded in the county where it is run. In other states, a brand is good statewide. Some brands that are still in use originated during the days when Texas was part of Mexico or when Texas was a republic. Even then, brand registration was required. The oldest brand in the Stiles collection is the **J Crossed W**, established by James Taylor White in Chambers County in about 1819. The brand is still used by descendants of the White who originated the mark.

"I don't have many of the original old irons, because as an iron wore out, a cowman would often cut the face off and use the handle again on a new stamp," Stiles said. "There are few hand-forged irons today. Most of them are welded."

Some brands were stamped on and some were run on with a running iron. The histories behind the branding irons are as varied and colorful as is the history of Texas and the West, for they are one and the same. The millions of cattle that have worn these marks burned on their sides were walking billboards, each with its own story—from the brand that was traded for a schooner of beer to the mark made to remind its owner of the sound of "katydids" he heard as a child. Brands are ironclad signatures of cattlemen, great and small, past and present.

Leonard Stiles stated, "I have been lucky in my career. I've worked for two outstanding organizations during the last fifty years—the Texas & Southwestern Cattle Raisers Association and the King Ranch."

During his eleven years as a field inspector for the Association and the following years with the historic King Ranch, Leonard's trail took some curious turns. Stiles's story is as colorful as those of his branding irons. When he left the Association in August 1961, he joined the King Ranch of Kingsville, Texas. In 1972, he was named manager of the Santa Gertrudis Division, a position he held for over sixteen years until he retired in 1988. Leonard and Mary still lived on the ranch at the time of his death on September 8, 2001.

Leonard Stiles and his branding irons are a part of the history of the cattle industry, the King Ranch, and the American West.

Jane Pattie

Aledo, Texas

Bud Penn takes a calf to the branding fire on the Sid Richardson Estate's Dutch Branch Ranch southwest of Fort Worth, ca. 1965.

Cowboys rope a calf for branding on Spencer & Judkins' 3 Ranch in Menard County, Texas, ca. 1929.

Fort Worth was a supply stop for crews taking cattle up the trail to Kansas in the 1870s and became a major cattle trading center when the Texas & Pacific Railway reached town in 1876. By 1878, the Fort Worth Stockyards had been organized and had shipped 2,200 cars of cattle. From then on, hundreds of thousands of cattle passed through the historic stockyards during their glory days, and Fort Worth became known as *Cowtown*. These hands chute brand cattle with a minimum of effort.

Part One

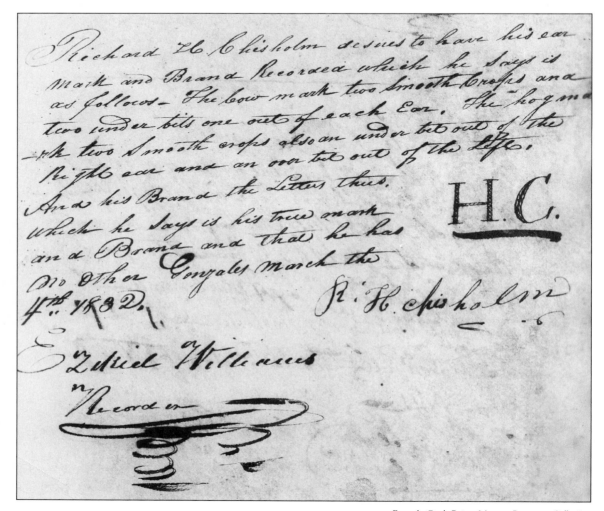

In 1832, Richard H. Chisholm recorded his brand, **HC Bar**, and ear marks, "two smooth crops and two under bits, one out of each ear," as seen in this early registration certificate in the Gonzales County records.

Chapter 1
Burned on Their Hides

Will James wrote in his memorable book, *Smoky the Cowhorse*: "He wondered if somebody'd stole Smoky and the bunch, but he put that off, figuring that no horse thief would steal horses packing as well known a brand as the Rocking R unless he was a daggone fool." And so has "figured" every stockman since the days when civilization centered around the Nile River in Egypt and the Tigris and Euphrates rivers in the Middle East, and those ancient peoples burned brands on their cattle.

The brand, a mark of ownership used on cattle and horses by today's ranchers, was in use 4,000 years ago. Artisans carved and painted pictures depicting cattle roundups and brandings on the walls of Egyptian tombs beginning as far back as 1900 B. C.

The branding of stock was also known to the Mesopotamians who held the sand-swept lands along the Tigris and Euphrates rivers in today's Iraq and Iran. Ancient texts describe the process of branding, and cattle with brands on their hips or shoulders are depicted in carvings seen on the ruins of temple walls.

Once man mounted a horse, he was no longer earth-bound, and that fact changed history. It was only natural for him to put his mark on his mount as a form of pride as well as identification. In medieval times, even swans were branded with hot irons.

In Europe in the sixth-century, the Franks had laws that governed the branding of horses. Laws also required owners to brand their livestock in thirteenth-century Spain as well as in Germany and France during the sixteenth century. Even Genghis Khan's fierce Mongolian horde that swept through the eastern world in the twelfth and thirteenth centuries knew the value of horses and burned brands on their hides to show ownership.

Branding was not required by law in England, but it is said that English horses were branded during the Dark Ages, and during Elizabethan times, the Irish and Welsh branded their stock. However, that practice of establishing ownership of livestock was not brought to the American colonies by the English, but it could have been brought to Colonial America by Dutch settlers who had learned it when the Spaniards occupied the Netherlands. It soon became the custom in the colonies to brand the stock, and all brands were registered. Connecticut enacted the first colonial branding law in 1644. However, the Spanish conquerors of the Aztecs were the first to introduce branding to the Western Hemisphere on the hips and shoulders of their cattle and horses.

The Spanish mounts of the sixteenth century were acknowledged to be the finest riding horses in Europe. In 1519, when Hernán Cortés first set foot in the Western Hemisphere in what is now Mexico, he and his men had sixteen horses with them. He was soon a forerunner of the cattlemen of today, for he and his contemporaries introduced the three essential segments of the ranching industry—horses, cattle, and the branding iron.

Cortés may have brought the first horses to Mexico, but it was Christopher Columbus who brought the first cattle to the Western Hemisphere. He unloaded less than one hundred head on the Caribbean island of Hispaniola in 1493.

No more cattle were brought from Spain until 1503 when Queen Isabella ruled that all ships sailing for the West Indies were to carry livestock. Transporting large animals by ship has always been difficult, and it was especially so in those days. It is no surprise that less than 1,000 had arrived by 1512.

The cattle thrived and multiplied in the warm climate and lush environment of the Indies, and they soon flourished not only on Hispaniola but also on Cuba, Puerto Rico, and Jamaica. It was animals from these herds that were taken to Mexico and that eventually spread into North and South America.

The first cattle in New Spain were six heifers and a bull that Gregorio de Villalobos shipped from Santo Domingo and unloaded at the new Spanish port of Veracruz in 1521. That was the beginning of more to come from the islands to Veracruz and the Panuco Delta in the 1520s. The coastal lowlands along the Gulf of Mexico became a cattle breeding area. It is reported that the herds almost doubled in fifteen months. The animals were tended by black slaves or mixed-blooded people brought with them from the Indies. Castilian *caporales* or foremen oversaw the operation.

Photo by Watt M. Casey, Jr.

Noted Texas historian and author Dan Kilgore reports that Nuño de Guzmán, governor of the Province of Panuco, issued licenses to the Spanish settlers granting them the right to capture Indians as slaves and trade them for cattle in the Indies. The exchange was one cow for eighty Indians.

They say that crime doesn't pay, but it did in the case of a converted Portuguese Jew, Luis de Carvajal, who came to New Spain as a conquistador. He was awarded a grant by the crown in 1579 and received a royal commission to colonize 600 square miles, the northeastern part of Mexico from the Panuco River north across the Rio Grande and into Texas up to the present site of San Antonio. All recipients of such grants were required to stock them with cattle. Carvajal established three ranches, one near Tampico and two others near Panuco. The conquistador prospered from his cattle, but he also made yearly expeditions throughout his land capturing up to 1,000 Indians that he sold as slaves in the City of Mexico. Perhaps he became too prosperous and made enemies. He was imprisoned by the Inquisition for not denouncing his sister as a Jew, and he died penniless in 1591.

Before his fall from favor, Carvajal had brought in settlers and founded two towns on his grant, Cerralvo, called León, and Monclova. After his incarceration, the Indians drove his colonists back to more settled areas. His cattle were left on their own to run wild and multiply. It is likely that some of those herds spread up the coast and waded the Rio Grande to the grasslands of Texas. There were no minerals on the grant to attract development, so the vast lands remained vacant until the mid-1700s.

When silver was discovered in the mountains of Mexico, other Spanish conquistadors established many large haciendas near the mining areas and furnished the miners with beef and draft animals. Cortés was one of the Spanish *ganaderos* whose stock grew sleek and fat on the grasses of Mexico's central plateau. They wore his **Three Crosses** brand. Oddly enough, not only cattle and horses felt the sting of the hot iron, but so did the native slaves. The Spanish conquistadors forced the conquered Indians to work as herdsmen on their *estancias* or cattle ranches and often branded them on the cheek with a G for *guerra*, prisoner of war. Spanish law forbade the Indians to own a horse, so they herded cattle on foot—at least for a while. In the beginning, the cattle were relatively tame. During the day, they were herded while they grazed and then they were penned at night, as was done in the areas of Estremadura and Salamanca in Spain.

The municipal council in the City of Mexico created a registry of brands in 1530, and it required a livestock owner to have a permit to own a brand or earmark. Ranch hands were forbidden to own a branding iron, and no one could alter an original brand with a running iron. A running iron is a straight rod or a rod with a curved end with which any design can be made.

Spanish cattle flourished in Mexico. Prior to 1539, cattle ran on vacant land which was common pasture and open range, and they multiplied rapidly. In the 1550s, *estancias* were established along the route of conquest between Veracruz and the City of Mexico and then spread to the north and west as the crown awarded land grants for cattle raising. The market was not meat but hides, and thousands of cowhides were exported to Spain each year.

The Spanish soldiers often married Indian women, and there was soon a community of *mestizos*. As Spanish ranchos spread northward into the semi-arid Sonoran desert, the animals required more grazing land. They were branded and turned out on open range, no longer herded during the day and corralled at night. Soon, no herdsman could handle the half-wild animals on foot, so despite the law, the *mestizo* was now mounted. Ranching spread into the west of Mexico in the Jalisco area, where the classic methods of working cattle horseback were developed, and the *vaquero* was born.

In 1541, Don Francisco Vasquez de Coronado led a large party of 1,500 soldiers, settlers, and priests up the Rio Grande into the province that is now New Mexico in search of gold and treasures and to establish a settlement. They had rams and ewes as well as 1,000 horses and 500 branded cows. From that time on, cattle and horses spread north into the Borderlands as did the Spaniards. But it was the church and its efforts to Christianize the native peoples of this wild land that spread the Spanish cattle into Florida, California, Arizona, New Mexico, and especially Texas.

During the days of Spanish rule, a rancher was required by law to brand his horses and cattle. He petitioned the district *alcalde* to secure a brand. He had to own 150 head of cattle, and he often bought them "on time" from a nearby mission. The padres were the cattlemen of that day. The rancher designed his brand and registered it with the *juez de paz*—the justice of the peace. He was required to have two irons—one to brand his stock and a bar iron to cancel the brand when he sold an animal. He also had to register his required earmark with the *juez de paz*, and it, too, had to be approved and recorded.

Spain claimed the land that is now Texas, but it was all but forgotten until the French La Salle sailed past the Mississippi River and landed by mistake on Lavaca Bay in Spanish territory. However, that must not have fazed him for he established Fort St. Louis in today's Jackson County, and that got the Spaniards' attention. In answer to the French encroachment, the viceroy of Mexico sent an expedition into Texas to establish missions. He wanted to convert the "savages" but also establish friendly relations with them, so the Indians would keep Spain informed of the movements of the French.

Alonso de León, the governor of Coahuila to the south of Texas, led the expedition of 110 soldiers, 400 horses, 200 cows and carried supplies of flour, muskets, powder, and shot. They headed north toward Texas on March 28, 1690, with instructions to discourage the French intruders. Father Damian Manzanet was with de León to see to the men's spiritual needs and to locate sites to establish missions.

Following the expedition, the story was told throughout New Spain that de León had left a bull and a cow plus a stallion and a mare at every river they crossed. There is no verification of that, but after Father Gaspar José de Solis traveled from Cuero through East Texas to Louisiana in 1763, he told of seeing many wild Castilian horses and cattle, and where else would they have come from? Perhaps de León planned to establish herds for future colonization.

The Spanish first built the mission San Francisco de los Tejas near the Neches River in East Texas in 1690. Nearby, they built Mission Santísimo Nombre de María, but both were short lived. The Indians were hostile toward the padres and the few soldiers who were left to guard against the French. There was sickness and crop failure, so the missions were abandoned in 1693. The Spanish just picked up and left in the night. They did not even take time to gather their cattle. They left them to run wild and propagate undisturbed. But the Spanish returned to East Texas in 1716, and once more established several new missions.

Then they founded a mission and presidio at San Pedro Springs in 1718 as a stopping place halfway between the presidios in northern Mexico and the East Texas missions. This presidio, San Antonio de Bexar, and the mission, San Antonio de Valero, better known today as the Alamo, were the beginnings of the city of San Antonio. In 1721, the church was also granted the right to establish four other missions along the San Antonio River. Once again, the Franciscan padres brought their cattle, horses, and sheep with them. All five missions flourished as did their flocks of sheep and herds of cattle.

But it was Mission Espíritu Santo near the present town of Goliad, Texas, that became wealthy through its stock. By 1778, it owned between fifteen and twenty thousand head of cattle that grazed on the open range. It was Texas's first large ranch.

The Spaniards had brought with them not only their stock but their methods of working and their equipment—and their branding irons. At first, they did not come to settle the land, but to find Indian converts and workers.

This was only successful among non-warlike Indians, who were eventually exterminated. But for a while, under the strict eyes of the priests at missions such as Espíritu Santo, thousands of cattle thrived and multiplied. Cattle and horses spread across the land, and in so doing, the horse came to the fearsome and deadly Apaches and to the Comanches, who became the most efficient light cavalry in the world.

By the late 1700s, the Spanish frontier in Texas, New Mexico, and Arizona retreated, because of the Apaches and Comanches, but some tough settlers stayed, and Spanish and Mexican brands are still seen in South Texas and throughout the Southwest.

A Spanish brand began with a design, perhaps based on the flamboyant written signature of the Spanish grandee. Then each son added a bar or a curlicue. As each generation added to the brand, it became larger and quite fancy. It had no specific name but was known by the name of the family who registered it. The earliest brand issued in the province of Texas of record in the Spanish Archives at the University of Texas, was granted to Don Juan Joseph Flores by the governor of the province on July 1, 1762.

Many brands were granted to the brave rancheros who defied the wilds of the new province. In 1765, Miguel Hernandez de Hoyos was granted a brand by the Alcalde of San Fernando de Bexar. This mark was burned on twenty-four mares and a stallion, a gift from the young man's parents. The herd was the offspring of three wild mares he had captured in 1748 as a boy.

In 1791, Don Juan Barrera recorded his brand in Goliad. Only a few months later, Spanish soldiers captured horses wearing this brand from the Indians, and they returned them to Don Barrera—methods not so different from present-day operations by Texas and Southwestern Cattle Raisers Association (TSCRA) inspectors.

When Mexico declared its independence from Spain in 1821, Spanish cattle and horses still grazed across southern Texas and along the coastal plains, and many remained on the land as did their owners.

After the Spaniards left, the Comanches became Mexico's problem. Mexico needed a buffer between them and the dreaded Comanches, and they established an impresario system and allowed Anglo settlers to enter Texas. The Anglos would take the brunt of the Indian attacks. The first group to settle in the southeast area of Texas came with Stephen F. Austin in 1821. They soon adopted the Mexican equipment and methods of stock raising and adjusted them to suit their needs and personalities. As will be noted from many of the brands in the Stiles collection, the Anglo settlers soon discarded the intricate Spanish and Mexican brands for simplicity. Many of today's South Texas ranching families came to Texas with Austin or came when Texas was a republic. Some came before. Even after Mexico gained its independence from Spain, the Spanish brand laws remained in force in Mexico and in the provinces of Coahuila-and-Texas, New Mexico, and Alta California.

It was Spanish cattle that crossed with the European breeds later brought to Texas by the early Anglo settlers that resulted in the vast herds of Longhorn cattle that became the bonanza to many cowmen during the end of the nineteenth century.

Texas enacted its first branding law in 1848. It required stock owners to record their brands and earmarks with the clerk in the county where their ranch was located. The county clerk was required to keep an up-to-date book of the brands in the county, as they do today.

In 1860, the Civil War interrupted life in Texas as it did throughout the country, stock ran free and multiplied for four years while their owners were away fighting. After the war, men returned home to Texas and often found they owned no more than the clothes on their backs and a strong will. But opportunity was there in the form of the wild Longhorn cattle waiting to be claimed by the stamp of a hot iron. Many cattle kings got their starts in just such a way.

The cowmen found that in working their newly acquired cattle, they needed sturdy, dependable horses. The Western horse answered their needs. He was a mixture of the Arabian and Barb of the Spanish horses and the English Thoroughbred of the colonists. The end product retained the brains and toughness of one and the speed of the other—the perfect cowhorse.

Just as each cattleman marked his wild Longhorns with a large brand so that it could be seen from a distance, he used a smaller one on his horses. They burned many a mark on a cow or horse with a cinch ring or a running iron heated gray-hot in a fire of twisted mesquite wood or dried cow chips. So despite the depredations of rustlers and marauding Indians, these early-day, determined cowmen clung to their land and their herds.

During this time, cattle and horses mingled on the open range, so brands were particularly important. Following the Civil War, when ranchers combined their herds to drive them up the great cattle trails from South Texas to Missouri, Kansas, Nebraska, Wyoming, and Colorado, a road brand was added to the existing brands in the herd in order to identify their particular herd in case of a stampede. Even after the cattle trails closed, brands continued to be important and they remain so today.

As Texas cattle ranchers moved westward away from encroaching civilization, they recognized the necessity of banding together to protect their livestock against rustlers. On a brisk February day in 1877, a group of North Texas cattlemen met in the town of Graham, eighty miles northwest of Fort Worth, to discuss their problems with cow thieves and decide how to control them. They formed The Stock-Raisers' Association of North-West Texas and divided the territory represented by the members into six districts.

The ranchers in each district joined together to handle their cattle on their district's open range. As a group, they determined when the spring grass could support a roundup, and they appointed certain men to gather the cattle and watch for strays. The men in a district gave notice to their neighbors before they began their drive after a roundup.

Each member was required to register his brand and mark, name, address, and location of his ranch. In 1881, George B. Loving of Fort Worth, Texas, published a book, *The Stock Manual*, which listed the brands of the principal stockmen of western and northwestern Texas. It listed 600 brands used on cattle and horses, and a revised edition was published in 1882. But the "men with long ropes" were still busy. The organization could not make honest men out of dishonest men with running irons.

The cowmen took the law into their own hands and hired cattle detectives to ride their country and put a stop to rustling. Then in 1883, the Association officially hired "range inspectors." They were furnished with lists of the members' brands and stationed along the trails and at shipping centers and markets to watch for strayed and stolen stock.

Sam H. Cowan, hired by the Association in 1893, was the first full-time attorney to look after the cattlemen's interests. He tried theft cases throughout Texas, Oklahoma, Kansas, and New Mexico, and he also dealt with the legislature, railroad freight rates, and other legal matters. There soon was more to the Association business than catching cow thieves, but rustling still remained a primary concern as it is today.

Cattlemen in other parts of the state formed similar organizations. One by one, many of them were absorbed by the Association, and by 1921, they were known as the Texas and Southwestern Cattle Raisers Association. Today's TSCRA has members state-wide and throughout Oklahoma. The area is now divided into thirty-one districts, each with a well-trained field inspector. Eighty market inspectors work all cattle and horse sales and slaughter plants, and there are two horse inspectors. With today's computers, ownership and brands can be checked immediately. The inspectors work closely with county sheriffs and local and state law enforcement officers. Each inspector also carries a Special Texas Ranger commission, giving him jurisdiction to work throughout the state.

Just as during trail-driving days more than 125 years ago, only a brand on an animal's hide is proof of ownership. Since a cowboy's horse was and is the most important part of his equipment, each rancher was anxious that not only his cattle could be identified by his brand, but also his horses. A man designed his brand to be distinctive and hard to alter. Some were practical, many imaginative, and all were important whether the cowman numbered his animals in the tens or in the thousands.

The numerous cattle and horse brands listed in that early *Stock Manual* as well as in more recent brand books, are as varied as their owners, most of whom began with little more than grit and pure cussedness. Often with no more than one cowpony and a running iron, a man scratched a toehold in the frontier and hung on until he often numbered his stock in the thousands and his acres in the ten of thousands. Those early day ranchers were a breed of men as tough as the lanky Longhorns and the wiry range horses that carried their brands.

Longtime TSCRA inspector Graves Peeler worked with J. Frank Dobie and Fort Worth oilman and rancher Sid Richardson to save the endangered Longhorn. They established the beginnings of the herd now at Fort Griffin State Park near Albany, Texas. Peeler also started a herd on his McMullen County Ranch. By 1952, it had grown to 250 head as seen above.

Chapter 2
All Trails Led to Cattle Work

Cattle and the coastal plains and South Texas brush country were interwoven in the fiber of slender, quiet-spoken Leonard Stiles of Kingsville, Texas, whose life was the land and its ranching heritage. He learned the art of brush popping early, and he became a cowman of wide experience and extraordinary experiences—a man who knew Texas cattle and cattle brands—a man whose integrity and knowledge of the cow business earned the respect of his peers.

The vast King Ranch of South Texas influenced his life long before he joined its staff in 1961, in fact, even before he was born near Raymondville, just down the railroad track south of the ranch's Norias Division. His paternal grandfather was a horticulturist in California who met visiting Texas cattlemen, Robert J. Kleberg and John G. Kenedy, in San Francisco. Perhaps they were there to promote the railroad they and other local Texas ranchers and businessmen were building from Corpus Christi to Brownsville. They persuaded him that there was a good future in South Texas. Stiles took their advice and went to Texas where he became involved in the booming real estate business in the valley. His son joined him there in 1907.

At this time, operation of the King Ranch was in the capable hands of Henrietta King, widow of its founder, Captain Richard King, who had died April 14, 1885. Her ranch manager and son-in-law was Robert Justice Kleberg. In order to build the St. Louis, Brownsville & Mexico railroad and bring the world closer to the ranch, Henrietta King donated one-half interest in 75,000 acres, a right-of-way across her land, and land for the townsite of Kingsville.

The first train puffed its way down the tracks in 1904 and opened the valley for settlement and business. Horticulturist Stiles lived in Raymondville and thrived in the real estate business, while his son operated a date and citrus farm.

Opportunity in the Texas valley beckoned adventurous people from near and far. The Maddy family from Medford, Oklahoma, whose daughter would become Leonard Stiles's mother, loaded their belongings into a covered wagon and set out for the promised land.

"My mother, her brothers, and my grandfather and grandmother rode in a wagon from up near the Kansas line. They came through Fort Worth on south and then followed the railroad track through Kingsville down to Raymondville," said Leonard. "I'm not sure how they went from Riviera south, because there was no highway open across the King Ranch at that time. Anyway, while the Maddys were in Raymondville, my mother and father met and were married. My grandparents didn't stay in Texas long. They went back to Kansas. My Uncle Harvey went with them, but he returned to Raymondville, where he operated a store for many years.

"He was telling me about their trip down here," Leonard recalled. "They followed the railroad track on the west side and were between Driscoll and Robstown, towns that were established on the railroad. They camped there for the night, and it came a rain storm and Agua Dulce Creek flooded. They were left stranded on a little island for a month because of the black mud. They

could walk into town and get groceries, but they couldn't get the team and wagon out. Some people lived up the creek a little ways, and my grandfather walked up there and borrowed a milk cow. They milked her all the time they were there. Even at that time, travel by team and wagon was difficult, and they had their share of high water, mud, and hardships."

Leonard Stiles's mother and father were married, and he was born September 14, 1920, near Raymondville.

Photo by Watt M. Casey, Jr. Leonard's mother died when he was six, and the Stiles family moved to La Morena Ranch at San Margarita near the Sauz Division of the King Ranch. Leonard attended a school between San Margarita and San Perlita. Then, due to the Depression, the family moved around while Leonard's father looked for work. They lived for a short while in Bandera and San Antonio and finally settled on a farm in Atascosa County near Amphion.

Leonard quit school and left home to look for a job when he was sixteen. He headed back to his old stomping grounds in the Raymondville country. Rancher Rocky Reagan had leased the lower end of the 60,000-acre Yturria Ranch. It was 30,000 acres of thicket, and he had 1,500 head of steers on the land. Yturria had been a railroad station, and if a man rode five miles due east to *Punta del Monte*, there was a big lake and a large camp house and a number of small houses built in a circle. Young Stiles went there looking for a job but was told they had no need of extra help. He went back to the road, flagged down the bus and headed back home.

A man got on the bus and sat on the steps at the front near where Leonard sat. They got to talking, and he asked the boy, "Where are you headed?"

The young man told him he had been looking for a job. He explained, "I used to live here and worked up at the Esparancha Ranch."

"That's right across from where I'm working as foreman for Rocky Reagan," the man replied. He was in charge of the place where Leonard had been told they needed no help. The foreman hired Leonard and took him home with him that night.

"As it turned out," Stiles later recalled, "Mr. Reagan had gotten this man out of the penitentiary, and he was one of the best brush hands I ever saw. He had been sent up for horse stealing, but he denied he did it. He told me he'd never go back to the pen. He had a good record, so Mr. Reagan sponsored him, and he was released in his custody. Will Bailey made a good hand.

"Years later when I was with the Cattle Raisers Association and worked in Brazoria County, Lee Murray, a Quarter Horse man who lived near Angleton, told me, 'We used to get convicts out of the pen and work them. We paid them and fed them. I had one man who was the best hand I ever saw. He was a cowman and a brush hand. You're from the valley. Did you ever hear of Duke Bailey?'"

Leonard asked him if he was talking about Will Bailey. He described him, and that was Will. He asked several ranchers in the area about him, and they all thought he was a top hand.

Stiles thought so, too. He worked with Bailey and Fase Huala. "*Fase* means your shirt tail is out," he said. "He was long-legged, short-bodied, and tough! He could whip that brush and cat claw! We were roping steers and doctoring one day and had some cattle in a trap when some fellow took a shot at me. It made me so mad, I headed for the house to get a rifle that Mr. Reagan had left there. If Mr. Will hadn't stopped me, I would have made a terrible mistake. He took me to the sheriff's office, and we reported the incident. Since I didn't recognize the man, nothing ever came of it."

Leonard went home that Thanksgiving. He told his Uncle Harvey that he would like to go out to La Morena and see ol' Tomás and all his *amigos*. "Who did I see there but the man who had shot at me!" he said. "He didn't come over and I let it pass. It wasn't long, however, until someone killed him. If it hadn't been for Will Bailey, I would have been in trouble. I learned a lot from Will. He was a good cowman and a good friend."

While Leonard's family lived south of San Antonio near Amphion, they bought their groceries in Poteet at the Hooge store. Leonard took a shine to pretty, dark-haired Mary Hooge, and the couple was married on January 24, 1942. Stiles was working for Kellog Construction Company, hanging steel on the world's highest refinery structure that was being built on Goose Creek near Baytown when he received his draft notice. He had one month to take care of affairs before he reported to Fort Sam Houston in San Antonio in July.

His first assignment was as one of twenty-five soldiers sent as guards on an equipment train from Denver to San Diego, California. By the time the train arrived at its destination, all the men but Leonard and Marco Sacolitz had jumped the train and gone AWOL.

Next he was sent to Camp Coleman at San Francisco, where he met his company. They were loaded onto a troop ship, the *Ile de France*, on December 7, 1942, and sailed for New Zealand and points west. He was gone for three and a half years.

Seven days out of Pearl Harbor, Mary presented him with their first daughter, but he didn't get the telegram sent by her brother until the ship arrived in Kharramshahr, Iran, on the Persian Gulf. Leonard was with the Army Corp of Engineers who moved supplies in to build a road to Tabriz and on through the mountains into Russia. The Germans occupied western USSR and were approaching Iran's northern border. Iran's oil fields had to be protected and a road opened from the Persian Gulf to get supplies to the Russian border. That was the Americans' job.

From Kharramshahr, they moved north to Ahwaz and further north to Qum, a huge underground city of markets where all kinds of handmade goods were sold.

There was a mishap with equipment one day, and the Colonel told his aide, "Get hold of that g.d. Texan!" Leonard never knew why he was chosen. He was sent with a civilian, Vernon Castle, to Tabriz in northern Iran to repair a drag line. Everyone there was a civilian except Leonard, and he was assigned to a man by the name of Helmpke, who had been in the area for a while. Helmpke was in charge of road-building equipment—drag lines, buckets, shovels, northwest rigs, as well as a 100-ton lowboy to move it all with. They also had a tractor they called a Walter Snow Plow. It had nine speeds forward, and four mph was its first speed. It was used to move the drag lines. That's where Stiles learned to handle heavy equipment.

Leonard was Helmpke's aide and under his orders. It turned out that he was a government agent. Leonard was never told who Helmpke worked for, and he never asked. He drove him up and down the road, and Helmpke would have him stop at the stations and he'd go inside. As it turned out, he was investigating thefts from the supply trains.

The Russians had set up an assembly plant at Kharramshahr. Boatloads of parts went through the Suez Canal because German Field Marshal Erwin Rommel and his Afrika Korps held North Africa and controlled the Mediterranean. The Americans maintained the road from Kharramshahr through Tabriz to Russia so that supplies could get to and from Russia.

"We often passed convoys of as many as six hundred trucks full of supplies going north to the Russian border," Leonard recalled.

When the war was over, Stiles was ready to go back to Texas. After he arrived home in November 1945, he and his family lived in Poteet where he worked for his brother-in-law for a year. He then took a job in Cuero working for Rufus Taylor, the Chief of Police. Taylor needed someone who could speak Spanish, and Leonard could. He had grown up with Hispanic friends and neighbors.

"What I knew about law enforcement during those early days, I learned from Rufus Taylor," Stiles often said.

While working in Cuero, Leonard met Texas & Southwestern Cattle Raisers Association inspector, Lester Stout, at Victoria. Stout had trouble with some of the Mexican people who worked on local ranches. They were butchering calves at night to barbecue. After work, Stiles often rode with Stout while he investigated these cattle theft cases. He became acquainted with other inspectors, and that type of work really interested him. When an opening for an inspector came up in the Hebbronville district, Stout encouraged Stiles to put in his application. Leonard did, and Henry Bell, secretary and general manager at the time, went to Cuero to interview him. He hired him on April 1, 1950. At that time, the Association didn't pay a lot of money, but it was more than Stiles was making at the police department.

Leonard and Mary attended the Cattle Raisers convention that spring, and when members from Brazoria and Matagorda counties learned of his background in law enforcement, they went to Henry Bell and asked to have Stiles assigned to their district. So instead of Hebbronville, Bell sent Leonard to West Columbia in Brazoria County

"I had never even heard of West Columbia," Leonard laughed when he told of it. "I had been reared in the valley with Mexican people, and I spoke Spanish and knew how they thought, but I knew absolutely nothing about black people, and there were a lot of them in my new district."

In typical Stiles fashion, he set about meeting the local law enforcement officers, learning the ways of the people of the area, their history, the ranchers and their brands, the back roads, and who did what when—all the things necessary to be effective as a field inspector. In the beginning, he just worked three counties, and his home base was to be Sweeny in Brazoria County. Lester Stout took Leonard and Mary there to buy a house, but Leonard moved to West Columbia by himself for a while until school was out. The Stiles family had grown to four children, and the youngest ones were twins.

"I went right to work, because I had a lot to learn," he admitted. "I had heard of an ex-inspector named Graves Peeler, as had most everyone in law enforcement or the cattle business, but I didn't know him. My district had been his when he worked for the Association. When he quit to work as manager of the Nash Ranch in Brazoria County, Harold Graves took over the district. Harold lived at Brazoria and had been with the sheriff's department. If I recall, he just worked for the Association until they could find someone to take Mr. Peeler's place. He knew all the ranchers in the area, and Mr. Bell told me to get in touch with him. He was a great help to me, and I needed all the help I could get!

"My early success can be attributed to the help of men such as Harold Graves and my good friend, Sheriff Jack Marshall of Brazoria County, and ranchers such as Jack Phillips. I knew I had a lot to learn.

"I kept hearing about Graves Peeler. When I'd ask for advice, I'd hear, 'Graves Peeler did it this way,' and they'd tell me a story about Graves Peeler. He was a legend. I decided I needed to know the man."

By that time, Peeler was living south of San Antonio on his ranch near Christine, and Stiles made a trip to meet him. They became great friends. "He was one of the biggest helps I had. When I'd get a case that I couldn't work out, I'd head for Mr. Peeler's. I'd often get there way in the night and wake him up, or I'd crawl in bed until the next morning when I'd talk to him about my problems. He could sure figure them out. He was a natural-born lawman and highly respected by all. People in my district would wonder how I'd solve some of those cases, but they never knew where I was getting my information and advice.

"Mr. Peeler would sit there and listen. He just drilled a hole through me, looking at me while I talked. He never said a word but just let me get it out of my system. Then he'd tell me what to do and who I could trust and who I couldn't trust. I didn't always do everything he suggested, because law enforcement had changed since his day, and I could have gotten in deep trouble. But his knowledge was always sound."

Leonard was soon making dents in the cow stealing in his district, Brazoria, Matagorda, Fort Bend, and Austin counties. At times he worked Harris and Jackson counties and part of Galveston County, which was G. O. Stoner's district, but some of Leonard's people pastured a lot of cattle there. It was not open range, but that was during the steer era, and during those years, thousands of head of steers were moved into large, leased salt grass pastures along the coast. Various ranchers leased the land jointly and threw all their cattle together. Kiddo Tacquard in

Galveston County leased a lot of country that he in turn leased to steer men from Huntsville, and then he took care of their cattle. They would buy steers from auctions around the area and then ship them down to the salt grass country. Other ranchers such as the Swickheimers and Ike Gross shipped many a steer in and out of that area, too.

From the Cattle Raisers Museum Permanent Collection

One Houston company leased 40,000 acres that is now covered in houses to the steer men. It had been the Bob Henderson ranch. The ranchers burned off the sacahuiste grass, and the land ran lots of cattle. At that time, cowmen shipped two- and three-year-old steers by rail to fatten on the grasslands of Kansas. They loaded them from pens at stations such as Hitchcock, north of Galveston, and Van Vleck near Bay City in Jackson County. By the time the steers reached the East Coast in finished condition, they were often four- or five-year-olds. The operation was expensive, and it soon wasn't feasible, because other ranchers began butchering their animals before they were two. But for a while, a lot of money was made in the steer business.

When the steer market came to an abrupt end, it broke many a cowman, but while it lasted, it was a lucrative business. It kept the coastal region's inspectors jumping. The district's inspector was to be at the shipping pens anytime a shipment was made, and he still had to keep up with regular shipments from other points along the railroads.

Leonard laughed when he told of one such shipment made by longtime Matagorda County cattleman, Will Cornelius, whose main ranch was near Markham. Leonard was still new to the district when Cornelius sent word that he would be shipping on a certain day from a ranch he had south of Bay City. Leonard was to be at the pens on the spur that ran to Wadsworth.

As Stiles told it: "Mr. Will Cornelius was quite a cowman. He was an old-timer and all of us younger people respected him and were real quiet around him. I sure wanted to do a good job that day, and I knew I had to look at every head as they were loaded, because I had understood Mr. Cornelius to tell me, 'Leonard, every cow here carries my brand, but there's one in particular that you need to watch for—the N cow. I know she's in the herd, and I want you to be sure you see her.'

"Mr. Will had a bunch of sons who all became my good friends, but I was only acquainted with them at the time. One of them warned me, 'Don't get up there and scare these cattle while we're loading. Mr. Will will get after you.' I sure didn't want that!

"Well, I hid behind posts and strained my eyes and did my best to see every cow that went up into those train cars. Finally it got toward the last, and I hadn't seen that one cow. I knew she hadn't gone by me. She just wasn't there.

"All the business was taken care of and the papers were signed, and I was sort of standing around. I wanted to tell Mr. Will that I hadn't seen that particular cow, but he had not mentioned it. After a while, he looked around at me. 'Leonard, did you find that cow?'

"I hated to admit to failure. 'No sir, I didn't.'

"'Well, she went on there!'

"'Mr. Will, I didn't see her,' I admitted.

"'She was the last one we loaded—the one I was telling you to watch for—the *end* cow!'

"The Cornelius men laughed and laughed. The joke was on me," Stiles grinned. "I just had to laugh, too."

That was one branding iron Leonard never found for his collection, either—the end one. Most of his irons were given to him by friends and members of the families who used them. There are a few exceptions, such as the first iron he acquired, the **Fleur de Lis L**. It had hung from a post in a hundred-year-old building used as a post office at Cedar Lake for as long as anyone could remember. J. B. Roberts had a store in the building for forty years and used the iron to stoke the fire in a pot-bellied stove that sat in the middle of the room. Leonard was interested in the brand and traced it back to rancher Billy Seardon, who had first registered it in Matagorda County after buying cattle carrying that brand.

"Back in those days," Leonard explained, "traders would come through the country driving a small herd of bulls, horses, mules, milk cows—trading from one ranch to the next." Leonard learned that Elton Leggett was Billy Seardon's son-in-law. The old rancher was on his death bed when Leggett asked him about the brand. He said he had bought some cattle with that brand on them, but he didn't know where it originated.

Another brand Stiles recalled that originated elsewhere and was acquired through a trader was the **AD Connected**. "I worked on a theft case in South Carolina. I brought two irons back to Texas with me. I showed one of the irons, an **AD Connected** from Annadale Plantation to Jack Marshall, the Brazoria County sheriff, who also branded **AD Connected**. He said his people had had that brand since 1862 when they bought mules branded **AD Connected** from a trader. The mules had come from the Carolinas by ship to New Orleans, where both horses and mules were unloaded and driven cross-country and traded. Annadale was an old, old plantation that had long been known for its mules. It is possible that that is where the Marshall brand originated. Old Mr. Marshall liked the design and registered it in Brazoria County. The Marshall family had stamped it on many a cow. That's how brands travel."

As ranchers learned of Stiles's interest and his knowledge of brands, they began contacting him and giving him irons for his collection. That was the case in 1963 when workmen in Houston were excavating for a new building for Humble Oil Company, as Exxon was known then. They demolished old buildings from the site that was known as Allen's Landing that dated back to 1860. Twelve feet down, they unearthed a piece of metal. Charles K. Sikes of Welton Becket & Associates, architects of the project, recognized it was a branding iron. Through banker, Dub Black, Sikes contacted Stiles in Sweeny, Texas. The brand was bent, but Leonard identified it as the **JP Connected** brand of Joseph Polley, who had come to Texas from Virginia as a teamster with Stephen F. Austin in 1823.

"Polley was awarded large grants of land and eventually became a cattle baron," Stiles said. "In fact, I learned that the partnership of Polley & Allen had had a set of pens on the site of the new building, and when I checked the county records, I found where Polley registered the **JP Connected** brand in 1840 in old Harrisburg, which is now part of Houston. Harrisburg became the county seat when Harris County was established in 1840. Polley also branded **JHP Connected**, and he owned land that is now the Battle Island Ranch in Brazoria County which belonged to Jack Phillips when I was there. As time went on, Polley moved west to Cibolo Creek east of San Antonio, where he lived out his life.

"Pete, Jay, and Milam Frost, respected ranchers west of Houston, all said that the **JP Connected** was a Frost brand, and it was—in their county. But I'm convinced the iron found in the excavation was Polley's."

Leonard had realized the antiquity of this method of showing ownership of livestock when he was in Iran and Iraq and first saw the carvings of branded cattle on temple walls in what had been ancient Babylon. He had visited the remains of the ancient city of Ur, that was possibly settled as early as 4,000 B.C. He thought of those marks of ownership and realized that fire branding had not changed much through the centuries.

"I really became interested in brands as an inspector, when various ranchers told me the histories of their brands—it was their families' histories." As Stiles went about Association business, he began watching for old irons, and the ranchers were often glad to give them to him. That started his collection. He considered every iron important, whether its owner had only a few cattle or they numbered in the thousands.

Photo by Jane Pattie

During the end of October each fall, friends and neighbors of the 6666 Ranch of King County, Texas, gathered for the S. B. Burnett Estate's annual colt branding, ca. 1962.

These cowhands place the mark of ownership—the rancher's brand—on a calf, ca. 1925.

Chapter 3
"That Damned Texan is no Preacher"

Bob Kleberg, president and chief executive officer of the King Ranch, was a race horse man. He was well-known by Quarter Horse people in Texas and the southwest for his quarter-milers such as Miss Princess and Nobodies Friend, but the King Ranch colors were also seen at the Thoroughbred tracks. King Ranch Thoroughbreds raced in all the big races—the Kentucky Derby, the Preakness Stakes, the Belmont Stakes, the Santa Anita Handicap, plus many others where they ran against the toughs—or the toughs ran against them. They were speed demons. There was Stymie; Assault, the 1945 Triple Crown winner; his half-brother, Middleground, winner of the 1950 Kentucky Derby and Belmont Stakes; Rejected; To Market; High Gun; Better Self; and many others. Through Kleberg's love of horse racing, he became good friends with another racing aficionado, New York financier, Harry Guggenheim.

Guggenheim was also in the cattle business. He owned two plantations in South Carolina—one at Wando and the other near Georgetown. Bob Kleberg was Guggenheim's guest at Cain Hoy, his Wando plantation. The New Yorker showed the Texan his Hereford cattle and told him how many cows he could run in the pasture they were in.

"You don't have that many cows here," Kleberg said. "And another thing. That calf that's bawling is looking for its mother. I don't see any tight-bagged cow. There's something wrong here."

Guggenheim admitted that he had a friend and neighbor who had been telling him that his cattle were disappearing. He had sent his accountant down to count them, and the man didn't find any shortage. Bob Kleberg wasn't surprised. "Let me send a man over here that no one knows and have him snoop around. We can find out what's going on." Guggenheim agreed.

Kleberg returned to Texas, and he contacted the old-time cattle detective, Graves Peeler, and told him what was happening. Peeler said, "I can't go, but I've got a boy who will do a job for you." Peeler called Leonard Stiles and asked him to come to Christine.

Peeler explained the situation and told Stiles, "I'll tell Mr. Bob and he'll call the Association and get them to give you a leave of absence." Leonard agreed to see what he could learn.

It was all arranged, and Texas Governor Price Daniel and the TSCRA sent Stiles to South Carolina to do some undercover work. Governor Daniel gave Leonard a letter to the South Carolina governor. Stiles was to investigate the reported disappearance of cattle from the Cain Hoy Plantation that belonged to absentee owner Guggenheim. According to Guggenheim's friend and neighbor who had contacted the owner, he suspected that the manager, a fellow from

Texas, was involved. Stiles was the man they sent to catch the thief. One Texan might catch another, if the manager were the culprit.

When Leonard left his home in Sweeny, he had $1,000 Bob Kleberg had given him for expenses and the governor's letter in his pocket. Not even his family knew where he was going.

As Stiles tells the story—

I don't say I was sent to Carolina to work undercover, because I was never good at that sort of thing, but I arrived under the pretense of looking for a job. I eventually worked with state law enforcement, but first, I had to do some detective work on my own. I was a stranger in town, and my business there caused much speculation. The locals decided at first that I was a Baptist preacher attending a big convention being held in Charleston, but I let it be known that I was job hunting. There was no way to hide that I was from Texas, and I came to be called "that Texan," and later, "that damned Texan."

As I nosed around, I found there was more going on than just cattle stealing, and there were more people involved than just the foreman. In fact, there was another Texan. Before it was all over, I was really ashamed of the Texans.

I first checked on the CPA who counted the cattle and who was convinced his tally was correct even though the owner's neighbor could see it wasn't. The manager, who I'll call Jenkins, had set up an umbrella at the pens near the end of the chute and put the man at a table in the shade. He kept the accountant's glass full of good whiskey and gave him a list of cattle to check as they ran them past him. He paid him $25 a day for his hard work, which was good money for that time. The accountant didn't know a heifer from a bull, and he had about as much business checking cattle as I would have keeping his books. Toward the end of the day, the foreman told him they would have to gather another pasture and pen the cattle for him to check the next day, which made sense to the accountant.

He returned the following morning and found the pens full of cattle awaiting his count. Unknown to him, he counted the same cattle a second time. It was just as the foreman had said, he wrote in his report to the owner. All the cattle were there and he found no irregularities.

Then I showed up. Word soon got around that I was asking too many questions, and I wasn't what I appeared to be. But they still couldn't figure out what I was up to.

On my arrival, I had called the governor's office to tell him of my assignment and of the letter I carried. He told me that it was not necessary for me to come to Columbus. He would send an officer from South Carolina Law Enforcement Division (SCLED) to work with me. The man they sent was a jam-up fellow, equivalent to a Ranger

Captain in Texas. We worked on that case for six weeks, and everyday, we uncovered new evidence. It all pointed to Jenkins.

The SCLED officer and I stopped in the Charleston Police Department one day where he knew the sergeant. Before I could stop him, he told the officer what I had uncovered. I knew that was a mistake. The sergeant had recognized me as "that damned Texan" the minute we walked in the door. I could tell by his look that there was something funny going on. I had my suspicions but I needed more proof, so I didn't say a word right then. I just played dumb. I had to pick up the foreman and get his confession first.

By the time we got back to the ranch, the sergeant had gotten word to Jenkins and he had rolled out. I knew I had to find him, but first I had to learn how he had disposed of the stolen cattle. I checked all the sales and learned that the cattle had not been sold through the local auctions.

The real break came when we found the man who had driven a truck hauling cattle from the ranch. He was a black man who worked on the place, and he was only following the foreman's orders. Jenkins had him convinced that we were sent there to kill him, and he made himself scarce. When we did catch up with him, we did some tall talking to make him believe that wasn't true, but we finally let him think it was in order to get his cooperation. Then he got to talking.

"I knowed something was wrong," the man admitted, "because the cows on my truck were just a'bawlin', and their calves were back on the ground a'bawlin'. Mr. Jenkins told me to load those cows up, and I did. I took them to town to the abattoir."

I didn't know that an abattoir was a slaughterhouse, and he didn't know what a slaughterhouse was. I couldn't understand his dialect, and I was glad to have the SCLED man with me.

We convinced him that we believed him, and it would be easier on him if he would help us. Now that we had him, we couldn't turn him loose. The man couldn't read and he didn't know town names or highway numbers, but we loaded him in our car, and he certainly knew where he had taken the cattle and other loads of stolen property. I soon was putting two and two together. The foreman was in deep trouble with liquor, women, and gambling. He was paying his debts by stealing from his employer, at first a few cattle at a time, and that was so easy that he was also selling other things such as fertilizer.

We learned from the black man that another Texan was involved, the overseer of Guggenheim's plantation near Georgetown. Jenkins would have the black man take a load of fertilizer to the Georgetown plantation where the overseer would give him a check for the load but would send him on to a store in North Carolina, where the store owner would give him a second check. The store owner then unloaded the fertilizer, knowing it was stolen, and the two Texans split the profits, and Jenkins paid on his gambling debts. It was all falling into place.

As we were to learn, the police sergeant's father operated the abattoir that was accepting the stolen cattle. The sergeant was the man Jenkins was in debt to and the one strong-arming him for the money. The sergeant and his father were benefiting from Guggenheim's losses.

Jenkins never dreamed we'd find the black man. While we had him in the back seat of the car, I questioned him and the other officer drove as he directed us. We wound up in Augusta, Georgia.

"Hold up a minute," he said. "Drive back through town." We did. "That house over there—we unloaded half a load of fertilizer there." He didn't know who lived there.

We stopped and the officer stayed in the car with the truck driver. I walked up the front steps and knocked on the door. I waited. I had no idea who would answer. And who should it be but Jenkins! I rarely went armed, and I had no pistol. I was just as slick as I could be. Jenkins walked back over to a bed and lay down where he had been when I knocked. I noticed he slipped his hand under the pillow, and I knew what he had in it. I thought I had had it for sure.

I did some tall talking and convinced him that we knew what had been going on and who was involved. The best thing for him to do was to confess. I said that I knew he had been a jam-up operator for a long time, and due to circumstances, he had gotten in over his head. He told me that besides his gambling debts, his girl friend was sick in the hospital, and his car was in the garage and he owed on that. I think he was on the verge of suicide.

"The best thing for you to do is to go to Columbus and report in at the SCLED office tomorrow at 1:00. I'll be there waiting. We've got enough on you for me to take you in, but if you'll come in on your own, you will save the state a lot of time and money, and it will go easier on you. If you don't, every time we find something else, it will make it that much harder." I convinced him. He said he'd be there.

I had been given $1,000 for expenses when I started on the case, and I gave Jenkins some of that money to get his car out of the garage and make the trip to Columbus. When I got back in the car and told the SCLED man what I had done, he just shook his head.

"Tex, I don't know about you!"

The next day, I was at SCLED headquarters at 1:00 as promised, but Jenkins didn't show. He hadn't appeared at 1:15, and I was beginning to get nervous. But about five minutes later, he walked in, much to my relief. The SCLED people handled it from there. Jenkins freely made his confession in his own words and finally stood trial and served his time.

The others involved got off Scot free. The attitude of those South Carolina people was that the man from New York had lots of money, and he didn't contribute to their needs, so they didn't give a damn whether they sent any local people to the penitentiary or not, even if they were thieves.

I had done my job, and I was ready to get back home to Texas and pursue cow thieves in my own district. There, at least, I could understand what they said and by this time, I knew how they thought!

• • •

That wasn't Stiles's only work out of state. The Association also sent him to Mississippi to solve a puzzling case.

"Cattle were disappearing from a ranch that was near the Gulf of Mexico. As far as the owners were concerned, their cattle were being stolen, but I proved to them that that was not the case.

The ranch was right on Bay St. Louis, where the tide came in and out, and the mosquitoes, horseflies, and other bugs were just as thick as could be. Those insects annoyed the cattle and pushed them right down onto the bank of the bayou or cut. Then the cattle pushed each other off into the water. That wasn't always a problem. I saw places where an animal could be pushed off into the water but could swim out and get back up the bank. A cow can float for a long time—even hours. If a tide carries her, she can just float with it. They lost a lot of cattle this way.

"The only thing was that the water was deep enough for boats to travel along there. And after a cow fell in the water and she was floating, if one of those Frenchmen came along in a boat and it was the right time of day or night, he just knocked her in the head and dragged her away and butchered her. This probably happened in some other cases, too. I couldn't say for certain, but knowing that part of the country and some of those people, that sort of solved the mystery as to where all the cattle were going.

"The same thing happened back near my district in Texas at Hoskin's Mound between Freeport and Galveston. Tide waters had cut the bank so steep that when and if a cow fell in, she couldn't get back out. She generally wore herself out until she drowned."

There was never a case that couldn't be solved. One thing Leonard learned was not to ever let up or give in. People might come to him and beg for the thief, but if he could prove he was guilty with the evidence he had, he would try him.

"If you ever favor a suspect in any way, it will carry on and from then on, you have lost your credibility. That's best left to the judge and jury to determine if he's guilty or innocent from the evidence."

Stiles dealt with all kinds of thieves—some who would catch a calf, tie it up, and load it in the back of their car. They were "Saturday night butchers," who killed a calf for a barbecue, and they were hard to make a case on. Others stole several hundred head. There was one thief who could load cattle in his trailer, no matter how wild they were, with one dog. He even picked up a trailer-load of cattle in sight of two Border Patrolmen. He was so blatant that they thought he was the owner.

"Sheriff Tiny Gaston was a big man and all muscle," Stiles said. "One time he called me to go with him to the police department in Houston. They had picked a woman up for prostitution, and she told them that she was from Fort Bend County in my district. Her husband had worked for Pete Finley. Finley had a resort-type operation where people from Houston held big parties and political gatherings and such."

Pete Finley lived at the front gate. He had some Hispanic workers out of Houston who would come clean up the place after these parties, but this woman's husband had worked there full time. He had left her and their children and gone to the car racetrack where he was making big money, but he wasn't sending her any of it. That's why she was in Houston working as a prostitute.

"When Tiny and I got to the Police Department, I spoke to her in Mexican, and you would have thought I was her best friend. She really spoke as good English as I do. She explained that she had to make a living. Here she was at the jail, her husband was out free, and he had butchered Pete Finley's calves. Well, that got my attention."

That was back in the veal days. Pete had a herd of cattle at his place, and the Houston market was a top market for veal. He had this Hispanic—the woman's husband—creep-feeding his calves. When the time came to go to market, he'd pen the cattle and cut off thirty calves and take them to market. Then there would be thirty bawling cows looking for their babies. That's when the husband did his own butchering. No one counted to see how many mama cows were bawling.

Pete Finley and Leonard were friends, and when Stiles told him what was happening, he said, "You're crazy, Leonard. He couldn't have gotten past me at the gate." But they counted cattle, and he was short. They compared dates and determined that when Pete shipped was when the man got the calves. But where did he butcher them?

The woman said, "My husband butchered them right here, and we put the meat in the car so we could get by Mr. Finley at the gate."

"What did he do with the hides?" asked Leonard.

"He buried them—right out there at the woodpile." Stiles looked dubious. "I can show you. I'm telling the truth," she insisted.

Leonard laughed as he told about looking for the hides—the little bitty Mexican woman running around the woodpile, jabbering—Tiny Gaston, as big as the barn door, with his arms draped over the clothesline pole, and Leonard wielding the shovel, digging under the woodpile where the woman indicated. "It was the funniest picture you ever saw!" Stiles laughed. But he found the hides.

"That taught me something," he said later. "From then on, if I worked a butchering case, I'd always look for fresh dirt at the suspect's woodpile."

Pete Finley filed on the man in Harris County, and he spent time in prison.

For eleven years, Stiles worked day and night developing cow stealing cases. It was a demanding job both mentally and physically. He was sometimes away from home two weeks at a time. He worked late and started early, so he often just slept in the jail rather than drive a long distance home. He was likely to be anywhere in his district, and the thieves knew it.

"It gets in your blood," Stiles admitted. "I enjoyed it. Then I got to the point where the ol' boy I would be after would know me and what I was doing. I took it that he was trying to beat me and I was trying to beat him. I'd just put in more hours until I caught him. I'd make a case and get him to court. Then some jackleg lawyer would come along and get him off. The judge would just sit there and let it happen. I'd wind up wanting to whip somebody. I knew if I stayed at that job, I was bound to do something I'd regret. I wanted no more to do with law enforcement. I had to make a change, but it had to be a job where I could support Mary and our five children."

The Stiles had made many good friends in Leonard's district and in the Association. It was a hard decision to make, but Leonard decided it was time to move on.

During branding time, cowhands come in all sizes, ca. 1985.

Courtesy of King Ranch Archives, King Ranch, Inc.

The barge "Lula Belle," outfitted with cattle pens, carried 515 King Ranch Santa Gertrudis steers from Texas up the Mississippi and Ohio rivers to the ranch's Pennsylvania property in 1963.

Chapter 4
That's How Brands Travel

Leonard Stiles had met Bob Kleberg through Graves Peeler, and when Mr. Bob offered him a job with the King Ranch, he thought about it. "We had made so many good friends while I worked for the TSCRA," Leonard reflected. "With five kids, we couldn't have made it without their help. The local cattle associations even supplemented my income to keep me there, or I would have had to move on much sooner. I didn't like that. It was a big decision, but I wanted out of law enforcement."

The original job opening at the King Ranch didn't materialize, so Stiles still had made no move when the Association sent him to the valley area to investigate a theft case. He went through Bishop, Texas, on his way to the valley, and Dick Kleberg was at the Caesar Pens, so he stopped. Richard Kleberg Jr. was Bob Kleberg's nephew and managed the Texas ranch. He became chairman of the King Ranch board of directors in 1969. Mr. Dick, as Leonard called him, asked him how things were going. "What's your status now?"

"I've got to make a change where I can make more money," Stiles said. "I'm either going to Florida with the Hudgins outfit or up to Colorado."

"Leonard, the day you turn in your resignation with the Association, your pay starts here at the King Ranch."

Stiles thought about the offer and accepted it. He had some cases to close before he turned in his badge, but he sent in his resignation. "I worked through July 1961 and was put on the King Ranch payroll on August 1, 1961. I didn't miss a day's pay."

The pay was better, but he didn't exactly get away from law enforcement for a while. He was security officer on the Santa Gertrudis Division, though as time passed, he took on other responsibilities. On March 20, 1972, Leonard was made manager of the Santa Gertrudis Division, and Joe Stiles, one of Leonard and Mary's two sons, was named manager of the ranch's Quarter Horse Division.

The King Ranch was known throughout the industry for developing the Santa Gertrudis breed of beef cattle. The cross of ⅝ Shorthorn and ⅜ Brahman produced a hardy breed that could cope with harsh climate and range conditions and still maintain growth characteristics that produce heavier weaning weights. This was developed by an intensive program of linebreeding and inbreeding to the blood of a single sire, a bull known as "Monkey," born on the ranch in 1920.

This concentration of blood lines was carried out by the ranch in a carefully controlled scientific program that lasted forty years with many generations of cattle. Careful selection in breeding Monkey's progeny fixed in the breed a predictable degree of uniformity and prepotence. All cattle in the King Ranch's foundation herd, both males and females, were direct descendants of the big, dark red bull, Monkey. It is a breed "dedicated to the economical production of quality beef in a wide spectrum of environments," wrote Jay Nixon in *Stewards of a Vision*, published by the King Ranch in 1986.

Courtesy of King Ranch Archives, King Ranch, Inc.

The first public auction of Santa Gertrudis bulls was held at the ranch in 1950, and in April of 1951, the Santa Gertrudis Breeders International (SGBI) was founded in Kingsville, Texas. From that time on, the big, red cattle not only grazed in the King Ranch pastures of South Texas and on other ranches throughout the United States, but they spread to cattle raising countries worldwide. While Dick Kleberg managed the 825,000-acre King Ranch in Texas, Bob Kleberg expanded their operations into South America, Australia, Spain, and Morocco and added an additional eight million acres to their responsibilities. The ranch also owned other properties in West Texas, Florida, Kentucky, Mississippi, and Pennsylvania.

In addition to Leonard's regular duties on the Santa Gertrudis Division, he made several trips for the King Ranch that proved memorable. One was in 1963, when he and his son Joe, then a teenager, accompanied 516 head of two-year-old Santa Gertrudis steers on an historic trip by water from Corpus Christi to Elizabeth, Pennsylvania, to the King Ranch's Buck and Doe Run Valley Farms.

"We lost only one animal," Leonard said. "We loaded the steers onto trucks at our Plomo Pens not far from headquarters and hauled them to Corpus. When we unloaded them onto the barge in Corpus, one steer ran down the ramp onto the barge and slipped on the deck. I think he hurt his back, because he soon got down. He died about Morgan City, Louisiana, and in order to get rid of the carcass, I cut him up and fed the fish and alligators."

The barge had been built to transport automobiles, and it stood about twenty feet higher than other barges. Cattle pens were built on the top two decks. "The floors sloped, which made it easy to use a pressure hose and wash the manure out of the pens and overboard, which we thought was no problem," Stiles continued. "We tried to keep the slush off of the decks because of the cool nights. The load was in the bottom of the barge where hay and sacks of feed for the trip were stowed."

They left Corpus with three men plus Joe and Leonard, but one man quit at Greenville, Mississippi.

A tug pushed the barge along the Intracoastal Canal to Morgan City, Louisiana, where they headed up the Atchafalaya River to Baton Rouge. There the cattle barge was cabled together in the center of twenty-nine other barges, four or five wide, to be pushed up the Mississippi River to Cairo, Illinois, by the tug *Northern*. There they would enter the Ohio River.

They made stops at ports along the river to leave barges and pick up others, but the huge flotilla traveled upstream twenty-four hours a day and averaged four miles an hour. Only a capable river captain can navigate the Mississippi because of the continual shifting and build-up of sandbars and the changing of the channel.

Leonard and Joe were feeding one day when the barge made a strange movement, accompanied by what sounded like loud shots. "We looked up and the men on the barges fell on the decks. Everyone was excited. We had hung up on a sand bar, and the cables that held the barges together were snapping," Leonard recalled. "Cables and bolts were flying everywhere like shrapnel. The only thing to do, we learned later, was to lie flat on the deck.

"We sat there for six days and nights while the Corps of Engineers dug us out. We rationed feed to the cattle, and because of the delay, we ordered more. After we were back underway, a ship came right up beside us, tied onto us, and transferred the feed.

"We passed the riverboat, *Delta Queen*, in the fog and her captain radioed, 'I can't see you, but I sure can smell you!'

"After we entered the Ohio River, we stopped at a town, and a crowd of people were there to see us. We had caused a stir during the entire trip and the news media were there all along the way. We were on deck when one of the hands pointed out a man in the crowd. 'He is with the Ohio River Authority, and he's going to get you for polluting,' the barge man said.

"Sure enough, the man filed on the ranch. He had been on board as a tourist, taking pictures of everything and of us washing the manure overboard. He objected to its contents of water and ground grain, but we could see big pipes from the refineries emptying black sludge into the river. That was apparently all right. We just let the manure stack up from there on.

"After we entered the Ohio River, we passed through fifty-two locks before we reached Elizabeth, Pennsylvania, near Pittsburgh. We unloaded the steers onto trucks for the final 236 miles to the King Ranch's property near Coatesville. The Buck and Doe Run Valley Farms was operated by Bob Kleberg's daughter, Helenita Groves."

The barge trip had taken thirty days of travel. "We could have made it in less time," Leonard said, "but the rivers were at a record low. Amazingly, the cattle gained weight. The only time they went off feed was while we were stuck on the sand bar for six days. They had gotten use to the movement while traveling."

This river transport was an experiment to see if it were feasible to ship cattle in this manner for fattening on the King Ranch's Pennsylvania property, and thus cut down on the rates charged by the railroads. This first trip did prove to be cheaper, but Leonard was warned by the unions that the ranch would have to deal with them on any trips after that.

They told him, "You know, Tex, we'd like to be friends, but next time you come up the river, come up with the union, 'cause we're scabbing when we have anything to do with you. We've helped you this trip, because it is the first time in history to do something like this, but next time is business!"

So that was the first and last barge trip up the Mississippi and Ohio rivers for King Ranch cattle. But there is an interesting side note to the trip. Elizabeth, Pennsylvania, where the cattle were unloaded, was the site of the shipyards that built two steamships for M. Kenedy & Co. of Brownsville, Texas, in 1850. The ships were designed to haul merchandise and passengers on the Rio Grande by one of the company's partners, Captain Richard King. The Captain even oversaw part of their construction, and in 1857, he ordered two more ships.

Captain King was also the founder of the King Ranch, so you can bet he would have thought it good business to ship **Running W** cattle by river. But the rules of the river had changed during the century that had passed, and that was the last barge trip up the Mississippi for cattle that still carry the Captain's brand. However, no one can deny its success. The King Ranch had once more made history, and Leonard and Joe Stiles were part of it.

Courtesy of King Ranch Archives, King Ranch, Inc.

Stiles passes the time on the barge by tossing a loop with a BIG rope which amuses his 16-year-old son, Joe Stiles, as Pat Miller looks on.

The Big House stands regally at King Ranch headquarters on the ranch's Santa Gertrudis Division in South Texas, ca. 1930.

Chapter 5
A Running W Escapee in Morocco

Leonard Stiles made two other long trips by ship with **Running W** cattle and horses—one in 1970 to deliver horses and Santa Gertrudis cattle to the King Ranch property in Morocco and another the next year to take animals to the King Ranch's property in Spain near the Portuguese border.

The trip to Morocco aboard the Dutch Steamship Company's M.V. *Ino* with El Moral, a seven-year-old chestnut stallion, eight Quarter mares, 140 Santa Gertrudis bulls, and thirty-six heifers, was "an accident looking for a place to happen" right from its beginning in Houston. If Leonard hadn't been so sick with the flu when he boarded the ship, the whole thing might have been funny. He laughed later when he looked back at the experience.

"Things went wrong from the start," he recalled. "There was so much graft on the Houston docks among the officials and longshoremen, that payoffs were required to get anything done. When we finally got underway and out into the Gulf of Mexico, we went through a bad storm and the roughest weather of the trip."

The ship's hatches had no covers and the waves washed in and drenched the animals and the hay stowed for their use. There was no ventilation in the hold, not even any fans, and no way to get rid of the accumulation of manure. The heat and the stench were almost unbearable. With a combination of the flu and being seasick, Leonard had to crawl on his hands and knees just to feed the stock.

The ship's crew could have cared less. "If you wonder if cattle and horses get seasick, I can tell you they do. They lie down and don't care what's happening around them. The trip was to be hell all the way," Stiles said.

The *Ino* had a scheduled stop in Martinique where it would take on water for the Atlantic crossing. When they arrived at Fort de France, the captain, a Spaniard, was drunk and almost plowed into the dock with his ship. Then the crew got into a fight and the local police took half of them to jail. In the excitement, the second in command failed to take on the full load of water before port authorities had the ship backed out into the bay. They got under way for North Africa short of water. Water was rationed during the crossing, and it was to be a long, hard trip.

One month later, Leonard sighted the shoreline of Morocco and anticipated the end of his troubles. The ship lay off the coast near Rabat and waited for the tide that would carry it inland ten miles up a river to the port of Kenitra. Stiles had made the animals ready for off-loading at

Kenitra and was on deck to see the farms and people who lived and worked along the river. While the ship docked, he leaned on the rail and watched. They had no more than tied up when a fight broke out on the dock, and once more, the police were quickly on the scene.

"It was something else!" Stiles said. "Those people fight over everything. The Moroccan dock workers were big, hefty guys, but all had turbans on their heads and wore what looked like their nightgowns," as Leonard called the Moroccan men's traditional clothing, the *djellabah*, an ankle-length robe. He soon learned that his trouble was not over.

"I had nothing to do with unloading the cattle, so I just watched. The ranch had sent small British lorries—short bed, bobtail trucks—to haul the cattle thirty miles to the nearby farm and the horses to Ranch Adarouch near Fez. The lorries looked like hog trucks with tailgates that let down and were held by chains on either side. Each one held only six bulls. I was skeptical, but that's all they had.

"I told those men, 'My god, I don't know how we're going to load these cattle on these little lorries!' I'm not sure they even understood me. They just nodded and grinned and backed a lorry into position and started loading the bulls. As the bulls crossed the tailgate and went to the front of the truck, the dock workers closed the gate and chained it like they did it every day.

"When animals are scared or in a strange place, no matter how wild they are, they'll usually stay together and you can handle them. But if one does break loose, he's gone!

"Everything was going along fine, and the men were doing things with those cattle I just couldn't believe. All of the sudden, one big bull just couldn't stand it any longer. The dock workers were closing the tailgate when that bull turned and came out right over the top of them, stepping on their heads. Down the dock he went! I mean, he took off! He scattered people everywhere. There was warehouse after warehouse up and down the dock, and the doors were open where they were loading or unloading. The bull finally slowed down enough to cut off and head into one of those open doors. He really scattered them! Workers came running out with their nightgown tails flying!"

Leonard had a dilemma. He had to catch that bull and he didn't even have a rope. The only one to be found was a big, heavy rope used to lash an automobile down on the ship's deck—not one for roping but it beat nothing. A policeman on the dock had a jeep and motioned for Leonard to get in. They raced down to the warehouse. When Leonard got out, the policeman left. He didn't plan to help.

Inside the warehouse, the bull had headed for the far end and bayed up in a corner. Stiles hurried all he could to get down there with the heavy rope.

"I didn't know what I could do afoot, but I had to do something. Those dock workers were big, stout fellows who knew how to handle heavy loads even if they were wearing dresses. I was counting on them for help when the time came.

"The bull was standing in the corner, pawing and daring someone to get close, and I hollered at the men to stay back. They didn't understand a word I said, so I finally resorted to sign language. They were wondering what a little guy like me could do with that big bull, and frankly, I was, too."

A forklift was parked nearby, and Leonard made it known that if the driver could take him in close and raise him up so that the bull couldn't hook him, maybe he could get a rope on the animal. He didn't want to be so high that the bull could run by him. He had to keep him in that corner.

Stiles built a loop and tied the other end of the rope to the forklift. The rope was so heavy it would be hard to throw, but if he could get close enough, he might be able to drop the loop over the big, red animal's head.

"The bull was in good position as we eased in toward him. Just as I swung my heavy rope and made my throw, he made a break to get past us. The forklift operator got excited and lifted me high, so my loop landed just in front of the bull's hips, which really was lucky. With the rope tied to the forklift and me up high, if I had caught him, he would have turned the whole works over.

"The warehouse was full of Moroccans, talking and hollering, and as the bull charged back through the building, he knocked them down and sent them flying! I don't know why someone wasn't killed. About that time, a man stopped a lorry in the doorway, so the bull ran past the door and bayed up again in the far corner. I had another chance at him.

"I decided it was best to stay off of the forklift. There were stacks of boxes and soft goods near him that I could run up on if I had to, so I would try it on foot. I hurried to get down to him before he left the corner, but that big coil of rope was about to weigh me down. I could barely swing the loop, and I knew I would just have one throw. He spotted me, and I could see him thinking, 'I know that guy, and I'm not staying around long!' He had already made a few runs at some of the Moroccans. They'd run off and then get right back in his way. They're crazy people!

"I got close to him, and here he came. I stepped aside and chunked it on him. I roped him around his shoulders, and I was hanging on. Man, he jerked me! I wasn't even slowing him down. I had a tiger by the tail. To my surprise, about thirty of those dock workers fell on that rope and grabbed hold. Then I worried that we were going to get that bull stopped, and he'd come right back up that rope. That's what he did. It flipped those guys and all I could see were arms and legs and their dress tails up over their heads, but they stayed with him. I knew I had to get another rope on him fast. They were all hollering, and there was such a roar in that tin building that I couldn't hear myself think.

"The men finally got the rope around a post and stopped the bull. I motioned to one fellow to get me another rope, and he did. I got up to the bull once more, and when he came around the post after me, I stuck it on him real pretty-like. A bunch of men fell on the rope, and now we had two ropes on him. Things were looking better. We choked him down, and he got to staggering. I ran up to him and grabbed him by the tail and pulled it up between his legs and reared back on it. I had him now.

"I motioned for the men to slack off on the ropes, because he was struggling to breathe, but they were afraid he would get loose from me. Of course, once they gave him some slack, he quit fighting. They had never seen this done before, and they didn't know how a little guy like I am could hold that big bull down by myself. They were hollering and cheering. They thought I was a miracle worker!

"I kept trying to get one of the biggest guys to come over and take my place holding the bull's tail, so I could get a rope and sideline him and tie him down. They were all reluctant. All of the sudden there was another big ruckus, and they were all fighting again. Here I was, a little guy, holding that big brute down and they were fighting about who was going to help me. I couldn't tell if they wanted to or didn't want to. When the fight was over, I still had the bull. I never could get one of them to get the drift of holding the bull down, but one man finally brought me a rope. I was out of breath, but I could see I was alone from here on in.

"I kept my knee in the bull's loin in case he tried to kick. By holding his tail with one hand and working with the other, I finally got the rope on one front leg and pulled it up to the bottom hind leg. With those two secure, I finally got all four feet tied. Then I had to sit there and wait while the Moroccans jabbered and sang again. That suited me. I needed to blow for a minute."

From the Cattle Raisers Museum Permanent Collection

The next problem Leonard had was deciding what he was going to do with the bull. He found an empty pallet and motioned to his nightgowned constituents, explaining that they would use a rope and roll the bull up on the pallet. One of the big guys got the idea, and he tried to tell the others what to do. They got to arguing and fighting again. Leonard decided that was just their way of life, so he waited. When the fight was over, they rolled the bull onto the pallet, and the forklift operator raised the pallet and bull up while another man backed the lorry up. They slid the bull into the truck and closed the tail gate.

"I wanted to leave him tied down until we got back to the other cattle," Stiles explained.

The lorries, Leonard learned, were equipped with wire nets over the cabs where the drivers carried their blankets and camping equipment. After the bull was loaded, another fight determined which man could sit in the net and ride with the bull back down the dock.

"I was keeping an eye on the bull," Leonard said, "and I kept seeing a man's head pop up and down. It was that guy who was supposed to be in the net. I couldn't figure out what he was doing, so I crawled up to take a look. He was trying to take the rope off of that bull. The floor was so slick, I don't think the bull could have done anything, but if he could get footing, he could have jumped over the side and been gone. I finally got it into that man's head to leave the bull alone.

"We headed back down the dock with the bull in the lorry and that whole bunch of men fell in behind us, singing and carrying on. It was a sight!

"When we got back to the rest of the cattle that were now loaded in the lorries, I untied the bull and turned him into one of the trucks. He was glad to be in familiar company, but he wasn't half as relieved as I was," Stiles admitted.

During the month's trip, Leonard had fed 1,052 bales of hay and 393 sacks of grain. The cattle were delivered safely to the farm and the horses to Ranch Adarouch in the edge of the Atlas Mountains. Leonard admitted that his trip back to Texas was dull by comparison, and he was thankful for that.

Cattle were one of the earliest species of animals to be domesticated in the lands around the Mediterranean, and many of its ancient civilizations developed a form of bull worship. From this came bull vaulting as seen on the island of Crete 3,500 years ago, and even today's Spanish and Portuguese bull fighting had its foundation in that dim past. Mythology and legends evolved concerning men and bulls, such as the Greek myth that has been told for centuries of the Athenian youth, Theseus, and his conquest of the half-bull, half-man Minotaur.

Think of the stories related today by swarthy men dressed in *djellabahs* and with fezzes or turbans on their heads as they recall the slight foreigner who came to Morocco and out-witted the big, red bull. Finally, single-handed, he held him down until he subdued and captured him.

That's the stuff of legend.

But Leonard Stiles would have told you he was just a cowman doing his job.

Cowboys drive a "windy" of cattle to a round-up on the Smith Brothers ranch.

Chapter 6
Three Crosses to Mexico—Running W to Spain

For four centuries, branded stock had sailed across the Atlantic Ocean. Among the first were Hernán Cortés's horses and **Three Crosses**-branded cattle that traveled from Spain to America during the 1500s, and then the King Ranch's **Running W**-branded cattle and horses that made the crossing from America to Spain in 1971. Yet it was an adventure that was not all that common. Leonard Stiles of the King Ranch was the "trail boss" on the trip. He had made a similar trip to Morocco the year before that proved to be anything but common.

King Ranch España consisted of three properties west of Seville—Los Millares, Navalagrulla, and Guadiamar. King Ranch España was owned eighty percent by the King Ranch-Texas and twenty percent by private Spanish citizens. The cattle and horses sent to Spain in 1971 went to Los Millares, known for its brave bulls—the *Concha y Sierra* fighting bulls.

The ranch was established April 10, 1882, and again, was long known for its outstanding bulls. Ranches where fighting bulls are raised are known as *ganaderias*. At that time, there were 259 accredited *ganaderias* in Spain. At the turn of the century, the *Concha y Sierra* bulls were considered the best in Spain.

The purpose of sending Santa Gertrudis cattle to Spain was to increase beef production by crossbreeding with native breeds. The brave cattle were kept to themselves in their own pastures on Los Millares away from the native cattle and the Santa Gertrudis from Texas.

Plans for the shipment began in Texas more than eight months before the departure date in June 1971. The animals to be sent were 41 certified Santa Gertrudis bulls, 272 heifers that had been served through artificial insemination, and 16 registered Quarter Horses. They all had to be free of contagious and parasitic diseases before leaving. They were chosen from the various divisions of the King Ranch in Texas.

Feed and bedding went with them. There were twenty-three tons of cattle cubes and three tons of horse pellets plus 1,900 bales of hay. The cattle and horses were started on the feed they would eat while on board ship two weeks before shipment. Space was booked on the *M.S. Athene*, owned by C. Clausen Steamship Company Limited of Denmark. It would embark from Houston for Huelva, Spain, on June 2, 1971.

It took hours of planning and mountains of paper work as well as physical labor to choose the cattle and horses and ready them for the journey. Leonard Stiles was to accompany the animals as he had done the year before when the ranch sent stock to Morocco. This time, Peter McBride would also go along. On May 30, Stiles and ranch veterinarian Monte Moncrief flew to Houston to inspect the ship and talk with Captain Karsten and Chief Officer Dickneite. Pens and stalls had been built on board ship to accommodate the stock.

Meanwhile, back at the ranch, all the animals had been gathered and weighed. The 272 two-year-old heifers weighed an average of 760 pounds each; 40 bulls averaged 1,000 pounds, and the other bull weighed about 2,300 pounds. Sixteen horses averaged 976 pounds. It took twelve trailers to haul the animals to Houston and three other trailers to haul the feed. The 1,900 bales of hay and salt blocks were delivered by the shipping agent, Orlando Puig, at ship side. They also had 200 bales of bedding for the stalls. Leonard noted later that they needed more hay to feed, since the bales furnished by the agent were not as heavy as promised.

The animals were delivered to Port City Stockyards in Houston. Stiles, Dr. J. K. Northway, longtime veterinarian at the King Ranch, Peter McBride, and Chief Officer Dickneite flew to Houston in the ranch plane and began checking cattle at the Port City yards and vaccinating them for anthrax.

Stiles had a complete list of cattle and horses and the brands on each. Tuesday, June 1, the animals arrived by truck on the dock, and they began loading cattle, horses, and feed. They finished at 12:30 A.M. Wednesday morning and sailed at 1:05. Leonard kept a night watchman on duty throughout the night, but he himself checked the animals several times after sailing, and all was quiet. Most of the animals were down in the hold, but there was good ventilation. Leonard saw the lights of Galveston to the starboard at almost daylight, and an hour later, the pilot left the ship. They had traveled only fifty-two miles, but they were on their way.

Stiles began a feeding routine—grain and water in the morning; hay and water in the evening. There was no problem with water on this ship, as there had been on the trip to Morocco.

He moved some of the bulls and horses around to give them more room. On June 4, they passed near Key West. The ship's first mate and doctor checked all the animals for sickness or temperature. It was apparent that they had not seen Leonard's medicine kit! He was prepared for any emergency.

They sailed past the Bahamas and headed for the Azores. Everything was fine except the mares were cantankerous and biting themselves.

John A. Stryker photo from the Cattle Raisers Museum Permanent Collection

By the sixth day, a few of the cattle had swollen hips and one had slipped a horn, but most were eating all their ration and doing well. Leonard remembered seeing a school of small, black whales, sending up spouts of water in the vast Atlantic waters.

On the ninth day out, Stiles walked the mares and stallions around on deck, because their ankles were swelling from lack of activity. That night, the crew had trouble, and the steward was placed in jail. Peter and Leonard took turns standing watch through the night.

The next day, they were short handed, but everything was calm, and the sea was smooth. Stiles enjoyed watching the flying fish running in front of the ship. This crossing was easier than the last.

The following day, the flies arrived, but the animals were okay. The men thought they must have hatched in the hay or feed. The next few days were cool and calm, and the ship made good time. The captain wired the agent in Spain of their expected time of arrival, and the agent advised Michael Hughes with King Ranch España at the main office in Seville. Leonard continued to walk the stallions.

On the fifteenth day, the sea was rough. There was a problem on deck with a drunk sailor. That was the least of their trouble. That night, another drunk sailor wrapped a bull's tail around a pipe and pulled it off.

The ship maneuvered through rough water off the coast of Spain the next day, but they picked up the pilot late that afternoon and moved into the harbor west of Huelva where they dropped anchor about 11:30 P.M. Leonard brushed all the horses and by 5:30 A.M., all the animals were ready to off-load. Michael Hughes of King Ranch España came aboard, but they did not dock until 12:30 noon, and the paper work took some time. Twenty bob-tail trucks were at the dock to haul cattle and horses and the remainder of the feed to the ranch. Stiles noted that the trucks were similar to the ones they used in Morocco. It was 10:30 P.M. before all the animals were unloaded and left for the ranch, forty-five miles northwest of Huelva. Leonard and Pete went to a hotel for the night.

Hughes, Stiles, and Pete drove to Los Millares the next morning and spent the afternoon looking after the cattle and horses. The pastures were green and lush due to recent rains, but water was scarce, and the cattle had to be driven to water holes. Leonard and Peter stayed at the ranch for several days until Stiles was sure the cattle and horses were settled. When they left, they went to Seville and visited the King Ranch office there before flying to Casablanca, Morocco, to check the cattle and horses at Ranch Adarouch and King Ranch Moroc. Then it was back to Texas.

Stiles kept a diary of the trip, as he had done on each of the other trips, and he made a detailed report to the King Ranch office on his return to Texas. All things considered, it had been a successful trip. The animals arrived in good condition other than one bull was minus a tail.

On March 20, 1972, Leonard Stiles was named manager of the Santa Gertrudis Division of the King Ranch in Texas. Today's ranch complex on this headquarters division of the King Ranch properties stands at the site of Captain Richard King's original Santa Gertrudis Rancho. It was founded by the Captain and his partner, Texas Ranger Captain Gideon "Legs" Lewis, in 1853. They established a cow camp on a slight rise above a seep spring that feeds Santa Gertrudis Creek, near where today's Big House now stands. While negotiations and paper work were in process for the purchase of the 15,500-acre Rincon de Santa Gertrudis Grant, Captain Lewis oversaw the build-up of cattle and horse herds. His company of Texas Rangers guarded the stock and *vaqueros* from Comanches and marauding bandits for the first few months. This area was called the Wild Horse Desert, but the families who had been granted land there by the Spanish crown and later by the Mexican government, called it the Desert of the Dead and left it deserted for seventeen years.

At first, Captain King continued with his riverboat business, transporting goods along the Rio Grande, but he soon spent less and less time on the river. The land and its cattle drew him north, and before long, he left the river for good. He had begun negotiations to purchase the 53,000 de la Garza Santa Gertrudis grant when an irate husband shot and killed Legs Lewis in Corpus Christi on April 14, 1855. Lewis left no will and had no heirs, so the estate was settled by the Probate Court, and the land remained with Captain King.

The present King Ranch headquarters is located on the original site chosen by Richard King. Leonard Stiles assumed the management of the day-to-day operation of the 203,468-acre Santa Gertrudis Division on March 20, 1972, a position he held until he retired in 1988. The Santa Gertrudis is one of the four divisions that make up the King Ranch in South Texas, and at that time, they were operated as separate ranches, though all under jurisdiction of the main office at the headquarters ranch. The other three divisions are the Laureles, the Norias, and the Encino.

Stiles oversaw the feeding and care of the horses and cattle, including weaning, classifying, dipping, preventative medicines, branding, castrating, assisting in palpation and semen collection. He saw to the maintenance of fences, pens, windmills, pastures, tick and fly prevention, supply inventories and purchasing. It was a full-time job.

Many changes occurred during those years, and when Stiles retired and no longer had his days and nights filled with the problems of running the Santa Gertrudis, Stephen "Tio" Kleberg, a great-great-grandson of Richard King and the vice-president of King Ranch Inc., asked him if he would be interested in staying on and showing the ranch to interested visitors. No one knew the land and its animals and history better than Leonard did. Stiles agreed, and he and Mary continued to live on the ranch until his death, September 8, 2001.

Leonard Stiles had lived a full life. He had seen and done things that he never dreamed of when he was riding herd on Rocky Reagan's wild steers and learning the fine art of brush popping at *Punta del Monte*. Through his work as an inspector for the Texas and Southwestern Cattle Raisers Association and then with the King Ranch, he had the unique opportunity to meet ranchers from throughout the west and around the world and to acquire his unusual branding iron collection. He and his steadfast companion, Mary, then chose to place the irons in the Cattle Raisers Museum where all visitors could enjoy them and understand the lifetime of work that is represented by each of these ironclad signatures of ranch men and ranch women throughout Texas and the West.

Working close to the fire, cowboys brand calves in the corrals at the J. W. Merrell ranch in the Big Bend region of Texas, ca. 1920.

A typical branding scene was captured in this photo by Frank Reeves, ca. 1933.

Cowboys cross the Rio Grande with a herd belonging to W. R. Cartledge of Castolon in Texas's Big Bend country.

Part Two

Tom Saunders IV watches as farrier Edwin Eppenauer fires up the old forge at ranch headquarters to shape a branding iron.

Proof of Ownership
The Leonard Stiles Branding Iron Collection

For half a century, Leonard Stiles collected branding irons and meticulously recorded their histories—or lack of any in some cases—as told to him by the owners of the brands. Stiles assigned a number to each iron as he received it, and the number coincided with a numbered history in his files. He listed each brand, where and when it was recorded, by whom, the location it was branded on the animal, earmarks, when and where and from whom he received the iron, and additional brief comments. Some irons have little or no information. Stiles's remarks as he wrote them at the time he acquired each iron appear in the following list. The owners' names and spellings are his.

Through the years, as he acquired more information on an iron or its owner, he saved it in a brown, legal-sized envelope that had the name and number on it that matched the tag on the iron. Much of the information written by the author that appears in parentheses following Leonard's comments, comes from that additional data that includes articles from *The Cattleman Magazine* and other magazines, obituaries, newspaper clippings, and letters from the owners. Some is also taken from the numerous notes and scrapbooks that Stiles kept. The notes are meant as interesting highlights and not necessarily current information. As Stiles received an iron, he branded it on a board. When he exhibited his collection at banks and fairs and conventions, he also showed these boards full of brands.

Stiles knew the importance of earmarks on cattle. If an earmark was recorded with a brand and he was aware of it, he showed it in his files as part of the history of the brand. Some brands had no earmarks at all. No earmarks are shown in the following list of brands, but those that Stiles recorded can be researched in the Cattle Raisers Museum archives.

For centuries, earmarks have been registered at the time a brand was recorded. They are an important part of an animal's identification, but they alone are not proof of ownership, because they are too easy to change or cut away completely. There are more than 250 different types and combinations of earmarks, and their names are part of cow country lingo—half crop, over slope, punch, grub, V over bit, U under bit, swallow fork, under round, slit, split or jinglebob. It is easier to show the earmarks drawn on a small drawing of ears as they are on the registration form, than to describe them in words. In Stiles's records, he wrote, for example, on branding iron number 160, the **2 4** brand of George W. Armstrong of Needville, Texas: "The brand is placed on the left thigh and carries the following earmark: ⬭⬭." That is a quicker reference than writing out "a tip on the left and an under split on the right."

There are also many brands and many ways to design a brand. Letters or numbers may be single, double, or connected figures and referred to as standard, flying, hooked, barbed, running, walking, dragging, backward, rafter, swinging, rocking, lazy or lying down, tumbling, long, or up and down. Some are in boxes, diamonds, circles, and others are picture brands, such as the anchor, a rocking chair, a hat, a wineglass, a heart. A brand is read from left to right, then from top to bottom. It is read from outside to inside, such as **Circle A**. An owner can call a brand whatever he or she likes, no matter what someone else thinks it looks like. In the following collection, a few brands have no names listed, and it is not an oversight. Apparently Leonard did not receive that information. The names that are shown are as Stiles wrote them.

When a Texas brand is registered, the location where the brand will be placed on cattle or horses is also recorded and must be adhered to. One rancher might brand a **P** on the right hip and another rancher in the same county could brand a **P** on the left shoulder. They are two different brands. According to Texas law, a brand and earmarks must be recorded with the county clerk in the county where the brand is used, so there can be duplications of brands throughout the state.

Brand laws are determined by individual states and do not apply nationwide. A brand in Texas can be placed on either side of the animal, identified as left or right, on the hip, loin, thigh, rib, shoulder, jaw, or awls—anywhere on left (or right) side. No brand except a county brand is placed on the neck of an animal. According to the law, "The Secretary of State is required to furnish a printed list of the county brands to each County Clerk who must post the list in his or her office. The owner of horses and cattle, in addition to his private brand, may place the county brand on the neck of all horses and cattle which he owns." This additional brand is to make the sale of stolen livestock more difficult. When horses or cattle branded with a county brand are moved to another county, the owner may counterbrand the stock with the new county brand. A county brand is one or two initials. For instance, McMullen County is **M.** and Matagorda County is **M.R.**, but not all counties were assigned brands. Some were exempt.

It is now necessary to re-record all marks and brands in the County Clerk's office every ten years on an announced date. If a brand is not re-recorded by its owner during the six month period following the announced date, it is available to anyone for use on a first come basis.

Branding irons are as varied in design as are brands. For years, many brands were put on with a running iron, a rod curved at one end and heated to draw the brand. A heated cinch ring held with two green sticks also did the trick. In the 1870s, those tools were outlawed for a time, because they made the alteration of brands too easy and gave no proof who had done it if the thief were caught. They were considered to be rustlers' tools. A man who didn't mind running a brand on a maverick or unbranded stock was often called a "ring toter." However, many ranchers used running irons and could very efficiently run their brands on their cattle. There are several running irons included in the Stiles collections.

Before the stamp iron became popular, its forerunner was the dotting iron, as described by J. Evetts Haley in his classic biography, *Charles Goodnight, Cowman and Plainsman*. A brand was "dotted" on an animal using one or more of three irons—a straight edge or bar, a small half circle and a large half circle. A combination of these three designs made the brand. This method soon gave way to the stamp iron where a brand could be put on with one application.

Many branding irons were and are made on the ranch where they are used; others were made by local blacksmiths. The old ones were hand-forged and later ones are welded. Just as brands come in all sizes and shapes, their handles come in all lengths and configurations, though they have both become more uniform in modern times. Branding irons can be constructed of iron, steel, stainless steel, or copper. The earlier ones are made of iron or steel. The old brands were often large, since they were used on grown animals, and were "string out" brands placed on shoulder, rib, and hip. Now the TSCRA recommends that brands for grown cattle be four to five inches high and horse brands two inches high. A calf brand should be only two to three inches tall.

The most important part of the iron is the face of the brand. A brand should be as simple as possible, since intricate patterns cause a concentration of heat which causes the brand to burn out and blotch. All sharp edges should be filed off, and the face should be no wider than $\frac{3}{16}$ to $\frac{3}{8}$ inch for grown cattle, $\frac{3}{16}$ to $\frac{1}{4}$ for calves, and $\frac{1}{8}$ to $\frac{1}{4}$ inch on horse brands. When the iron is burned up and becomes too thin, it will cut deep and leave a thin scar that will cover over with hair. Before that happens, it is time to cut the brand off of the handle and replace it with a new one.

Handles were made in many lengths and often out of whatever was available. Some had a circle on the handle end to help in applying it, and some were folded back to form a handhold. Others were flared to hold a wooden handle or pointed so a corn cob could be stuck on for insulation. The brands themselves were usually welded onto the handles but a few in the Stiles collection are bolted together. Each iron is unique in its construction.

Some ranchers now use other methods to mark their cattle such as freeze branding, but the irons in the Stiles collection were heated in a gas heater or in a bed of coals as has been done for decades. The color of the face determines when it is ready for branding. It should be an ashy gray. If it is black, it is too cold to properly mark, and cherry red is too hot and will burn too deep, leaving a sore that is hard to heal and often, a blotched brand.

When the work is finished, the branding irons should be thoroughly cleaned. A bucket of sand and a wire brush will remove carbon buildup from burned hair. Then the irons should be reshaped with a file and stored in a container of oil. In the days when the cowboys stayed at the chuck wagon, the irons were carefully wrapped and stored in the wagon. Those were the days when the cattle were roped and dragged to the branding fire. Some ranchers now use squeeze chutes or tilt tables, but on many ranches, the old ways are still followed.

Carol Williams of Fort Worth, Texas, was Educational Coordinator when Leonard and Mary Stiles brought their branding irons to the Cattle Raisers Museum, and she laid the groundwork for publishing a catalog that would be helpful to museum visitors. Carol has since moved on to other endeavors, and Dr. Cheri Wolfe, Museum Director, has taken that dream a step further with the publishing of this book.

The following branding irons are listed in the order that Leonard Stiles received them and in no other order. Most of them represent Texas cattlemen, but there are brands from other states and other countries. Many of these brands have been carried on the hides of thousands of cattle and many on only a few, but each iron is important.

Texas Counties Represented
in the Leonard Stiles Branding Iron Collection

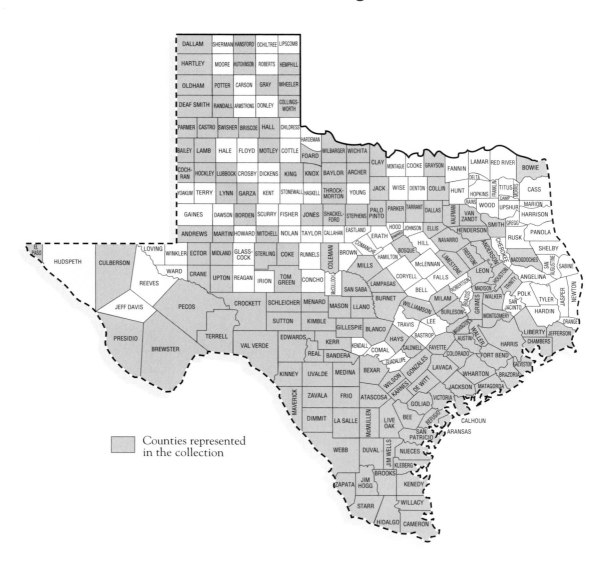

Counties represented
in the collection

The Brands

The following 1,096 brands are listed in numerical order as Stiles received them and the comments are his. Where I have added information, my comments are in parenthesis after his. No ear marks are shown but brand locations are included when known. *Source* indicates when Stiles received the iron and from whom.

Nº 1   J H Connected
D. K. Poole

The **JH Connected** brand, placed on the left hip of cattle, was recorded in Brazoria, Matagorda, Wharton, Live Oak, and Jackson counties by D. K. Poole of Bay City, Texas. Poole, a rice farmer and cattleman, operated the Cox Ranch in southwest Brazoria County, one of the first areas to be settled by Anglos in Texas, and he pastured cattle near LaWard. He sent many steers to Kansas and Oklahoma grass. Poole also branded the **Double Half Circle** on the left side and left hip and the **Half Circle A** on the left hip.

Source: Poole Ranch foreman L. L. "Monk" Chiles, 1954.

Nº 2   Open A
R. J. Nunley

The **Open A** brand is recorded in Zavala, Uvalde, Medina, Webb, Frio, LaSalle, and McMullen counties by R. J. "Red" Nunley of Sabinal, Texas. It is branded on the left hip and left thigh. The Nunley Ranch, located between Freer and Encinal, ships from Encinal. Nunley and Dolph Briscoe Sr. were partners for years. Many steers which go to northern and western markets carry this brand.

Source: R. J. Nunley, 1958, while I was working on a case with TSCRA Inspector Leon Vivian.

(R. J. Nunley, a director of the TSCRA for many years, was born in Trickham, Brown County, Texas, on January 6, 1912. He died during a deer hunt at his Encinal ranch on December 28, 1983. Former Texas Governor Dolph Briscoe Jr., his partner in the cattle business since 1954, said, "Nunley was the best cowman in Texas.")

Nº 3   LH Seven
Emil H. Marks

The **LH Seven** brand was recorded in 1898 in Harris and Fort Bend counties by Emil H. Marks of

Barker, Texas, and is placed on the right hip. Marks used this brand on his Longhorn cattle in the old days, and he still runs it on Longhorn steers. From 1926–1929, it was an E. H. Marks and W. A. Paddock partnership brand.

Source: Emil Marks, Barker, Texas, 1956, while I was on a theft case in that area.

(Emil Marks wrote to Leonard Stiles: "I wanted the 7L brand, but it was already recorded in Harris County, so I registered the LH7 brand in 1898. I was seventeen years old, a green country boy. My grandfather, Gothilf Marks, recorded ⋂ wet hat brand in 1851 in Harris County, and it is still used by my grandson, Milo Marks."

Gothilf Marks brought his family by ship from Germany to Texas in 1843. Their destination was Indianola, but there was yellow fever and smallpox there, so the ship sailed to Galveston. Gothilf's son, August Texas Marks, was born on the way to Galveston.

A. T. Marks drove cattle up the trail to Kansas on several trips. He married and Emil was born in 1881. Both August and his wife died when Emil was a boy. The youngster went to live with his uncle, Rufe Muske, where he broke horses and herded cattle for $15 a month. He became an adept cowman, and in later years, 6,670 head of cattle carried his brand at one time.

During branding in about 1918, Marks put on a small ranch rodeo for entertainment. For the next forty-one years, the LH7 Rodeo was an annual tradition, and people came from miles around. Marks was also a founder of the Salt Grass Trail Ride that opened the Houston Fat Stock Show each year.

Emil Marks was an early convert to the use of Brahman blood in his cattle so they could withstand the rigors of the Texas coast, but he always kept a herd of Longhorns as his father had. Marks was almost eighty-eight years old when he died in 1969. He was still doing what he loved—working with cattle and horses. He, like his Longhorns, was a rare breed and the backbone of the Texas cattle industry.)

D

№ 4   D
A. H. Pierce

The **D** is an old brand of the Pierce Ranch, Pierce, Texas, recorded by A. H. "Shanghai" Pierce in Wharton, Matagorda, and Brazoria counties. It is placed on the left hip or left shoulder.

The original brand, the **DK**, registered by Daniel Kinchloe in 1847, was purchased with a herd of cattle from a man named Kuykendall during the 1870s in the Texas Panhandle by Shanghai Pierce, who registered it in 1880, 1881, and 1887. The **K** was dropped because of "blotting," and the **D** alone could be made with a running iron. During trail driving days, 50,000 head of Pierce's cattle wore this brand. Pierce was known for his banking business and as a trail driver and rancher.

This iron has an unusual twisted handle and was made for Pierce by a local blacksmith. Some of the ranch's irons were made on the convict farm near Wharton.

Sam T. Cutbirth was manager of the 85,000-acre ranch when P. A. Lundy and I counted 14,000 head of cattle during the division of the Estate in February and March, 1956.

Source: Frank Anderwald, Pierce Ranch foreman, 1956.
See brand number 452.

(Able Head "Shanghai" Pierce was one of Texas's most colorful cowmen. He left his home in Rhode Island and stowed away on a schooner leaving New York for Texas on June 29, 1853, his nineteenth birthday. It was hard to hide his six foot four inch frame and the loud, nasal twang of his voice, so he mopped the decks to earn his passage. He disembarked at Lavaca, Texas. One of his first acquaintances, Captain Richard Grimes, gave the young man work on his ranch that was managed by his son, Bradford. The younger Grimes proved to be a hard task-master. Perhaps the experience sharpened Pierce's mind. It taught him lessons in the cattle business that he never forgot.

Pierce served in the Civil War as regimental butcher in Company D, 1st Texas Cavalry, because "he was adept at finding cattle." Shanghai liked to brag that he was "the same as a Major General—in the rear on advance and in the lead on retreat!"

After the war, Abel and his brother, Jonathan, returned to Texas and became partners in the cattle business. El Rancho Grande in Matagorda and Wharton Counties was the first of the vast Pierce holdings. When Shanghai died on December 26, 1900, at the age of sixty-seven, he owned 200,000 acres and 20,000 head of cattle, plus he had more that $1,300,000. Shanghai Pierce was a rip-snortin' Texas legend.)

№ 5   Lazy Eleven
T. J. Poole Ranch

The **Lazy Eleven** brand was first recorded in 1889 by the T. J. Poole Ranch in Matagorda and Brazoria counties. Many cattle between the Colorado and Bernard Rivers carrying this brand on their left sides were shipped to northern and western markets. When Poole pastured stock in South Texas, the local Mexican people referred to the brand as the **Panther Scratch**.

Poole, whose ranch covers 20,000 acres, was a director and an honorary vice-president of the TSCRA from the 1930s to the 1960s. He also brands the **Bar P** behind the left shoulder, the **Backward C** on the left hip, and the **Open A** on the left loin. Mrs. Poole brands the **JF Connected** and the **JF Connected Bar** on the left hip.

In 1929, Poole was the first rancher in the area to ship steers to Oklahoma and Kansas grass to fatten. In later years, he was partners with his brother, Donald K. Poole.

Source: L. L. "Monk" Chiles, T. J. Poole Ranch foreman, 1954.
See brand numbers 33, 130, 139, and 333.

(Thomas Jefferson Poole Jr. of Bay City, Texas, died September 2, 1969, at the age of eighty-five. He was a fourth generation Texas rancher. He was born September 12, 1883 in Corsicana, the son of Fannie Louise Grimes Poole and Thomas J. Poole Sr. His grandfather was William Bradford Grimes, the son of Captain Richard Grimes who settled in the Texas Republic in 1837 on the Tres Palacios Ranch, which became known as the WBG Ranch.

T. J. Poole Jr. was in his teens when he took over management of the WBG Ranch. When the ranch was sold, Poole and his father leased several thousand acres east of the Colorado River. They later formed the Poole Cattle Company and leased the George Sargent Ranch and in 1916, bought the adjoining 15,000 acres in southwest Brazoria County known as the "Cox Ranch.")

№ 6   Running W
Fred S. Robbins

The **Running W** brand was recorded in Matagorda County in 1875 by Fred S. Robbins, whose family were early settlers of the county, having arrived in 1838. The Robbins Ranch is on the Colorado River and the Intracoastal Canal near Matagorda Bay. The old, rectangular ranch house still stands, and some of the original bloodlines remain in the cattle now run by Robbins' son-in-law, H. W. Savage Sr. The brand name comes from the name of a pasture on the river. The most cattle to carry the brand at one time were 900 head. Before Robbins died, he willed the brand to his son Palmer Robbins.

Source: Hamilton Savage, 1954.
See brand numbers 38, 248, 253, 347, and 487.

№ 7   Crescent Five
J. W. Munson

The **Crescent Five** brand was first recorded in 1883 in Brazoria County by J. W. Munson. Houston Munson sold the ranch near Baileys Prairie to David Bintliff of Houston, Texas, in 1954, two years before he died in San Antonio. Houston Munson Jr. now lives in Gonzales.

Source: Houston Munson, Munson Ranch, 1954.

Nº 8 UT
Morrison and Briscoe

The **UT** is a Morrison and Briscoe brand recorded in LaSalle County. It carries no ear mark.

Source: R. J. Nunley, Encinal, Texas, 1958, while working on a case with TSCRA Inspector Leon Vivian.

Nº 9 PK
W. A. Paddock

The **PK** brand is the first and last letters of the name Paddock and was recorded in 1919 in Harris County by W. A. Paddock. As many as 6,000 head of cattle carried his brand at one time. Stuart Sherar, manager of this old ranch, operates an up-to-date feeding and breeding program.

Source: Emmett Felts, foreman of the Lower Ranch, 1957.

(This ranch was sold to R. E. "Bob" Smith of Houston in 1966.)

Nº 10 UHL Connected
Milligan Brothers

The **UHL Connected** brand was recorded in 1879 by Milligan Brothers in Brazoria and Matagorda counties. This old saddle iron carried by the Milligan brothers during the open range days is smaller and shorter than a regular branding iron.

Source: Cecil Milligan, who took it from the attic of the old Milligan Store in Bay City, Texas.

Nº 11 Lazy E
Harold Graves and Jordie McNeill Sr.

The **Lazy E** is a partnership brand recorded in 1910 in Brazoria County by former TSCRA Inspector Harold Graves and his brother-in-law, Jordie McNeill Sr.

Source: Harold F. Graves, 1957.

(Harold Graves, the son of Dr. Joseph and Fannie Foote Graves, was born on February 4, 1893, in the Graves family home on the Brazos River near old town Brazoria. During World War I, he was a machine gunner in Europe with the 36th Division. He was discharged in 1919 and returned to Brazoria County where he operated a store and managed a ranch near Cedar Lake. During the oil boom days, he worked in the oil fields near West Columbia.

Graves became a rancher and worked as an inspector for the Livestock Sanitary Commission during the 1920s tick fever outbreak. He was also a deputy sheriff, TSCRA Inspector, and a knife collector. His letter to Stiles in the archives is written on the back of a "wanted" poster. Graves died November 28, 1978, following a short illness.)

Nº 12 TF
A. P. George Ranch

The **TF** brand was recorded in 1890 in Fort Bend County and is used on the A. P. George Ranch. Before George bought the ranch, it was known as the TF Ranch.

Source: Paul Henry, George Ranch foreman, 1954.

See brand numbers 26, 66, 73, 74, and 77.

(The George Ranch is on land that was one of Stephen F. Austin's original land grants, homesteaded by Henry Jones in 1822. One of Jones' great granddaughters married A. P. George, and they operated the ranch until 1961. It is now a 474-acre historical park owned by the George Foundation and administered by the Fort Bend Museum Association.)

Nº 13 Comet
Alonzo Peeler

The **Comet** was an Alonzo Peeler brand recorded in Atascosa County in 1916. The partnership of Jennings and Peeler branded the **J P Connected**. Peeler died in 1961 and was buried on a hill in Atascosa County overlooking the Hall Ranch.

Source: Alonzo Peeler, Christine, Texas, 1956 while we were on a deer hunt with J. P. Phillips and Bill Curtis on the Hall Ranch.

See brand number 115.

(Alonzo Peeler was from an old ranching family, and he had ranched on his own since he was twenty years old. At the time of his death, he owned 27,000 acres. Two of his brothers, Graves and Travis, were TSCRA Inspectors.)

Nº 14 AP Bar Connected
Adolph Poenisch

The **A P Bar Connected** brand was recorded in 1910 in McMullen County by Adolph Poenisch of Tilden, Texas.

Source: Adolph Poenisch while on a Brazoria County Cattleman's Association trip, 1957.

(In a letter to Stiles, Poenisch wrote, "I chose this brand to distinguish between my father's cattle and mine. My father branded a **Fish Hook P***, recorded in the 1880s in Nueces County, and* **1O***, recorded in Grayson County.")*

Nº 15 Bar X
David C. Bintliff Interests

The **Bar X** brand was recorded by David C. Bintliff Interests, Houston, Texas, in Webb, Austin, and Brazoria counties in Texas, Otero County in New Mexico, and Carroll Parish in Louisiana, and in Guatemala. A Negro man had originally registered the brand in Brazoria County, and Bintliff purchased it for $25.00. It is now used on the old Houston Munson Ranch.

Source: 1955 in Laredo from C. B. "Jeff" Jeffries, foreman of the Bintliff Interests in Webb County and later foreman in Brazoria County.

(Bintliff Interests had 15,000 cattle on seven ranches in 1969.)

№ 16   Arrow S
Dan Harrison Ranches

The **Arrow S** brand was recorded in 1928 in Atascosa, Sutton, Edwards, McMullen, Live Oak, and Fort Bend counties by the Dan Harrison Ranches.

Source: ranch foreman on the Harrison Ranch at McCoy, Texas, 1957.

See brand number 103.

(Dan J. Harrison Jr. of Houston, Texas, was an independant oilman, a Quarter Horse breeder, and rancher. At the time of his death, January 14, 1980, he ran Herefords, Brahmans, and crossbred cattle on four Texas Ranches—Harrison Ranch at Fulshear, Pilloncillo Ranch at Catarina, Harrison Ranch at Sonora, and Arrow S Ranch at Campbellton. Harrison was a TSCRA director from 1964–1980.)

№ 17   Lazy D
W. E. "Bill" Gunn

W. E. "Bill" Gunn of Freeport, Texas, recorded the **Lazy D** brand in Brazoria County in 1900. Gunn, who worked for a packing company in Houston, bought top registered Hereford and Angus bulls and experimented with breeding, feeding, and when to sell. His cattle run on salt grass and in marsh area. He is well-informed about livestock.

Source: Bill Gunn, 1956.

№ 18   Spade
Renderbrook Spade Ranch

The Spade Ranch gets its name from the **Spade** brand, which it has used since 1889. This brand was first recorded in Texas by Henry Sanborn and J. F. Evans, better known in his day as "Spade" Evans. Their ranch was twenty-three sections located on Saddler Creek, ten miles east of Clarendon, Texas, in Donley County where they recorded the brand in 1883.

In 1888, Isaac L. Ellwood, manufacturer of barbed wire in DeKalb, Illinois, purchased the Spade Ranch, stock, and brand. In 1889, he acquired Dudley and John Snyder's Renderbrook Ranch in Mitchell, Sterling, and Coke counties. He moved the Spade stock to the Renderbrook Ranch south of Colorado City. This ranch became known as the Renderbrook Spade Ranch, and the **Spade** brand has been used there since the original cattle were acquired. Ellwood purchased additional land from the Snyders in Lamb, Hockley, Lubbock and Hale counties. He soon owned nearly 400,000 acres.

The **Spade** brand is now recorded in Mitchell, Sterling, Coke, Hockley, and Borden counties, and it is placed on the left side of cattle. It is also branded on the left forearm of horses in San Miguel County, New Mexico.

Source: Frank H. Chappell Jr., Lubbock, Texas, and retired manager, Otto Jones, at an Inspector's meeting at the Spade Ranch near Sterling City.

(Otto F. Jones had worked for the Spade Ranch for sixty-two years when he retired in 1969. He was born in Nolan County November 30, 1888, while his father, Bill Jones, was foreman of the H Triangle Bar Ranch. Otto went to work for the Spade Ranch in 1907 and three years later, he was wagon boss. In 1912, he was made ranch manager, the position he held until he retired. Otto Jones died in 1974.)

№ 19   Half Circle G Bar
W. C. Gilbert

The **Half Circle G Bar** brand on the right hip was recorded in 1898 in Jefferson County by W. C. Gilbert, a rancher and rice farmer. Many old time rodeos were held at the Gilbert Ranch before his death in 1958.

Source: Willie Gilbert, 1957 Inspector's meeting in Beaumont, Texas.

№ 20   Star
Henderson Coquat

The **Star** brand was recorded in Live Oak, La Salle, and Webb counties by Henderson Coquat and branded on the left side or left thigh of registered Charolais cattle.

The first of the Coquat Ranches was in LaSalle County, purchased in 1939. Next he acquired land in Webb County. He was instrumental in the formation of the American-International Charolais Association. Coquat was convinced that crossbred cattle were the market product of the future, and his ideal cross was registered Brahman and registered Charolais, a hybrid that worked well under harsh conditions of the country. Coquat died in 1958, but his breeding program continued, supervised by his nephew, Tom Coquat, and then by Henderson's son, Bob Coquat.

Source: a Brazoria County Cattleman's Association trip in 1957.

(Coquat was the son of a French seaman, reared on a small stock farm in Live Oak County. He became successful in oil and gas exploration and production, real estate, investments, and ranching.)

№ 21   M
Coquat Ranch

The **M** brand was recorded by the Coquat Ranch in Webb County.

Source: Tom Coquat, 1957.

See brand numbers 34, 35, and 116.

(Henderson Coquat's nephew, Tom Coquat, was manager of the Coquat Ranches for twenty years until 1972 when he left to manage his own herds and those of others.)

№ 22   O T with a Tail
Milby B. Butler

Milby B. Butler of League City, Texas, brands the **O T with a Tail**, recorded in Galveston County in 1858 by his grandmother, Hepzie Butler. During the 1870s, there were more than 25,000 head of cattle carrying this brand. Hepzie gave the brand to her son, George W. Butler, when he was old enough to go into business for himself. Many people called George "O. T." because of his brand. Milby Butler, born in 1889, received the brand from his father, George, in 1905. Milby died during the early 1970s.

Source: Milby Butler, 1958, while on a trip with Longhorn men Graves Peeler, Harold Graves, and Jack Phillips.

(*Milby Butler helped establish some of the first registered Brahman cattle in that area. He crossed them with native cattle and English breeds that had been introduced to Texas while his son, Henry, concentrated on Longhorns. Milby's father, George Butler, had built stock pens on the Butler Ranch adjoining the G.H.& H. Railroad. Thousands of Longhorns were shipped through those pens. During one period, 49,000 head were shipped to Cuba alone.*)

№ 23   Seven L Connected
Cecil K. Boyt

The **Seven L Connected** brand was recorded in 1934 in Liberty County by Cecil K. Boyt of Devers, Texas. Boyt is an honorary Vice-President of the TSCRA and ranch manager of cattle, rice, and oil for the estate of his father, E. W. Boyt. The Boyts exported more than 2,000 registered Brahmans to South America. Elmer W. Boyt, a pioneer of the cattle-rice economy of the Texas Gulf Coast, died in 1958. The E. W. Boyt Estate's brand was the **Lazy U**. Cecil Boyt also operates his own rice and livestock interests and maintains three herds of registered cattle—Gray Brahmans, Red Brahmans, and Shorthorns.

Source: Cecil Boyt, 1959, after his son and I found his iron in a barn on their ranch.

See brand numbers 245, 255, and 335.

№ 24   Doorkey
Dyer Moore Ranch

The **Doorkey** brand was recorded about 1850 in Fort Bend and Brazoria counties. This iron was buried in a concrete foundation at the Dyer Moore Ranch in Fort Bend County by Oscar Scott when he was a young man. After hearing of my collection, Scott dug the iron up and gave it to me. The metal in it is over 100 years old. He also gave me a number of other Moore brands. Dyer Moore was an important figure in the early history of Brazoria and Fort Bend Counties.

Scott lived his last few years on the Moore Ranch near Guy, Texas, in Fort Bend County. He was seventy-eight years of age when he died about 1959.

Source: Oscar Scott, 1957.

№ 25   Walking Stick
H. A. "Shoat" Dromgoole and Son

The **Walking Stick** brand is recorded in Colorado County by H. A. "Shoat" Dromgoole and Son. The Dromgoole Ranch on the Colorado River near Garwood, Texas, is rich river bottom. They've handled many cattle and also have good roping horses, pecans, and sheep.

Source: H. A. Dromgoole, 1957.

See brand numbers 85–90.

№ 26   Z
A. P. George Ranch

The **Z** brand is recorded by the well-known A. P. George Ranch of Fort Bend County. The manager is Hilmar Moore of Richmond, Texas, a TSCRA Director. The ranch raises Santa Gertrudis cattle from the King Ranch and stands a King Ranch stallion. Mr. Berry handles their registered cattle and show cattle.

Source: Paul Henry, ranch foreman.

See brand numbers 12, 73, 74, and 77.

№ 27   Six
Dolph Briscoe Sr.

The **Six** brand was recorded by Dolph Briscoe Sr. of Uvalde, Texas, in Dimmit, Webb, and Uvalde counties.

Source: Dolph Briscoe Jr., 1957.

See brand number 28.

(*Mrs. Dolph Briscoe Sr., the former Georgie Briscoe, was born in 1888 on the family homestead in Fort Bend County, deeded to her family by the Mexican government in 1832. She was the daughter of Mr. and Mrs. William Montgomery Briscoe. Her great uncle was a signer of the Texas Declaration of Independence. She married her distant cousin, Dolph Briscoe, on October 1, 1913, in Fulshear in Fort Bend County.*)

№ 28   Nine
Dolph Briscoe Sr.

The **Nine** brand was recorded by Dolph Briscoe Sr. in Dimmit, Webb, and Uvalde counties in 1920. This is the same iron used to make the **Six** brand.

Source: Dolph Briscoe Jr.

№ 29   Swinging Eleven
Joe Finley Jr.

The **Swinging Eleven**, branded on the right hip, was recorded in 1932 to replace the Corbota brand, registered in 1909 and used previously by the Callaghan Land and Pastoral Company. It is recorded by Joe Finley Jr. of Encinal, Texas, in Mexico and in Webb and LaSalle counties where it is used on purchased purebred cattle. The ranch runs 20,000 head of Hereford cattle on 270,000 acres.

Source: Joe Finley Jr.

See brand numbers 732, 737, 743, 765, 771, and 773.

(*The original owner of the Callaghan Ranch was an Irish sea captain, Charles Callaghan, who was a blockade runner during the Civil War. After the war, he homesteaded eighty acres between San Antonio and Laredo and started a sheep ranch that grew to 70,000 acres. On December 20, 1874, the thirty-eight-year-old Callaghan died of pneumonia, and the land passed to his heirs.*

In 1888, the Callaghan Ranch was sold to David Beals, George Ford, and Thomas A. Coleman, who was named manager of the property. Beals and Ford died and when Coleman retired, he was replaced by Joe Finley Sr. In 1943, the place became a cattle ranch, and in three years, it covered 200,000 acres. Finley and his son, Joe Finley Jr. eventually purchased the ranch.)

№ 30 CU
Sugarland Industries

The **CU** brand is registered in Fort Bend County by Sugarland Industries, Sugarland, Texas, and is branded on the left shoulder or left side. Tom James was head of Sugarland Industries when I worked for the Association. TSCRA Inspector G. O. Stoner made a cattle theft case years ago when brands were changed on **CU** cattle.

Source: ranch foreman, Sugarland Industries's Bassett Blakely Ranch on the Brazos River, 1957.

№ 31   C J Six Connected
Henry Banker

The **C J Six Connected** brand was recorded by Henry Banker in 1880 in Fort Bend, Wharton, Brazoria, and Jackson counties and is placed anywhere on the left side. This particular iron was used by Banker in the early days when he would leave Needville, Texas, on a train going north to buy steers. He carried this iron with him, broken down in a suitcase. After buying steers, he would brand them, come back home and get his crew together—men and wagons—and return for the cattle. By branding them on the spot, he knew he would get the steers he bought.

Source: eighty-nine-year-old Henry Banker, 1955 when he still had a wonderful memory. He died in 1959.

№ 32   T J
Tom Booth

The **T J** brand, recorded by Tom Booth in Fort Bend County, was an old brand bought with some cattle and used along the Brazos River bottoms near the town of Booth, Texas. Tom Booth died about 1959.

Source: Paul Henry at the A. P. George Ranch, 1956.

№ 33   Flat Top Three
Tom Poole

The **Flat Top Three** brand is recorded by Tom Poole in Matagorda County and is used on the Cox Ranch, located on the Bernard River and the Intracoastal Canal near Freeport, Texas. The iron was about fifty years old when given to me.

Source: L. L. "Monk" Chiles, T. J. Poole Ranch, 1954.
See brand numbers 5, 130, 139, and 333.

№ 34   Walking Stick
Tom Coquat

The **Walking Stick** brand was used by Tom Coquat on registered Charolais cattle in Webb County.
Source: Tom Coquat, 1957.
See brand numbers 20, 21, 35, and 116.

№ 35   Bar D Y
Tom Coquat

The **Bar D Y** brand was recorded in Webb County by Tom Coquat and used on registered Charolais cattle.
Source: Tom Coquat, 1957.
See brand numbers 20, 21, 34, and 116.

№ 36   O U
Shirley A. Beard

The **O U** brand was originally a partnership brand recorded in 1924 in Fort Bend County by the Beard Brothers, Shirley A. Beard and Sid Beard, of Needville, Texas. It is branded on the left side. When Sid Beard died in 1933, S. A. Beard bought his interest in the **O U** brand and has used it ever since.

Source: Shirley Beard, 1956.
See brand numbers 219 and 220.

(Shirley Beard's original brand, made from his initials, was recorded in 1912. While he was working for T. W. Davis, Davis sold cattle to T. Martin in Missouri City, Texas, and had ten dogie calves left, which he gave to Beard. From these calves, Beard grew a herd of 150 head. During the 1924–1925 freeze, he lost half his herd, so he sold the rest. He then went into partnership with his brother.)

№ 37   Frying Pan
Renderbrook Ranch

The **Frying Pan** brand was recorded in 1881 in Potter and Randall counties by J. F. Glidden and H. B. Sanborn and used on cattle on 250,000 acres. When the partnership was dissolved in 1894, I. L. Ellwood, owner of the Spade Renderbrook Ranch, bought part of the land and all of the stock, and registered the brand in the Spade Renderbrook counties. Otto Jones was Renderbrook Ranch manager for fifty years.

Source: Frank Chappell Jr. of Lubbock and Otto Jones at TSCRA Inspectors' meeting at the Spade Renderbrook Ranch, Sterling City, Texas.

See brand number 18.

*(Otto Jones wrote a letter dated May 22, 1960, to Leonard Stiles giving the history of the Frying Pan brand that was acquired when the Spade Renderbrook Ranch purchased the Frying Pan stock and some of the land, making the Ellwood holdings almost 400,000 acres. He wrote, "I. L. Ellwood bought Glidden's outfit and brand. There never were any **Frying Pan** cattle here at Renderbrook but several old **Frying Pan** horses were here when I arrived in 1907." Otto Jones died in 1974 at eighty-six years of age.)*

№ 38   Running W
Fred S. Robbins

The **Running W** brand was recorded in 1875 by Fred S. Robbins in Matagorda County. The Robbins family were early settlers, having arrived in 1838. Robbins Ranch is located on the Colorado River and the Intracoastal

Canal near Matagorda Bay. The old rectangular ranch house still stands, and some of the original bloodlines remain in the cattle run on the ranch by Robbins' son-in-law, H. W. Savage Sr.

Source: Ham Savage.

See brand number 6, 247, 248, 253, and 347.

Nº 39   O Y Connected
Otto H. Yauch

The **O Y Connected** brand, the owner's initials, was recorded in 1910 by Otto H. Yauch in Brazoria County. Two hundred cattle carried this brand at one time. Otto's son, Glen Yauch, a past President of the Brazoria County Cattleman's Association, lives on the Brazos River at East Columbia and now uses the brand. J. P. S. Griffith of West Columbia is ranch foreman.

Source: received in 1955.

Nº 40   H T
Hilmar Moore and Milton Robinowitz

The **H T** is a partnership brand recorded by Hilmar Moore and Milton Robinowitz in Fort Bend, Brazoria, Duval, Wharton, Galveston, Austin, Harris, and Jackson counties. It is placed on the left loin.

Source: Milton Robinowitz, Richmond, Texas, 1955.

See brand number 41.

*(Hilmar Moore was the 37th president of the TSCRA and the mayor of Richmond for thirty-four years. He was a fifth generation rancher and an agribusinessman in Richmond. Moore was a direct descendant of one of Stephen F. Austin's "Old 300." The historic Moore brand, the **L C Connected**, originated in 1875 and was the initials of Lottie Dyer, Hilmar's grandmother.)*

Nº 41   Open A
Hilmar Moore and Milton Robinowitz

The **Open A** is a partnership brand used on steers and recorded by Hilmar Moore and Milton Robinowitz in 1940 in Fort Bend, Brazoria, and Duval counties.

Source: received in 1956.

See brand number 40.

(Milton Robinowitz was a TSCRA director beginning in 1966.)

Nº 42   Pitchfork
Stewart Savage

The **Pitchfork** is an early day brand designed by Amelias Savage and recorded in Matagorda County by Norman Savage in 1843. It was used by several members of the Savage family, each placing the brand in a different location or direction on an animal. It is pictured here as used by Stewart Savage.

Source: Francis Savage, 1959.

Nº 43   T T Diamond
Frank Harris

Frank Harris of West Columbia, Texas, uses the **T T Diamond** brand, placing it on the left hip. He operates the T Diamond Ranch in Brazoria County. This brand was originally recorded in 1886 by Robert McFarland of Columbia Prairie, Texas, Mrs. Harris's father. He used the brand in the open range days on cattle running between the Bernard and Brazos rivers.

Source: J. Frank Harris, 1957. This iron was borrowed to brand cattle and never returned.

See brand number 72.

(Harris was born in Gonzales County October 20, 1895, and he moved to West Columbia from Houston in 1937. He produced the Houston Fat Stock Show and Rodeo in 1958 and 1959, the Texas High School State Championship Rodeo in Halletsville for twenty-five years, the National High School Finals in 1969, and the Texas Prison Rodeo for five years.)

Nº 44   Flying V
Mrs. Kittie Nash Groce

The **Flying V** brand was recorded in Brazoria, Fort Bend, Frio, McMullen, Atascosa, and Live Oak counties by Mrs. Kittie Nash Groce of East Columbia, Texas. It was placed on the left hip. It is now used on the Nash Ranch between the Brazos and Bernard Rivers by her heir, Baldwin N. Young of West Columbia.

Source: W. A. "Bill" Curtis, Groce Ranch foreman, 1956.

See brand numbers 123, 142, 143, 458, and 492.

(When Kittie Nash Groce's father died in 1930, Kittie and her mother, Houston socialites, moved to the country and took over the ranch during the Great Depression. They knew nothing of cattle, and Kittie hired the knowledgeable Graves Peeler as ranch manager. His wisdom guided the Groce Ranch from 1930–1944. When he left to ranch on his own, he had increased the number of cattle on her ranch by four times, improved the pastures, and established a good breeding program. Bill Curtis replaced him as ranch manager and continued his work. Kittie Groce generously shared her good fortune through many lasting contributions to the town of West Columbia.)

Nº 45   Running W
Captain Richard King; King Ranch

The **Running W** brand is recorded by the King Ranch, Kingsville, Texas, in Kleberg, Hidalgo, Jim Wells, Willacy, Brooks, Nueces, Kenedy, and Cameron Counties, Texas, and also in Osage County, Oklahoma, and Coahuila, Nuevo Leon, Mexico. It was first registered in 1869 in Nueces County by Captain Richard King. It is placed anywhere on either side on cattle and horses. In Spanish, this brand is called *La Viborita* or the "Little Snake."

Source: Charlie Burwell, foreman of the King Ranch's Laureles Division, 1956.

See brand numbers 93, 584, 731, and 980.

(Captain Richard King was a steamboat pilot who arrived on the Rio Grande in 1845. He entered the shipping business with Mifflin Kenedy. The two made a fortune in their freight business. But it was in the Nueces Strip—a hot, humid, barren land between the Nueces River and Rio Grande—that Richard King built the ranching empire known today as the King Ranch. The land was part of a Spanish grant known as the Rincon de Santa Gertrudis.

In 1862, he had purchased the cattle and land of William Mann's estate. Mann's brand was the **Running M**. *It is possible that King simply inverted the* **Running M** *to create the* **Running W**, *the King Ranch's famous brand. King and his wife, Henrietta, survived the hardships of the area, the Civil War, and bandit raids. By 1867, the ranch covered 146,000 acres and carried thousands of head of cattle. The ranch's faithful, hard working Mexican cowhands became known as Kineños.*

When King died in 1885, Henrietta, took over the management of the ranch with the help of her able son-in-law, Robert Justus Kleberg. From that time to the present, the ranch has remained with King's descendants through Alice King Kleberg and her husband, Robert J. Kleberg. It has been a leader in the ranching industry as the founder of a major American beef breed, a producer of top performance and running horses, and a source of technology that has led to many significant advances in livestock production and wildlife management. Today, the ranch covers 825,000 acres of South Texas.)

Nº 46   Fleur de Lis L
Billy Searden

The **Fleur de Lis L** brand was the first iron in my collection. J. B. Roberts had a store in Cedar Lake, Texas, and he used the iron to poke the fire in a wood stove. I expressed an interest in it, and he gave it to me. At that time there was no known history on the brand. I have since found that it belonged to Billy Searden, who about 1890 bought cattle bearing this brand from some forgotten cowman. It has been branded on numerous cattle in Matagorda County for many years. It is now used by Mr. and Mrs. Elton Leggett. She is Searden's daughter.

Source: J. B. Roberts, 1952.

Nº 47   Mashed O
Lee Swickheimer

The **Mashed O** brand was recorded in Brazoria, Goliad, Lavaca, and Blanco, Texas, and used mostly on Hereford steers by Lee Swickheimer of Fannin, Texas. It was placed anywhere on the left side but usually on the left loin. Swickheimer died about 1960.

Source: Lee Swickheimer, 1955.

(While a TSCRA Inspector, Stiles solved a theft case of **Mashed O** *cattle. The Swickheimer Ranch, founded in Goliad County by Mr. & Mrs. George J. Swickheimer, was managed for*

many years by their son Lee, and following his death, by another son, George G. Swickheimer. The Swickheimers were leaders in the fight against screw worms and in the advancement of ranching methods.)*

Nº 48   Backward C C
Walter Crosby

The **Backward C C** brand was recorded in 1858 in Brazoria County by Zelia Ann Eliza, Samuel McGaw, and William Henry Crosby. It is now recorded by Walter Crosby of Jones Creek, who always had a horse to loan me when I was working in the area. Walter Crosby died in 1965.

Source: Walter Crosby of Freeport, 1956.

Nº 49   Two Dash
Roy Martin

The **Two Dash** brand is used by Roy Martin of Cotulla in LaSalle County on registered Red Brahman cattle.

Source: Roy Martin at the Martin Ranch, 1957.

Nº 50   Backward L Backward Seven
L Seven Ranch

The **Backward L Backward Seven** brand is placed on the left side of L Seven Ranch cattle in Colorado and Wharton counties and in Coahuila, Mexico. This large ranch is owned by William N. Lehrer, Garwood, Texas, who runs Hereford cattle and is a rice farmer.

Source: Bub Shaw at Garwood, Texas, 1958.

Nº 51   Screwplate
Frank Turner Jr.

The **Screwplate**, branded on the right side of cattle, is recorded in Brazoria County by Frank Turner Jr. The Turner Ranch is located at Rosharon, Texas, near the entrance to the Ramsey State Prison Farm. Turner is an inspector in South Texas for the Federal Land Bank.

Source: Turner made this one-piece iron and a pair of spurs he gave me, 1957.

See brand number 135.

Nº 52   Mashed O
Swickheimer Ranch

This is a **Mashed O** brand recorded by the Swickheimer Ranch.

(The Swickheimer ranch house near Goliad is recognized as a Texas Historical Site.)

No 53   Key
Dolph Briscoe Jr.

The **Key** brand is recorded in Uvalde County by Dolph Briscoe Jr. of the Briscoe Ranch. Source: Les Brown, Briscoe Ranch foreman, 1957.

(Briscoe served as president of TSCRA from 1960–1962 and as Governor of Texas from 1973–1979.)

Nº 54   V E Connected
J. H. Dingle

The **V E Connected** brand was recorded in Brazoria County in 1911 by J. H. Dingle of Freeport, Texas. Dingle, an early settler of the area, ranches on the Brazos River. He chose this brand because it was a "simple brand that wouldn't blot."

Source: J. H. Dingle, 1957.

See brand number 141.

Nº 55   Open A Six Connected
Charlie L. Brandes

The **Open A Six Connected** brand was recorded in Brazoria and Victoria counties in 1850 by Charlie L. Brandes of Victoria, Texas. It was branded on the left hip. This iron was found on the Bernard River on the Cox Ranch in Brazoria County in 1954.

Source: L. L. "Monk" Chiles, 1954.

Nº 56   Seven H L Connected
Dr. Mark Poole

The **Seven H L Connected** brand was recorded in 1929 and is used by Dr. Mark Poole, who was a missionary in the Belgium Congo and is now a doctor in Bay City, Texas. Poole escaped from the Congo and returned to the States about 1959. The Poole cattle are in Brazoria and Matagorda counties on the Cox Ranch and on the Northern Headquarters Ranch. Tom Poole maintained this brand for Dr. Poole while he was in Africa.

Source: L. L. "Monk" Chiles, 1954.

Nº 57   Rafter Six
E. L. Bass

The **Rafter Six** brand was recorded by E. L. Bass in Brazoria and Matagorda counties in 1947 and is placed on the left rib. The Rafter Six Ranch of Sweeny, Texas, is owned by Elbert Lee "Cowboy" Bass of Houston.

Source: E. L. Bass, 1953.

(E. L. Bass recorded the brand, H with an Upside Down F, in 1918 in Bay City and used it on 500 head of cattle. When a refinery dumped a tank car of poison into the creek in about 1948, it poisoned Bass's cattle. Jordie McNeill was one of three men appointed by the court to investigate the damages.)

Nº 58   I C I
E. P. Womack Jr.

The **I C I** brand is recorded in Brazoria County by E. P. Womack Jr. of West Columbia, Texas. It is placed on the left hip or left loin. The Womack Ranch is on the west side of the Brazos River above East Columbia.

Source: E. P. Womack Jr., 1955.

Nº 59   Double Crescent
Barry Barber

The **Double Crescent** brand is recorded by Barry Barber in Matagorda and Brazoria Counties, and the cattle are pastured on the Poole Ranch.

Source: L. L. "Monk" Chiles, foreman of the Poole Ranch, 1955.

Nº 60   Gancho or Hook
Henderson Coquat

The **Gancho** or **Hook** brand was recorded by Henderson Coquat in Live Oak, LaSalle, and Webb counties.

Source: Bob Coquat, Three Rivers, Texas, 1957.

See brand numbers 20, 21, 34, and 35.

Nº 61   P Six
Pinchback Ranch

The **P Six** brand was used in Colorado County by the Pinchback Ranch near Garwood, Texas.

Source: an old-timer who knew the Pinchback people, 1957.

See brand number 62.

Nº 62   J Eight
Pinchback Ranch

The **J Eight** brand was used in Colorado County by the Pinchback Ranch near Garwood, Texas.

Source: an old-timer who knew the Pinchback people.

See brand number 61.

Nº 63   O Cross Connected
Roy Parks

The **O Cross Connected** brand was recorded by Roy Parks of Midland, Texas, in Midland, Ector, and Shackleford counties. It is usually placed on the left side. The **P** brand, recorded in Bosque County before the Civil War by LeRoy Parks, is placed on the animal's jaw.

Mr. Parks, an outstanding Hereford rancher, served as TSCRA president from 1954–1956.

Source: while attending a 1956 Inspectors' meeting at the Parks Ranch.

Nº 64   Nine
Dolph Briscoe Jr.

The **Nine** brand is recorded by Dolph Briscoe Jr. of Uvalde, Texas, in Uvalde, Dimmit, and Webb counties. Briscoe was president of the TSCRA from 1960–1962 and the son of Dolph Briscoe Sr., the Association president from 1932–1934.

Source: Dolph Briscoe Jr., 1957.

See brand number 53.

Nº 65   Three Dash
W. M. Sells

The **Three Dash** brand, placed on the left hip, is recorded in Jackson and Calhoun counties by W. M. Sells of Midway, Texas, on Karankawa Bay. The brand was recorded in 1892 by Olie Traylor, Monroe Sells's mother. The largest number of cattle carrying this brand at one time was 2,000 head. Monroe Sells was a law officer and assisted in several area theft cases. He also worked with us in 1961 during Hurricane Carla.

Source: W M. Sells, 1953.

Nº 66   Lazy D
A. P. George Ranch

The **Lazy D** brand is recorded in Fort Bend County by the A. P. George Ranch. The cattle are usually branded on the left loin.

Source: Paul Henry, 1957.
See brand numbers. 12, 26, 73, 74, and 77.

Nº 67   Horseshoe E Connected
H. R. Smith

The **Horseshoe E Connected** brand was recorded by H. R. Smith in 1884 in Brazoria County.

Source: W. A. "Bill" Curtis, Nash Groce Ranch manager, 1957.

Nº 68   Seven P L Connected
J. S. Abercrombie

The **Seven P L Connected** brand is recorded by J. S. Abercrombie of Houston, Texas. Ranches are located in Atascosa, McMullen, and Live Oak counties. This brand, also used in Old Ocean, Brazoria County, is usually placed on the left hip or the left loin. This brand originated with the Seven P L Ranch at Campbellton, one time owned by the Tom Peeler family.

Source: Raymond Glick.
See brand number 113.

Nº 69   B R

There is no information on the **B R** brand.

Nº 70   Lazy L
George Culver

The **Lazy L** brand was recorded by George Culver in Matagorda County. Culver handled a lot of steers, and he often sold steers to the Poole Ranch to go north to market. The Culver family still ranches in that area. In 1965, chemical plants and summer homes were fast taking over that good ranching land known as the salt grass area.

Source: a nephew of Mrs. George Culver, 1952.

Nº 71   Pitchfork
Hamilton Savage

The **Pitchfork** brand, designed by Amelias Savage, was recorded in 1843 by Norman Savage in Matagorda County. The brand is usually placed on the left hip or may be placed on the left thigh or side. It is used by Hamilton Savage of Bay City, Texas. The cattle are run in pastures along the Colorado River near Matagorda. The largest number of cattle at one time under the brand was 2,000 head.

Norman Savage was Hamilton Savage's grandfather. After Norman's death in 1878, his wife used the brand until her death in 1930. "Ham" Savage has used the brand since and is known and respected as a top cowman. I enjoyed catching wild cattle with him in the Colorado River bottoms.

Source: Ham Savage, 1955. Ham Savage died in 1965.
See brand numbers 42, 104, 239, 349, and 350.

Nº 72   T Diamond Connected
Frank Harris

The **T Diamond Connected** brand, placed on the left hip, is used by Frank Harris of West Columbia on his T Diamond Rodeo stock in Brazoria County. The brand was first recorded in 1886 by Robert McFarland and used in the early days by the McFarland family on Columbia Prairie.

When I went to work for the TSCRA in that district in 1950, I stayed at Frank Harris's home for the first week. He also later stored my branding iron collection in a barn on the T Diamond Ranch for several years. Harris pastured Santa Gertrudis cattle for Allen & Allen of Kingsville during the 1956–1957 drought. His rodeo stock is used at the Houston Fat Stock Show, San Antonio Rodeo, and many other rodeos across Texas as well as in Louisiana. He bought good bucking horses in Wyoming, Montana, and Colorado. This iron was borrowed to brand cattle and was not returned.

See brand number 43.

Nº 73   Circle
A. P. George Ranch

The **Circle** brand is recorded by the A. P. George Ranch in Fort Bend County and placed on the left hip or side. The George Ranch raised Santa Gertrudis cattle from the King Ranch and also had a King Ranch stallion and a Prince Albert bull. Mr. Berry handled the registered cattle and the show stock. I knew both A. P. George and Mrs. Mamie George. Hilmar Moore of Richmond, a TSCRA Director and an able man, manages this great ranch.

Source: foreman Paul Henry, 1957.
See brand numbers 12, 26, 66, 74, and 77.

JHD No 74 J H D Connected
A. P. George Ranch

The **J H D Connected** brand is used by the A. P. George Ranch in Fort Bend County. J. H. Davis originated it, thus the initials in the brand.

Source: George Ranch foreman, Paul Henry, 1957.

See brand numbers 12, 26, 66, and 73.

S No 75 S
Henry Jones

The **S** brand was recorded by Henry Jones of Fort Bend County, an early rancher and friend of the A. P. George Ranch.

Source: Paul Henry, A. P. George Ranch foreman, 1957.

Z No 76 Z
George Culver

The **Z** brand is recorded in Matagorda County by George Culver of Wadsworth, Texas. It was originally used by the Stewart Brothers.

Source: Mrs. Culver's nephew, 1955.

7HL No 77 7 H L Connected
A. P. George Ranch

The **Seven H L Connected** brand is recorded by the A. P. George Ranch in Fort Bend County and is placed on the left shoulder. Mrs. Jane H. Long first recorded the brand in 1838.

Source: George Ranch foreman, Paul Henry, 1957.

See brand numbers 12, 26, 66, 73, and 74.

(Jane Long came to Texas in 1819 with her husband, General James Long, who was killed in Mexico City. An historical marker at her old home near Richmond, Texas, states, "She was known as the pioneer of Anglo-American women in Texas.")

B4 No 78 B 4
Buller family

The **B Four** brand is recorded by the Buller family in Wharton and Fort Bend counties. I worked several cattle theft cases with Deputy Sheriff Marvin Buller of Columbus, a long time peace officer in Colorado County. He died March 20, 1979.

Source: Marvin Buller, 1954.

SO No 79 S O
Polly Ryon Estate

The **S O** brand was recorded by the Polly Ryon Estate in Fort Bend County.

Source: Paul Henry, A. P. George Ranch foreman, 1957.

(Polly Ryon was the daughter of Henry Jones, who established what is today the A. P. George Ranch near Richmond, Texas. Through her efforts, the ranch grew and prospered. Ryon's daughter, Mamie, married A. P. George, whose name the ranch bears.)

JO No 80 J O
J. W. Slavin

The **J O** brand was recorded in 1859 by J. W. Slavin of Fort Bend County and was used on cattle along the Brazos River near Booth and Thompson, Texas.

Source: T. W. Oberhoff, 1957.

ЯF No 81 Backward R F
Ed R. Frnka

The **Backward R F** brand is recorded in Lavaca, Colorado, and Wharton counties by Ed R. Frnka of Garwood, Texas. It is placed on the left hip or the left side of steers going to northern and western feedlots.

Source: W. R. "Bill" Frnka, Cedar Post Ranch, 1957.

See brand numbers 82, 83, and 84.

F No 82 F Quarter Circle
Frnka Ranch

The **F Quarter Circle** brand was recorded in Lavaca and Colorado counties in 1925 by the Frnka Ranch of Garwood, Texas.

Source: W. R. "Bill" Frnka, 1957.

See brand numbers 81, 83, and 84.

⫟ No 83 Lazy F
W. R. Frnka

The **Lazy F** brand was recorded in 1930 in Colorado and Dimmit counties by W. R. "Bill" Frnka of Garwood, Texas, who used it on steers going to grass in Kansas.

Source: Bill Frnka, Cedar Post Ranch, 1957.

See brand numbers 81, 82, and 84.

WF No 84 W F Connected
Ed R. Frnka

The **W F Connected** brand was recorded by Ed R. Frnka in Colorado County.

Source: Ed Frnka's son, W. R. "Bill" Frnka, Cedar Post Ranch, 1957.

HD No 85 Half Circle H D Connected
H. A. Dromgoole & Son

The **Half Circle H D Connected** brand, placed on the left side, was recorded in Colorado and Wharton counties by H. A. "Shoat" Dromgoole & Son of Garwood, Texas.

Source: Dromgoole Ranch on the Colorado River, 1957.

See brand numbers 25, 86–90, and 109.

A No 86 Round Top A
H. A. Dromgoole & Son

The **Round Top A** brand was recorded in Colorado County by H. A. "Shoat" Dromgoole & Son of Garwood, Texas.

Source: Dromgoole Ranch, 1957.

See brand numbers 25, 85, 87–90, and 109.

№ 87 H
H. A. Dromgoole & Son

The **H** brand is recorded in Colorado County by H. A. "Shoat" Dromgoole & Son of Garwood, Texas.

Source: Dromgoole Ranch, 1957.

See brand numbers 25, 85, 86, 88–90, and 109.

№ 88 Frying Pan
H. A. Dromgoole & Son

The **Frying Pan** brand was recorded in Colorado County by H. A. "Shoat" Dromgoole & Son of Garwood, Texas.

Source: Dromgoole Ranch, 1957.

See brand numbers 25, 85–87, 89, 90, and 109.

№ 89 T
H. A. Dromgoole & Son

The **T** brand was recorded in Colorado County by H. A. "Shoat" Dromgoole & Son of Garwood, Texas.

Source: Dromgoole Ranch, 1957.

See brand numbers 25, 85–88, 90, and 109.

№ 90 Goose Egg
H. A. "Shoat" Dromgoole & Son

The **Goose Egg** brand was recorded in Colorado County by H. A. "Shoat" Dromgoole & Son of Garwood, Texas.

Source: Dromgoole Ranch on the Colorado River, 1957.

See brand numbers 25, 85–89, and 109.

№ 91 Five Point Star
Texas Department of Corrections

The **Five Point Star** brand of the Texas Department of Corrections, formerly the Texas Prison System, Huntsville, Texas, is recorded in Fort Bend, Brazoria, Madison, Houston, Walker, and Harris counties. It was originated by a Legislative Act during the 1930s that stated that all prison system stock must be branded with a star. In 1936, under the management of O. J. S. Ellingson, the prison system had approximately 6,000 head of Brahman-cross cattle. In 1956, the Star brand was on 14,229 beef cattle and 3,263 dairy cows on 73,133 acres.

The brand is also used on the Longhorn herd owned and managed by the Texas Parks and Wildlife Department and kept at Fort Griffin Historical Park near Albany.

Source: Warden C. L. McAdams, Ramsey State Farm, 1958.

*(According to the Brazoria County records in Angleton, a **Five Point Star** brand was recorded by Joab H. Barttin in 1849.)*

№ 92 M L Connected
Mary and Leonard Stiles

The **M L Connected** brand, recorded by Mary and Leonard Stiles in DeWitt County in 1948, is branded on the left rib of cattle at Cuero in DeWitt County and on the W. E. Gunn Ranch at Freeport in Brazoria County.

(This is the brand of Leonard and Mary Stiles who donated this branding iron collection to the Cattle Raisers Museum in Fort Worth. The design came from the initials of their names.)

№ 93 Running W
King Ranch

The **Running W** brand, owned by the King Ranch of Kingsville, Texas, was first recorded in 1869 in Nueces County by Captain Richard King and is placed anywhere on either side of cattle. It is registered in Kleberg, Hidalgo, Jim Wells, Willacy, Brooks, Nueces, Kenedy, and Cameron counties in Texas, Osage County in Oklahoma, and in Coahuila, Nuevo Leon, Mexico. In Spanish, this brand is known as *La Viborita* or "Little Snake." This particular iron is a calf brand.

Source: Charlie Burwell, foreman of King Ranch's Laureles Division, 1956.

See brand number 45.

№ 94 Little h Little b Connected
Humphries & Burson

The **Little h Little b Connected** brand was recorded in 1930 in Liberty and Briscoe counties by the Humphries & Burson partnership.

Source: Howis Partlow, Liberty, Texas, 1957.

№ 95 Ace of Clubs
Lee M. Pierce

The **Ace of Clubs** brand is used by Lee M. "Tick" Pierce of Blessing, Texas, on his ranch in Matagorda County. It was first recorded in 1885 by A. B. Pierce Sr. After his death, his wife used the brand on a few cows tended by Walter Stanford. She sold her cattle, and the brand was not used again until Tick Pierce started in the cattle business in 1951. He recorded it in 1953. The brand's name is taken from the Ace of Clubs Ranch in the Collegeport area, owned by Lee Pierce's father. It is believed to be an old brand bought on cattle years ago. It was also a partnership brand at one time.

Source: Bill Curtis, manager of the Nash Ranch, Brazoria County.

See brand number 446.

№ 96 Dot P L Dash
G. Lock Paret

The **Dot P L Dash** brand was recorded in Baton Rouge, Louisiana, in 1940 by G. Lock Paret of Lake Charles and branded on 400 registered Brahman cattle on his ranch at Ragley, Louisiana.

№ 97 Seven Eleven
M. D. Huebner

The **Seven Eleven** brand was recorded in 1907 by M. D. Huebner of Bay City, Texas, after a family partnership was terminated. Each fall, the Huebners drive their cattle, often a herd of 1,500, from the Bay City area to the mouth of the Colorado River where they swim across to Matagorda Island and winter on the island's salt grass. I made this trip one spring when the Huebners brought their cattle home from the island.

Source: Dudley Huebner, 1956.

Nº 98   Three D brand
D. Waggoner & Son

The **D71** brand was registered in 1871 in Wise and Clay counties by D. Waggoner & Son. The **Three D** brand was recorded in 1881 and is run on Hereford cattle in Wilbarger, Foard, Archer, Baylor, Wichita, and Knox counties. The 1956 TSCRA Inspectors meeting was held at the Waggoner Ranch south of Vernon, Texas. Ranch manager, John Biggs, was president of the TSCRA at the time.

Source: Paul Waggoner, 1956.

*(The **D71** brand was apparently discontinued on Waggoner cattle after 1881 but was used as a horse brand. In Loving's 1881 Brand Book, Waggoner's cattle brand is shown as **SL**, but it was used only a short time and then replaced by three reversed Ds—one on the hip, on the side, and on the thigh. Today, a single reversed **D** is stamped on the right hip of the cattle on the 500,000-acre ranch that is still operated by the Waggoner family.)*

Nº 99   Dash S Dash
Thad Smith Jr.

The **Dash S Dash** brand is recorded by Thad Smith Jr. of Barker, Texas, in Harris, Waller, Liberty, and Galveston counties. This was an old brand that belonged to Smith's grandfather, G. S. Fred H. Smith, who recorded it in Harris County in 1900. Thad Smith Sr. recorded it in Harris County in 1904 and placed it on the left side. Thad Smith Jr. brands on the right side. The S represents the name "Smith," and the dashes were added to protect against cattle rustlers.

Nº 100   Diamond A
Warren P. Allee

The **Diamond A** brand is recorded in Dimmit County by TSCRA Inspector Warren P. Allee of Carrizo Springs, Texas. J. E. Baylor gave Allee's wife, Mabel, a grey horse branded **Diamond A** as a wedding gift in 1941. Warren Allee was a TSCRA Inspector from 1937–1980, and I worked several theft cases with him.

Nº 101   Cloverleaf
Don Stiles

The **Cloverleaf** brand was recorded in DeWitt County in 1938 by my brother, Don Stiles, of Cuero, Texas.

Source: Don Stiles, 1955.

(The Stiles Cattle Company — Mr. and Mrs. Don Stiles Sr. and sons, Don Jr., Harvey, and Clint—is a combination cattle order buying firm and ranching enterprise that runs about 3,000 mother cows.)

Nº 102   S Cross S Bar
R. B. Stiles and David Stiles

The **S Cross S Bar** brand, recorded by R. B. Stiles and David Stiles in 1936 in Atascosa County, was used on commercial cattle and some dairy cattle at Amphion, Texas.

Source: Don Stiles, 1954.

Nº 103   T Y T Connected
Dan Harrison

The **T Y T Connected** brand on the left hip or left side of cattle is used by Dan Harrison of Houston in South Texas. It was recorded about 1944 in Sutton, Edwards, McMullen, Live Oak, Fort Bend, and Brazoria counties and is used on the Arrow S Ranch and the Pilloncillo Ranch.

Source: from Harrison's McCoy Ranch, 1956.
See brand number 16.

Nº 104   Seven V Bar
Mrs. H. W. Savage

The **Seven V Bar** brand used by Mrs. H. W. Savage Sr. of Bay City, Texas, was recorded about 1917 in Matagorda County and is placed on the left hip. Two hundred cattle carried the brand at one time. Her father used the **V Bar** brand in the early days where she now lives on the Colorado River. She added a **7** to the **V Bar**.

Source: Mrs. H. W. Savage Sr., 1956.
See brand numbers 42, 71, 239, 349, and 350.

Nº 105   H E Connected
R. W. Henderson

The **H E Connected** brand was recorded by R. W. "Bob" Henderson of Houston, Texas, in Brazoria, Galveston, Henderson, and Montgomery counties and placed on the right thigh. About 4,000 head of cattle carried the brand on the old Turnbow Ranch near Alvin. I helped Henderson count and sell the cattle and brand in 1957 to Ed Deloney, a one-armed man, who shipped them to England.

Source: Bob Henderson, 1957.

Nº 106   J H D Connected
J. H. P. Davis

The **J H D Connected** brand was recorded by J. H. P. Davis in Fort Bend County.

Source: A. P. George, father-in-law of J. H. P. Davis.

Nº 107   Four H Half h
Hampil Estate

The **Four H Half h** brand was recorded by the Dr. Hampil Estate in Brazoria County. Hampil was an early settler on the Bernard River and at one time, the doctor for the prison. The Hampil place is next to the Hard Scrabble Ranch and the Cox Ranch. I worked wild and spoiled cattle there with Monk Chiles, who works the Hampil cattle and now leases the pasture.

Source: L. L. "Monk" Chiles.

J2 Nº 108 J Two
Joe Wadsworth

The **J Two** brand was recorded by Joe Wadsworth of Victoria County.

Source: Joe Wadsworth, 1954, during the division of the Wadsworth-McDaniel cattle.

Nº 109 Walking Stick Bar
H. A. Dromgoole

The **Walking Stick Bar** brand was recorded by H. A. Dromgoole in Colorado County.

Source: H. A. Dromgoole, 1957, at his home on the Colorado River.

See brand numbers 25 and 85–90.

6666 Nº 110 Four Sixes
S. B. Burnett Estate

The **6666** brand is recorded in King, Hutchinson, and Carson counties by the S. B. Burnett Estate of Fort Worth, Texas.

(Samuel Burk Burnett was born in Missouri in 1849 and moved with his family to Texas in 1859. Young Burk drove his father's cattle to market during the 1860s. About 1871, he purchased 100 head of cattle carrying the 6666 brand from Frank Crowley in Denton County. Burnett recorded the brand in Wichita County in 1875, on the Kiowa-Comanche Reservation in 1881, in Carson and Hutchinson counties in 1902, and in King County in 1903. The 6666 brand represents the S. B. Burnett Estate to this day. The story is told that Burk won the brand and cattle in a poker game by holding four sixes—but that is just a colorful tale.

In the late 1800s, Burnett ran cattle on leased land in Indian Territory. When the area was to be opened for settlement, he bought the Dixon Creek Ranch in the Texas Panhandle from the White Deer Lands Trust in 1902 and the 140,000-acre 8 Ranch in King County from the Louisville Land & Cattle Company of Louisville, Kentucky, and moved his cattle back to Texas.

Burk Burnett soon owned 320 sections in fee, and he built a ranching empire that still exists in King and Carson counties. It has been continued by his granddaughter, the late Anne Burnett Tandy, and his great-granddaughter, Anne W. Marion of Fort Worth. The Estate's cattle still carry the 6666 brand. The horses are branded L on the left shoulder, their dam's number on the left jaw, and the year foaled on the left butt.)

Nº 111 M L Connected
W. J. Swickheimer

The **M L Connected** brand on the left hip was recorded in Goliad, Brazoria, and Lavaca counties in

1895 by W. J. Swickheimer. The brand was designed from Mrs. Swickheimer's initials.

Source: Lee Swickheimer of Fannin, 1957.

See brand numbers 47 and 52.

ZC Nº 112 Z C Connected
Dolph Briscoe Jr.

The **Z C Connected** brand belonged to Dolph Briscoe Jr. of Uvalde, Texas.

Source: Briscoe Ranch foreman, Les Brown.

See brand numbers 53 and 64.

Nº 113 Seventy-four Connected
J. S. Abercrombie.

The **Seventy-four Connected** brand was recorded by J. S. Abercrombie in Gonzales and Atascosa counties and is placed on the left hip or left side. The 74 Ranch is north of Campbellton, Texas, and was part of the 7PL Ranch owned by Abercrombie. The 74 Ranch is presently owned by Abercrombie's daughter, Josephine Bryan of Houston.

Source: Raymond Glick, 1953.

See brand number 68.

Nº 114 Half Moon
Runnels-Pierce Estate

The **Half Moon** brand was recorded by the Runnels-Pierce Estate in Matagorda, Brazoria, and Wharton counties. It was used by the Pierce-Sullivan Pasture and Cattle Company in the late 1800s, during the days when colorful cattleman, A. H. "Shanghai" Pierce, was still in command. I made a tally of cattle during the division of the Pierce Estate in 1956. After the division, the Runnels took the **Half Moon** as their brand and used it mostly on the Duncan Ranch east of the Colorado River along the Matagorda and Colorado county line.

Source: Frank Anderwald and Sam Cutbirth, Runnels-Pierce Estate, 1956.

(John Runnels, a director of the TSCRA since 1981, is the great-grandson of Shanghai Pierce, early day trail driver and rancher. Pierce was said to be as "uncouth as the cattle he drove" and he referred to his Longhorns as "ol' mossyhorns." He was a top cowman and a shrewd businessman and one of Texas's most colorful cattlemen.)

Nº 115 Spur
Alonzo Peeler

The **Spur** brand, placed on the right hip, was recorded in 1928 by Alonzo Peeler of Christine, Texas, in Atascosa County. Peeler died in 1961 and was buried on a hill overlooking the Hall Ranch. The partnership of Jennings & Peeler recorded the U brand and used it from 1912–1918.

Source: Alonzo Peeler, 1957, while on a deer hunt.

See brand number 13.

Nº 116   Four S Connected
Scott Brothers

The **Four S Connected** brand was recorded in Webb County, Texas, and was used on registered Charolais cattle on the Coquat Ranch by the Scott Brothers.

Source: Bob Coquat of Three Rivers, 1957.

No 117   L
George E. Light Jr. & Sons

The **L**, branded on the left loin, was recorded in LaSalle and Dimmit counties in 1940 by George E. Light Jr. & Sons of the Light Ranch, where 6,200 cattle have carried this brand at one time. It is a hold-over from the L 7 Cattle Company. In 1968, the Light Ranch sold 20,000 acres to the Texas Parks & Wildlife Department to be used as a reserve. George Light Jr. was a Director of the TSCRA in 1959.

Source: George Light III, 1958, while I was receiving Poole Brothers' cattle in Pearsall with Monk Chiles.

Nº 118   Seven
George E. Light III

The **Seven** brand on the left side of cattle was recorded by George E. Light III of the Light Ranch in 1950 in Dimmit, LaSalle, and Webb counties. About 2,500 head have carried this brand at one time. George E. Light Jr. & Sons brand an **L**, and George E. Light III turned that brand over to use as a **7** and branded it in a different location.

Source: George Light III, Cotulla, Texas.

(George E. Light III became a TSCRA director in 1954.)

Nº 119   T Bar
Tom Coleman, Jr.

The **T Bar** brand was recorded in 1928 in Dimmit, LaSalle, and Webb counties by Tom Coleman Jr. This brand originated from the **T** brand of the earlier Coleman-Fulton Pasture Company of which his father, Thomas Atlee Coleman of San Antonio, was a partner with C. W. Fulton and J. M. and T. H. Mathis, all of Rockport. That company was founded in 1871, and the owners fenced 123,000 acres, said to be the first large pasture fenced in the state.

The company's superintendent, Joseph F. Green, and John M. Green of Encinal, leased the 224,000-acre Catarina Ranch in Dimmit, LaSalle, and Webb counties in 1896. They branded a **T** on the right hip until 1900. The brand was easy to change, so they rebranded the existing livestock with a another **T** on the left hip, and younger animals were branded on the left side and left hip.

Source: Light Ranch, 1958, where Coleman once ranched.

Nº 120   M J Connected
Mrs. Mary Jane Sterling

The **M J Connected** brand was registered by Mrs. Mary Jane Sterling in 1860 in Liberty County.

She was the mother of Governor Ross Sterling (1931–1933).

Source: Jim Sterling of Dayton, Texas, 1957, through Graves Peeler.

Nº 121   O S
G. O. Stoner

The **O S** brand was recorded in Liberty, Harris, Chambers, and Victoria counties in 1877 by George O. Stoner, father of TSCRA Inspector G. O. Stoner of Houston, Texas. The most cattle to carry the **O S** brand at one time were 1,000 head. The Stoner Ranch in Victoria County, where G. O. Stoner was born in 1888, is now part of the O'Connor Ranch. Stoner, a TSCRA Inspector from 1910 to 1957, helped me when I began working for the Association. He died August 30, 1972.

Source: G. O. Stoner, 1957, at his ranch in Harris County. *See brand number 976.*

Nº 122   H M Connected
Milton Hensley

Source: The   **H   M   Connected** branding iron came from Milton Hensley of Boling, Wharton County, Texas, 1955.

Nº 123   Diamond S
Smith & Nash

The **Diamond S** brand was recorded in Brazoria County as a partnership brand of Smith and Nash and used on the Nash Ranch.

See brand numbers 44, 142, 143, 458, and 492.

Nº 124   Seven V Bar
Buster Roberts

The **Seven V Bar** brand was recorded by Buster Roberts of Katy, Texas, in Harris, Fort Bend, and Waller counties. Roberts was an inspector for a Houston loan association and a deputy sheriff in Fort Bend County.

Source: Buster Roberts, 1955.

Nº 125   Fifty-five Bar
J. P. Williams

The **Fifty-five Bar** brand is recorded in Brazoria County by J. P. Williams of Sweeny, Texas.

Nº 126   Lazy P
Lykes Brothers Inc.

The **Lazy P** brand was recorded in Webb, Duval, Brewster, and Presidio counties by the Lykes Brothers, Inc. of Houston, Texas. It is placed on the left side or left loin.

Source: ranch foreman Roscoe Seago, 1958, at Cameron Duncan Ranch, Freer, Texas. He also gave me a .44 magnum, short-barrel rifle with a hexagon barrel.

(The five Lykes brothers built their extensive cattle holdings during the Spanish-American War when they developed a cattle

import and export company in Havana, Cuba. The brothers owned and directed large ranches in Texas, Florida, and Cuba. They also established the Lykes Brothers Steamship Company.)

№ 127   Goose Egg
Pickering & Poole

The **Goose Egg** brand was recorded in Brazoria County and used on the Cox Ranch by the partnership of E. E. Pickering and Tom Poole. Pickering was born in 1883 on the Pickering Ranch in Victoria County near the town of Placedo. He was a pioneer cattleman and ran a large scale ranching operation from 1912 to 1949 when he retired. He was co-founder of the town of Placedo and died at 85 years in 1968.

№ 128   Little h
Dick Byers

The **Little h** brand was recorded by Dick Byers at Altair in Colorado County. The ranch is leased by J. H. Clipson of Eagle Lake, Texas.

Source: Dick Byers, 1957, when he was eighty-one and still living on the ranch.

№ 129   T Bar
Taylor Brothers

The **T Bar** brand was recorded in 1860 by the Taylor Brothers in Wharton County on the Colorado River. W. T. Taylor made his own branding irons in the blacksmith shop. He chose a letter of the alphabet that was easily shaped. When the property was divided in 1900, the herd consisted mainly of full-blood Devon cattle which ran over a wide range and were probably not registered.

Source: Glen Taylor, 1958.

See brand numbers 213, 214, 218, 219, 228, and 230.

№ 130   J F Connected
Mrs. T. J. Poole Jr.

The **J F Connected** brand, placed on the left hip, is used by Mrs. T. J. Poole Jr. in Brazoria and Matagorda counties. Francis E. Grimes first recorded it in 1856 in Matagorda County.

See brand numbers 5, 33, 139, and 333.

№ 131   U Dash
Bob Stringfellow

The **U Dash** brand was recorded by R. E. L. "Bob" Stringfellow in Brazoria County and used by Mrs. Stringfellow on her ranch at the mouth of the Brazos River near Freeport. The brand is placed anywhere on the left side.

Source: Mrs. Bob Stringfellow, 1957.

See brand number 132.

№ 132   V Dash
Bob Stringfellow

The **V Dash** brand was recorded in Brazoria County by Bob Stringfellow and used by Mrs. R. E. L. "Bob" Stringfellow on her ranch at the mouth of the Brazos River near Freeport. It is branded anywhere on the left side.

Source: Mrs. Bob Stringfellow, 1957.

See brand number 131.

№ 133   W B G
W. B. Grimes

The **W B G** brand was recorded by William Bradford "Bing" Grimes in Brazoria and Matagorda counties in 1852. Grimes owned a factory on the Tres Palacios where cattle were butchered for tallow and hides. Later, he had 15,000 cattle under this brand on free range that he drove or shipped to Kansas between 1875 to 1885. The brand was discontinued about 1900.

Source: Tom Poole, 1956, Bay City, Texas.

№ 134   Two Little hs
Jimmy Hill and Walter Crosby

The **Two Little hs**, branded on the left hip, was recorded in 1940 in Brazoria County by Jimmy Hill and Walter Crosby. Crosby, of Freeport, Texas, died in 1965.

Source: Walter Crosby, 1958.

№ 135   Screw Plate
Frank Turner Jr.

The **Screw Plate** brand was recorded in 1912 in Brazoria County by Frank Turner Jr. and is placed on the right side. The Turner Ranch is at Rosharon near the entrance to the Ramsey State Prison Farm. Turner is an inspector for the Federal Land Bank in Houston. He made this one-piece iron, ▼, that was stamped twice to make the brand.

Source: Frank Turner, 1957. He also gave me a pair of spurs he made.

See brand number 51.

№ 136   C
Robinowitz Brothers

The **C** brand was recorded by the Robinowitz Brothers in Fort Bend, Austin, Harris, Galveston, Brazoria, Jackson, and Wharton counties. It is placed on the right side or shoulder of steers.

Source: Milton Robinowitz, 1957, at his Fort Bend County ranch.

See brand number 162.

№ 137   Flat Top Three
George D. Culver Ranch

The **Flat Top Three** brand was recorded by the George D. Culver Ranch in Matagorda County.

Source: Mrs. George Culver, Wadsworth, Texas.

Nº 138   Backward C Dash
Poole & Robinowitz

The **Backward C Dash** is a Poole and Robinowitz partnership brand recorded in the Gulf Coast counties of Brazoria and Galveston and branded on the left side of steers going to northern and western markets.

Source: Monk Chiles at the Northern Headquarters Ranch, Matagorda County, 1953.

See brand numbers 40, 41, 136, and 162.

TJP

Nº 139   T J P
T. J. Poole Jr.

The **T J P** brand is recorded by T. J. Poole Jr. in Wharton, Matagorda, and Brazoria counties. His father, T. J. Poole Sr., used the brand in this area about 1900.

Source: T. J. Poole Jr., Bay City, Texas.
See brand numbers 5, 33, 130, and 333.

Nº 140   Backward F Bar
A. G. Dingle

The **Backward F Bar** brand was recorded by A. G. Dingle in Brazoria County in 1920. Because the **F** brand was taken, he chose the **Backward F Bar**. He used it on registered Brahman cattle near Brazoria, Texas. Dingle is a Freeport businessman. Although ranching is his hobby and 150 head were the most to carry his brand at one time, he is a great believer in Brahman cattle and has contributed to the improvement of the breed.

BF

Nº 141   B F
A. F. Shannon

The **B F** is an early day brand recorded by A. F. Shannon in Brazoria County in 1837. The Shannon Ranch, near the Gulf of Mexico, was on the Velasco side of San Luis Pass where Shannon owned a ferry that operated from Velasco through the pass to Galveston. The ranch was a stopping place for travelers between the two towns.

Source: information from Mona Dingle.

TLC

Nº 142   T L C
Nash Ranch

The **T L C** brand was recorded by the Nash Ranch in Brazoria County.

See brand numbers 44, 123, 143, 458, 492, 501, and 505.

Nº 143   Box
Nash Ranch

The **Box** brand was recorded by the Nash Ranch in Brazoria County.

See brand numbers 44, 123, 142, 458, 492, 501, and 505.

Nº 144   Bracket M
Owner unknown

This **Bracket M** branding iron was found on the Bernard River near Sweeny, Texas, in 1954.

Nº 145   Goose Egg
Poole & Pickering

The **Goose Egg** was a partnership brand of Poole & Pickering recorded in Matagorda County. This iron was found on the Cox Ranch, apparently left there when a herd of steers or cows were bought and branded with the **Goose Egg**.

See brand number 127.

Nº 146   W Diamond L Connected
Mrs. Walter Crosby

The **W Diamond L Connected** brand was recorded in Brazoria County in 1930 by Mrs. Walter Crosby, and is placed on the left thigh or the left hip. I recovered a cow with this brand sixty miles from where she belonged.

Source: Walter Crosby, 1958.

Nº 147   O Bar
W. A. Hoskin

The **O Bar** brand is used by W. A. "Bill" Hoskin of Brazoria County. Elizabeth Barrett first recorded it in 1841. W. D. Hoskin purchased her cattle and brand at a Sheriff's Sale in 1871 and recorded the brand in 1874. He used it on many cattle at Hoskin's Mound on the Gulf Coast before it became Bill Hoskin's brand.

Source: W. A. Hoskin, Angleton, Texas.

JHC

Nº 148   J H C Connected
John H. Craig

The **J H C Connected** brand was recorded by John H. Craig in Brazoria and Matagorda counties in 1920, but it has been used since 1899. It is branded on the left hip or the left side. About 750 cattle were the most to carry the brand at one time.

Source: John Craig, West Columbia, Texas.

Nº 149   Sloping L
Lester Bunge

The Sloping L brand was registered in 1937 in Colorado, Lavaca, and Wharton counties and also in Greenwood County, Kansas. Lester Bunge runs it on the left hip or left shoulder of Brahman cattle.

Source: Mr. and Mrs. Lester P. W. Bunge, Garwood, Texas.

(Lester Bunge died in El Campo, Texas, at the age of eighty-six years.)

Nº 150   O Bar
John C. Moyle

The **O Bar**, branded on the left hip, was recorded by John C. Moyle in 1924 in Montgomery County.

This is the first iron used by Moyle when he came to Texas from Pennsylvania. It is homemade from a pipe collar and a bar. In the early 1930s, Ray D. Moyle added another bar and recorded two more brands in Brazoria County—Ō and ‖O.

Source: Ray D. Moyle, Rosharon, Texas.

№ 151   P L Connected
Louis M. Pierce Jr.

The **P L Connected** brand was recorded in Brazoria County by Louis M. Pierce Jr., Houston businessman and rancher. Pierce brands on the right side or right hip. He is also a noted Quarter Horse breeder, and has many fine cutting horses.

Source: Louis Pierce, 1957, Oak Tree Ranch near Rosharon, Texas.

(Pierce also recorded the brand in Maverick and Atascosa counties where he had other ranches and ran commercial cattle. Pierce has served as president and chairman of the board of the Houston Livestock Show and Rodeo and has been an honorary director of the TSCRA since 1990.)

№ 152   E Cross
Cornelius Cattle Company

The **E Cross** brand on the left hip was recorded by the Cornelius Cattle Company in Matagorda County in 1908. W. D. "Will" Cornelius used it on many cattle along the Gulf Coast. In 1965, the brand was also on cattle at Gin Gin, Australia, operated by Leonard and Boo Cornelius.

Source: Will Cornelius, his Markham, Texas ranch, 1953.

(The Cornelius family have been longtime Texas ranchers in the Matagorda Bay area. George William Cornelius was a trail driver in the 1870s, and his son, W. D. Cornelius Sr., was a charter member of the American Brahman Breeders Association. Today's commercial cow-calf operation is carried on by family members.)

See brand numbers 153 and 154.

№ 153   K X
Cornelius Cattle Company

The **K X** brand was recorded by Cornelius Cattle Company in Matagorda County in 1886, and it is placed on the left hip. It is well known among cowmen and especially among the cowboys who rode **K X** horses.

Source: W. D. "Will" Cornelius, 1958, at his Markham, Texas, ranch.

(W. D. Cornelius married Mary Ethel Johnson in 1919. About 1940 Will and his wife formed a partnership with their two sons and a daughter that operated as Cornelius Cattle Company. Will died in 1960, and the ranch was divided.)

See brand number 152 and 154.

№ 154   O O Bar
Johnny Walker & W. D. Cornelius

The **O O Bar** partnership brand was recorded by Johnny Walker and W. D. Cornelius in Matagorda

and Colorado counties in 1925 after the "Big Freeze," when many cattle in this area were lost.

Source: W. D. Cornelius, 1958.

№ 155   Half Circle L
J. D. Hudgins

The **Half Circle L** brand was recorded in 1885 in Wharton County by M. F. Taylor, the nephew of J. D. Hudgins. He sold the brand and cattle to J. D. Hudgins & Brothers in 1901, and the brothers sold their interests to J. D. Hudgins in 1906. He retained the brand because of its neatness and it does not blot. It has been used on the Hudgins's registered Brahman cattle since the beginning of their herd in 1915. The brand is known in many countries. South American cattlemen call it the **Parasol** or **Quitasol** brand, and some will not buy a bull unless it carries that brand.

As many as 4,000 cattle at one time have grazed the 10,000 acres of deeded land and 15,000 acres of leased land on the Hudgins Ranch. Edgar Hudgins was the first to encourage me to display my branding iron collection.

Source: Edgar Hudgins, Hudgins Ranch, 1958.

(Joel Hudgins homesteaded the Wharton County land in 1839. The name J. D. Hudgins is synonymous with fine Brahman cattle and the founding of the American Brahman Breeders Association. J. D. Hudgins, Inc., located at Hungerford, Texas, is carried on by family descendants. The Hudgins operation has advertised in The Cattleman magazine continuously since the beginning of the publication in 1914.)

№ 156   7 V L Connected
Pat A. Richmond & Brothers

The **7 V L Connected** brand was recorded in 1930 in Matagorda and Jackson counties by Pat A. Richmond & Brothers of Palacios, Texas.

Source: Pat Richmond, 1957, Karankawa Bay Ranch.

№ 157   T Up T Down
T. P. Brundrett

The **T Up T Down** is an early brand of Brazoria County, used since about 1900. It first belonged to Charles Brundrett and his son, W. T. C. Brundrett. When they left the county in the 1930s, George Kennedy obtained the brand. In 1954, he returned it to T. P. Brundrett, grandson of its original owner, who recorded it in 1954 as placed on the left loin. Eight hundred cows have carried the brand at one time.

Source: T. P. Brundrett, Angleton, Texas, 1958.

№ 158   2 C
J. R. Farmer

The **2 C**, branded on the left thigh, is recorded in Fort Bend County by J. R. Farmer of Richmond, Texas. D. W. Armstrong originally recorded it in 1850 and branded 300 calves a year in Fort Bend and Wharton counties.

Source: J. R. Farmer, 1957, Pecan Grove Ranch near Richmond.

See brand number 159.

JF

Nº 159   J F
Jordan Farmer

The **J F** brand was recorded in 1850 by Jordan Farmer in Fort Bend and Wharton counties. It is placed on the left thigh.

Source: J. R. Farmer, 1957, Pecan Grove Ranch near Richmond.

See brand number 158.

24

Nº 160   24
George W. Armstrong

The **24** brand was recorded in Fort Bend and Wharton counties and used in the Bernard River bottoms by George W. Armstrong of Needville, Texas. It is placed on the left thigh. Mrs. Frank Vaughn of Bishop was an adopted daughter of George Armstrong. Her daughter inherited the Armstrong land and cattle, and Mrs. Vaughn looked after her interests until she was twenty-one years old.

Source: Frank Vaughn, 1957, Armstrong Ranch.

FT

Nº 161   F T
Frances Teas Vaughn

The **F T** brand was recorded in Fort Bend County by Frances Teas Vaughn of Corpus Christi, Texas, the daughter of George W. Armstrong.

Source: Frank Vaughn, 1957.

Nº 162   Wagon Box
Buls & Robinowitz

The **Wagon Box** brand was recorded in 1935 by Robinowitz and Buls of Damon, Texas, in Brazoria and Fort Bend counties.

Source: George Buls, Damon, Texas, 1957.

See brand numbers 40, 41, and 138.

⊢

Nº 163   Lazy T
Senior Ranch

The **Lazy T** brand is recorded in Fort Bend and Harris counties by the Senior Ranch near DeWalt, Texas.

Source: Bill Senior, 1957.

ED

Nº 164   E D
Tom Darst

The **E D** brand was recorded in 1838, by E. H. Darst and is still run by Tom Darst in Fort Bend and Wharton counties. This is an old iron and was bronzed to preserve it. The brand is one of the oldest in Texas to still be used by the same family. It was of greatest importance about 1900 under the ownership of Darst's wife, Mary E. Darst, who ran about 1,000 cattle. The brand is placed anywhere on the left side.

Source: Tom Darst, Darst Ranch, 1958, after we broke a theft ring in that area.

See brand numbers 172 and 187.

Nº 165   Flying N
Edwin R. Spencer

The **Flying N** brand was recorded in Matagorda and Colorado counties by Edwin R. Spencer of Columbus, Texas.

Nº 166   Hat Three
Ralph. B. McCauley

The **Hat Three** brand was recorded in Matagorda County in 1864 by Thad Tarver, who later traded it to Ralph B. McCauley for a schooner of beer. The original iron is being preserved by R. B. McCauley of Needville, Texas. The **Hat Three** brand, placed on the right hip, is used in Matagorda, Fort Bend, and Wharton counties.

Source: iron is a copy from R. B. McCauley, 1958, after we broke a theft ring in which a running iron was used to change this brand.

E

No. 167   F G Connected
Fred Grunwald

The **F G Connected** brand was recorded by Fred Grunwald in 1912 in Fort Bend County.

Source: Fred Grunwald, 1958, after we broke a theft ring in which this brand was changed with a running iron.

UE

Nº 168   U E Connected
Ben H. Wheeler

The **U E Connected** brand, placed on the left hip, was recorded in Matagorda County in 1869 by Ben H. Wheeler's father who got the idea for the brand design from the sound made by locusts—"Ue, ue, ue." He used this brand in the Blessing area on Tres Palacios Bay in the early days.

Source: Ben H. Wheeler

∩

Nº 169   Open A
Dallas Hillboldt

The **Open A** brand was recorded by Dallas Hillboldt of Sealy, Texas, in Austin, Colorado, Waller, Galveston, and Fort Bend counties and is placed on the right hip. A man had shot Hillboldt, and Hillboldt carried the .45 slug on a chain.

Source: Jack Hillboldt, 1958, soon after Dallas Hillboldt's death.

Nº 170   Lazy Y
J. Laurence Ducroz

The **Lazy Y** brand was recorded in Brazoria County in 1910 by J. Laurence Ducroz and is branded anywhere on the left side on his registered Brahman cattle.

Source: Charlie A. Ducroz, Brazoria, Texas, who died in 1976.

See brand numbers 171, 173, and 183.

№ 171   Lazy H
J. Laurence Ducroz

The **Lazy H**, recorded in 1910, was branded anywhere on the left side of registered Brahman cattle by J. Laurence Ducroz of Brazoria County.

Source: Charlie A. Ducroz, Brazoria, Texas.
See brand numbers 170, 173, and 183.

№ 0172   L D
R. H. Darst Estate

The **L D** brand of the R. H. Darst Estate was recorded in Fort Bend County by R. H. Darst about 1890. He purchased the brand and cattle carrying it from Lizzie Domon—hence the **L D** brand, which had probably been recorded years before the purchase. As many as 1,000 cattle at one time carried this brand on their left thighs.

Source: Bobbie Darst, Beasley, Texas, 1958.
See brand numbers 164 and 187.

№ 173   C Half Circle
Charlie A. Ducroz

The **C Half Circle** was recorded by Charlie A. Ducroz of Brazoria in 1901 and was used in Brazoria and Matagorda counties on registered Brahman cattle.

Source: Charlie Ducroz, 1958.
See brand numbers 170, 171, and 183.

№ 174   J Dash
John H. Adams

The **J Dash** brand was recorded by John H. Adams in 1883 and was branded on the left hip in Brazoria, Matagorda, and Refugio counties.

Source: John Adams, Alvin, Texas, 1958, when the brand had been used by his family for over seventy-five years.

№ 175   Lazy U
E. W. Bailey Sr.

The **Lazy U** brand was recorded by E. W. Bailey Sr. in 1925 in Matagorda County. Bailey and his daughter, Hallice, (Mrs. Noel E. Adams), and V. L. Letulle of Bay City, formed a partnership some years ago and branded **IOU**. When their partnership was dissolved, Bailey changed his brand to the **Lazy U**, which he retained until his death. After Hallice Bailey married Noel Adams, she recorded **Lazy U** Bar in Brazoria County.

Hallice Bailey Adams wrote, "My father's original brand, recorded sometime after 1900, was **Seven Up, Seven Down**, which at one time was well-known in Matagorda County."

Source: John H. Adams, 1958.

№ 176   Little h G Bar
Grupe Ranch

The **Little h G Bar** brand was used in the early days in Brazoria County by the Grupe Ranch near Liverpool, Texas.

№ 177   M O R
Moore Ranch

The **M O R** brand was recorded by the Moore Ranch in Brazoria County and is usually branded on the right loin but can be placed anywhere on the right side. It is used in the Alvin area on half-breed Brahman and Jersey cattle, many of which are sold to South American buyers. The Moore Ranch has 2,500 to 3,000 good cattle at Hoskin's Mound where Emmet Crainer is foreman. Moore sometimes hired local football players to work as cow hands for the summers.

Source: Warren Moore, 1958.
See brand numbers 179, 180, and 181.

№ 178   B B
I. J. Westbrook

The **B B** brand was recorded by I. J. Westbrook in Matagorda County in 1942. This brand is the initials of Westbrook's two daughters.

№ 179   Bar U
W. N. Moore

The **Bar U** brand was recorded in 1950 in Brazoria County by W. N. Moore and is placed on the right shoulder or right hip, mainly on steers.

Source: W. N. Moore, 1958.
See brand numbers 177, 180, and 181.

№ 180   Dash M
W. N. Moore

The **Dash M** brand, recorded in 1950 in Brazoria County by the W. N. Moore Ranch, is placed on the right loin or anywhere on the right side.

Source: Warren Moore, Alvin, Texas, 1958.
See brand numbers 177, 179, and 181.

№ 181   Seven U Connected
W. N. Moore

The **Seven U Connected** brand, placed on the right hip, was recorded in Brazoria County by W. N. Moore of Alvin, Texas.

Source: Warren Moore, 1958.
See brand numbers 177, 179, and 180.

№ 182   V P Connected Bar
H. E. Brigham

The **V P Connected** Bar brand, recorded in Brazoria County by H. E. Brigham, is placed on the right side of cattle. Brigham ranches on the Varner Livestock

Company land in West Columbia, Texas. Governor Hogg's secretary knew Harvey Stiles, who grafted pecan and fig trees from Alvin and Algoa, Texas.

Source: Mr. and Mrs. Harry E. Brigham, West Columbia, Texas.

(The Varner-Hogg Plantation is now a State Historic Park. It features a Greek Revival plantation home built during the mid-1830s by Columbus R. Patton, a planter from Kentucky. The land was originally part of the Stephen F. Austin colony and was obtained as a land grant by Martin Varner. It was last owned by James Stephen Hogg, first native-born governor of Texas.)

Nº 183   D Bar
Laurence Ducroz

The **D Bar** brand was recorded by Laurence Ducroz of Brazoria County in 1874. His ranch was on the Bernard River, and his son, Charles A. Ducroz, now runs it.

Source: Charlie Ducroz, 1958.

See brand numbers 170, 171, and 173.

Nº 184   Bar Cross
Jack Garrett

The **Bar Cross** brand is recorded in Brazoria County by Jack Garrett of Danbury, Texas, who brands it on the left hip of fine Brahman cattle. In 1964, he crossbred Brahmans with Herefords and Angus on 10,000 acres, twenty miles south of Houston.

Source: John Travis "Jack" Garrett, 1957.

Nº 185   Brand name unknown
Hancock Brothers

This is a Hancock Brothers' brand, recorded in Wharton, Colorado, Lavaca, and Jackson counties. They now use it on many cattle on a large ranch near the old town of Providence City, Texas.

Source: Eddie Balusek, Hancock foreman, during a matched calf roping at the Hancock Ranch, 1958.

Nº 186   Seven U Connected
J. L Myatt

The **Seven U Connected** brand was recorded by J. L. Myatt, El Campo, Texas, in Wharton, Jackson, and Matagorda counties, Texas, and on his Arkansas Land & Cattle Company ranch in southeastern Arkansas. It is placed on the left hip, loin, or side. Myatt came from Tennessee to Texas to ranch in 1903. He hated a cow thief, and he and his manager, Artie Bittner, were good men to have backing you. Bittner gave my son, Joe, a good roping mare that Joe named Artie. Jesse Lee Myatt died in 1970, and Bittner died in Wharton in 1978.

Source: Artie Bittner.

Nº 187   V S
Mrs. Vivian Darst

The **V S** brand was first recorded by Mrs. Vivian Darst of Richmond, Texas, in Matagorda County. It is now used in Brazoria and Fort Bend counties. Vivian Sargent Darst died in 1965.

Source: Tom Darst, during the recovery of cattle stolen from the ranch.

See brand numbers 164 and 172.

Nº 188   G K Connected
Dr. Guy Knolle

The **G K Connected** brand was recorded by Dr. Guy Knolle of Houston, Texas, in Harris, Fort Bend, and Washington counties.

Source: Dr. Guy Knolle, 1958, after I recovered his stray cattle near Beasley.

Nº 189   96 Connected
Bascom Munson

The **96 Connected** brand is recorded in Brazoria County by Bascom Munson of Baileys Prairie, Texas. This is an early-day brand of Munson's family.

Source: W. Bascom Munson, Angleton, Texas.

See brand number 190.

Nº 190   Munson M
Bascom Munson

The **Munson M** brand is recorded by Bascom Munsom in Brazoria County and is placed on the left hip.

Source: Bascom Munson, Angleton, Texas, 1958.

See brand number 189.

Nº 191   Rocking Triangle T
McBride and Stiles

The **Rocking Triangle T** brand was recorded in 1955 by McBride & Stiles of Cuero, Texas, in DeWitt County.

Source: My brother, Don Stiles of Cuero, Texas, 1958.

Nº 192   Circle H
A. W. Henderson

The **Circle H** brand was recorded in Wharton and Colorado counties by A. W. Henderson of Ganado, Texas. Sheriff H. R. "Mike" Flournoy purchased cows with that brand in 1955 from A. W. Henderson and was given the iron, but he never recorded the brand in his name.

Source: Mike Flournoy, Wharton, Texas, 1960.

See brand number 193.

(Mike Flournoy was elected sheriff of Wharton County from 1954–1979, but he died of a heart attack on December 29, 1978. His wife, Rose, succeeded him as sheriff and served out his term and resigned December 3l, 1979. It is said that the sheriff in the stage play and movie, The Best Little Whorehouse in Texas, was based on Flournoy.)

№ 193   Flowered Top T
H. R. "Mike" Flournoy

The **Flowered Top T** brand, used by Sheriff Mike Flourney of Wharton, Texas, was recorded in 1900 in Wharton and Colorado counties by his father, J. T. Flournoy. The most cattle carrying this brand at one time were 400 head.

Source: Mike Flournoy, 1960.
See brand number 192.

№ 194   S F
J. J. Fenn

The **S F** brand was recorded in 1852. It is now used in Brazoria, Galveston, Fort Bend, and Harris counties and in Louisiana by J. J. "Button" Fenn & Sons of Rosharon, Texas. It is placed anywhere on either side of cattle.

Source: Button Fenn, 1958.

№ 195   Diamond L Connected
C. A. Vollbaum

The **Diamond L Connected** brand was recorded in 1900 in Brazoria County by C. A. Vollbaum of Brazoria, Texas, and is used along the Brazos River.

Source: C. A. Vollbaum at his ranch, 1958.

№ 196   7 U
Paul Bledsoe

The **7 U** brand was recorded in 1955 by M. Osburn, Angleton, Texas, in Brazoria County. It is now used by Paul Bledsoe of Sweeny and placed on the left hip.

Source: Paul Bledsoe, 1958.

№ 197   Lazy H C
Harry Culver

The **Lazy H C** brand was recorded in 1878 in Matagorda and Brazoria counties by Harry Culver of Wadsworth, Texas, and is placed on the left hip or anywhere on the left side.

Source: Harry Culver, 1957, at his ranch.
See brand number 198.

№ 198   Forty Seven
Culver Ranch

The **Forty Seven** brand was recorded by the Culver Ranch of Wadsworth, Texas, in Matagorda County.

Source: Harry Culver, 1957.
See brand number 197.

№ 199   B K
Bill Klahn

The **B K** brand was recorded in 1935 in Matagorda County by Bill Klahn of Bay City, Texas. The most cattle to carry the brand were fifty head. Klahn had no cattle when I received the iron.

Source: J. B. Roberts at a store in Cedar Lake, 1957.

№200   7 H B Connected
Thomas W. Bundick

The **7 H B Connected** brand was recorded by Thomas W. Bundick of Markham, Texas, in Matagorda County in 1929. The Bundick branding irons were found in an old barn on the Bundick property.

Source: Mrs. Blanche O'Connor, Bay City, Texas.
See brand numbers 201 and 202.

№ 201   T B
Thomas W. Bundick

The **T B** brand was recorded in Matagorda County in 1857 by Thomas W. Bundick of Markham, Texas.

Source: Mrs. Blanche O'Connor, Bay City.
See brand numbers 200 and 202.

№ 202   Seven B
Thomas W. Bundick

The **Seven B** brand was recorded in 1857 in Matagorda County by Thomas W. Bundick of Markham, Texas.

Source: Mrs. Blanche O'Connor, Bay City.
See brand numbers 200 and 201.

№ 203   I S I
Mrs. Blanche O'Connor.

The **I S I** brand, placed on the left hip, was recorded in 1929 in Matagorda County by Mrs. Blanche O'Connor, sister of the well-known cowman, Louis Wolf.

Source: Mrs. Blanche O'Connor, 1957.

№ 204   J P Connected
J. G. Phillips Jr.

The **J P Connected** brand is recorded in Brazoria County by J. G. "Jack" Phillips Jr. of West Columbia, Texas. It is branded on the right hip of Longhorns and Red Brahman cattle on his Battle Island Ranch. The brand was first recorded in the county in 1843 by Joseph H. Polley.

Source: Jack Phillips, 1958.
See brand numbers 205 and 211.

(Jack Phillips Jr. was a longtime Gulf Coast cattleman whose grandfather, James Ray Phillips, came to Texas from Georgia in 1829 and went into the cattle business on a land grant from the Mexican Government. Jack Phillips Jr.'s Battle Island Ranch got its name from a duel that was fought here in the early days. Phillips was a director of the Brazoria County Cattleman's Association, a charter member and past president of the Texas Longhorn Breeders Association, and a director and honorary director of the TSCRA until his death in 1994.)

№ 205   J H P Connected
J. G. Phillips

The **J H P Connected** brand is recorded in Brazoria County and used by J. G. "Jack" Phillips Jr.

of West Columbia, Texas, on his ranch, which was begun in 1840. Phillips was well known for his herd of 200 Longhorns, some with horns that spanned six feet. This brand was first recorded in Bexar County in 1850 by Joseph Henry Polley.

Source: Jack Phillips, 1958.

See brands 204 and 211.

Brand № 206   Five Down Five Up
John Gayle Sr.

The **Five Down Five Up** brand was recorded in Brazoria County in 1916 and is placed on the right hip, thigh, or loin. John Gayle Sr. uses it along the Brazos River near East Columbia.

№ 207   Bar Seven Bar
John Gayle Jr.

The **Bar Seven Bar** brand was recorded in Brazoria County in 1925 by John Gayle Jr. It is placed on the right hip, thigh, or loin of Gayle cattle along the Brazos River near East Columbia, Texas.

№ 208   N Seven Connected
Louis Wolf

The **N Seven Connected** brand was recorded in 1929 in Matagorda County by Louis Wolf of Markham, Texas, and is placed on the left hip.

Source: Wolf's sister, Mrs. Blanche O'Connor, 1957.

№ 209   Seven D Dash Connected
D. R. Bolling

The **Seven D Dash Connected** brand was recorded by D. R. Bolling of Palacios, Texas, in 1941 in Jackson, Calhoun, Matagorda, and Wharton counties. It is branded on the left hip or anywhere on the left side. The most cattle to carry the brand at one time were 300 head.

Source: Dave Bolling at the picturesque old Bolling Ranch on the Carancahua River, 1957.

№ 210   J V
Thelma Craig

The **J V** brand was recorded in Brazoria County in 1920 by Thelma Craig of East Columbia, Texas.

Source: Craig's brother, Jack Phillips, at his ranch, 1958.

№ 211   Seven Four Connected
Phillips & Gayle Sr.

The **Seven Four Connected** is a partnership brand of Jack Phillips & John Gayle Sr., recorded in about 1900 in Brazoria County.

№ 212   O N
Grace Pierce Heffelfinger

The **O N** brand was recorded in 1870 in Matagorda County by Grace Pierce Heffelfinger of Blessing, Texas, the granddaughter of A. H. "Shanghai" Pierce. Her husband, William Walter "Pudge" Heffelfinger, played football at Yale. He died at eighty-nine in 1957.

Source: Grace Heffelfinger, Live Oak Ranch, 1958.

№ 213   Cross C
W. T. Taylor & Brothers

The **Cross C** brand was recorded in 1860 by W. T. Taylor & Brothers in Wharton and Colorado counties and was their main brand. They chose a letter that was easily shaped. In 1900, the brothers divided the property and cattle, which were mostly purebred Devons. Mrs. Glen Taylor, nee Ida Brooks, wrote in 1960, "I doubt that they registered the cattle. They ran over a wide range. I estimate that there were 3,500 head at the time of the division in 1900."

Source: Glen Taylor, 1958.

See brand numbers 129, 214, 218, 228, 229, and 230.

№ 214   T
W. T. Taylor & Brothers

The **T** brand was recorded in 1860 in Wharton and Colorado counties by W. T. Taylor & Brothers. **T** was chosen for Taylor and because it was easy to shape in their blacksmith shop where Taylor made his own irons. The **T** brand was a cull brand.

Source: Glen Taylor at his Don Tal ranch in Wharton County, 1958.

See brand numbers 129, 213, 218, 228, 229, and 230.

№ 215   Arrow H Connected
C. Herman Booth

The **Arrow H Connected** was recorded in 1935 in Brazoria County by C. Herman Booth of Manville, Texas. It is branded on the right hip.

Source: Herman Booth at his ranch, 1958.

№ 216   D C L
Raymond Henry

The **D C L** brand was recorded in 1876 in Austin County by Raymond Henry.

Source: Sid Talley of Rosenburg, Texas, in 1958. Talley was a great help to me during troubled times from cattle thieves while I was a Field Inspector.

№ 217   Dash Seven Connected
Austin Williams

The **Dash Seven Connected** brand was recorded in 1876 in Brazoria County by Austin Williams of West Columbia, Texas. Williams worked for Jordie Farmer and was as good a cowhand as I've ever known. He was black as tar and big as a mule. He used a long rope, because his white cattle were some of the wildest in the area. The brand was placed on the left thigh with a bar iron.

Nº 218   Hip O
Mrs. L. G. Smith & M. D. Taylor

The **Hip O** brand was recorded by Mrs. L. G. Smith of Boling, Texas, and M. D. Taylor in 1906 in Wharton County. The **O** was branded as a ring around the animal's hipbone. It was easily read, and it retained its shape as the animal increased in size. About 100 cattle carried this partnership brand. Mrs. Smith later married M. D. Taylor.

Nº 219   A Up A Down
Beard Ranch

The **A Up A Down** brand was recorded in Fort Bend County in 1865 by the Beard Ranch near Needville, Texas. During the days when cattle were branded on the range, a cowman carried an iron with him at all times. This brand, placed anywhere on the left side, was chosen because it could be made with a bar, and a bar was easy to carry. The Beard Ranch began with seven heifers and grew to a herd of 600 mother cows. The brand has been in the Beard family since they started in the cow business. Mr. Shirley Beard died in 1965.

Source: Mr. and Mrs. Shirley Beard of Needville, 1957.
See brand number 220.

Nº 220   U
S. A. Beard

The **U** was recorded in Fort Bend County about 1935 by S. A. Beard to use as a partnership brand with Abe Robinowitz. As many as 800 steers carried the brand at one time. It was placed on the left side.

Source: S. A. Beard, 1957.
See brand number 219.

Nº 221   Seven H O Connected
M. C. Otto

The **Seven H O** Connected brand, placed on the left side, was recorded in Fort Bend County in 1915 by M. C. Otto of Needville, Texas.

Source: Mrs. Monroe Otto, 1958, Henry Banker's daughter.
See brand numbers 222 and 223.

Nº 222   O H L Connected
Mrs. M. C. Otto

The **O H L Connected** brand was recorded in 1925 in Fort Bend County by Mrs. M. C. Otto and is branded on the left side. The **O H L Connected** iron is the same iron used to brand the **Seven H O Connected**, M. C. Otto's brand.

Source: Mrs. Monroe Otto, 1958.
See brand number 221 and 223.

Nº 223   Seven U B Connected
Monroe Otto

The **Seven U B Connected** brand was recorded by Monroe Otto of Needville, Texas, in 1915 in Fort Bend County.

Source: Mrs. Monroe Otto, 1958.
See brand numbers 221 and 222.

Nº 224   Fifteen Bar
Samuel Selkirk

The **Fifteen Bar** brand was first recorded in 1869 in Matagorda County and is branded on the left hip by Samuel Selkirk. It was used on cattle on Selkirk Island, known to five of us boys as "Wild Cow Island," where we roped out fifty-two head of wild cows and bulls in 1956. Selkirk sold out to Hamilton Savage, who sold out to Graves Peeler of Christine, Texas. The cattle were moved to the Peeler Ranch in McMullen County.

Souce: Selkirk, 1956.

Nº 225   R Z
Ruth, Russell, and Zuleika Stanger

The **R Z** brand was recorded in Brazoria County in 1925 by Russell Stanger Sr. for his children, Ruth, Russell, and Zuleika Stanger.

Source: Russell S. Stanger Sr., about 1958.

(Russell Stanger was a member of a pioneer Brazoria County ranching family and was a well-known Longhorn cattle breeder. His father, Richard H. Stanger, was born in Galveston in 1847. He was orphaned at an early age and worked as a cowhand for a year until he saved $100. He bought fifty acres and had a small herd of Longhorns. He soon owned a butchering operation, two cotton gins, a syrup mill, and a gristmill.

Russell Stanger was born November 1, 1890, in Brazoria County. As a young man, Stanger roped Longhorns along the Brazos River bottoms. He ranched on Baileys Prairie and kept a small herd of Longhorns, but his main herd was Brangus with some registered Angus and Brahman cattle. Stanger died in 1978.)

Nº 226   Rocking K
Fred Koenig

The **Rocking K** brand was recorded in 1940 in Fort Bend, Wharton, and Brazoria counties by Fred Koenig of Rosenburg, Texas, who leased the Huntington tract next to Clements State Prison Farm.

Nº 227   V Bar
Jack K. Hillboldt

The **V Bar** brand was recorded by Jack K. Hillboldt in 1890.

Source: Jack Hillboldt, Sealy, Texas.

№ 228   Half Diamond H
M. D. Taylor

The **Half Diamond H** brand was recorded by M. D. Taylor in 1898 in Wharton County. Probably 500 head of cattle carried the brand.

Source: Mrs. T. G. Taylor, Boling, Texas.

See brand numbers 129, 213, 214, 218, 229, and 230.

№ 229   T
Taylor Brothers

The **T** brand was recorded by W. T. Taylor & Brothers in Wharton County.

Source: Mrs. T. G. Taylor, Boling, Texas.

See brand numbers 129, 213, 214, 218, 228, and 230.

(Mrs. T. G. Taylor of Boling, Texas, furnished the information on the Taylor brands. She wrote that the **Cross C** *was the Taylor family brand from 1860–1900, and the* **T** *was a cull brand.)*

№ 230   J
T. G. Taylor

The **J** brand was recorded by Glen Taylor of the Don Tal ranch in Wharton County and was carried by 250 cattle.

Source: Mrs. T. G. Taylor, Boling, Texas.

See brand numbers 129, 213, 214, 218, 228, and 229.

№ 231   Screwplate
J. D. Sutherland & Son

The **Screwplate** brand was recorded in 1920 in Matagorda County by J. D. Sutherland & Son of Wadsworth, Texas. It may be branded anywhere on the right side.

Source: Sutherland at his ranch, 1958.

№ 232   Double H
Moore Brothers

The **Double H** brand was recorded in Fort Bend County by the Moore Brothers of Richmond, Texas. Hilmar G. Moore was a good and fair man. He was mayor of Richmond, a director of the TSCRA, and manager of the A. P. George Estate.

Source: Hilmar Moore, 1958.

See brand numbers 40, 234, 465, 466, and 467.

(The Moore brothers, Hilmar and John, are from a pioneer South Texas ranching family. All four of their great-grandfathers came to Texas with the original Austin colony in the early 1820s. Their grandfather, John M. Moore Sr. was a well-known cattleman who developed the Braford breed of cattle, served in both the Texas House of Representatives and the U.S. Congress. Their grandmother, Lottie Dyer Moore, was also from a pioneer ranching family. The Moore brothers continued the family ranching interest.)

№ 233   Lazy T
Melvin Harper

The **Lazy T** is a partnership brand recorded in 1930 in Matagorda County by Melvin Harper, manager of Lewis & McDonald's Buckeye Ranch. This brand is used on top bucking stock in the rodeo arenas. It was chosen because it is easy to put on and can be made any size. It is carried by 500 head of stock.

Source: Melvin Harper, Buckeye Ranch, 1958.

№ 234   H D
John M. Moore Jr.

The **H D** brand, placed on the right side, was recorded in 1915 in Fort Bend and Brazoria counties by John M. Moore Jr. It was first recorded in 1870. Moore's grandfather, James Foster Dyer, bought the Hodge-Darst cattle and their **H D** brand in the 1870s. He ran thousands of cattle with this brand during the open range days. About 700 head now carry the brand.

Source: 1958.

№ 235   Upside Down Derby
Buckeye Ranch

The **Upside Down Derby** brand was recorded in Matagorda County by J. L. Lewis and E. L. McDonald. The Buckeye Ranch, Buckeye, Texas, now uses it. About 2,000 head carry this brand.

Source: foreman, Melvin Harper, 1958.

№ 236   Bar J F
Johnny Ferguson

The **Bar J F** brand was recorded in Wharton County by Johnny Ferguson of Mackay, Texas, and is branded anywhere on the left side. Some of the top Quarter Horses and racehorses in the country carry this brand. Ferguson says, "The brand is my initials and is on 1,020 head of stock."

Source: Sonny Bahner, Ferguson Ranch manager, 1958.

(The Ferguson Ranch was known for its famous racehorses and stallions, horses such as Go Man Go, Top Deck, Hustling Man, and Mae West.)

№ 237   Meatblock
H. A. Norris

The **Meatblock** brand, placed on the left hip, was recorded in Matagorda County by H. A. Norris of Bay City, Texas. It was first recorded 1897 by J. E. Thompson of Bay City.

Source: Harry A. Norris in 1958.

(Harry Allen Norris, eighty years old, Bay City rancher and rice farmer, died in Houston in 1969.)

Nº 238   Hat
Mrs. S. F. Perry

The **Hat** brand of Brazoria and Calhoun counties was first recorded in 1854 by Captain H. W. Hawes at the old town of Saluria, Texas, where Hawes went in an effort to save his slaves. His heirs carried on the brand after his death. His daughter, Mrs. S. F. Perry of Freeport, uses the **Hat** straight, and his son, A. E. Hawes, uses the **Hat** upside-down.

Source: Stephen F. Perry Jr., at his ranch on the Bernard River, 1958.

See brand numbers 250, 251, 272, 310, and 504.

Nº 239   Six Bar
Galen M. Savage

The **Six Bar** brand was recorded in 1857 in Matagorda County by Greenberry Savage. Norman Savage who settled in Matagorda County in the early 1800s designed the brand. Two thousand cattle have carried this brand at one time. Galen M. Savage & Son brand on the left hip.

Source: Galen Savage at his ranch near Bay City, Texas, 1959.

See brand numbers 42, 71, 104, 349, and 350.

Nº 240   Five A
Aster Vallet

The **Five A** brand was recorded in 1906 in Fort Bend, Harris, and Galveston counties by Aster Vallet of Beasley, Texas. It is branded on the right hip.

Source: Aster Vallet, 1959, after I recovered stolen cattle.

Nº 241   Lazy S J Connected Bar
James Stallsby

The **Lazy S J Connected Bar** brand was recorded in 1928 by James Stallsby of Dayton, Texas, who runs cattle in the deep woods of East Texas.

Source: James Stallsby, 1959.

Nº 242   Trunk Handle
Jack Reeves

The **Trunk Handle** brand was first recorded in Matagorda County in 1938 by Nancy Partain. Jack Reeves later purchased it from a Mr. Collins, and in 1975, about 500 cattle still wore this brand. Reeves brands the **Trunk Handle,** and Mignon Doman of Bay City, Texas, brands the **Trunk Handle** with a bar under it.

Source: Jack Reeves at his Markham, Texas, ranch, 1959.

Nº 243   E B Bar
Emil Balusek

The **E B Bar** brand was recorded in 1929 in Matagorda County by Emil Balusek of El Maton, Texas. Balusek, who died in 1960, was a blacksmith and made branding irons.

Source: in 1959.

Nº 244   Lazy E
E. D. Upham III

The **Lazy E** brand was recorded about 1930 in Brazoria County by E. D. Upham III, whose family were early settlers.

Source: E. D. Upham III, 1959.

Nº 245   Seven L Connected
Cecil K. Boyt

The **Seven L Connected** brand was recorded in 1930 in Liberty and Chambers counties by Cecil K. Boyt of Devers, Texas, who was an honorary vice-president of the TSCRA.

Source: Cecil Boyt, 1959
See brand numbers 23, 255, and 335.

Nº 246   O
George Northington Jr.

The **O** brand was recorded in 1933 in Wharton and Colorado counties by George Northington Jr. of the Red Barn Ranch, Egypt, Texas. It is placed on the left side of good crossbred cattle that run along the Colorado River bottoms. The most cattle to carry this brand at one time were 500 head. The Northingtons are longtime ranchers in Wharton County and were the developers of the town of Egypt.

Source: George Northington Jr., Red Barn Ranch, Egypt, Texas.

See brand number 261.

(Northington to Stiles: "I used as my brand **77–7** *on the left side and* **7** *on the left hip, recorded in 1905. Then Buffalo Bill came along with the 101 Ranch Circus, and wanting to be a big shot or appear so, I took the* **101** *brand on the left side and used it until 1933 when I dropped the ones and recorded the* **O** *on the left side that I still use. Some people call my brand a* **Circle***, some a* **Full Moon***, some a* **Hoop of Cheese***, and some another name that I don't care to mention."*

Northington continued about other brands used in Wharton County by his family:

"Jan. 2, 1860, Andrew Northington, my great-grandfather, recorded **Half Circle N** *on left hip.*

"July 28, 1860, Mentor Northington, my grandfather, recorded **Single N** *on left hip.*

"May 2, 1878, W. A. Northington, my uncle, recorded **Double N** *on left hip.*

"October 18, 1880, Mentor Northington & Sons, my grandfather, father & uncle, recorded the **Half Circle U Bar** *on left hip. Mentor died in 1887, and my father, G. H. Northington Sr., continued to use the brand. Early in 1900, my father bought out his brother, W. A. Northington, and dropped the* **Half Circle U Bar** *and used the* **N N** *brand. In the early 1930s, he dropped one N and just branded the* **Single N** *until his death in 1938.*

"Early in 1900, Mentor Northington, my brother, used an **M**

on the left side and **N** on the left hip, and when my father passed away, Mentor dropped the **M** and just used the single **N**.

"About 1890, G. H. Northington Sr. and G. C. Duncan formed a partnership in the cattle business and usually ran about 1,500 head. They would feed out 300 head of four-year-old steers every winter, fattening them mostly on cottonseed, and they fed them in the bottom along the Colorado River. Their brand was **D + N** on the left side. Across the river from them was Shanghai Pierce with his spread, and he branded **D** on the left side. When the river was low, their steers would go across and mix with Pierce's, and several times Pierce only saw the **D** and overlooked the **+N** and shipped some of their steers. They changed their brand to **6 + N**, so he could not make that mistake again.")

Nº 247   U I
U I Cattle Company

The U I Cattle Company and brand are now owned by W. W. Rugeley of Bay City, Texas, in Matagorda County. The Samuel Robbins family, originators of the **U I** brand, moved from Petersburg, Virginia, to Texas, and arrived in the Matagorda area in 1838. Samuel's sons, Chester H. and Frederick W. Robbins, recorded the **S R** as a partnership brand in 1852. After their deaths in 1875, the **U I** brand was recorded by Mrs. Chester Robbins and the **U U** brand was recorded for the Estate of Frederick Robbins. The **S R** cattle were divided equally between the two. By 1890, some 3,000 head of **U I** cattle roamed across 19,000 acres in Matagorda County near the mouth of the Colorado River. Mrs. Chester Robbins lived to be ninety-nine years old and owned the **U I** brand until her death on January 15, 1935.

Source: Savage Cartwright, foreman U I Ranch, 1959.
See brand numbers 6, 38, 248, 253, and 347.

Nº 248   C
U I Cattle Company

The **C** brand was recorded by Fred F. Robbins in 1935 in Matagorda County and is branded on the left hip of cattle and the left loin of horses on the U I Cattle Company's ranch at Wadsworth, Texas.

Source: ranch foreman, Savage Cartwright, 1959.
See brand numbers 6, 38, 247, 253, and 347.

Nº 249   Sixty-Two
R. M. Middleton

The **Sixty-Two** brand was recorded in 1906 by R. M. Middleton in Chambers, Liberty, Jefferson, and Galveston counties. It is branded on the right hip or anywhere on the right side.

Source: Mayes Middleton of Liberty, Texas, at his ranch, 1959.

Nº 250   Diamond One
S. S. Perry Sr.

The **Diamond One** brand was recorded on February 12, 1884, in Brazoria County by S. S. Perry Sr. of Peach Point Plantation at Gulf Prairie, Texas. It is placed on the right side of cattle.

Source: Stephen S. Perry Jr., 1959, who was eighty-two years old and still very active in the cattle business.
See also brand numbers 238, 251, 272, 310, and 504.

Nº 251 "the Perry brand"
Mrs. James F. Perry

The Mexican brand of Stephen F. Austin, now known as the Perry brand, is recorded in Brazoria County, the oldest county in Texas, by the Perry Ranch, owned by Stephen Perry Jr. When Austin traveled to Mexico City in 1833, he sent 150 head of cattle with this brand to his sister, Mrs. Emily Austin Perry at the 12,000-acre Peach Point Plantation. The brand was recorded in 1838 in Brazoria County by James F. Perry in his name. It has been used ever since on the Peach Point Ranch and is carried by 500 to 600 cattle. This was the first Anglo brand to be recorded in Texas and is now in the name of Emily Austin Perry's great-great-grandson, Stephen Perry.

Source: Stephen Perry, 1959 when the iron was approximately eighty-five years old.

Nº 252   V Three
Vallet Ranch

The **V Three** brand was recorded by the Vallet Ranch in 1921 in Fort Bend and Galveston counties. It is placed on the right hip.

Nº 253   C Square
Chloe Rugeley

The **C Square** brand is recorded by Chloe Rugeley of Bay City, Texas, and is used on cattle on the U I Cattle Company Ranch. The brand was first recorded in 1888 in Matagorda County and was given to her by her grandfather, Fred S. Robbins. It is placed on the left hip.

Source: Savage Cartwright, U I Cattle Company Ranch foreman, 1959.
See brand numbers 6, 38, 247, 248, and 347.

Nº 254   Screwplate
R. O. Middlebrook

The **Screwplate** brand was recorded by R. O. Middlebrook in 1855 in Liberty and adjoining counties. It is branded anywhere on the right side. It is also used on the Middlebrook horses, well known for their stamina.

Source: R. O. Middlebrook.

Nº 255   Lazy U
C. K. Boyt

The **Lazy U** brand was recorded by C. K. Boyt of Devers, Texas, in 1916 in Liberty County. It was used at one time as a partnership brand by Bert McCloy and Cecil Boyt and placed on the left shoulder.

See brand numbers 23, 245, and 335.

(Cecil K. Boyt raised Brahmans, Brahman crossbreeds, and Quarter Horses on his Seven L Ranch at Devers, Texas, and was also involved in rice farming, oil, and real estate. He was a director and treasurer of the American Brahman Breeders Association, co-owner and vice-president of Devers Canal Co., and honorary vice-president of the TSCRA. Boyt died in 1974.)

Nº 256   J Crossed W
James Taylor White

The **J Crossed W** was the cattle brand of James Taylor White when he settled in Chambers County in 1819, and it is used today on the historic White Ranch near Anahuac as a partnership brand by James Taylor White V and George B. Hamilton Jr., great-great-grandsons of J. T. White. The brand is placed on the right hip. It was also recorded in Jefferson County in 1846.

A State of Texas Centennial marker near the old White Ranch in Chambers County gives its founding date as 1828. This brand is believed to be the oldest used continuously by one family.

Source: James White V, Stovall Ranch, 1959, while working in that area with Buck Eckols and Mayes Middleton.

(It is said that James Taylor White came to Texas in about 1820 when the land was still under Spanish domain. He started in the cattle business with twelve Longhorns and by 1831, his brand was on 4,000 head and the number grew. He pioneered ranching in southeast Texas. His market was New Orleans, and he drove his herds over the dangerous Opelousas Trail to Louisiana. After selling his cattle, he deposited the money in a New Orleans bank rather than risk losing it to robbers on his return trip. He soon had $150,000 in his account and was the richest man in southeast Texas. At one time, the White Ranch covered 100,000 acres. The family brand continues to be a Crossed W, but the ranch has been split through the years. However, White's descendants continue in the cattle business.)

Nº 257   Diamond
Tom Booth

The **Diamond** brand was recorded by the Booth Ranch in Fort Bend County.

Source: Tom Booth, 1959, at his ranch on Big Creek near the Booth Oil Field.

See brand numbers 259 and 260.

Nº 258   Turkey Track
Frank D. Sorrel

The **Turkey Track** brand was recorded in 1924 in Wharton County by Frank D. Sorrel of Wharton, Texas. The most cattle to carry this brand at one time were 200 head.

Source: Frank Sorrel, 1959.

See brand number 268.

Nº 259   T
Tom Booth

The **T** brand is used by Tom Booth in Fort Bend County.

Source: Tom Booth, 1959, through foreman, Leon Clayton.

See brand number 257 and 260.

Nº 260   T O
Booth Ranch

The **T O** brand was recorded by the Booth Ranch in Fort Bend County.

Source: Tom Booth, 1959, through foreman, Leon Clayton.

See brand number 257 and 259.

Nº 261   Spade
G. C. Duncan

The **Spade** brand was recorded in 1884 in Wharton County by G. C. Duncan as **Spade** on the left side and **7 4** on the left hip and known as **Spade 7 4**. Later, Duncan dropped the **7 4** from use on his cattle and only used it on the left shoulder of horses. G. C. Duncan died in 1889. F. B. and Donald Duncan still use the **Spade** brand.

Source: George Northington, 1959.

See brand number 246.

(Green C. Duncan came to Texas from Kentucky and settled on land in Wharton County left to him by a half brother. He entered into a stock and mercantile partnership with G. H. Northington and became a prominent rancher in South Texas. He also served in the Texas legislature.)

Nº 262   Crossed W
James T. White

The **Crossed W** brand was first used about 1820 by James Taylor White when he settled in Chambers County. Between 1820 and 1850, from 10,000 to 12,000 head of cattle carrying this brand ran on 115,000 acres. James T. White II and the White Estate used the brand from 1875 to 1904, and it is now used by J. T. White IV and his son, J. T. White V, who represent the fourth and fifth generations. This is one of the oldest brands in the state to have had continuous use in the same family.

Source: Jamie White, Stowell, Texas, 1959, while working in that area with Mayes Middleton and Buck Eckols. Jamie White died in 1976 at the ranch near Galveston.

See brand number 256.

Nº 263   J H Backwards-Nine
Connected
David Middleton

The **J H Backwards-Nine Connected** brand was first

recorded in 1865 in Chambers, Liberty, and Jefferson counties by David Middleton of Wallisville, Texas, and he used the brand until his death in 1877. It was recorded by R. M. Middleton in 1949 in Chambers and Jefferson counties.

Source: Mayes Middleton at his ranch, 1950s.

(Dave Middleton, a great-grandson of the original David, was a member of an East Texas oil and ranching family and a breeder of Beefmaster cattle on the Middleton Ranch. He also served as a director of the TSCRA from 1980 until his death in 1982.

The first David Middleton came to Texas from England by way of Canada. He arrived in Texas in 1836, in time to fight for her independence from Mexico, and then both he and his wife died of smallpox, leaving a baby son, Archie. Archie later established the Middleton Ranch on land awarded by the state to his father for his part in the revolution. Archie's son, Mayes Middleton, expanded the family's holding when he purchased the Spohn Ranch west of Encinal, Texas, a year before he died in 1960.

His son, Dave, was ranch manager of his father's estate. He said, "Crossbreeding has always been a way of life. I grew up crossbreeding Brahman cows with British bulls, breeding for heifers with stamina to stand this harsh climate and steers that the market wants."

*At one time, thirteen brands were used on the Middleton Ranch. They were consolidated into one brand—the **J H Backwards-9**. It was chosen because it can not be put on upside down.)*

№ 264   Lazy S Five Connected
Ike Gross

The **Lazy S Five Connected** brand is used mainly on horses by Ike Gross of Houston in many counties along the Gulf Coast.

Source: Ike Gross, 1959.

See brand numbers 269, 279, and 663.

№ 265   Bar V
B. L. Vineyard

The **Bar V** brand was recorded by B. L. Vineyard of Wharton, Texas, in Matagorda and Wharton counties.

№ 266   Pitchfork
C. T. Blankenburg

The **Pitchfork** brand was recorded by C. T. Blankenburg of El Campo, Texas, in Wharton and Matagorda Counties. It is branded on the left shoulder.

Source: C. T. Blankenburg, 1959.

№ 267   S
Fred Sterritt

The **S** brand is used by Fred Sterritt of Liberty, Texas, in Chambers and Jefferson counties. Many years ago, it was used by a cattleman in the area, and this very old iron was dug up in the town of Liberty.

Source: Buck Eckols of Liberty, 1959.

№ 268   Half Circle S Bar
Frank D. Sorrel

The **Half Circle S Bar** brand is recorded by Frank D. Sorrel of Wharton, Texas, in Wharton County. It was first recorded in 1888 by M. Sorrel. Upon his death in 1952, his cattle and brand became the property of Frank Sorrel. The most cattle to carry this brand at one time were 700 head.

Source: Frank Sorrel at his ranch, 1959.

See brand number 258.

№ 269   Ninety Bar
Ike Gross

The **Ninety Bar** brand is recorded in Harris, Galveston, Brazoria, and Jim Wells counties by Ike Gross of Houston, Texas, and used on many cattle along the Gulf Coast.

Source: Ike Gross, 1954.

See brand numbers 264 and 279.

№ 270   Two Little h
Alex Border

The **Two Little h** brand was recorded by A. R. Hudgins in 1874 in Wharton County. It was used after that by Will Border and wife, Jennie Hudgins Border, in Wharton County. It was recorded next by Alex Border of Hungerford and placed on the right hip of registered Brahman cattle. Alex Border died in 1963.

Source: Alex Border, 1959.

№ 271   Lazy D T
C. R. Davis

The **Lazy D T** brand is recorded by C. R. "Roy" Davis in Wharton and Matagorda counties. It is placed on the left hip.

Source: C. R. Davis, 1959 at his ranch near Louise, Texas.

№ 272   V
Stephen S. Perry Jr. & Philip McNeil

The **V** brand is a partnership brand recorded in 1927 in Brazoria County by Stephen S. Perry Jr. and Philip McNeil and used on the Perry Ranch on the Bernard River. Perry pastured cattle for the King Ranch in 1954.

Source: Stephen Perry, 1959.

№ 273   Upside Down R
W. E. Rauh

The **Upside Down R** brand was recorded by W. E. "Bill" Rauh of El Campo, Texas, in Wharton County. It is branded on the left side, loin, or hip on Santa Gertrudis cattle.

Source: Rauh Ranch foreman, Lee Martin, 1958.

See brand number 274.

№ 274   Sloping Eleven
Rauh Ranch

The **Sloping Eleven** brand was recorded in Wharton County by the Rauh Ranch of El Campo, Texas, and is placed on the left side, hip, or loin of Santa Gertrudis cattle.

Source: Lee Martin, Rauh Ranch foreman, 1958.

See brand number 273.

№ 275   I C U
J. E. Thompson

The **I C U** brand has been in use since about 1860. It was recorded in 1897 in Matagorda County by J. E. Thompson of Bay City, Texas, given to him by his father who got the brand from a Mrs. Armstrong. It is also recorded in Fort Bend and Brazoria counties. Thompson was a small rancher with about 200 cattle, and he raised good horses and mules, which also carried the brand. Mr. and Mrs. Gus Brown of Bay City now use this brand.

Source: Mr. and Mrs. Gus Brown, 1959.

№ 276   Half Circle M
A. R. Hudgins

The **Half Circle M** brand was recorded by A. R. Hudgins in Wharton County.

Source: Alex Border, 1959.

See brand number 270.

№ 277   P Five
Buck Eckols

The **P Five** brand, recorded by the Pruett family in 1820 in Liberty and Chambers counties, is now used by Buck Eckols of Liberty, Texas. The same earmarks are used now as in 1820—a crop to the left and an underhalf crop to the right. The brand was transferred from Ed Pruett to Buck Eckols in recent years.

Source: Buck Eckols, 1959.

(Buck Eckols was an inspector for the TSCRA from 1943 to 1973.)

№ 278   Upside Down Derby
Sam Dailey

The **Upside Down Derby** brand was recorded by Sam Dailey of Rosenburg, Texas, in Fort Bend County. It is placed on the left thigh.

Source: Sam Dailey, 1959.

№ 279   Drawknife
Ike Gross

The **Drawknife** brand on the left loin was recorded in Harris, Galveston, Brazoria, and Jim Wells counties by Ike Gross. This brand is on many head of cows and steers in coastal counties. Gross's philosophy on cattle business: "Shave your buying and sell high."

Source: 1959.

See brand numbers 264 and 269.

№ 280   H A
V. T. Harper

The **H A** brand was recorded in Matagorda County in 1915 by V. T. Harper of Markham, Texas. The brand represents the first two letters of his name.

Source: Melvin Harper, 1959.

№ 281   Hard Scrabble N
Tommy Hinkle

This brand, the **Hard Scrabble N** or the **Running N**, and the ranch that it represented were both known as "Hard Scrabble." The brand was recorded in 1867 in Brazoria County when the ranch was established by Christopher Randolph Cox who ran from 2,000 to 5,000 cattle carrying this brand on 10,000 acres. Cox named the ranch and the brand for a town in his home state of Kentucky. After Cox died, the ranch was sold to T. J. Poole Sr. of Bay City, Texas. The brand is now placed on registered Brahman cattle by Tommy Hinkle of Brazoria, whose land is on the Bernard River near the Cox Ranch.

№ 282   Half Circle C Bar
Alex Border

The **Half Circle C Bar** brand was recorded in 1924 in Wharton County by Alex Border.

Source: Alex Border, 1959.

See brand numbers 284 and 286.

№ 283   T U
Bill Banker

The **T U** brand is recorded by Bill Banker of Hungerford, Texas, in Wharton, Jim Wells, and Fort Bend counties. It is branded on the left hip. It is also used by John Damon of Sweeny in Brazoria County.

Source: Bill Banker, 1959.

№ 284   Question Mark
Alex Border Jr.

The **Question Mark** brand was recorded in Wharton County in 1942 by Alex Border Jr. of Hungerford, Texas, who used it on registered and commercial cattle. Border died in 1964.

See brand numbers 282 and 286.

№ 285   g m Connected
Golston & McLaughlin

The **g m Connected** partnership brand was recorded in 1958 in Wharton County by Golston and McLaughlin and was used on the Golston Ranch. In a letter dated 1960, Golston stated that the brand is no longer in existence.

Source: 1959.

№ 286   h
Sid Border

The **h** brand was recorded by Sid Border of Hungerford, Texas, in Matagorda County in 1908.

Source: Alex Border, 1959.

See brand numbers 282 and 284.

№ 287   T E Connected N
Mrs. Elizabeth Dawdy

The **T E Connected N** brand was recorded in Matagorda County in 1878 by J. R. Rowles who came to Texas from England in 1875 and settled in Matagorda County. He worked for W. B. Grimes in his slaughterhouse until he purchased land from D. M. Wheeler and established his ranch. At his death, the brand went to his daughter, Elizabeth, and her husband, Jack Dawdy, prominent ranchers in the county. Mrs. Dawdy died in 1964.

№ 288   Spanish X
W. O. Hudgins

The **Spanish X** brand was first recorded in Brazoria County in 1885 by Mrs. William Seaburn. W. O. Hudgins recorded it later and placed on the left hip of crossbred Brahman cows in the Slop Bowl area near Velasco, Texas.

Source: W. O. Hudgins, Angleton, Texas, 1956.

See brand numbers 291, 196, and 302.

(Hudgins ran cattle on the Stratton Ridge salt grass prairies from his teenage years until shortly before his death in 1986 at his home in Oyster Creek.)

№ 289   H Four Connected
Andrew Moller

The **H Four Connected** brand was recorded in Texas in 1850 by Andrew Moller. It originated in Ireland as a Rawls brand. The Moller brand is now used in Brazoria County and also in West Texas, California, Arkansas, and Mississippi.

№ 290   Seven F
L. L. "Brownie" Rhodes

The **Seven F** brand was recorded by L. L. "Brownie" Rhodes in Brazoria and Matagorda counties and is used on cattle near Velasco, Texas. It is branded on the left hip. Rhodes owns good cow dogs.

Source: Brownie Rhodes, 1959.

№ 291   Seven H Y Connected
W. O. Hudgins

The **Seven H Y Connected** brand was recorded in Brazoria County by W. O. Hudgins and is placed on the left thigh.

Source: W. O. Hudgins, 1959.

See brand numbers 288, 296, and 302.

№ 292   Seventy-Four Connected
Adrian Moller

The **Seventy-Four Connected** brand was originated in Germany by Gottfreidt Moller, who landed in Texas at Dollar Point in 1820. L. J. Moller recorded it in 1884 and branded it on the left hip. It is now used in Brazoria County by Adrian Moller, Angleton, Texas, and it is branded on the left side.

Source: Adrian Moller, 1959.

№ 293   I K E
Ike Laughlin

The **I K E**, branded on the right hip, was recorded in Matagorda County by Ike Laughlin of El Campo, Texas, who runs cattle on the Tres Palacios River near Palacios.

Source: 1959.

№ 294   Backward L
Lafayette Ward

The **Backward L** brand was recorded in Jackson County by Lafayette Ward of San Antonio, Texas, and used on the Ward Ranch at LaWard. In 1965, he sold the brand to Baur of Port Lavaca. Ward was a director of the TSCRA.

Source: Roy Davis and Tom Holstein, 1959.

№ 295   N U Connected
W. Joel Bryan Jr.

The **N U Connected** brand was recorded in Brazoria County by W. Joel Bryan Jr., Lake Jackson, Texas. He branded it on the left hip of cattle on Bryan Beach for many years.

Source: 1959.

See brand number 299.

№ 296   Bar L Seven
W. O. Hudgins

The **Bar L Seven** brand was recorded by W. O. Hudgins in Brazoria County and is branded on the left thigh.

Source: W. O. Hudgins, 1959.

See brand numbers 288, 291, and 302.

№ 297   Five Half Circle Connected
George Kennedy & Armour Munson

The **Five Half Circle Connected** brand was recorded in Brazoria County by George Kennedy and Armour Munson of Angleton, Texas, and is branded on the left flank, hip, or thigh.

Source: George Kennedy, 1959.

№ 298   Circle L
Frank H. Lewis

The **Circle L** brand was recorded in 1933 in Matagorda County by Frank H. Lewis of Bay City, Texas. It is placed on the right hip.

Source: Frank Lewis, 1959.

See brand number 315.

Nº 299　V Six
W. J. "Joel" Bryan Jr.

The **V Six** brand was first recorded in 1874 by J. P. Bryan in Brazoria County. It was next recorded by his grandson, W. J. "Joel" Bryan Jr., who branded on the left hip. Then Joel's oldest nephew, J. P. Bryan Jr., ran the brand for fifteen years, and it is now owned by one of Joel Bryan's grandchildren, W. J. Bryan III.

Source: 1959.

See brand number 295.

Nº 300　B D
Bill Daniel

The **B D** brand was recorded in 1818 in Liberty County by Bill Daniel's family. His Plantation Ranch on the Trinity River was colonized in 1818 while Texas was under Spanish rule. The Daniel family has been in the cattle business ever since. The brand is used on registered Red Brahmans and Shorthorn cattle.

Source: Bill Daniel, 1959.

(Plantation Ranch is an historic Texas ranch, owned by Bill Daniel, past Governor of Guam and brother of Price Daniel, Governor of Texas from 1957–1963.)

Nº 301　G M
C. A. Moller & Son

The **G M** brand, placed on the left hip, was recorded in Brazoria County by C. A. Moller & Son.

Source: G. Moller, 1959.

Nº 302　E B Connected
Mrs. W. O. Hudgins

The **E B Connected** brand is recorded by Mrs. W. O. Hudgins in Brazoria County and placed on the right thigh. She runs Brahman cattle on her ranch near Velasco, Texas. This old brand was established by Swen Burgstin and was first recorded in 1851. Then Henry Seabourn recorded it in 1857.

See brand numbers 288, 291, and 296.

Nº 303　H Crook
J. B. Hawkins

The **H Crook**, branded on the right hip, was recorded in Matagorda and Brazoria counties in 1866 by James B. Hawkins. The Hawkins Ranch of Bay City, Texas still uses it in Matagorda County. An average herd of 4,500 cattle carry the brand. There has been little change in the operation of this 25,000-acre ranch since its founding in about 1850. The Hawkins Ranch still uses the original brand and ear mark, an overbit in the left and a swallowfork in the right.

Source: Frank Lewis, Hawkins Ranch, 1959.

Nº 304　Dash R
U. S. Government Drought Relief Program

The **Dash R** brand was used by the U. S. Government during the 1930 drought on cattle shipped from West Texas to the Gulf Coast in a drought relief program.

Source: Frank Lewis, Bay City, Texas.

Nº 305　U
J. E. "Ed" Winston

The **U** brand was recorded in Fort Bend and Brazoria counties by J. E. "Ed" Winston of Richmond, Texas, and is branded on the left hip.

Source: Ed Winston's daughter, Mrs. Marjorie Murphee of Richmond, 1959.

Nº 306　T A
Kiddo Tacquard

The **T A** brand was recorded in 1856, by J. H. and Henry George Tacquard in Galveston County. H. G. "Bish" Tacquard Jr. gave his son, Kiddo Tacquard, 500 head of cattle and the brand. It and Tacquard's **T 2** brand are the oldest brands in Galveston County that are still run on the same place, the Hall's Bayou Ranch.

Source: Kiddo Tacquard of Alta Loma, Texas, 1959.

See brand number 307.

(Kiddo Tacquard was a well-known cowman and rodeo performer and official. Tacquard pastured many steers on his salt grass pastures during the 1950s. He died at ninety-two in June 1995.

The Tacquard brothers—Henry, George, and the youngest, Jacques—arrived in Galveston, Texas, from France in 1846 when Jacques was ten years old. They left Galveston and sailed in a small boat across the bay to the mainland and up Hall's Bayou to find high ground to settle on. Jacques soon went to Mexico but returned to Texas after the Civil War. He became one of the largest landowners in Galveston County. Henry's grandson, Kiddo, lived in the house where his father, Bish, was born in 1860 and where he was born in 1903. Bish and Kiddo had a cow/calf operation. They owned 220 acres where headquarters is, but leased 52,000 acres.)

Nº 307　T Two
Kiddo Tacquard

The **T 2** brand was first recorded in 1860 in Galveston County by Kiddo Tacquard's grandfather, Henry George Tacquard, after he and his brothers arrived in Texas from France. The **T 2** and **T A** brands are the oldest brands in Galveston County still being used by the same family on the same ranch. Each brand was on 500 cattle in 1900.

Source: Kiddo Tacquard, 1959.

See brand number 306.

Nº 308   J A Connected
Sargent Ranch

The **J A Connected** brand was recorded in Matagorda County by the George Sargent Ranch in 1854 and is still used on the Sargent Ranch.

Source: Mrs. Joe Sargent Smith, Richmond, Texas, 1959.
See brand number 309.

Nº 309   h Up h Down
Sargent Ranch

The **h Up h Down** brand is a Sargent Ranch brand recorded in Matagorda County.

Source: Mrs. Joe Sargent Smith, Richmond, Texas, 1959.
See brand number 308.

Nº 310   Hat
Mrs. Stephen F. Perry

The **Hat** brand was recorded in 1854 by Captain H. W. Hawes at the old town of Saluria, Texas. Mrs. Stephen F. Perry of Freeport, daughter of Captain Hawes, now uses the **Hat** brand in Brazoria and Calhoun counties. Captain Hawes's son, A. E. Hawes, uses the **Hat Upside Down.**

Source: Mrs. Stephen F. Perry, 1959.
See brand numbers 238, 250, 251, 272, and 504.

Nº 311   Cross L
L. M. Slone

The **Cross L** brand was recorded in 1925 in Jackson and Matagorda counties by L. M. Slone of Bay City, Texas. It is branded on the left hip.

Source: L. M. Slone, 1956.

Nº 312   Bar H
John A. Means

The **Bar H** brand, made with a bar iron, was recorded by John Means's grandfather in Wharton and Galveston counties. The brand was chosen because it could be easily made with a running iron.

Source: John A. Means, Louise, Texas, 1959.

Nº 313   Heart
John Matthews

The **Heart** brand was recorded about 1860 in Matagorda County by John Matthews. Approximately 300 cattle on 2,000 acres wore the brand in 1895. Mrs. Jack Matthews, daughter-in-law of the original owner, still runs the brand.

Source: Jack Matthews, Bay City, Texas.

Nº 314   Circle
H. G. Gilmore

The **Circle** brand is recorded in Matagorda County by H. G. Gilmore of Bay City, Texas, and is branded anywhere on the left side.

Nº 315   Circle L
Frank H. Lewis

The **Circle L** brand is recorded in Matagorda County by Frank H. Lewis of Bay City, Texas.
See brand number 298.

(Frank Lewis, a well-known Brahman breeder in Matagorda County, was president of the TSCRA from 1970-1972.)

Nº 316   Thirty-Six
Heard Ranch

The **Thirty-Six**, an early-day brand used on many cattle, was recorded in Wharton County by the Heard Ranch of Louise, Texas.

Source: through Deputy Marvin Powers, El Campo, 1959.
Same as brand number 327.

Nº 317   Half Circle U
Taylor Kemp

The **Half Circle U** brand was recorded in Wharton County by Taylor Kemp of Sweeny, Texas.

Source: Taylor Kemp, 1959.

Nº 318   Six E
J. D. Yelderman

The **Six E** brand was recorded in Fort Bend and Brazoria counties by J. D. Yelderman of Damon, Texas.

Source: Jake Yelderman, 1959.
See brand number 318.

Nº 319   L F Bar
Louis Fredrickson

The **L F Bar** brand was recorded in Colorado and Fort Bend counties by Louis Fredrickson. Fredrickson died in 1992.

Source: Louis Fredrickson, 1956.

Nº 320   N A Connected
Naomi C. Chappell

The **N A Connected** brand was recorded in Wharton and Matagorda counties in 1919 by Mrs. Naomi C. Chappell of El Campo, Texas. It is placed on the left hip. Mrs. Chappell gave my son Joe a fast, little half-Shetland pony named Hot Shot. Joe learned to ride on this little horse and won quite a few trophies and ribbons at different youth rodeos and horse shows.

Nº 321   C M
Philip McNeill

The **C M** brand was recorded before 1900 by Charlie Moss of Llano, Texas. After the 1900 storm on the Texas coast, Philip McNeill of Brazoria went to Llano and bought a herd of cattle from Charlie Moss that was branded **C M**. McNeill did not re-brand the cattle but continued to run the **C M** brand in Galveston and Brazoria counties and recorded it in 1900 or 1901. About 500 head carried the brand.

See brand numbers 322 and 323.

Nº 322   Hipbone
Philip McNeill

The **Hipbone** brand was recorded by Philip McNeill in Brazoria County about 1900 and was once on a herd of 1,200 cattle. The brand was chosen because it was easily read and would not blot. It is still being run on a few cattle owned by Philip McNeill's heirs.

See brand numbers 321 and 323.

Nº 323   Andiron
Perry McNeill

The **Andiron** brand was recorded in Brazoria County in 1875 by C. P. McNeill and wife. An andiron in their fireplace suggested the unusual design. During the 1880s and 1890s, they ran from 1,000 to 1,200 cattle with this brand on open range from west of the San Bernard River to the Matagorda County line and for twenty miles inland from the Gulf of Mexico. C. P. McNeill's grandson, Perry, later used the brand. Perry McNeil died in 1976.

See brand numbers 321 and 322.

Nº 324   I E Bar
E. E. Green

The **I E Bar**, branded on the left hip, was recorded in Colorado County by E. E. Green of Garwood, Texas.

Nº 325   Dash Sixty Bar
Ben Woodruff

The **Dash Sixty Bar** brand was recorded in Lavaca, Colorado, Jackson, and Wharton counties in 1929 by Ben Woodruff of Garwood, Texas.

Nº 326   Hay Hook
Bert Dwiggins

The **Hay Hook** brand was recorded in Wharton County by Bert Dwiggins of El Campo, Texas.

Nº 327   3 6
Heard Ranch

The **3 6** brand was recorded by the Heard Ranch in Wharton County.

Source: through Deputy Marvin Powers of El Campo, Texas, 1959.

See brand number 337. (Same brand as number 316.)

Nº 328   Bar Seventy-Six Connected
August Pilsner

The **Bar Seventy-Six Connected** brand was recorded in Colorado County by August Pilsner of El Campo, Texas.

Nº 329   A O Z
Alonzo O. Zarape

The **A O Z** brand, the initials of its originator, Alonzo O. Zarape of Buckeye, Texas, is recorded in Matagorda County.

Source: A. O. Zarape, 1959.

Nº 330   Five Cross
Lester Bunge

The **Five Cross** brand was recorded in Colorado and Wharton counties in 1876 by the Bunge Ranch of Garwood, Texas. I returned this iron to Mrs. Lester Bunge in 1959.

Nº 331   Open A Dash
J. M. Frost III

The **Open A Dash** brand was first recorded by J. M. Frost in 1883 in Fort Bend County. It has been in continuous use in Fort Bend, Harris, and Brazoria counties by members of the Frost family since that time. It is now used on cattle and registered Quarter Horses by J. M. Frost Jr. and J. M. Frost III of Sugarland, Texas, in Chambers, Liberty, Harris, Jefferson, and Brazoria counties.

Source: Jay Frost III at their Sugarland ranch, 1959.

Nº 332   Anchor
A. A. Giesecke

The **Anchor** brand is recorded by A. A. Giesecke of West Colombia in Brazoria County. Charles A. Giesecke first recorded the brand in Brazoria County in 1852 and used it until his death in 1864. His widow, Sarah Davis Giesecke, used the brand until her death in 1895. Then it was run by Charles E. Giesecke until he died in 1946 and it passed to A. A. Giesecke. He has branded it on the left hip of as many as 500 cattle through the years.

Source: A. A. Giesecke, 1959.

Nº 333   J F Connected
Mrs. T. J. Poole Jr.

The **J F Connected** brand is recorded in Brazoria and Matagorda counties by Mrs. T. J. Poole Jr. of Bay City, Texas. Mrs. Poole's father, Francis E. Grimes, first recorded it in 1856. The brand is used on the Cox Ranch and the Northern Headquarters Ranch where it is branded on the left hip.

Source: L. L. "Monk" Chiles, 1959.

See brand numbers 5, 33, 130, and 139.

Nº 334   Double Cross
L. L. "Monk" Chiles

The **Double Cross** brand is used by L. L. "Monk" Chiles of Brazoria, Texas. Chiles received the brand from Scott Taylor in 1930 and recorded it in Brazoria and Matagorda counties. The brand is placed on the left hip. This is the original iron.

Source: Monk Chiles, the Cox Ranch, 1959.

See brand number 354.

Nº 335   Half Circle F Four Connected
Mrs. E. W. Boyt

The **Half Circle F Four Connected** brand was recorded in 1886 by Mrs. E. W. Boyt of Devers, Texas.

Source: Cecil Boyt at the Boyt ranch, 1959, with the assistance of Buck Eckols and Mayes Middleton.

See brand numbers 23, 245, and 255.

Nº 336   Circle Seven
Joe Clyde Wessendorf

The **Circle Seven** brand was recorded in 1939 in Fort Bend County by Joe Clyde Wessendorf of Richland, Texas. It is placed on the left hip.

Source: Joe Clyde Wessendorf at his ranch, 1959.

Nº 337   Crossed Walking Stick
Heard Ranch

The **Crossed Walking Stick** brand was recorded in Wharton County by the Heard Ranch of Louise, Texas.

Source: Deputy Marvin Powers of El Campo, 1959.

See brand numbers 316 and 327.

Nº 338   Backward L Open A Connected
Marvin Powers

The **Backward L Open A Connected** brand was recorded in 1939 in Jackson and Wharton counties by Deputy Marvin Powers of El Campo, Texas.

Source: Marvin Powers, 1959.

Nº 339   A K Bar
Ed Holik

The **A K Bar** brand was recorded in Wharton County by Ed Holik of El Campo, Texas.

Source: Marvin Powers, El Campo, Texas, 1959.

Nº 340   A
Owner unknown

The **A** branding iron was found in Liberty County by a worker while digging the foundation for a new bank building in Liberty, Texas. The iron was found at the site of old cattle working pens. It is a small brand, and the iron is very old. The man who found it gave it to TSCRA Inspector Buck Eckols.

Source: Buck Eckols, Liberty, Texas, 1959.

Nº 341   H F Connected
Harper Brothers & Fitzgerald

The **H F Connected** was a partnership brand recorded in 1954 in Arkansas by Harper Brothers & Fitzgerald—thus the brand, **H F.**

Source: Buckeye Ranch, 1959.

Nº 342   H R Connected
Price Daniel

The **H R Connected** brand, placed on the right hip, was recorded in Liberty County by Texas Governor Price Daniel of Liberty, Texas. The most cattle to carry the brand at one time was about 300 head. The brand was originally recorded in 1860. As a fourteen-year-old boy, Governor Daniel purchased this brand from his neighbor, Miss Elba DeBlanc, and used it because it was easier to run than his first brand, the **4 H L F.** The **H R Connected** brand is appropriate because the Governor's ranch is named Holly Ridge from the vast number of holly trees on his headquarters tract.

(Price Daniel was governor of Texas from 1957–1963.)

Nº 343   Double Diamond
Fred A. Brock Jr.

The **Double Diamond** brand was recorded in Brazoria County about 1900 when Fred Brock Sr. bought a herd of cattle with that brand. The largest number of cattle to carry the brand at one time was 1,500 head. Fred A. Brock Jr. now runs cattle branded on the left loin with the **Double Diamond** in Brazoria County.

Source: Fred Brook Jr. at his ranch near Velasco, Texas, 1959.

Nº 344   I U
George W. Townsend

The **I U** brand was recorded by George W. Townsend of Bay City, Texas, in 1940 in Wharton, Matagorda, and Edwards counties. The most cattle to carry this brand on their left hips at one time were 800 head. Townsend said, "I chose **I U** because it was an open brand that would turn out smooth."

Source: George Townsend at the opening of the new Bay City coliseum, of which he was president.

Nº 345   F D Connected
Forest Damon

The **F D Connected** brand was recorded in 1896 in Wharton County by Forest Damon. This is an old iron.

Source: Sonny Bahner, Ferguson Ranch near Mackay, Texas, 1959.

Nº 346   Sixty Bar
Ben Woodruff

The **Sixty Bar** brand was recorded by Ben Woodruff in Wharton, Lavaca, and Jackson counties. It is placed on the left hip.

Source: Ben Woodruff at his ranch on the Colorado River, Garwood, Texas, 1959.

Nº 347   V Bar
Fred McC. Robbins

The **V Bar** brand was recorded in 1880 in Matagorda County by Fred McC. Robbins and is placed on the left hip. The brand has been used since that time on the

Robbins Ranch, which is the last ranch south on the Colorado River before it empties into the Gulf of Mexico. J. M. Frost also recorded the **V Bar** brand in 1883 in Fort Bend, Harris, and Brazoria counties.

See brand numbers 6, 38, 247, 248, and 253.

Nº 348   A Up A Down
Mrs. D. R. Bolling

The **A Up A Down** brand was recorded in 1900 by W. C. Melbourn in Matagorda, Calhoun, and Jackson counties. Will Melbourn passed it to his daughter, Mrs. D. R. Bolling of Palacios, Texas, in Matagorda County. The most cattle to carry the brand at one time were 2,000 head.

Source: 1959.

See brand numbers 209, 383, and 515.

Nº 349   Pitchfork
Savage family

The **Pitchfork** brand was recorded by Maranda Savage about 1838 in Matagorda County. It was chosen because it is clear and easy to read. The **Pitchfork** is used by several members of the Savage family, each branding in a different location or direction on an animal. This is one of the oldest brands in Matagorda County.

Source: Francis Savage, 1959.

See brand numbers 42, 71, 104, 239, and 350.

Nº 350   Triangle
Francis Savage & Sons

The **Triangle** brand on the left hip was recorded about 1940 by Stewart Savage & Sons in Matagorda County. Francis Savage & Sons, Triangle Cattle Company, Bay City, Texas, now use it. One thousand cattle are the most to have carried this brand at one time. Savage wrote, "The **Triangle** is easy to brand with no blotch."

Source: Francis Savage, 1959, at the Bay City Coliseum.

See brand numbers 42, 71, 104, 239, and 349.

Nº 351   Circle Dot
O. H. Ullman

The **Circle Dot** brand was recorded in Wharton County in 1940 by O. H. Ullman. The brand was then used on the Forrest Damon Ranch.

Source: Sonny Bahner, 1959, at the same time I received Damon irons 355 & 345.

Nº 352   Five X
Raleigh Sanborn

The **Five X** brand, first recorded in 1853 in Matagorda County, was later used by Raleigh Sanborn on many registered Brahman cows on the Sanborn Ranch near Sargent, Texas.

Source: Sonny Bahner at the Bay City Coliseum, 1959.

Nº 353   U Up U Down
Voss McCrosky

The **U Up U Down** brand was recorded by Voss McCrosky in 1929 in Matagorda County. It is placed on the left hip.

Source: Voss McCrosky, 1959.

Nº 354   Six Open A
L. L. "Monk" Chiles

The **Six Open A** brand was recorded in Brazoria and Matagorda counties by L. L. "Monk" Chiles and is branded on the left hip.

Source: Monk Chiles, 1959.

See brand number 334.

Nº 355   Seven T
Abel & Damon

The **Seven T** brand was recorded in Wharton County in 1908 as a partnership brand by Abel & Damon.

Source: Sonny Bahner, 1959.

Nº 356   J Open A
Mrs. Selina Phillips

The **J Open A** brand on the right hip was recorded in 1880 in Brazoria County by Price Phillips. Mrs. Selina Phillips's ranch was on the Brazos River near East Columbia, Texas. She died in 1966.

Source: Mrs. Selina Phillips, 1959.

Nº 357   Half Circle N
Mr. & Mrs. Buster. O. Nave

The **Half Circle N** brand was recorded in 1940 in Matagorda County by Mr. & Mrs. Buster O. Nave of Bay City, Texas. It is placed anywhere on either side of cattle.

Source: Buster Nave, 1959, Bay City Coliseum.

Nº 358   Seventy Four Connected
Seth Taylor Estate

The **Seventy Four Connected** brand was recorded in Matagorda County. It is used by the Seth Taylor Estate.

Source: through Voss McCrosky, 1959.

Nº 359   Bar U
Blair & Merrifield

The **Bar U** is a partnership brand recorded in Wharton County by Blair & Merrifield. The brand is made with two irons.

Nº 360   Five With a Tail
C. E. Johnson

The **Five With a Tail** brand was first recorded in 1870 in Colorado County by Bob Johnson and was a trail brand from Colorado County to Kansas. When Johnson lost his life on the trail, his Negro servant took his body back to

Texas in a wagon. The trip took forty-two days. C. E. "Ed" Johnson of Altair, Texas, now uses the brand in Colorado County and places it anywhere on the left side of cattle.

Source: Ed Johnson at his Altair Ranch, 1959.

Nº 361   C Cross J
John & Robert Stafford

The **C Cross J** brand was recorded in 1870 in Colorado County by John & Robert Stafford. It is branded on either hip or loin. The **J Cross Connected** brand, from which it originated, was recorded in Colorado County by James Wright in 1860 and in 1869 as a partnership brand by James E. Wright and R. E. Stafford.

Source: R. R. Wells, at Eagle Lake ranch, 1959.

See brand number 366.

Nº 362   Half Diamond 1
R. R. Wells

The **Half Diamond 1** brand was recorded in 1892 in Colorado County by R. R. Wells. It is placed on either hip, thigh, or side. The brand came into use after the deaths of John and Robert Stafford in 1892 in the Townsend-Stafford feud. Mrs. R. R. Wells is a granddaughter of John Stafford.

Nº 363   M J
Mascot Land & Cattle Company

The **M J** brand was recorded in Colorado and Wharton counties in 1914 by the Mascot Land & Cattle Company. In 1890, I. T. Pryor and H. Lee Johnson, owners of the company, recorded an **M** on the left rib. Lee Johnson bought Ike Pryor's interest in the company in 1914, and after that, Johnson branded a **J** on the left hip with the **M** on the left rib.

See brand number 376.

(Well-known trail driver Ike T. Pryor took cattle up the trail to Kansas during the 1870s and 1880s. In 1876, he bought a 200,000-acre ranch and 1,500 head of cattle. In 1884, he and his brother sent 45,000 head of cattle to market. He built up his cattle business and established the 100,000-acre 77 Ranch in Zavala County. Pryor served three terms as president of the TSCRA and one as president of the American National Livestock Assoc. in 1917–1918. The pioneer cowman died in 1937.)

Nº 364   F Down F Up
J. R. "Jordie" Farmer

The **F Down F Up** brand was recorded by J. R. "Jordie" Farmer in Brazoria County. This is an old brand from an early ranch family. Alexander Farmer recorded the **F** brand in 1850, and K. O. Farmer recorded the **2 9** brand on the left rib in 1891. These brands were used on wild, white Brahman cattle.

Source: Jordie Farmer, Farmer ranch near West Columbia, Texas, 1959.

Nº 365   Lazy L K
Jean Chiles

The **Lazy L K** brand on the left hip was recorded in Brazoria and Matagorda counties by Jean Chiles.

Source: L. L. "Monk" Chiles, 1959.

Nº 366   D O
John and Robert Stafford

The **D O** brand on either hip or loin was recorded in 1870 by John and Robert Stafford in Colorado County. The brothers were shot to death in Columbus, Texas, in 1891 in the Townsend-Stafford feud. The old Stafford brands are still used in Colorado County by the Stafford brothers' great-granddaughters. Mrs. R. R. Wells of Eagle Lake, Texas, is the granddaughter of John Stafford.

Source: R. R. Wells.

See brand number 361.

Nº 367   X 7
Leo A. Duffy

The **X 7** brand is recorded by Leo A. Duffy of El Campo, Texas, in Matagorda, Wharton, and Jackson counties. It was originally recorded in 1877 by Leo's father, G. A. Duffy, who chose the brand because "it doesn't blot and it could be put on with a wagon rod." As many as 2,000 head of cattle have carried the **X 7** at one time. It is placed anywhere on the left side.

Source: Leo Duffy.

Nº 368   Straddle Bug
Otto Eberspacher

The **Straddle Bug** brand was recorded by Otto Eberspacher about 1910. It is placed on the left side of commercial Brahman cattle in Brazoria County. It was chosen because "it is easy to make with a running iron." The most cattle to carry this brand at one time are 450 head.

Source: Otto Eberspacher at his Bastrop Bayou Ranch, 1959.

Nº 369   Lazy L K
Fred C. Cornelius

The **Lazy L K** brand was recorded in Matagorda and Jackson counties by Fred C. Cornelius during the 1800s and is placed on the left hip. A variation of this brand on the left hip was recorded in 1909 by F. & W. D. Cornelius & Company. The brand was transfered to Fred C. Cornelius Jr. in 1922. He used the **Flat Top 3** brand on his Brahman cattle and horses.

Source: Fred Cornelius Jr., 1961.

(Frederick Casper Cornelius Jr. was born in Midfield, Texas, in 1901 and died in 1979.)

Nº 370   J H J Connected
Bert M. Jamison

The **J H J Connected** brand on the right hip is recorded in Brazoria County by Bert M. Jamison whose ranch is near Angleton, Texas. The brand and ear mark were first recorded by J. H. Jamison in 1844. The Jamisons were early settlers in the county. "The brand was chosen probably because of my father's initials. My mother used it for many years before I took over. It was well-known during open range days of 1912 when 5,000 cattle carried the brand." —Bert M. Jamison Sr.

Source: Bert Jamison, 1959.

Nº 371   H E Connected
Gene Hammond

The **H E Connected** brand is recorded in Brazoria County by Gene Hammond of Sweeny, Texas. Gene lost his left arm, but he is one of the best "wild cow catchers" I know.

Nº 372   House Top J H J Connected
Johnny Jamison

The **House Top J H J Connected** was recorded in Brazoria County in 1913 by Johnny Jamison and placed on the right hip. The most cattle to carry this brand at one time were 300 head.

Source: Bert M. Jamison at his ranch, Angleton, Texas, 1959.

Nº 373   Open Box
John T. Gann Jr.

The **Open Box** brand on the left hip is recorded by John T. Gann Jr. in Ellis, Wharton, and Calhoun counties and in Arkansas. It was recorded by John T. Gann Sr. in Wharton County in 1894 and used by him as a holding brand until his death in 1948. The estate's cattle and brand were purchased by John T. Gann Jr. in 1951. The most cattle to carry this brand at one time were 1,800 head.

Source: John Gann Jr., 1959. Gann died in 1988.

Nº 374   Lazy S T
Stephen Taylor

The **Lazy S T** brand was recorded as No. 283 in the Matagorda Brand Book by Stephen Taylor in 1853. Pierce Estate foreman, Frank Anderwald, wrote, "This iron was found in a closet in the office where Shanghai Pierce died. Mr. Cutbirth gave me this iron and some others, and I checked the brand book in Bay City for their records."

Source: Frank Anderwald in 1959.

Nº 375   Seven L Connected Dash
W. A. Harrison

The **Seven L Connected Dash** brand was recorded by W. A. Harrison in 1914 in Wharton and Colorado counties.

Source: W. A. "Willie" Harrison, Wharton, Texas, 1959.

Nº 376   T V Connected
I. T. Pryor & H. Lee Johnson

The **T V Connected** brand was recorded in 1900 by I. T. Pryor & H. Lee Johnson in Colorado County and was branded on many steers going to Kansas.

Source: C. E. "Ed" Johnson.

See brand number 363.

Nº 377   Horseshoe J
Mrs. B. M. Jamison

The **Horseshoe J** brand was recorded in 1880 in Brazoria County by a Kellog of Boston, Massachusetts. D. B. & B. M. Jamison bought the brand about 1900. It was given to Mrs. B. M. Jamison when she married. About 250 cattle were the most that carried the brand at one time.

See brand numbers 270 and 372.

Nº 378   C H Connected
Harry F. Guggenheim

The **C H Connected** brand was recorded in Berkley County, South Carolina and used on the Cain Hoy Plantation and the Daniels Island Ranch, both owned by Harry F. Guggenheim of New York. This brand is run on approximately 1,000 Hereford cows. The Daniels Island Ranch can be seen from the Cooper River Bridge at Charleston. It is between the Wando and Cooper rivers.

Source: foreman Lynn Wardlow, formerly of Woodville, Texas, when I investigated a cattle theft ring in 1959.

Nº 379   Y Cross
Hugh F. Buffaloe

The **Y Cross** brand on the left hip was recorded in 1939 in Jackson and Matagorda counties by Hugh F. Buffaloe.

Source: Hugh Buffaloe, 1959.

Nº 380   A D Connected
Graham Reeves

The **A D Connected** brand was recorded by Graham Reeves of New Jersey. It is used on Santa Gertrudis cattle on Reeves's Annadale Plantation near Georgetown, South Carolina. Jack Marshall of Brazoria, Texas, who also brands the **A D Connected**, said his people got the idea for this brand years ago when they bought mules that were shipped from South Carolina to New Orleans to go to Mexico.

Source: Annadale foreman, Vernon "Buck" Ramsey, 1959.

Nº 381   V I V
Leon Vivian

The **V I V** brand is used by Leon Vivian of George West, Texas. His grandfather, Leon T. Vivian, first recorded the brand in 1840 in Live Oak, McMullen, Dimmit, and Duval counties. Loyd Vivian registered it in Goliad County. Leon Vivian was a Texas Ranger (1941–1945) and a

TSCRA Inspector (1938–1941 and 1945–1967) and was inducted into the Texas Ranger Hall of Fame. He was ninety years old when he died in 1985.

Source: Leon Vivian, 1955.

 Nº 382   D Cross
Gardner Duncan
The **D Cross** brand was recorded in 1890 in Colorado County by G. C. Duncan of Egypt, Texas. I. V. and Gardner Duncan recorded the brand in 1911 in Colorado and Wharton counties. Then it was recorded in Burnet County by I.V. Duncan and his brother, N. B. Duncan, who operated a partnership ranch until N. B.'s death in 1937. The brand is still used by N. B.'s son, Donald Duncan, on the Burnet County ranch.

See brand number 261.

(A partnership was formed about 1890 between G. C. Duncan and G. H. Northington Sr. They ran 1,500 head of cattle along the Colorado River, branding them with a **D Cross N** *on the left side. Across the river from them was Shanghai Pierce's ranch that branded a* **D** *on the left side. When the river was low, the steers would cross and mix up. Several times, Shanghai saw only the* **D** *and, overlooking the* **Cross N**, *shipped some of the partners' steers. Northington and Duncan changed their brand to a* **Six Cross N**, *so that Pierce could not make this mistake again. —from a letter to Stiles from G. H. Northington)*

 Nº 383   J O
Bolling Ranch
The **J O** brand was recorded in Matagorda and Jackson counties by the Bolling Ranch at Palacios, Texas, owned by Bob Bolling. This is the original iron used on the ranch, located in the forks of the Carancahua Bayou. Later J. W. Bolling recorded it as a horse brand, and it is now in the name of J. W. "Bill" Bolling Jr.

See brand numbers 209, 348, and 515.

 Nº 384   Running M
C. O. Moser
The **Running M** brand on the left hip was recorded by C. O. Moser in 1935 in Bowie County, Texas, and Washington County, Oklahoma. Note the "tail up and tail down" on the brand. It is now recorded by Norman Moser of DeKalb, Texas, a past president of the TSCRA.

Source: Norman Moser at the 1959 TSCRA convention.

See brand number 1064.

(Several generations of the Moser family have been actively involved in agricultural activities. C. O. Moser graduated from Texas A&M University in 1904. He became head of the Institute of American Fats and Oils and served as a Dallas County agricultural agent during World War I. Norman Moser was honorary director of the Meat Board and president of TSCRA from 1958–1960. Norman was also vice president of the American National Beef Cattleman's Association and chairman of the Texas Animal Health Commission.

He is a commercial cattleman in Bowie County and operates as Norman Moser Land and Cattle Company. His son, Chris, is also a past director of the TSCRA.)

 Nº 385   Seven U F Connected
J. F. Welder
The **Seven U F Connected** brand on the left rib is used by Leo Welder. James F. Welder recorded it in 1887 in Victoria and Refugio counties. In 1903, T. S. Welder recorded it for the J. F. Welder Heirs, Victoria, Texas.

Source: 1959 TSCRA convention. The brand was also recorded in 1914 in Duval County by J. E. Wood.

See brand numbers 667, 683, 688, 867, and 880.

(Members of the Welder family have been ranching in south Texas since the early 1800s. Empresario James Power established a colony in Mexican Texas with his partner, James Hewetson, in 1826. Power signed the Texas Declaration of Independence and was active in politics of the Republic. His grandson, James F. Welder, was born in San Patricio County in 1863. Welder entered the cattle business early and soon had extensive ranch holdings in four counties. He was also a financier and became president and chairman of the Victoria National Bank. Leo Welder, grandson of J. F. Welder, served as president of the TSCRA from 1962–1964.)

 Nº 386   J Cross Connected
Jim Clipson
The **J Cross Connected** brand on the right hip was recorded by the Clipson Brothers in Colorado County.

Source: Jim Clipson of Eagle Lake, Texas, 1959.

See brand number 394, 406, and 410.

 Nº 387   Cross Anchor
Charlie Burwell
The **Cross Anchor** brand was recorded in 1930 by Charlie Burwell in Nueces and Kleburg counties. It is branded on the left thigh, shoulder, side, or hip. It is on about 100 top Santa Gertrudis cattle.

Source: Charlie Burwell, 1959.

(Burwell was foreman of the King Ranch's Laureles Division from 1930 until his death in 1964.)

 Nº 388   B R Connected
Cal Farley's Boys' Ranch
The **B R Connected** brand was recorded in 1941 by Cal Farley's Boys' Ranch of Tascosa, Texas, in Oldham County. The Boys' Ranch brand is not primarily a cattle brand although it is used on some cattle. It is a trademark and the brand of an institution founded in 1939 for homeless and troubled boys. It has provided a home with love, care, and an education to more than 1,800 boys as of 1959. Carl Basham who lives at Boys' Ranch made this iron.

Source: Cal Farley, 1959.

(Cal Farley's Boys Ranch was established in 1939 at historical Old Tascosa, a town approximately forty miles northwest of Amarillo, Texas. Boys Ranch continues to help youngsters in need of a home.)

Nº 389   Dipper
J. C. McGill

The **Dipper** brand was recorded in 1928 by J. C. "Claude" McGill in every county in Texas from the Nueces River to the Rio Grande. McGill owned La Paloma Ranch in Kenedy County and El Ranchito in Jim Wells County.

Source: J. C. McGill, La Paloma Ranch, 1959.

See brand number 392.

(Claude and Frank McGill were well-known cattlemen in South Texas. They became partners in 1911 and formed McGill Bros. At first they operated on leased ranches, but in 1916, they bought the Santa Rosa Ranch in Kenedy County, where they developed the Braford breed of cattle. Both men served on the executive committee of the TSCRA. When Claude died in 1935, he left his interest in the business to Frank's children, who have continued with the ranches. Frank McGill was the nineteenth president of the TSCRA (1936–1938). He died in 1952.)

Nº 390   T C
Tom O'Conner

The **T C** brand was first used by Thomas O'Conner in 1837, but it was registered in 1848 in Refugio County and later in Goliad, Calhoun, Victoria, San Patricio, LaSalle, and Webb counties. The design came from his initials. During the 1880s, about 100,000 head of O'Conner cattle ran on half million acres. The most to carry this brand at one time were 25,000 head. The brand is still used by Thomas O'Conner's grandsons, Martin and Tom O'Conner, on the original ranch and is carried by 5,500 Herefords on 70,000 acres.

Source: Dennis O'Conner, Primo Stables in Victoria, Texas, 1959.

(South Texas rancher Tom O'Conner and A. P. Borden of the Pierce Estate imported the first commercial herd of Brahmans from India in 1905. O'Conner descendants still operate the ranch under the name "O'Conner Brothers.")

Nº 391   Lazy S
W. A. Blackwell

The **Lazy S** brand was recorded about 1912 by W. A. Blackwell in DeWitt and Karnes counties. The brand is owned by the W. A. Blackwell Estate and R. F. Blackwell of Cuero, Texas, and is used on good Hereford steers. The most cattle carrying this brand at one time were 4,000 head.

Source: Reiffert Blackwell, 1959.

Nº 392   Triangle
McGill Brothers

The **Triangle** brand was recorded by the McGill Brothers, J. C. and Frank, in 1911 in every county

between the Nueces River and the Rio Grande. It has been used by Frank McGill Jr. since 1952. Over 5,000 cattle carry the **Triangle** brand.

Source: McGill's El Ranchito in Jim Wells County, 1959.

See brand number 389.

Nº 393   A K Bar
A. S. Kahla

The **A K Bar** brand was recorded in 1922 in Brazoria and Galveston counties by A. S. "Swede" Kahla of Sweeny, Texas. The brand, placed on the right hip, is used on cattle on Bolivar Peninsula.

Source: 1958.

Nº 394   Little h
Jim Clipson

The **Little h** brand on the right hip was recorded in 1958 in Colorado County by Jim Clipson of Eagle Lake, Texas.

Source: Jim Clipson, 1959.

See brand number 386.

Nº 395   Triangle T
J. P. S. Griffith

The **Triangle T** brand on the left hip was recorded in 1953 in Brazoria County by J. P. S. Griffith of West Columbia, Texas. It is sometimes called the "Christmas Tree" brand.

Source: foreman Glenn Yauch, 1959.

Nº 396   E V A
Eva White

The **E V A** brand was recorded by Eva White of the Settegast Ranch in Fort Bend and Harris counties, Texas. This old iron was found at the Settegast Ranch in 1959.

Nº 397   Question Mark
J. B. Gary Estate

The **Question Mark** brand on the left hip was recorded by the J. B. Gary Estate in Wharton County. This old brand has been used on many cattle.

Source: J. B. Gary of Boling, Texas, 1959.

See brand number 399 and 408.

Nº 398   Six E
Jake Yelderman

The **Six E** brand was recorded by Jake Yelderman in Brazoria and Fort Bend counties. It is branded on the left rib.

See brand number 318, same brand.

№ 399   J, H J Connected
Gary Estate

The **J, H J Connected** brand was recorded in Wharton County by the Gary Estate of Boling, Texas.
See brand numbers 397 and 408.

№ 400   S
Clay Ogle

The **S** brand was recorded by Clay Ogle of Sweeny, Texas, in Brazoria County.
Source: Clay Ogle, 1958.

№ 401   D U
Charlie Williford

The **D U** brand was recorded by Charlie Williford of Fulshear, Texas, in Fort Bend and Brazoria counties.
Source: Charlie Williford, 1959.

№ 402   T Three Bar
Sam Morgan

The **T Three Bar** brand was recorded in Brazoria County in 1946 by Sam Morgan of Sweeny, Texas.
Source: 1959.

№ 403   Seventy-Five
E. N. Wilson

The **Seventy-Five** brand was recorded in 1884 in Brazoria County by E. N. Wilson. Ned Wilson found this iron in a field near Old Ocean and despite the similarity in the names, the brand was never in his family.
Source: Ned Wilson, 1959.

№ 404   C U
Settegast Ranch

The **C U** brand is recorded in Fort Bend County by the Settegast Ranch of Richmond, Texas.
See brand numbers 405, 411, and 412.

№ 405   Diamond Seven
found on Settegast Ranch

The **Diamond Seven** branding iron was found on the Settegast Ranch in Fort Bend County.
See brand numbers 404, 411, and 412.

№ 406   Diamond
Jim Clipson

The **Diamond** brand on the right hip was recorded in Colorado County by Jim Clipson.
Source: Jim Clipson in 1957.
See brand numbers 386, 394, and 410.

№ 407   Six D
C. T. Armstrong

The **Six D** brand on the left thigh is used by Mrs. C. T. Armstrong of Damon, Texas, and was

recorded in 1880 in Fort Bend and Brazoria counties. Mrs. Armstrong's father had used the brand as a **Six D** with a **bar** over it.
Source: 1959.

№ 408   J I J
Gary Estate

The **J I J** is an old-time brand recorded by the Gary Estate of Boling, Texas.
Source: J. B. Gary of Boling, 1959.
See brand numbers 397 and 399.

№ 409   Four
Owner unknown

The **Four** branding iron was found by Federal Game Warden Parkson on the bank of the Rio Grande in Zapata County. The owner is unknown.
Source: 1959.

№ 410   A Up A Down
Jim Clipson

The **A Up A Down** brand was recorded in Colorado County by Jim Clipson of Eagle Lake, Texas.
See brand numbers 386, 394, and 406.

№ 411   H Double Cross
Settegast Ranch

The **H Double Cross** brand was recorded in Fort Bend and Harris counties by the Settegast Ranch in 1885 as a trail brand for cattle going north to Kansas grass. This set of large irons was used on bought grown cattle. They were hanging in a barn and probably have not been used since 1905.
Source: Settegast Ranch, 1959.
See brand numbers 404, 405, and 412.

№ 412   H Double Cross
Settegast Ranch

The **H Double Cross** brand was recorded in Fort Bend and Harris counties by the Settegast Ranch. This set of small irons was used to brand calves.
Source: Settegast Ranch, 1959, when I received the large set of **H Double Cross** irons (no. 411).
See brand numbers 404, 405, and 411.

№ 413   Two T Connected
William B. Kennedy

The **Two T Connected** brand on the left hip was recorded in 1900 in Brazoria County by William B. Kennedy of Angleton, Texas. The brand came from cattle bought years ago in Wharton County by Kennedy's father from the father of W. E. "Jack" Thomas of Louise, Texas.

(This iron is the same as brand number 443 but varies in shape somewhat. Received from Jack Thomas.)

Nº 414   Seven H L Connected
George Seibel

The **Seven H L Connected** brand was recorded in 1925 in Brazoria County by George Seibel and run on Chocolate Bayou. The most cattle to carry this brand at one time was 150 head. The brand was first recorded in 1864 in Brazoria County by Jacob Seibel, who had also recorded the **E S** brand in 1856. The **Seven H L Connected** brand is put on with a running iron. I ran it on a board in the presence of George Seibel in 1960 at the Brazoria County Fair in Angleton, Texas.

Source: George Seibel, 1960.

See brand number 416.

Nº 415   C F
Cecil Finger

The **C F** brand was recorded by Cecil Finger of Alvin, Texas, in Brazoria County in 1900. It is placed on the left hip with a running iron. I ran the brand on a board in the presence of Cecil Finger at the Brazoria County Fair in Angleton in 1959.

Source: Cecil Finger, 1959.

Nº 416   Y L Connected Bar
Mrs. George Seibel

The **Y L Connected** Bar brand was recorded in 1923 in Brazoria County by Mrs. George Seibel. She had fifty cattle with this brand, which was placed on the left hip with a bar iron. I ran the brand on a board in the presence of George Seibel at the Brazoria County Fair in Angleton in 1959.

Source: George Seibel, 1959.

See brand number 414.

Nº 417   Seven U P Connected
J. A. "Archie" Martin

The **Seven U P Connected** brand was recorded in Brazoria County by J. A. "Archie" Martin of Sweeny, Texas. Walter Crosby and I handled the cattle after Archie Martin's death and all that weren't branded, I branded with a running iron.

Source: 1959, Brazoria County Fair.

Nº 418   T
Mrs. J. R. "Jordie" Farmer

The **T** brand was recorded in Brazoria County by Mrs. J. R. "Jordie" Farmer of West Columbia, Texas. It was first recorded by Isaac T. Tinsley in 1848, who also recorded the **Fifteen** brand. This **T** iron is old and believed to have been used many years ago in this country.

Nº 419   Half Circle J A Connected
Ed Cole

The **Half Circle J A** Connected brand was recorded in Brazoria County by Ed Cole of West Columbia and Alvin, Texas, and put on with a running iron. Ed Cole is an outstanding man and athlete. He competed in rodeos in saddle bronc riding, steer wrestling, and bull riding and has been All-Around Champion Cowboy numerous times. He was ranch foreman for the T Diamond Ranch at West Columbia.

Source: Ed Cole, 1959.

(Ed Cole was 1956 All-Around Champion Cowboy of the Southwestern Rodeo Association.)

Nº 420   Q
Albert J. May

The **Q** brand was recorded in 1932 in Wharton, Matagorda, and Fayette counties by Albert J. May of Wharton, Texas. This brand and a herd of 400 cattle were purchased from Bennie Quinns of Hockley, Texas. Before acquiring the **Q** brand, which is put on with a running iron, Albert May ran the **W F Connected** brand exclusively. A cow with that brand was given to him in 1889 when he was one month old by an uncle, Grover May. This brand was recorded in Albert May's name in Gonzales and Wharton counties.

Nº 421   V Seven
Andrew Melgaard

The **V Seven** brand was recorded in 1890 in Brazoria County by Andrew Melgaard of Brazoria, Texas. It was branded with a bar iron on the left side of many native Longhorn cattle along the Brazos River by Melgaard, an old-time native of Brazoria County. I ran this brand on a board with the permission of Mrs. Andrew Melgaard.

See brand number 425.

Nº 422   Flying V
Walter G. Dew

The **Flying V** brand was recorded by Walter G. Dew of Richmond, Texas, in Fort Bend County in 1943, in Harris County in 1945, and in Fayette County in 1960. It was first recorded by Walter's older brothers, H. S. Dew & Brothers, in Fort Bend County in 1905. Another brother, F. Y. Dew, bought out H. S. Dew & Brothers in 1920 and recorded the brand in Liberty, Fort Bend, and Harris counties. It was put on the left side with a running iron. I ran the brand on a board during the 1959 TSCRA Convention with the permission of Walter Dew.

Source: Walter Dew, 1965.

Nº 423   Backward E M Bar
Marcus Brothers

The **Backward E M Bar** brand was recorded in 1910 by the Marcus Brothers of Houston in Harris, Polk, and Liberty counties. It was put on with a running iron. With the Marcus Brothers' permission, I ran the brand on a board during the 1959 TSCRA convention in Dallas, Texas.

(Max Marcus was a lifelong rancher in eastern Harris County. He died at his home in Crosby, Texas, in June 1978.)

№ 424   C R Connected
J. H. "Tim" Tigner

The **C R Connected** brand on the right side was recorded in Brazoria County by J. H. "Tim" Tigner of Angleton, Texas.

Source: Timmy Tigner, Tigner Ranch, 1959.

№ 425   V Seven Connected
Andrew E. Melgaard

The **V Seven Connected** brand was recorded in 1890 in Brazoria County by Andrew E. Melgaard of Brazoria, Texas. It is on some of the few Longhorn cattle left in this country and being perpetuated by J. G. "Jack" Phillips. I put this brand on a board with a bar iron in 1959 with the permission of Mrs. Andrew Melgaard.

See brand number 421.

№ 426   Terrazas brand
Don Luis Terrazas

The **Terrazas** brand was recorded by Don Luis Terrazas who was the largest cattle rancher in the State of Chihuahua, Mexico, during the time that Porfirio Diaz was President of Mexico (1880–1920) and possibly before. It is said that the brand has no meaning but was simply made of pleasing lines and curves.

Source: TSCRA Inspector D. O. Roberts of El Paso, Texas, 1959.

(Don Luis Terrazas was a wealthy cattle baron in Mexico whose ranch extended from the Rio Grande to Chihuahua City, more than 235 miles to the south. More than 500,000 cattle grew sleek on this vast empire. It is believed the ranch inspired the song, El Rancho Grande. During the Mexican Revolution, Terrazas escaped to the United States where he died in 1923.)

№ 427   Half Circle H
William Randolph Hearst

The **Half Circle H** or **Babicora** brand belonged to newspaper publishing magnate William Randolph Hearst of California, who had cattle in Coahuila, Mexico, and in Arizona, New Mexico, and California for a number of years. The Babicora Ranch in Mexico was located on a high plateau in the Sierra Madres.

Source: TSCRA Inspector D. O. Roberts of El Paso, Texas, 1959.

№ 428   O J F Connected
Monte Marshall

The **O J F Connected** brand was recorded in Victoria County, Texas, by Sheriff Monte Marshall.

Source: TSCRA Inspector Lester Stout and Sheriff Marshall of Victoria, 1959.

№ 429   Backward C Dash
J. B. "Bert" McCloy

The **Backward C Dash** on the right hip was recorded in 1937 in Brazoria County by J. B. "Bert" McCloy of Angleton, Texas. McCloy had used a **C Dash** brand in Liberty County. When he moved to Brazoria County and the C Dash was already taken, he recorded the **Backward C Dash**. During the early 1920s and before, McCloy was a TSCRA Inspector in the Beaumont area. He was also a partner in the cattle business at one time with Bob Boyt of Devers, Texas. In 1956, McCloy had 1,000 head of cattle on his 8,000-acre ranch.

№ 430   W Bar
A. J. Wray

The **W Bar** brand was recorded in 1950 in Colorado County by A. J. Wray of Columbus and Houston, Texas.

Source: Charlie Kearney, Wray ranch foreman, 1959.

№ 431   L Open A
Leonard Meyer

The **L Open A** brand on the left side was recorded in Fort Bend County in 1946 by Leonard Meyer of Rosenburg, Texas.

Source: Leonard Meyer, 1959.

№ 432   Double J
Fred King

The **Double J** brand was recorded in Matagorda County in 1913 and used at Palacios by Fred King's father. The King family lived on the Mad Island Division of the Pierce Ranch for many years.

Source: Fred King, 1959, while I helped count cattle at the Runnels-Pierce Ranch during the division of the estate.

№ 433   Crescent V
Sartwelle Brothers

The **Crescent V** brand was recorded in Jackson, Matagorda, and Harris counties by the Sartwelle Brothers of Palacios and Houston, Texas. The Matagorda County ranch was on Carancahua Bay. J. W. Sartwelle died in 1965.

Source: J. W. Sartwelle, 1959.

(The history of the Sartwelle Brothers Ranch began in 1830 when Judge Silas Dinsmore, their ancestor, arrived in Texas from Mobile, Alabama. He received a land grant in 1832 in Matagorda County, and he received later grants in Calhoun, Lavaca, and Jackson counties. He entered the Texas War of Independence and then received the first "Letter of Mark and Reprisal" issued by the fledgling Texas government. It was a license for legalized piracy in the Texas Navy. "The Judge" must have done his job well, for he was elected the first Chief Justice in Matagorda County.

His daughter married William Lovell Sartwelle of New Hampshire in 1850. Their five grandsons established the Sartwelle

Bros. Ranch Co. on family land near Palacios in 1915. One of the brothers, James William Sartwelle, was prominent in the development of the Brahman breed of cattle. By 1920, Sartwelle and his brothers and sisters had a herd of 2,000 cattle, one of the largest grade herds of Brahmans in the country. The Sartwelle family continues to play an important role in the development of the Brahman breed and the cattle industry in Texas.)

Nº 434   P Hobble P
Sam Wilson

The **P Hobble P** brand is recorded in Waller County by Sam Wilson of Pattison, Texas. It was an early-day brand used by his family. Wilson is a well-known trainer and exhibitor of top cutting horses.

Source: Sam Wilson, 1959.

Nº 435   H L Connected
J. L. "Roy" Baker

The **H L Connected** brand was originally recorded in Smith County east of Dallas in 1915 by H. E. Lasseter. It is now used by J. L. "Roy" Baker of Bullard, Texas, on registered Charolais cattle. Roy Baker purchased a ranch and its brand and recorded the brand. The most cattle to have carried this brand at one time is 500 head. J. L. Baker gave me this iron at the East Texas Fair where I displayed my collection.

Source: J. L. Baker, Baker ranch near Encinal, Texas, LaSalle County, 1959.

Nº 436   Eight-eight Bar
Charlie Kearney

The **Eighty-eight Bar** brand was recorded in 1937 in Colorado County by Charlie Kearney of Columbus, Texas. It was first recorded in 1854 by Eli Klapp.

Source: 1959.

Nº 437   Backward E L Connected
Ernest and Sibyl LeBlanc

The **Backward E L Connected** brand was recorded in Brazoria County by Ernest and Sibyl LeBlanc of Sweeny, Texas. This iron was returned to the LeBlancs.

Source: at the Brazoria County Fair, Angleton, 1959.

Nº 438   T U
John Damon Sr.

The **T U** brand was recorded in Brazoria County by John Damon Sr.

Source: 1959, Damon Ranch near Old Ocean, Texas.

Nº 439   E Cross Connected
George E. King

The **E Cross Connected** brand was recorded in 1932 in Brazoria County by George E. King.

Source: George King, Rosharon, Texas, 1959.

Nº 440   A D Connected
Jack Marshall

The **A D Connected** brand is recorded by Sheriff Jack Marshall of Brazoria County, Texas. Marshall's people first recorded it in 1862 after they bought mules with that brand that came from South Carolina. It is made with a running iron.

Source: received at the Brazoria County Fair, 1959.

Nº 441   N Connected A L
Mrs. Gregg Laurence

The **N Connected A L** brand was recorded in 1915 in Matagorda and Brazoria Counties by Gregg Laurence of Bay City, Texas. Three hundred cattle carried this brand at one time. Mrs. Laurence's uncle, Allen Wynn, first used it in Bastrop and Williamson counties, possibly as early as 1880.

Nº 442   M
Laurence & Boettcher

The **M** brand, recorded in 1916 in Wharton, Matagorda, and Brazoria counties, was a partnership brand used by Gregg Laurence and Clem Boettcher for twenty-two years. The most cattle to carry the brand at one time were 1,300 head. The Boettcher family continued to use the brand in Wharton County

Nº 443   Two T Connected
A. E. "Jack" Thomas

The **Two T Connected** brand was recorded in Wharton and Jackson counties by A. E. "Jack" Thomas of Louise, Texas. Thomas's father had used it during open range days.

Source: Jack Thomas, 1959.

Nº 444   Lazy V
Baer Cattle Company

This brand, generally known as the **Lazy V** and sometimes the **Lazy Open A**, is recorded in Matagorda County by Arthur G. Baer of Bay City, Texas. It is used on cattle along the coast from Matagorda to the Brazoria County line. The 21,000-acre Baer Ranch was begun about 1870 by Gottlieb Baer, who first recorded the brand in 1870. The **Lazy V** has been carried by 5,000 head of cattle at one time. Baer Cattle Company also sold bucking bulls for RCA rodeos.

Source: Baer Ranch, 1959.

Nº 445   J P Connected Z
Peltier Brothers

The **J P Connected Z** brand was recorded in 1910 in Brazoria County by the Peltier Brothers of Danbury, Texas. It was recorded in a northern state before the Peltiers came to Texas. Twelve different additions to the brand designate the different brothers who use it.

Source: Walter Peltier, 1959.

№ 446   Ace of Clubs
Lee M. Pierce

The **Ace of Clubs** brand was used during the Civil War by Jonathan E. Pierce, brother of A. H. "Shanghai" Pierce. Jonathan's son, A. B. Pierce, recorded it in Matagorda County in 1885 and used it until he died. His wife continued to use the brand on a few cattle tended by Walter Sanford. After she sold the cattle, the brand was not used again until Lee M. Pierce of Blessing, Texas, recorded it in 1953.

Source: Lee Pierce, 1959.

See brand number 95.

№ 447   Five T
T. A. Binford

The **Five T** brand is recorded in Harris and Jackson counties by former Sheriff T. A. Binford of Harris County. T. D. Binford first recorded it in 1865 in Montgomery County. Upon his death in 1885, the brand was given to his grandson, Thomas Abner Binford who uses it on about 100 calves a year.

Source: T. A. Binford with the help of Ferdy Wirt, 1959.

(Binford served as sheriff of Harris County from 1917–1937.)

№ 448   Backward L Open A L Connected
Ferdy Wirt

The **Backward L Open A L Connected** brand was recorded in Harris and Montgomery counties in 1935 by Ferdy Wirt.

Source: Ferdy Wirt, 1959.

№ 449   Twenty-two
William Stafford

William Stafford came to Texas in 1822 and settled near San Felipe in Stephen F. Austin's colony. He then moved to Stafford Point on Oyster Creek. He recorded the **Twenty-two** brand in 1844 in Fort Bend County.

Source: Commissioner Johnny Davis of Stafford, Texas, 1959.

№ 450   Crescent
Silver Lake Ranches, Inc.

The **Crescent** brand is recorded by Silver Lake Ranches Inc. of Galveston, Texas, in twelve counties in Texas and in Osage County, Oklahoma. It was originally the brand of W. L. Moody of Galveston, Texas.

Source: Crescent V Ranch of Matagorda and Jackson counties, 1959.

№ 451   Half Circle S
W. H. Brooks

The **Half Circle S** brand was recorded in Brazoria County by W. H. Brooks in 1905 and was placed on the left side or left hip. Joe Zrubek found this iron on the old Turnbow Ranch in Brazoria County in 1959. Bob Henderson of Houston, Texas, now operates this ranch.

№ 452   D
A. H. "Shanghai" Pierce

The D brand was recorded in Wharton County by A. H. "Shanghai" Pierce. This old iron with a fancy twist in the handle was found on a convict farm on the Colorado River near Wharton, Texas, in 1959.

See brand number 4.

№ 453   Backward R H Connected
Unknown

The **Backward R H Connected** branding iron was found on the old Turnbow Ranch in Brazoria County in 1959 by Joe Zrubek. Bob Henderson of Houston, Texas, now operates this ranch.

Source: Bob Henderson.

№ 454   R
G. R. Laney

The **R** brand was recorded by G. R. Laney of Wills Point, Texas, in Van Zandt County in 1929. Laney made this original branding iron in 1929. I displayed my branding irons at the East Texas Fair in Tyler and acquired this iron.

Source: TSCRA Inspector T. O. Tinsley, 1959.

№ 455   B
John R. Martin

The **B** brand is recorded by John R. Martin of Van Zandt County. It was originally recorded by the Blair Cattle Company in 1875 and has been passed down through generations of relatives and is still used. John Martin made this iron in about 1940.

Source: John R. Martin, 1955.

№ 456   Half Circle X Bar
Foster Ranch

The **Half Circle X Bar** brand was recorded in 1880 in McMullen County by the Foster Ranch on San Miguel Creek. Graves Peeler found it.

Source: Graves Peeler, 1959.

№ 457   Seven Cross L Connected
Tom J. Boone

The **Seven Cross L Connected** brand on the left hip was recorded in Brazoria, Fort Bend, and Matagorda counties by Tom J. Boone of West Columbia, Texas.

Source: Tom Boone's ranch, 1959.

№ 458   C
Mrs. Kittie Nash Groce

The **C** brand was recorded in Brazoria County by Mrs. Kittie Nash Groce of East Columbia, Texas. It was a jaw brand used on horses.

Source: Graves Peeler.

See brand numbers 44, 123, 142, 143, and 492.

Nº 459   M A Connected Half Circle
Webb-Andersen

This **M A Connected Half Circle** branding iron belonged to Mrs. Wilbur Webb Jr. (Marentze A. Webb) of Danevang, Texas, and was the original iron used by Mads Andersen. This unusual iron was at the Smith Ranch at Louise, Texas, and was brought to my attention by Lee Howell of Houston, who bought the Smith Ranch in 1959.

The **M A Connected Half Circle** brand was originally used in Wharton County in 1895 by Mads Andersen, who was born in Fyn, Denmark in 1857. He immigrated to Nebraska in 1880 and moved to Wharton County, Texas, in 1894. He first branded his cattle in 1895 because the Pierce Ranch cattle were grazing open range, part of which was Mads Andersen's. He made this branding iron which weighs about seven pounds.

Source: Mrs. Wilbur Webb Jr., 1959.

Nº 460   Diamond With a Tail
Ewing Halsell

The **Diamond With a Tail** brand was recorded in Maverick County in 1898 by Ewing Halsell of San Antonio, Texas. He also used it in Oklahoma, Kansas, and New Mexico.

Source: foreman Roy Sturgis at Halsell's Farrios Ranch in Dimmit County, 1959, while I was there working with TSCRA Inspector Warren Allee.

(*Ewing Halsell died in 1965. He was a member of a pioneer Texas ranching family and was a well-known cattleman with large ranch holdings in several states. He was a longtime director of the TSCRA. The Halsell Foundation, located in San Antonio, supports many charitable causes in Texas.*)

US

Nº 461   U S
H. P. Stockton Estate

The **U S** brand is recorded in Wharton County by the H. P. Stockton Estate of Louise, Texas. Stockton's father used this old-time brand during open range days.

Source: through Johnny Garrett of Louise, 1959.

Nº 462   Running M
Captain W. C. "Bill" McMurrey

The **Running M** brand was recorded in Dimmit County in 1910 by W. C. "Bill" McMurrey.

Source: Captain McMurrey's foreman on his ranch near Carrizo Springs, 1959. I was working a theft case with TSCRA Inspector Warren Allee.

(*Bill McMurrey had a long record as a law enforcement officer. He was a deputy sheriff, a U. S. Mounted Customs Inspector, and for six years, a Texas Ranger. He was made Captain of Company D of the Texas Rangers in 1935. When he retired from the Rangers, he went into ranching full time. He operated three ranches in South Texas—the Santa Anita in LaSalle County, the Palo Blanco in Dimmit County, and the Santa Niño in Zapata County.*)

Nº 463
F Lightning   Albert Bell Fay

The **F Lightning** brand was recorded by Albert Bell Fay of Houston, Texas, in 1950 and used on his ranches in Liberty and Matagorda counties.

Source: Fay ranch at Cedar Lake, 1959.

Nº 464   Eight Point Star
Stern Estate

The **Eight Point Star** brand is recorded in Fort Bend County by the Stern Estate of New York and used on the Stella Ranch at Fulshear, Texas.

Source: Stella Ranch manager Smith, 1959.

Nº 465   Backward L D Connected
Mrs. Lottie Dyer Moore

The **Backward L D Connected** brand on the right thigh was recorded in Fort Bend County by Mrs. Lottie Dyer Moore in 1870 and is used on the Dyer Moore Ranch on the Brazos River. The iron was buried in concrete in 1900 by Oscar Scott, now deceased, and was found and given to me with three other irons.

Source: Dyer Moore, Moore Ranch, 1959.
See brand numbers 232, 234, 466, and 467.

(*Lottie Dyer was from a pioneer Texas family, and her grandfather was a signer of the Texas Declaration of Independence. She married John M. Moore Sr. in 1883. He acquired vast land holdings and developed the Braford breed of cattle.*)

JFD

Nº 466   J F Connected D
J. F. D. Moore

The **J F Connected D** brand was recorded in Fort Bend County in 1839 by J. F. Dyer. Allen & Dyer who ran cattle on 25,000 acres in Fort Bend County recorded it as a partnership brand in 1874. In 1908, J. F. D. Moore recorded it and branded it on the right thigh or right side.

Source: Dyer Moore, 1959, with three other irons.
See brand numbers 232, 234, 465, and 467.

M

Nº 467   M
John M. Moore

The **M** brand was recorded by John M. Moore in 1870. It was used mostly on bought cattle.

Source: Dyer Moore at the Moore Ranch, 1959.
See brand numbers 232, 234, 465, and 466.

Nº 468   Lazy J
J. T. Cornelius

The **Lazy J** brand was recorded in Matagorda County in 1945 by J. T. Cornelius of Midfield, Texas.
See brand numbers 469, 470, 475, and 476.

№ 469   J Lazy J
Ardell Cornelius

The **J Lazy J** brand was recorded in Matagorda County in 1948 by Miss Ardell Cornelius of Midfield, Texas.

See brand numbers 468, 470, 475, and 476.

№ 470   Five F Connected
F. Cornelius Sr.

The **Five F Connected** brand was recorded in Matagorda County in 1898 by F. Cornelius Sr. of Markham, Texas (W. D. Cornelius's father). Jim Cornelius of Midfield still has one of the original irons.

№ 471   Bar B Bar
Percy Barbee

The **Bar B Bar** brand was recorded in Brazoria County in 1940 by Percy Barbee of Sweeny, Texas. "I could not get **Bar B** at the time I registered my brand, so I had to take **Bar B Bar**," wrote Barbee.

№ 472   Diamond
Rusty Thomas

The **Diamond** brand was recorded in Colorado County in 1948 by Rusty Thomas of Eagle Lake, Texas.

Source: Rusty Thomas, 1959. I worked on a cattle theft case in the area for Thomas and Winterman.

№ 473   Pot Hook A
Mrs. C. S. Mitchell

The **Pot Hook A** brand is an old-time brand recorded in Jackson County and used on cattle on Carancahua Bay for many years. Mrs. I. N. Mitchell II originally recorded it in 1860.

Source: Mrs. C. S. Mitchell (Mary E. McNeill of Brazoria County), 1959, at Jordie McNeill's ranch near Brazoria, Texas.

№ 474   Mexican brand
Owner unknown

This Mexican brand was found in Zapata County by Harold Slayton of Beeville, Texas. Slayton gave it to Lonnie Stewart of Three Rivers.

Source: Lonnie Stewart, 1959.

№ 475   Backward F X
Jim T. Cornelius

The **Backward F X** brand was recorded in 1870 in Matagorda County and is now used by Jim T. Cornelius of Midfield, Texas.

Source: Cornelius Ranch, 1959.

See brand numbers 468, 469, 470, and 476.

№ 476   Backward F Lazy X
Juanita Cornelius

The **Backward F Lazy X** brand was recorded in 1944 by Juanita Cornelius in Matagorda County.

Source: Jim Cornelius, 1959.

See brand numbers 468, 469, 470, and 475.

№ 477   Double A Bar
A. M. Askew

The **Double A Bar** brand was designed "from my initials" by A. M. Askew of Houston, Texas, and recorded in 1945 in Fort Bend, Waller, and Brazoria counties. It was branded on registered Charolais show cattle. Five hundred head of Askew cattle carried this brand at one time, and approximately 1,000 head have been sold. In 1960, he had both Charolais and Charbray cattle.

Source: Billy Bates, Askew Ranch near Richmond, Texas, 1959.

№ 478   Crutch
Oscar G. Probst

The **Crutch** brand was recorded by Oscar B. Probst of Cuero, Texas, in 1943 in Dewitt and Goliad counties. The most cattle to carry this brand at one time were 175 head. Probst chose the brand because he used a crutch for sixty years.

№ 479   Forty-seven Connected
Marvin N. Burns

The **Forty-seven Connected** brand was recorded in 1952 by Marvin N. Burns of Angleton, Texas, in Brazoria County. The most cattle to carry this brand at one time were about eighty-five head.

Source: Mrs. Marvin Burns, 1959.

№ 480   T
Tom Brady

The **T** brand was recorded in Dimmit County by Sheriff Tom Brady of Carrizo Springs, Texas. Brady used it on a ranch that retired Texas Ranger Captain Bill McMurrey now leases.

Source: Sheriff Brady and Inspector Warren Allee, Carrizo Springs, 1959.

№ 481   A O Connected
Buster Oliver

The **A O Connected** brand was recorded in 1885 by A. Oliver in Victoria County. Buster Oliver, a deputy sheriff in Matagorda County, now uses the brand.

Source: Buster Oliver, 1959.

№ 482   J Y Connected Dash
Jimmy Weaver

The **J Y Connected Dash** brand was recorded in Calhoun County in 1930 by Jimmy Weaver of Port Lavaca, Texas.

Source: Jimmy Weaver at the 1959 Matagorda County Fair.

Nº 483　Backward E E
Percy V. Corporon

The **Backward E E** brand on the left hip was recorded in 1914 in Matagorda County by Percy V. Corporon of Palacios, Texas. The Corporon Ranch lies between Palacios Bay and the Colorado River near Collegeport, Texas. Corporon first registered this brand when he was fourteen or fifteen years old and branded his first cow with it.

Nº 484　X L Connected
Ted Mangum

The **X L Connected** brand was recorded in Wharton and Matagorda counties by Ted Mangum and used on commercial and registered Brahman cattle.

Source: Ted Mangum, Hungerford, Texas, 1959.

Nº 485　Upside Down T
C. A. Mewis

The **Upside Down T** brand is recorded in Austin County by Colbert A. "Boody" Mewis of Bellville and Sealy, Texas. He also uses the brand on many cattle in Arkansas and Mississippi.

Source: Boody Mewis at the Sealy Auction Ring, 1959.
See brand number 494.

(Mewis was a well-known South Texas rancher and founder of the Sealy Livestock Auction Company. He died in 1983.)

Nº 486　Rafter Cross Connected
Adolph Novak

The **Rafter Cross Connected** brand was recorded in Brazoria County in 1917 by Adolph Novak of Danbury, Texas. The Novak family now uses the **Rafter Cross Connected** followed by an initial to signify a certain member of the family.

Source: Adolph Novak at his ranch, 1959.

Nº 487　Dragging X
Elmer Cornett

The **Dragging X** brand was recorded in Matagorda County by Elmer Cornett of Blessing, Texas. It is placed on the left hip.

Source: 1960.

Nº 488　Dash E J
Stanton's Hereford Ranch

The **Dash E J** brand, recorded in Brazoria and Blanco counties by Stanton's Hereford Ranch of Alvin, Texas, was first recorded in 1912 by George Stanton's father.

Source: George Stanton at his store in Alvin, 1960.

Nº 489　V Seven Connected
Gus Lee

The **V Seven Connected** brand was recorded in Matagorda County in 1938 by Gus Lee of Blessing, Texas. It is also recorded in Jackson County and placed on the left loin or left hip.

Source: Gus Lee.

Nº 490　Half Circle O
Sheriff J. L. Watson

The **Half Circle O** brand was recorded by Sheriff J. L. Watson in 1920. His father originally used the brand.

Source: J. L. Watson at Edna, Texas, 1960.
(Watson was sheriff of Jackson County from 1941–1969.)

Nº 491　Circle X Connected
Dave Lundquist

The **Circle X Connected** brand was recorded in Colorado, Wharton, and Jackson counties in 1915 by Dave Lundquist of Garwood, Texas.

Source: Lundquist Ranch, Garwood, Texas.

Nº 492　Flying V
Kittie Nash Groce

The **Flying V** brand is recorded by Kittie Nash Groce of the Nash Ranch of East Columbia in Brazoria County.

Source: ranch manager W. A. "Bill" Curtis at the Nash Ranch, 1960. Bill Curtis died in 1966.
See brand numbers 44, 123, 142, 143, and 458.

Nº 493　F Double Cross
Fondren Estate

The **F Double Cross** brand is recorded in Harris and Fort Bend counties by the Fondren Estate of Houston, Texas.

Source: Fondren Ranch foreman, Joe Davis, Stafford, Texas, 1959.

(Walter W. Fondren was one of nine founders of Humble Oil and Refining Company in 1917. His son, Walter Jr., president of the Fondren Foundation, also owned extensive business and ranching holdings in Houston and in Harris and Fort Bend counties. He died in 1961. The Fondren Foundation continues to operate in Houston as a charitable and civic institution.)

Nº 494　Lazy T
C. A. Mewis

The **Lazy T** brand is recorded in Austin County by C. A. "Boody" Mewis of Bellville, Texas.

Source: Boody Mewis at the Sealy Auction barn, 1959.
See brand number 485.

№ 495 Horseshoe Bar
Spike Baty

The **Horseshoe Bar** brand was recorded in 1957 in Dimmit County by Spike Baty of Asherton, Texas. The Baty ranch is near Carrizo Springs.

Source: Spike Baty, Baty ranch, 1960.

№ 496 H H
Lieutenant Herman Hale Jr.

The **H H** brand on the left side of cattle was recorded in Fort Bend County in 1935 by Lieutenant Herman Hale Jr. of Houston, Texas.

Source: foreman at Hale Ranch, Needville, Texas, 1960.

№ 497 One Seventy-six Connected
John J. Seerden

The **One Seventy-six Connected** brand was recorded in Matagorda County in 1870 by John J. Seerden of Wadsworth, Texas. His son now uses the brand. This iron was seventy-five years old when he gave it to me.

Source: John Seerden at Bay City, 1960.

№ 498 Lazy U
M. U. Borden

The **Lazy U** brand was recorded in Brazoria County by Milam Borden in 1930 and is now used by M. U. Borden of West Columbia, Texas.

Source: Borden Ranch, located on the Brazos River, 1960.

№ 499 G T Connected
Graves Peeler

The **G T Connected** brand was recorded in Brazoria County in 1934 by Graves Peeler while he was foreman of the Kittie Nash Groce Ranch. Peeler still uses it on his ranch in McMullen County.

Source: W. A. "Bill" Curtis and I found this iron on the Groce Ranch in 1960.

See brand number 858.

(Graves Peeler was a TSCRA Inspector from 1920–1930 before he became manager of the Groce Ranch.)

№ 500 W C
C. S. Traylor

The **W C** brand was originated by William Coleman who sold a herd of cattle and the brand to J. C. Traylor in 1880. Mrs. J. C. (Charlette) Traylor used the brand for many years until her death in 1928. Her grandson, C. S. Traylor of Port Lavaca, Texas, now uses this brand and earmark in Jackson and Calhoun counties. The **W C** brand is put on the left hip and still carries the original earmark—an under half crop to the left and an underbit to the right.

Source: C. S. Traylor, 1960, through TSCRA Inspector Lester Stout.

№ 501 Cross S
Unknown

The owner of the **Cross S** brand is unknown.

Source: Billy Holt, Francitas shipping pens in Jackson County.

№ 502 B X
Joe Jennings

The **B X** brand is believed to belong to an old Negro, Joe Jennings, who was still living in 1960.

Source: W. A. "Bill" Curtis, the Nash Ranch, 1960.

№ 503 N H B Connected
Mrs. Herman Hale

The **N H B Connected** brand was recorded in Fort Bend County in 1935 by Mrs. Herman Hale of Houston, Texas.

Source: Hale Ranch, 1960.

№ 504 Bar b Open A
S. S. Perry Sr.

I received the **Bar b Open A** iron from S. S. Perry Sr. at his Peach Point Ranch in Brazoria County a short time before his death in 1960.

See brand numbers 238, 250, 251, 272, and 310.

№ 505 C
Nash Ranch

The **C** brand was recorded in Brazoria County as a jaw brand used by the Nash Ranch on horses and cattle while Graves Peeler was managing the ranch.

Source: Graves Peeler and I found this iron at the Nash Ranch, 1960.

See brand numbers 44, 123, 142, 143, 450, and 492.

№ 506 Seven V P Bar Connected
Varner Livestock Company

The **Seven V P Bar Connected** brand was recorded in Brazoria County by the Varner Livestock Company of West Columbia, Texas.

Source: Hogg-Varner Ranch, 1960.

№ 507 J A
J A Cattle Company

The **J A** brand was recorded in 1877 by the partnership of Charles Goodnight and John Adair. The brand was selected by Goodnight and represented John Adair's initials. In 1885, there were approximately 65,000 cattle wearing this brand on their left hips. An estimated 16,000 calves were branded annually. The ranch at one time covered 1,500,000 acres, and the **J A** brand was recorded in Randall, Swisher, Briscoe, Donley, Armstrong, and Hall counties. In 1960, the ranch was 400,000 acres in Armstrong, Donley, and

Briscoe counties and operates as the J A Cattle Company, Clarendon, Texas.

Source: TSCRA Inspector Alan Jeffries of Clarendon, Texas, 1960.

See brand number 574.

(In 1869, John Adair, an Irishman, married Cornelia Wadsworth Ritchie, a young widow from New York visiting Europe. They moved to New York, but Adair found living there unsuitable. In 1874, the Adairs journeyed West and while in Colorado, met Charles Goodnight, the great Texas trail driver. Goodnight told them of the grasslands of Palo Duro Canyon in Texas and of its potential for cattle raising.

In 1876, the Adairs and Goodnights traveled to Texas and the Palo Duro. Finding it all that Goodnight had said, they formed a ranching partnership for ten years. The Adairs provided the money to purchase the land and cattle, and Goodnight provided the know-how to raise and market the cattle.

John Adair died in 1885, but Mrs. Adair continued in partnership with Goodnight and took a keen interest in the ranch. In 1886, the partnership was terminated, but Goodnight stayed on as manager until Mrs. Adair found a suitable replacement. The land and cattle were divided, but Mrs. Adair's part included the headquarters and the J A brand. Cornelia Adair died in 1929.

M. H. W. Ritchie, Mrs. Adair's grandson, managed the ranch from 1935 until his death in 2000. It is now owned by Monte Ritchie's daughter, Cornelia Ritchie Bivins, of Amarillo, Texas.)

№ 508   Mill Iron
William E. Hughes

The **Mill Iron** brand was recorded in 1881 in Baylor County by the Continental Land and Cattle Company. It is also recorded in Hall, Wheeler, Collinsworth, Childress, Cottle, and Motley counties. Colonel William E. Hughes bought the brand, and when he died, it went to his wife. At her death, it went to a granddaughter, Annie C. Hughes of Denver, Colorado. In 1890, an estimated 25,000 calves were branded with the **Mill Iron** brand. At this time (1960), the brand is recorded by the Mill Iron Ranches of Denver. It is used in Cottle, Collingsworth, Motley, and Hall counties in Texas.

Source: TSCRA Inspector Alan Jeffries, 1960.

*(The original owner of the **Mill Iron** brand was a man named Simpson who had a small herd of cattle on the Pease River in north Texas. The Continental Cattle Company had bought the Hashknife holdings in Baylor County in 1881 when they purchased the cattle and the **Mill Iron** brand, which became the company's official brand. The Mill Iron Ranches also had a feeding ranch in Montana and branded 10,000 to 12,000 calves annually. By 1890 Colonel William E. Hughes was the sole owner. They absorbed the Hashknife Ranch in Baylor County and the Rocking Chair Ranche in Collingsworth County in 1896. In 1913, Hughes began to reduce his land and cattle. By 1918, he had sold most of his holdings and closed out the brand. At his death, a limited operation went to his heirs.)*

№ 509   R O
W. J. Lewis

The **R O** brand and ranch were purchased in 1917 by W. J. Lewis of Clarendon, Texas, from Mrs. Alfred Rowe, the widow of the founder of the Rowe Ranch. It is recorded in Motley, Donley, Hall, Oldham, Briscoe, Gray, Armstrong, and Hartley counties. It was started in 1878 in Donley and adjacent counties by the Rowe Brothers, and in 1905, it was transferred to Alfred Rowe. An estimated 15,000 cattle wore this brand on the left hip between 1889 and 1905.

Source: TSCRA Inspector Alan Jeffries, 1960.

*(Alfred Rowe, an Englishman born in South America, began the R O Ranch. In 1882, following the advice of Charles Goodnight, he purchased stock and range and recorded the **R O** brand in Donley County. His ranch, with headquarters near Clarendon, covered 100,000 acres by 1900 and ran 10,000 cattle. Alfred Rowe died on the Titanic when it sank in April 1912.)*

№ 510   T
Tom Coleman

The **T** brand was used by Tom Coleman many years ago while he was a partner in the Fulton Pasture Company of Rockport, Texas. Between 1870 and 1897, twelve to fifteen thousand cattle wore the brand. TSCRA Inspector Warren Allee and I found this iron in 1960 at the Glass Ranch in Dimmit County near Carrizo Springs, Texas. We believe it was Coleman's. Frank and Roy Baker now operate the ranch.

See brand numbers 513 and 520.

№ 511   Lazy Us
Hugh Fitzsimons

The **Lazy Us** brand was recorded in Dimmit, Maverick, Kerr, and Llano counties, Texas, and in Clay County, Missouri, by Hugh Fitzsimons of San Antonio, Texas.

Source: Fitzsimons's San Pedro Ranch near Carrizo Springs, 1960.

№ 512   J
Owner unknown

The **J** iron was used in Harris and Fort Bend Counties, but the owner is not known. It appears to be very old.

Source: 1960. Found on the Paddock Ranch at Barker, Texas, by Emmett Felts.

№ 513   Thirty-three
Tom Coleman

The **Thirty-three** brand was used by Tom Coleman on the Glass Ranch in Dimmit County and South Texas.

Source: Inspector Warren Allee and I found the iron on the ranch in 1960.

See brand numbers 510 and 520.

Nº 514   Nineteen Half Circle
Mrs. George Culver

The **Nineteen Half Circle** brand was recorded in Matagorda County by Mrs. George Culver of Wadsworth, Texas.

Nº 515   J O
J. W. Bolling Jr.

The **J O** brand is recorded by J. W. Bolling Jr. in Jackson County. It was first recorded by Bob Bolling and was the original brand of the Bolling Ranch located in the forks of the Carancahua River. Later it was used by J. W. Bolling as a horse brand and is now used by J. W. "Bill" Bolling Jr.

Source: Dave Bolling at the Bolling Ranch, 1958.
See brand numbers 209, 348, and 383.

Nº 516   D S
Sullivan Cattle Company

The **D S** brand was recorded in Brooks and Kleberg counties by the Sullivan Cattle Company of Palacios, Texas.

Source: Junior Moore in Falfurrias, Texas, 1960.

Nº 517   J I Bar
J. I. Hailey Ranch

The **J I Bar** brand is recorded in Karnes and Live Oak counties by the J. I. Hailey Ranch of George West, Texas.

Source: 1960 on a Brazoria County Cattleman's Association trip.

Nº 518   Cross Triangle
A. D. Cobb

The **Cross Triangle** brand was recorded in 1943 in Bee County by A. D. Cobb and used on the Cobweb Ranch.

Source: A. D. Cobb of Beeville, Texas, 1960.

Nº 519   V R Connected
R. C. Roddy

The **V R Connected** brand was recorded in Wharton County by R. C. Roddy of Hungerford, Texas.

Source: Edgar Hudgins at the Hudgins Ranch, Wharton County, 1960.

Nº 520   Three
Coleman Ranch

The **Three** brand was used in Dimmit County by the Coleman Ranch of Carrizo Springs, Texas. Inspector Warren Allee and I found this small saddle iron on the Glass Ranch in 1960. The iron is very old and was probably carried many years ago by the Coleman Ranch's Mexican cowboys.

See brand numbers 510 and 513.

Nº 521   Backward E P
Ed Pickering

The **Backward E P** brand was recorded by E. E. Pickering on March 22, 1858, in Victoria County. It is used now by Ed Pickering in Victoria and Jackson counties.

Source: eighty-one-year-old Ed Pickering at the TSCRA convention in Austin, Texas, in 1960 with the help of Inspector Lester Stout.

Nº 522   W Bar
Catto-Gage Ranch

The **W Bar** brand is recorded in Brewster County by the Catto-Gage Ranch of Marathon, Texas.

Source: at the Laredo Feedlots, 1960, while on a Brazoria County Cattleman's Association trip.

(Alfred Stevens Gage was a pioneer cattleman in the Big Bend area of Texas. He and his brother had 75,000 acres near Marathon, and after his brother died, Gage's capable management enabled the ranch to prosper and grow to 400,000 acres. After his death in 1928, his daughters, Dorothy Forker and Roxana Catto operated the ranch for many years. Today, most of the original land holdings remain under the management of Gage's descendants.)

Nº 523   R Y Connected
Roy Yeager

The **R Y Connected** brand was recorded in 1900 in Zapata and Jim Hogg counties and is used by Roy Yeager of the Hebbronville Auction Ring.

Source: 1960, Brazoria County Cattleman's Assoc. trip.

Nº 524   Cross Bar
Horace Caldwell

The **Cross Bar** brand was recorded in 1920 in Nueces and Kleberg counties by Horace Caldwell.

Source: 1960, Brazoria County Cattleman's Assoc. trip.

Nº 525   S R
Stratton Ranch

The **S R** brand was recorded in Nueces County by the Stratton Ranch of Corpus Christi, Texas, which was once a large cattle ranch. This iron is very old.

Source: Horace Caldwell, 1960.

Nº 526   Circle A
Seedling Plantation

The **Circle A** brand was recorded in 1863 by the Seedling Plantation of Mississippi. It is now used by the International Paper Company of Hancock County, Mississippi.

Source: Ex-sheriff Flip Johnson, 1960, while I was on a possible cattle theft on an island owned by International Paper Company where they run cattle.

See brand number 544.

Nº 527   T E D Connected
Ted Mangum

The **T E D Connected** brand was recorded in 1942 in Wharton County by Ted Mangum.

Source: Ted Mangum, 1960, at the J. D. Hudgins Ranch, Hungerford, Texas.

Nº 528   Backward C Bar C
Caldwell & Caldwell Ranch

The **Backward C Bar C** brand was recorded in 1942 in Corpus Christi in Nueces County by the Caldwell & Caldwell Ranch.

Source: Horace Caldwell, 1960.

Nº 529   Three R
Hollis M. Sillavan

The **Three R** brand was recorded in Washington County in 1951 by Texas Ranger Hollis M. Sillavan.

Source: Ranger Sillavan, at Columbus, Texas, 1951.

Nº 530   Pitchfork
Driscoll Ranch

The **Pitchfork** brand is recorded by the Driscoll Ranch in Nueces County. The Driscoll Ranch joins the northeast corner of the King Ranch's Santa Gertrudis Division.

Source: Horace Caldwell, 1960, on a Brazoria County Cattleman's Assoc. trip.

Nº 531   D Three
Sullivan Cattle Company

The **D Three** brand is recorded in Kleberg and Brooks counties by the Sullivan Cattle Company of Falfurrias, Texas.

Source: Junior Moore and Seth Wood of the Maraposa Cattle Company, 1960.

(The Sullivan Cattle Company had its beginnings in the early 1890s and has long been known for its top herds of Beefmasters.)

Nº 532   J M Connected
El Indio Land & Cattle Company

The **J M Connected** brand is recorded in Brooks County by El Indio Land & Cattle Company of Falfurrias, Texas, owned by John Maher of Houston.

Source: Jack Lindsey, foreman of the Reed Roller Bit Company, 1960, on a Brazoria County Cattleman's Assoc. trip.

Nº 533   P E
P. E. Pearson

The **P E** brand was recorded in 1945 in Wharton and Matagorda counties by P. E. Pearson of Richmond, Texas. He also used the **P E P** brand on Sandy Creek Ranch.

See brand number 565.

Nº 534   Brand name unknown
Mason Briscoe

This brand was registered in Fort Bend County in 1875 by William Briscoe of Richmond, Texas.

Source: Mason Briscoe while on a Brazoria County Cattleman's Assoc. trip, 1960.

Nº 535   Seventeen
John & George McNeal

The **Seventeen** brand was recorded in 1892 in Brazoria County. It is used by John & George McNeal of West Columbia, Texas.

Source: a nephew of John McNeal.

Nº 536   Double Bar R
Roy Schmidt

The **Double Bar R** brand was recorded in 1930 in Fort Bend County by Roy Schmidt of DeWalt, Texas.

Source: 1960.

Nº 537   M Six
J. A. McFaddin Estate

The **M Six** brand is recorded in Victoria County by J. A. McFaddin Estate of Victoria, Texas. It was recorded in Jefferson County in 1840.

Source: TSCRA director Claude K. McCan, 1960.

(The McFaddin Ranch near Victoria has a rich history dating back to pre-Civil War times. James McFaddin had herds of both cattle and horses in Refugio County by 1856, and after the Civil War, he relocated in Victoria County and established a ranch. The McFaddin Ranch was one of the first in the county to use barbed wire and the first to have practically full-blooded Brahman cattle. James McFaddin died in 1916. His grandson, Claude McCan and Claude's uncle, Al McFaddin, took charge of the ranch. They crossbred Brahmans and Herefords and became known for their excellent cattle.

McCan took over full management of the ranch in 1925, operating it and the Welder-McCan Ranch until his death in 1974. Al McFaddin served as president of the TSCRA from 1912–1914, and Claude McCan served from 1942–1944.)

Nº 538   S Wrench
W. Roy Wright & Son

The **S Wrench** brand was recorded in about 1897 in Colorado County by J. F. Wright. It is now used by his son and grandson, W. Roy Wright & Son of Hempstead, Texas. The most cattle to carry the brand at one time was 800 head. The brand had been in the family for many years prior to the time they moved to Texas in 1896.

Nº 539   T U
W. S. Riggs

The **T U** brand was recorded in Brazoria County in 1920 by W. S. Riggs. Two hundred head have been the most cattle to carry it at one time. Riggs chose this brand because it is easy to run and had little chance to blot.

Source: W. S. Riggs, 1960.

Nº 540   J Little h Connected
George Light et al

The **J Little h Connected** brand is used by George Light of Cotulla, Texas, and associates. It is recorded in Webb County at Laredo, and in Blyth, California, by El Vaquero Cattle Company—Bank of America, George Light, and Catto-Gage Feedlots.

Source: iron in 1959 and information in 1960 at the Laredo Feedlots.

Nº 541   T O Connected
Joe A. Wyse

The **T O Connected** brand was recorded in Matagorda County in 1910 by Joe A. Wyse of Cedar Lake, Texas. It is also registered in Kentucky.

Source: 1960.

No. 542   Backward E N Connected
Mrs. Pearl Jamison Rucks

The **Backward E N Connected** brand is recorded in Brazoria County by Mrs. Pearl Jamison Rucks of Angleton, Texas.

Source: 1960.

(Mrs. Rucks died in a fire at her home on February 9, 1966. She was the daughter of James Jamison who settled in Brazoria County about 1840.)

Nº 543   T 6
J. B. Otto

The **T 6** brand is recorded in Fort Bend and Brazoria counties by J. B. Otto of Needville, Texas.

Source: Mrs. J. B. Otto, 1960.

Nº 544   Circle B
B. D. "Flip" Johnson

The **Circle B** brand was recorded in Hancock County, Mississippi, in 1915 by ex-Sheriff B. D. "Flip" Johnson. In 1960, I investigated a cattle theft case on an island near Point Clear and Lake Shore, Mississippi. The stolen cattle belonged to Gene Beckendorff of Sealy, Texas.

Source: Flip Johnson, Mississippi, 1960.
See brand number 526.

Nº 545   Three X
Mrs. Armell Baker

The **Three X** brand is recorded in Victoria County by Mrs. Armell Baker of Inez, Texas.

Source: with the help of TSCRA Inspector Lester Stout, 1960.

Nº 546   L H Seven Connected
J. L. Smith

The **L H Seven Connected** brand was recorded in Brazoria County in 1945 by J. L. Smith of Rosharon, Texas.

Source: 1960.

Nº 547   Six H
Dippel Brothers

The **Six H** brand was recorded in 1900 in Fort Bend, Austin, and Wharton counties by the Dippel Brothers of Needville, Texas.

Source: 1960.

Nº 548   Diamond C
Harris Masterson

The **Diamond C** brand was recorded in Fort Bend County by Harris Masterson of Houston and Rosenburg, Texas. The foreman of the Diamond C Ranch is T. C. Vines.

Source: Diamond C Ranch, 1960.

Nº 549   J H Connected
Dora Hudgins

The **J H Connected** brand was recorded in Wharton County by Dora Hudgins of Hungerford, Texas.

Nº 550   2 6 Diamond
Mrs. Mit Dansby

The **2 6 Diamond** brand was recorded in Brazos County in 1943 by Mrs. Mit Dansby of Bryan, Texas. The most cattle to carry this brand at one time were 300 head. The brand originated from the **2 6** brand of Mrs. Dansby's family and the Diamond from her husband's brand. The **2 6** brand was recorded in Brazos County in 1859 by her great-grandmother, Mrs. Artillery McCulloch. It was recorded next by Artillery's son, John McCulloch, in 1880 and then later by Mrs. Mit Dansby's father, William Irvin McCulloch.

See brand numbers 553, 558, and 560.

Nº 551   Lazy A
M. W. Marshall

The **Lazy A** brand was originally recorded in Victoria County in 1932 by Sheriff M. W. Marshall. On September 30, 1943, all brands and marks became void and were again recorded in 1945. The brand is placed on the left hip, left thigh, or the left loin. The most cattle with this brand at one time were 150 head.

Source: Sheriff M. W. Marshall, Victoria, Texas, 1960.

Nº 552   H U Connected
Mrs. Hub Muske

The **H U Connected** brand was recorded in Waller County in 1890 by Mrs. Hub Muske. This is an old iron.

Source: Roy Muske of Brookshire, Texas, 1960.

See brand numbers 555 and 559.

(The Muske family were prominent ranchers in Waller County. Roy Muske began crossbreeding Brahmans and Herefords in 1918. His father, John Frederick Muske, came to Texas from Germany in the 1850s. By the late 1800s, Muske's herd of Longhorns was one of the best in the area.)

№ 553   One Diamond D
H. P. Dansby Estate

The **One Diamond D** brand, recorded in Brazos County in 1943 by the H. P. Dansby Estate, was originally recorded in 1870. It now belongs to Mit Dansby of Bryan, Texas. The brand is a combination of several old family brands. The most cattle to carry this brand at one time were 400 head.

See brand numbers 550, 558, and 560.

№ 554   Three Rails
Bill Briscoe

The **Three Rails** brand was recorded in Fort Bend County in 1945 by Bill Briscoe of Richmond, Texas.

№ 555   H U B
Hub Muske

The **H U B** brand was recorded by Hub Muske of Brookshire, Texas, in Waller County in 1875.

Source: Roy Muske.

See brand numbers 552 and 559.

№ 556   Bar One Bar
Mason Briscoe

The **Bar One Bar** brand was recorded in 1918 in Fort Bend County by Mason Briscoe of Richmond, Texas.

Source: Mason Briscoe at his ranch, 1960.

№ 557   H H Connected
H. H. Moore & Son

The **H H Connected** brand was recorded in Grimes, Washington, and Brazos counties in 1930 by H. H. Moore & Son of Navasota, Texas. It is placed on the left side or the left shoulder. The **H L Connected** brand is also used by him on steers.

Source: the Moore Ranch, 1960.

(H. H. Moore ran a cow/calf and steer operation and was closely associated with Texas A&M University. He held a Special Texas Ranger commission for thirty years. At the time of his death in 1988, he was an honorary director of the TSCRA.)

№ 558   2 6
W. I. McCulloch

The **2 6** brand has been used in Brazos County by relatives of Mrs. Mit (Esther McCulloch) Dansby for many years. Her great grandmother, Mrs. Artillery McCulloch, first recorded the **2 6** brand in 1859 in Brazos County. Mrs.

Dansby's grandfather, John McCulloch, recorded the brand in 1880, and Mrs. Dansby's father, William Irvin McCulloch, also recorded the brand.

See brand numbers 550, 553, and 560.

*(The 2 6 brand has been used by the McCulloch family since 1859. The various children often added a **Bar** before, after, or beneath the 2 6 brand.)*

№ 559   Seven H U Connected
Roy Muske

The **Seven H U Connected** brand was recorded in Waller County in 1912 by Roy Muske of Brookshire, Texas. This brand was first recorded in Waller County by Mrs. Hub Muske in 1890.

Source: Roy Muske.

See brand number 552.

№ 560   Six Diamond
Mit Dansby

The **Six Diamond** brand was recorded in Brazos County in 1943 by Mit Dansby of Bryan, Texas. It is a combination of his father's brand, a **Diamond**, and part of his wife's brand, a **Six**. The **Six Diamond** has been used on about 300 cattle.

See brand numbers 550, 553, 558, and 561.

№ 561   Diamond Bar
Mit Dansby

The **Diamond Bar** brand was recorded in Brazos County by Mit Dansby of Bryan, Texas.

See brand numbers 550, 553, 558, and 560.

№ 562   Box
Fred Goth

The **Box** brand was recorded in Fort Bend County by Fred Goth of Needville, Texas.

Source: 1960.

№ 563   Three
Charles S. Lips

The **Three** brand was recorded in Brooks County by Charles S. Lips of Encino, Texas.

Source: ranch foreman Murray Potts, 1960.

№ 564   Y 6 Connected
W. D. Parker

The **Y 6 Connected** brand was recorded in Waller and Fort Bend counties by W. D. Parker of Houston, Texas.

Source: Parker ranch foreman Jim Luman, Brookshire, Texas, 1960.

PEP

Nº 565   P E P
Sandy Creek Ranch

The **P E P** brand was recorded in 1945 in Wharton, Matagorda, and Fort Bend counties and is used by the Sandy Creek Ranch of Richmond, Texas. It was chosen for the ranch by the late J. F. Hutchins. It is believed that the brand has never been used by any other ranch.

Source: "Pep" Pearson, Richmond, Texas, 1960.
See brand number 533.

IC

Nº 566   One C
Ben Prause

The **One C** brand was recorded about 1898 in Colorado County by Ben Prause of Bernardo, Texas.

Source: Ben's son, George Prause of Cat Spring, Texas, 1960.
See brand number 567.

Nº 567   Cross P Connected
George Prause & Son

The **Cross P Connected** brand was recorded in Colorado and Austin counties in 1945 as a partnership brand of George Prause & Son, Cat Spring, Texas. Prause wrote, "I chose this partnership brand because I was already branding **P**, and we could tell which were partnership cattle." About 600 head carried the **Cross P** brand at one time.

Source: George Prause, 1960.
See brand number 566.

Nº 568   H R Connected
H. R. Cullen

The **H R Connected** brand was recorded in Colorado County by H. R. Cullen of Houston, Texas.

Source: 1960.

Nº 569   Open A Bar S Connected
A. H. Seaholm

The **Open A Bar S Connected** brand was recorded in Colorado County in 1945 by Edgar Litzman. It is used by A. H. Seaholm of Eagle Lake, Texas, in Colorado and Wharton counties. One hundred-fifty head of cattle carry this brand.

Source: A. H. "Pappy" Seaholm, 1960.

Nº 570   K
George W. Keith

The **K** brand was recorded in Colorado County by George W. Keith of Eagle Lake, Texas. Keith brought this brand with him from North Dakota about 1900.

Source: A. H. Seaholm, 1960.

Nº 571   Bar Eleven
Andrew Briscoe

The **Bar Eleven** brand was recorded in Fort Bend County in 1945 by Andrew Briscoe of Richmond, Texas.

Source: Andrew Briscoe, 1960.

Nº 572   V F Connected
Vernon Frost

The **V F Connected** brand was recorded in Fort Bend and Chambers counties by Vernon Frost of Houston, Texas.

Nº 573   Four
C. M. Frost

The **Four** brand is recorded in Fort Bend, Harris, and Brazoria counties by C. M. Frost of Houston and Fulshear, Texas. He uses it on the Figure 4 Ranch. His grandfather, Samuel Miles Frost, used it in those counties beginning about 1825. His father branded it for many years, and then C. M. Frost inherited it. It was branded on the greatest number of cattle between 1888 and 1924.

Source: Pete Frost, 1959.
See brand number 572.

Nº 574   J A
J A Cattle Company

The **J A** brand was recorded in Randall, Swisher, Briscoe, Donley, Armstrong, and Hall counties in 1877 and is owned by the J A Cattle Company, located near Clarendon, Texas.

See brand number 507.

Nº 575   Backward L C
Louis Crouch

The **Backward L C** brand is recorded in Matagorda and Caldwell counties and used by Louis Crouch of Lockhart, Texas.

Source: Crouch Ranch foreman, Leonard Hemphill, 1960.

Nº 576   A D
Dittmann Harrison

The **A D** brand, recorded in Colorado and Wharton counties in 1855 by August Dittmann, is now in use on the Harrison Ranch of Columbus, Texas.

Source: 1960, Dittmann Harrison. His wife, Sherry, is the daughter of Texas Ranger Dan Hines.

Nº 577   Crescent One
F. W. Neuhaus III

The **Crescent One** brand was recorded in 1848. It is owned by F. W. Neuhaus III and recorded in Lavaca, Fort Bend, Harris, and Brazoria counties.

Source: 1960 when the iron was about forty years old.

Nº 578   D
Burton Dunn

The **D** brand was recorded in 1883 by Pat Dunn. It is owned by Burton Dunn and used on Padre Island, Mustang Island, Jim Wells, Nueces, Brooks, Cameron, Willacy, Kenedy, and Kleberg counties. The **D** brand is placed on the left thigh or left hip. The brand was put on my board by Pat Dunn's son, Burton Dunn of Corpus Christi, Texas.

(Pat Dunn was known as the "Duke of Padre Island," because he grazed cattle on the island from 1884 to 1937—longer than any other rancher. Padre Island had abundant grass, and it was first used for pasturing cattle by Padre Nicholas Balli in the early 1800s. It is 117 miles long and 25 miles wide. Cattle were sometimes barged from the mainland but usually waded across the shallows of the Laguna Madre near Flour Bluff.

Pat Dunn died November 26, 1937. His son, Burton, and Dave Coover of Corpus Christi took over the grazing rights on the island. The causeway, built to Padre Island from the mainland, brought a change to a century of the island pasture.)

№ 579   Y
John B. Harney

The **Y** brand was recorded in Nueces County by John B. Harney of Corpus Christi, Texas. It was also recorded in Falfurrias in Brooks County in 1936 by Ed Rachal.

№ 580   K Eight
owner unknown

No information on the **K Eight** brand.
Source: Harold Graves of Brazoria County.

№ 581   K Z
owner unknown

No information on the **K Z** brand.
Source: Harold Graves of Brazoria County.

№ 582   R Double Bar
Roy Schmidt

The **R Double Bar** brand was recorded in Fort Bend County in 1940 by Roy Schmidt of DeWalt, Texas.

№ 583   Wet Hat
E. H. "Emil" Marks

The **Wet Hat** brand was owned by E. H. "Emil" Marks of Barker, Texas. His grandfather, Gothilf Marks, recorded it in 1851, and it is used by Emil's son, Milo Marks. Emil Marks died in 1968.
Source: Emil Marks, Sealy, Texas, 1960.
See brand number 3.

• • •

In 1960, Leonard Stiles acquired the branding iron collection that had belonged to the late Sheriff John Harney of Nueces County with the help of Charlie Burwell, manager of the King Ranch's Laureles Division in Nueces and Kleberg counties. Mrs. Harney gave Stiles her husband's collection of forty-five historic branding irons (between numbers 584 and 645) that had mostly been used in Nueces County. Stiles and Sheriff Harney's son, a sergeant for the Corpus Christi Police Department, retrieved the irons from a barn where they were stored.

In an effort to identify and date the irons, Stiles and ex-TSCRA Inspector Travis Peeler searched the Nueces County brand books, including the original book of 1836, for information on these brands, which in many cases proved to be sketchy or nonexistent.

The Harney irons are indicated with an asterisk following the number.*

№ 584*   Running W
King Ranch

The **Running W** brand is owned by the King Ranch of Kingsville, Texas, and is used in Kleberg and Nueces counties. After working together for thirty years, Mifflin Kenedy and Captain Richard King dissolved their partnership in 1870. According to the terms of the division, a new brand was to be acquired by each partner for the counterbranding of the sorted herds. Richard King chose a clean-cut, simple mark destined for fame—the **Running W**. In Spanish, the brand was called *La Viborita* or "Little Snake." The earliest official registration of the **Running W** was February 9, 1869, in Nueces County. Whether the **Running W** had its origin north or south of the Rio Grande is a question that remains unanswered.

It is believed that Captain King may have arrived at the brand from the letter **M**. In 1862, King purchased the land and cattle of William Mann's estate. With the purchase came three brands, one being a **Running M**. It is possible that King simply inverted the **Running M** to create the **Running W**, which became his distinctive mark. The **Running W** is an open-spaced, neat, attractive brand that can be easily run and is hard to alter.

See brand numbers 45, 93, 731, and 980.

№ 585*   Dragging Open A
Owner unknown

The **Dragging Open A** brand was used in Nueces County.

№ 586*   Bow and Arrow
John Rabb

The **Bow and Arrow** brand was registered in Nueces, Live Oak, Jim Wells, Webb, and San Patricio counties in 1857 by John Rabb. The cattle carry the earmarks of an underhalf crop in each ear.
Source: information from M. P. Wright Jr., Robstown, Texas.

№ 587*   Brand name unknown
B. A. Berrnett

This brand was recorded in 1859 and used by B. A. Berrnett in South Texas.

№ 588*   J H L Connected
John Huffpowers

The **J H L Connected** brand was recorded by John Huffpowers in Nueces County in 1866.

Nº 589   Boot
Paul Barber

The **Boot** brand was recorded in Lavaca County in 1917 by Paul Barber. This iron was lost while on exhibit at Six Flags Over Texas in Arlington, Texas.

Nº 590*   Laurel Leaf
Mrs. Sarita Kenedy East

The **Laurel Leaf** brand belonged to the late Mrs. Sarita Kenedy East of Sarita, Texas. It was recorded in Nueces and Cameron counties in 1868 and 1880 by Captain Mifflin Kenedy. He sold the brand in 1882 to an English syndicate, and they used it until the turn of the century when the syndicate sold its land to Mrs. Henrietta King. Robert Driscoll bought their cattle and the **Laurel Leaf** brand. Driscoll gave the brand to John G. Kenedy, and it was used by the Kenedy Pastoral Company on horses. After Kenedy's death, the brand came into the possession of Mrs. Arthur S. East (Sarita Kenedy). The brand received its name from Captain Mifflin Kenedy's ranch, "Laureles" — The Laurels.

Source: John Harney collection, 1960. In addition, I received a small **Laurel Leaf** branding iron found on the Laureles Ranch in 1960. An old cowhand, Juan Silva, who is still living in 1961, remembers when the brand was being used.

See brand number 646 and 979.

Nº 591*   Brand name unknown
Desderio Galvan

This brand was registered in Nueces County in 1872 by Desderio Galvan.

Nº 592*   C
Isaiah Clayton

The **C** brand was recorded by Isaiah Clayton in 1884. It also belonged to Juan Saens. A **C** brand was also recorded in Nueces County by Berta C. Cunningham of the Chapman Ranch and was placed on the left rib. Mrs. Ruth E. Cowles of the Chapman Ranch recorded a **C** brand on the left jaw.

Nº 593*   Horseshoe L
W. W. Wright

The **Horseshoe L** brand on the left side was recorded in Duval County by W. W. Wright of San Diego, Texas.

Nº 594*   Bar Six
Morris McElroy

The **Bar Six** brand was recorded in Nueces County in 1930 by Morris McElroy.

Nº 595*   Brand name unknown
Owner unknown

No information on this brand, but it is thought to be from Nueces County.

Nº 596*   Brand name unknown
Owner unknown

No information on this brand, but it is from Nueces County.

Nº 597*   O
Albert Rachal & Brothers

The **O** brand was recorded in Nueces, LaSalle, and Brooks counties in 1882 by Albert Rachal & Brothers.

(Albert Rachal was said to have crossed more cattle out of Mexico than any other cowman. He was said to "Rachal 'em out.")

Nº 598*   Brand name unknown
Owner unknown

No information on this brand, but it is from Nueces County.

Nº 599*   J F Connected Two
Joseph Fitzsimmons

The **J F Connected** brand was recorded by Joseph Fitzsimmons in 1857 and used in South Texas.

Nº 600*   W R Connected
M. P. Wright

The **W R Connected** brand on the left side was recorded in 1888 by M. P. Wright in Banquete, Nueces County, Texas. M. P. Wright Jr. of Robstown recorded it in Nueces, Live Oak, Jim Wells, and San Patricio counties.

(Well-known rancher, M. P. Wright Jr., died in May 1968. It is said that he was the owner of the largest purebred herd of Longhorn cattle in the world. His grandfather was the colorful "W 6" Wright who came to South Texas from Mississippi and settled in 1858.)

Nº 601*   H K Connected
Henrietta M. King

The **H K Connected** brand was the first of the King Ranch brands officially recorded in Nueces County. Richard King filed it in the name of "Mistress Henrietta M. King, wife of Richard King" on March 20, 1859. It was recorded again in Nueces and Jim Wells counties in 1883 by Richard King II when his parents gave him the Agua Dulce Ranch and the brand. The brand was used on the various holdings by the descendants of Richard King II. This iron was in the John Harney collection. Mrs. Minerva King Patch, daughter of Richard King II, gave the iron to Sheriff Harney.

See brand number 891.

(Richard King III was the grandson of King Ranch founder, Captain Richard King and his wife, Henrietta King. He was a banker in Corpus Christi and was named trustee of his grandmother's estate when she died in 1925. His father, Richard King II, had died in 1922.

King was the manager of and a partner with his two sisters, Minerva King Patch and Mary King Estill, in the 150,000-acre Santa Fe Ranch in Brooks, Hidalgo, and Kenedy counties that they inherited from their grandmother. They also inherited 71,680 acres in

Crane, Crockett, Edwards, Upton, and Val Verde counties that was later sold. The **H K Connected** brand was used on all R. King & Company stock.

The Santa Fe Ranch was transferred to the King Ranch in 1956, and the Agua Dulce was sold to Belton Kleberg Johnson, a great-grandson of Captain King. Richard King III died in 1974.)

№ 602*   Diamond S Bar
Owner unknown
The **Diamond S Bar** brand was used in Nueces County, but the owner is unknown.

№ 603*   Brand name unknown
Owner unknown
No information on this brand, but it is from Nueces County.

№ 604*   Brand name unknown
Ed Rachal
This brand was recorded in Brooks and LaSalle counties by Ed Rachal of Falfurrias, Texas. It was branded anywhere on the left side of cattle and horses.

№ 605*   B
W. D. Bluntzer
The **B** brand was recorded in 1900 in Nueces County by W. D. Bluntzer of Bluntzer, Texas.

№ 606*   G
William Gallagher
The **G** brand was recorded by William Gallagher in 1875 in Nueces County, Texas.

№ 607*   H S
Robert Schallert
The **H S** brand was recorded by Robert Schallert in South Texas.

№ 608*   S
Mrs. Johanna Shaw
The **S** brand was recorded in 1865 in Nueces County by Mrs. Johanna Shaw.

№ 609*   Half Circle Backward
E H Connected
Edward Harney
The **Half Circle Backward E H Connected** brand was recorded in Nueces Town in 1878 by Edward Harney.

№ 610*   Five
J. P. Miller
The **Five** was a road brand recorded in 1873 in Nueces County by J. P. Miller.

№ 611   Half Circle K Bar
Charlie Kaechele
The **Half Circle K Bar** brand was recorded in Colorado, Wharton, and Harris counties by Charlie Kaechele of Wallis, Texas. The brand was placed on the left ribs of commercial Hereford cattle on the Bernard River. Mr. Kaechele was an old-time cowman who fed many steers. He lived all his life at Wallis and was killed by a train in front of his house in 1960.
Source: 1960.

№ 612*   Half Circle M
I. D. Magee
The **Half Circle M Brand** was recorded in 1915 at Nueces Town, Texas, by I. D. Magee.

№ 613   Bar K
Karl Leediker
The **Bar K** brand was recorded in Houston County by Karl Leediker of Crockett, Texas, a director of the TSCRA.
Source: Karl Leediker, 1960.
See brand number 619.

№ 614*   Brand name unknown
Owner unknown
This brand is from Nueces County. Its name and owner are unknown.

№ 615*   Y Four Connected
M. J. Allen
The **Y Four Connected** brand was recorded in Nueces County in 1878 by M. J. Allen.

№ 616*   F
Dave Odem
The **F** brand was recorded in San Patricio County in 1875 by Dave Odem.

№ 617   P Bar
Buck Pyle
The **P Bar** brand was recorded in Pecos County by Buck Pyle of Sanderson and San Antonio, Texas.
Source: Buck Pyle, 1960.
(Forest Barnett "Buck" Pyle was born in Memphis, Texas, on January 12, 1896, and he spent his childhood in Clarendon. In 1915, his family acquired the 210,000-acre Longfellow Ranch in Pecos County. Buck Pyle and J. M. West of Houston formed the West-Pyle Cattle Company in 1924, and the Longfellow Ranch was included in their partnership with Pyle as manager. During the next forty years, the partnership acquired additional ranch holdings of more than one million acres from New Mexico to the Gulf Coast. The company was known for its purebred cattle and good horses. The partnership was dissolved in 1964. Buck Pyle died in 1989 at the age of ninety-three.)

No 618   Long X
Reynolds Land & Cattle Company

The **Long X** brand was recorded in the West Texas counties of Hartley, Culberson, and Throckmorton and in Bernadillo and Valencia counties in New Mexico by the Reynolds Land & Cattle Company of Fort Worth, Texas.

(G. T. and W. D. Reynolds first recorded the **Long X** *brand, made with a bar iron, in Throckmorton County in 1882. The Reynolds brothers, George T. and William D., came to Texas in 1846 as young children. After serving in the Civil War, the two entered into a partnership and began acquiring cattle and land in Shackleford, Haskell, and Throckmorton counties. The Reynolds family had formed a strong friendship with the Matthews family in nearby Albany. Sallie Ann Reynolds Matthews tells the story of these two great ranching families in the 1936 book* Interwoven.

The Reynolds family was of strong, pioneer stock. In 1867, George Reynolds was traveling to Haskell County when Indians attacked him and shot him in the stomach with an arrow. He pulled the shaft out, but the arrowhead remained imbedded in the muscles of his back. It was there for fifteen years until a Kansas City surgeon finally removed it in 1882.

That year, 1882, the brothers established the Reynolds Cattle Company in the Davis Mountains of West Texas with headquarters near Kent. Their Long X Ranch became noted for its fine Hereford cattle. The company also established an Angus cattle operation in Dallam and Hartley counties in the Texas Panhandle. At the time of George Reynolds' death in 1925, the company ran cattle on more than 450,000 acres. Reynolds Cattle Company headquarters has been located in Fort Worth since 1902.)

No 619   Bar L
Karl Leediker

The **Bar L** brand was recorded in Houston County by Karl Leediker of Crockett, Texas, a director of the TSCRA.

Source: Karl Leediker, 1960.
See brand number 613.

No 620   D E E
G. F. Plummer

The **D E E** brand was recorded in 1920 in Galveston County by G. F. Plummer of Alta Loma, Texas. This is the first iron Plummer had when he went into the cow business in 1920. When Plummer retired, Doug Latimer of Alvin bought him out. In 1963, Latimer had 200 cows in that brand.

Source: G. F. Plummer.

No 621   M K Connected
Kenedy Ranch

The **M K Connected** brand was recorded in Kenedy County, Texas, in 1882 by the Kenedy Ranch.

(In 1882, Mifflin Kenedy sold his Laureles Ranch and cattle to a syndicate from Dundee, Scotland, doing business as the Texas Land & Cattle Company, Ltd. One month later, he began buying land and organized the Kenedy Pasture Company with headquarters of his new ranching operation on the old La Parra land grant south of Baffin Bay.

Mifflin Kenedy's son, John G. Kenedy, managed the ranch, and he and his family lived there. Mifflin Kenedy lived in Corpus Christi when he died in 1895.)

No 622*   Comet or Frying Pan
Flim & Brown

The **Comet** or **Frying Pan** was recorded in 1928 in Nueces County as a partnership brand by Flim & Brown at Banquete, Texas.

No 623*   Little t
Weil Ranch and Palangana Ranch

The **Little t** brand was recorded by the Weil Ranch and the Palangana Ranch of South Texas. A *palangana* is a pulley over a dug well. The brand was placed on the left hip or anywhere on the left side of cattle. Weil also recorded the **C C** brand in Jim Hogg County. It was placed on the left hip or anywhere on the left side of cattle and carried the same earmark as the **Little t**. Weil died in March of 1966.

(The Spanish word palangana *also means "basin." This iron may have come from the John Harney collection.)*

No 624*   M Y Connected
Owner unknown

The **M Y Connected** brand is from Nueces County.

No 625*   Y
A. L. Magee

The **Y** brand was recorded in Nueces County by A. L. Magee in 1876.

No 626*   A
N. O. Adams

The **A** brand was recorded by N. O. Adams in 1881 in South Texas.

No 627*   Circle R
Rand Morgan

The **Circle R** brand was recorded in 1938 in Nueces County by Rand Morgan.

No 628*   Heart
Walter Pettigrew

The **Heart** brand was recorded in Nueces County in 1856 by Walter Pettigrew.

№ 629*   Flying Y
Ed Rachal

The **Flying Y** brand was recorded in Brooks and LaSalle counties by Ed Rachal of Falfurrias, Texas. It was begun in 1867 in Liberty County by Mrs. Anais Rachal. Her son, E. R. Rachal, later recorded it in several counties. In 1936, Anais Rachal's grandson, Ed Rachal, used it in Brooks, Duval, Nueces, and eight adjacent counties. At that time, the brand was carried by 6,500 cattle on 84,000 acres of leased land. It was placed anywhere on the left side of cattle and horses. Ed Rachal was born in 1903 and died in 1964.

See brand number 579.

№ 630*   L R
Mrs. J. A. Roark

The **L R** brand was recorded in 1917 in Nueces County by Mrs. J. A. Roark.

№ 631   Circle J T J
Unknown

The **Circle J T J** brand is from Brazoria County.

Source: Harold Graves.

№ 632*   3 0
N. G. Collins

The **3 0** brand was recorded in 1871 by N. G. Collins and used in South Texas.

№ 633*   1 8
Owner unknown

The **1 8** brand is from Nueces County, and the owner is unknown.

№ 634*   Brand name unknown
J. R. Dickson

This brand was recorded in 1885 by J. R. Dickson of Collin County, Texas.

№ 635*   X I Bar
R. F. Whitworth

The **X I Bar** brand was recorded by R. F. Whitworth in Nueces County.

№ 636   Pitchfork
Robert Driscoll

The **Pitchfork** brand was recorded in Nueces County in 1885 by Robert Driscoll. The Driscoll Ranch joins the northeast corner of the King Ranch's Santa Gertrudis Division.

(Robert Driscoll Sr. was one of the founders and directors of the St. Louis, Brownsville & Mexico Railway, chartered on January 12, 1903, and built from Sinton, Texas, 160 miles to Brownsville. The town of Bishop was built on land that had been part of the Driscoll Ranch, and Robstown was established in the center of one of Driscoll's pastures.)

№ 637*   J H Connected Half Circle
Joe C. Harney

The **J H Connected Half Circle** brand was recorded in Nueces County in 1957 by Joe C. Harney.

№ 638   Walking S
Linda Stiles

The **Walking S** brand was recorded in Brazoria County in 1958 by Linda Stiles. It is put on with a running iron.

(Linda Stiles is a daughter of Mary and Leonard Stiles, the collector of these irons.)

№ 639   J S Connected
Joe Stiles

The **J S Connected** brand was recorded in Brazoria County in 1960 by Joe Stiles. It is put on with a running iron.

(Joe Stiles is a son of Mary and Leonard Stiles, the collector of these irons.)

№ 640   Triangle K Connected
J. B. Roberts

The **Triangle K Connected** partnership brand was recorded in Matagorda and Brazoria counties in 1925 by J. B. Roberts and R. E. Dineyard. They dissolved the partnership in 1929, and Roberts recorded the brand in his name in Matagorda County.

№ 641   E V E Connected
Armour Munson

The **E V E Connected** brand was recorded in Brazoria County by Armour Munson of Angleton, Texas. It is put on with a running iron. Munson is an expert with a running iron, making all brands as precise as with a stamp iron. He has done it this way since the early days. The Munson cattle run on Weedy and Bailey's Prairie to the Fort Bend County line near Juliff on the Brazos River.

Source: Armour Munson, 1960.

(Joe Munson uses this same brand but inverts it. See brand number 643.)

№ 642   Bar M
Mrs. Joe Munson

The **Bar M** brand was recorded in Brazoria County by Mrs. Joe Munson of Angleton, Texas, and is put on with a running iron.

Source: Armour Munson, 1960.

№ 643   E V E Connected
Joe Munson

The **E V E Connected** brand was recorded in Brazoria County by Joe Munson of Angleton, Texas, and is put on with a running iron.

Source: Joe Munson, 1960.

(Joe Munson uses the same brand as Armour Munson but inverts it. See brand number 641)

Nº 644   T J C Connected
Mrs. Mary P. Bingham
The **T J C Connected** brand was recorded in Brazoria County by Mrs. Mary P. Bingham of Houston, Texas.
Source: Armour Munson, 1960.

Nº 645*   Brand name unknown
Owner unknown
No information on this Nueces County brand.

Nº 646   Laurel Leaf
Kenedy Pastoral Company
The **Laurel Leaf** was the Laureles Ranch brand some years ago. It was recorded in Kleberg and Nueces counties by Mifflin Kenedy when he bought the Laureles Ranch from Charles Stillman in 1868. Kenedy sold the ranch and the brand to Texas Land & Cattle Company, Ltd. of Dundee Scotland in 1882. The syndicate began selling their cattle and land to Henrietta King's Santa Gertrudis Ranch in 1901, and they completed the deal in 1906. The **Laurel Leaf** brand went with the ranch, but Mrs. King returned the brand to John G. Kenedy. The **Laurel Leaf** brand was registered in Nueces and Kleberg counties by the Kenedy Pastoral Company. A small **Laurel Leaf** iron that is a jaw brand is also in the collection.
See brand number 590 and 979.

(For some time, Captain Richard King had thought of buying the Laureles Ranch, which adjoined his Santa Gertrudis Ranch on the east and ran to the Laguna Madre shore. King delayed in his plans, and Mifflin Kenedy made a deal to purchase the Laureles from its owner, Charles Stillman, in 1868. It was some years later that Henrietta King bought the ranch. She completed the final transaction for the Laureles in 1906. It is now one of the four divisions of the King Ranch. Ex-Texas Ranger Charlie Burwell took charge of the 255,026-acre division from Dick Kleberg in 1930.)

Nº 647   Twin V
Tom B. Saunders III
The **Twin V** brand on the left side was recorded in Parker County in 1930 by Tom B. Saunders III who uses the brand on his ranch southwest of Weatherford, Texas. It originated years earlier for use on a ranch in the Texas Panhandle.
Source: Tom Saunders III of Fort Worth, 1960.

*(The Saunders name has been synonymous with the livestock industry since early trail driving days, beginning with the brothers George and W. D. Saunders. Tom Saunders II, father of Tom III, is credited with modernizing cattle shipments in 1918 by transporting cattle to market in trucks. The **V C** brand was also used by the Saunders family, who has been in Texas since 1850. Tom Saunders III was a noted cattle feeder and livestock broker. The TSCRA director died in Fort Worth in 1974.*

Today, the Saunders Ranch near Weatherford is operated by Tom B. Saunders IV, who runs Simmental cattle.)

Nº 648   Lazy D
T. L. Davidson
The **Lazy D** brand was recorded in Wharton and Matagorda counties by T. L. Davidson.

LET

Nº 649   L E T
Owner unknown
There is no information on the **L E T** branding iron.

Nº 650   J B Connected
John S. Bowser
The **J B Connected** brand was recorded in Harris, Fort Bend, and Austin counties by John S. Bowser of Simonton, Texas. The brand passed from John Bowser to Harvey A. Bowser of Houston and is a mule brand.
Source: Otto Schultze at the Simonton Ranch, 1960.

32

Nº 651   3 2
C. H. Meninkie
The **3 2** brand was recorded in Waller County by C. H. Meninkie of Hempstead, Texas.

BZ

Nº 652   B Z
Fritz and Anna Berthold
The **B Z** brand was recorded in Colorado and Columbus counties in 1940 by Fritz and Anna Berthold. It was first registered by Anna's father, Mr. Reichert. The most cattle to carry this brand at one time were 150 head. Fritz Berthold died in 1960. Only one branding iron was made and this is the original iron.
Source: 1960.

Nº 653   D R Connected
R. D. McDonald
The **D R Connected** brand was recorded in Harris and Brazoria counties by R. D. McDonald of Houston, Texas. Foreman Bill Ragland and I made this iron with the approval of R. D. McDonald.

52

Nº 654   5 2
W. J. "Jack" Worsham
The **5 2** brand belongs to W. J. "Jack" Worsham of Sulphur Springs, Texas. It has been in the Worsham family for over 100 years and was used by his great-grandfather, grandfather, and as a partnership brand between his father and uncle.
Source: Jack Worsham, 1960.

Nº 655   Brand name unknown
J. E. & J. M. Pickering
This brand was recorded in Victoria County in 1901 and also in Jackson, Matagorda, and Wharton counties by J. E. and J. M. Pickering.

Nº 656   F Bar
Jay Fimble
The **F Bar** brand was recorded by Jay Fimble in Victoria County.
Source: Jay Fimble, Victoria, Texas.

Nº 657   M H Connected
Milton Hensley
The **M H Connected** was the brand of Milton Hensley.

Nº 658   Half Circle H I
Laura A. Armstrong Jorden
The **Half Circle H I** branding iron was found by Waldo Edling of West Columbia, Texas, on the Bernard River. County records show that Laura A. Armstrong Jorden of West Columbia recorded it in Brazoria County in 1939.
Source: Waldo Edling.

Nº 659   S Bar
Herbert E. Smith
The **S Bar** was recorded by Herbert E. Smith whose ranch is near Sterling City, Texas. This brand is made with two irons, an **S** and a **Bar**.
Source: Herbert Smith, 1960, through Leonard Cornelius.
See brand numbers 660 and 669.

Nº 660   S
Herbert E. Smith
The **S** brand was recorded by Herbert E. Smith of Big Lake, Texas, whose ranch is near Sterling City. The same **S** iron is used to stamp brand number 669.
Source: Herbert Smith, 1960, through our mutual friend, Leonard Cornelius.
See brand numbers 659 and 669.

Nº 661   Seven Coming Seven Going
Billy Smith
The **Seven Coming Seven Going** brand was recorded in Brazoria County in 1945 by Billy Smith of West Columbia, Texas.
Source: Billy Smith, 1960.

Nº 662   S T
Thomas C. Holeman Jr.
The **S T** brand has been used continuously since before 1840 when it was recorded by Thomas C. Holeman and wife in Refugio County. Before 1840, it was used by Susan Teal in Victoria County. Anthony Sideck recorded it in Refugio County in 1882, and then John Sideck ran cattle with the **S T** brand in the county.
Source: Thomas C. Holeman Jr., 1960, at a Victoria, Texas, bank where my branding irons were on exhibit.
(John Sideck's grandfather, John B. Sideck, Anthony's father, came to Texas from Louisiana in 1820 and was one of Victoria County's earliest settlers. John was born in Refugio County in 1846 to Anthony and Catherine Fagan Sideck. He operated Sideck Properties in Refugio County. John never married, so when he died in 1914, he left his estate to his cousin, Mrs. Thomas C. (Rose) Holeman.)

Nº 663   Draw Knife
Ike Gross
The **Draw Knife** brand was recorded in Harris, Brazoria, Matagorda, Brooks, and Galveston counties by Ike Gross of Houston, Texas.
See brand numbers 264, 269, and 279.

Nº 664   Seven I L
L. A. Huber
The **Seven I L** brand is recorded in Austin County by L. A. Huber of Bellville, Texas. It is made by using only one iron—L .
Source: Huber Ranch near the old Kleberg home, 1960.
See brand number 694.

Nº 665   M
Owner unknown
There is no information on the **M** brand.

Nº 666   Bar X
Albert E. Gates
The **Bar X** brand was recorded in Webb County in 1929 for the Gates Cattle Company by Alonzo E. "Lonnie" Gates of Laredo, Texas, "for my children, Albert E., Alonzo W., and Mrs. D. S. (Anita) Elliott."
See brand number 672.
(Lonnie Gates' great grandfather, John Gates, left Virginia and was in Shelby County, Texas, in 1835. The Gates family later settled in the Crystal City area, where they ranched and owned a store. Lonnie, the oldest of seven children, took to cow work rather than merchandising, and in 1902, when he was eighteen, he struck out on his own. He leased land and stocked it with Longhorns. He was soon able to buy 4,020 acres in Webb County for less than a dollar an acre. That was the beginning of Lonnie Gates's successful and respected career as a rancher. He formed a partnership with his children and grandchildren. Lonnie acquired the Espejo Ranch in Webb County in the mid-1930s and sold it in the 1950s to his three children. The 73,000-acre Espejo Ranch was managed by his son, Albert E. Gates. The 57,000-acre Alamo Ranch southwest of Fort Sumner, New Mexico, was owned by Lonnie and his nine grandchildren with grandson A. S. "Tex" Elliott as foreman. The Gates ranches, known for their excellent cattle, are continued by Lonnie Gates' descendants.)

№ 667   Seven A Connected
Welder Cattle Company

The **Seven A Connected** brand was recorded by Jay Welder of the Welder Cattle Company of Victoria, Texas.

Source: Wesley Vivian at a Victoria bank where I had a branding iron exhibit.

See brand numbers 385, 683, 688, and 867.

№ 668   U Backward Seven
Connected
Owner unknown

There is no information on the **U Backward Seven Connected** brand.

№ 669   S Bar
Herbert E. Smith

The **S Bar** brand is recorded by Herbert E. Smith of Big Lake, Texas, and used on his ranch near Sterling City. Smith works for the Texas Highway Department at Bay City.

Source: Herbert Smith, 1960, through our mutual friend, Leonard Cornelius.

See brand numbers 659 and 660.

№ 670   U C
Owner unknown

There is no information on the **U C** brand.

№ 671   F
Owner unknown

There is no information on the **F** brand.

№ 672   A Bar
Alonzo E. Gates

The **A Bar** brand was recorded in Webb County in 1910 by Alonzo Edward Gates of Laredo, Texas. "I have used the **A Bar** brand since I started in the cattle business in 1910," Gates wrote.

Source: A. E. Gates

№ 673   Circle S
O. H. Saver

The **Circle S** brand was originally recorded in 1840 in Tennessee and later in Victoria County, Texas.

Source: O. H. Saver, 1960.

№ 674   Open A
Tyree Vawter

The **Open A** was a trail brand recorded in Grayson County by Tyree Vawter of Sherman, Texas.

See brand number 684.

№ 675   J Dot
John Hunter & Sons

The **J Dot** was a trail brand recorded in Grayson County in north Texas in 1865 by John Hunter & Sons of Sherman. The ranch at that time was near Gunter, Texas. This brand is still in use.

№ 676   C H E Connected
Koontz Ranch

The **C H E Connected** brand was recorded in 1870 in Victoria County by Henry Clay Koontz of the Koontz Ranch at Inez, Texas. Captain Hugh Jordan designed the brand. As many as 5,000 cattle have carried this brand at one time on the 11,000-acre ranch. It is still in use.

(The Koontz Ranch, founded by Henry Clay Koontz Sr., is known for its excellent Brahman cattle. Koontz was a director of the American Brahman Breeders Association, and many of his cattle were shipped to foreign countries to be used as foundation breeding stock. His descendants continue the ranching operations today.)

№ 677   J P Connected
W. L. Pickens

The **J P Connected** brand was recorded in North Texas in Grayson County by W. L. Pickens of Sherman, Texas.

№ 678   C Dash
Louis Kolle Jr.

The **C Dash** brand was recorded in Jackson and Victoria counties in 1922 by Louis Kolle Jr. of Victoria, Texas.

Source: received at the Victoria Bank.

№ 679   I T I
H. S. Thompson

The **I T I** brand was recorded in Wharton County in 1930 by H. S. Thompson of El Campo, Texas.

№ 680   Dash Seven
Lee Hudgins

The **Dash Seven** brand is recorded by Lee Hudgins of Sherman in Grayson County, Texas, and in Oklahoma.

See brand number 685 and 699.

(The Hudgins Ranch was founded by Harry M. "Pete" Hudgins and was known for its fine cattle in Grayson, Fannin, and Cook counties. Today, the ranch is operated by Hudgins' son, Lee, and grandson, Pete.)

№ 681   J P Connected
Joseph H. Polley

The **J P Connected** brand was recorded in Harris, Brazoria, Fort Bend, and Bexar counties in 1840 by Joseph H. Polley of Harrisburg, Texas.

(This iron was found buried ten feet down by an excavating crew while digging the site of the Humble Oil and Refining building in Houston in 1962. Stiles was contacted by the architect to research the owner of the iron. He determined it was Joseph Polley, who had accompanied Stephen F. Austin on his first trip to Texas. The architect gave the iron to Stiles for his collection. Stiles learned that Polley had had cattle pens at the site.

Polley also recorded the **JHP Connected** *brand in Bexar County in 1850. By 1859 and 1860, he owned more cattle than anyone else in Texas. 150,000 head carried his brand and roamed the 150 miles from the San Antonio River to the Rio Grande.)*

№ 682 S M S
Swenson Land & Cattle Company

The **S M S** brand was recorded in Jones County in 1882 by the Swenson Land & Cattle Company of Stamford, Texas.

(The Swenson Ranches were established by Swante Magnus Swenson, a native born Swede who emigrated to Texas in the 1850s. He bought land and entered the mercantile business before going into ranching in 1882. Three ranches were established and managed by Swenson's sons, Eric and Swen Albin. Those ranches were known as the Throckmorton, Mount Albin, and Flat Top.

In 1883, the Swensons acquired the Ellerslie Ranch and later the Espuela Ranch. They also donated land for the city of Stamford, a city that continues to be a center of ranching activity and the site of the Texas Cowboy Reunion each July.

Under the management of Frank Hastings, the ranch bred fine Hereford cattle and made innovations such as mail-order buying of cattle, selling cattle by the pound instead of by the head, and dehorning cattle when they were young.

In 1978, the heirs of the Swenson Land & Cattle Company divided the ranch into four companies: Swen R. Swenson Cattle Company, Tongue River Ranch Company, Throckmorton Land & Cattle Company, and SMS Ranch Company. Swen R. Swenson Cattle Company kept the original **SMS** *brand. Today, the Swen R. Swenson Ranch is managed by Gary Mathis.)*

№ 683 Upside Down L Little L
John J. Welder

The **Upside Down L Little L** brand was recorded in 1932 in Victoria, Bee, San Patricio, and Calhoun counties by John J. Welder. The brand is registered in ten locations.

Source: Jay Welder at the Victoria bank where my collection was displayed.

See brand numbers 385, 667, 688, and 867.

(John J. Welder, a member of a prominent South Texas ranching family, and the brother of James F. Welder, built the Victoria National Bank. He was the first Texas rancher to practice tick eradication.)

№ 684 Double V
Tyree Vawter

The **Double V** brand was recorded In Grayson County by Tyree Vawter of Sherman, Texas.

See brand number 674.

№ 685 Dash
Harry Hudgins

The Dash brand was recorded by Harry Hudgins of Sherman, Texas. It is a transit brand.

See brand numbers 680 and 699.

(Trail or road brands were used when cattle were in transit to a different location.)

№ 686 3
Owner unknown

The 3 brand is a road brand from Sherman, Texas.

№ 687 T L Connected
Charlie Brandes

The **T L Connected** brand is recorded in Brazoria and Victoria counties by Charlie Brandes of Victoria, Texas.

Source: received at the Victoria Bank, 1960.

№ 688 L Little L
Welder Cattle Company

The **L Little L** brand was recorded in 1932 in Victoria County by the Welder Cattle Company. It is the same brand as number 683 but put on right side up.

See brand numbers 385, 667, 683, and 867.

№ 689 Seven Y
Otto Borchers

The **Seven Y** brand was recorded in Lavaca, Dewitt, Jackson, and Gonzales counties by Otto Borchers of Yoakum, Texas.

№ 690 T A Connected
A. C. Thompson

The **T A Connected** brand was recorded in Wharton County in 1913 by A. C. Thompson of El Campo, Texas.

Source: 1959 at El Campo.

№ 691 R
Rudisell & Pickins

The **R** brand was recorded in Grayson County by Rudisell & Pickins of Sherman, Texas.

№ 692 Brand name unknown
E. W. Farmer

This brand was recorded in Fort Bend County in 1891 by E. W. Farmer of Richmond, Texas. It was found under the chute at an abandoned set of pens on the Bernard River near Boling, Texas.

Source: Farmer ranch foreman, Dick Clawson, 1959.

Nº 693   J A Connected
Charlie Brandes

The **J A Connected** brand was recorded in Victoria and Brazoria counties by Charlie Brandes of Victoria, Texas.

See brand number 687.

Nº 694   T A L Connected
L. A. Huber

The **T A L Connected** brand was recorded in Austin County by L. A. Huber of Bellville, Texas. Only one iron, the **L**, is used to make this brand and other brands owned by Mr. Huber. This is a very old iron.

Source: Huber Ranch near the old Robert Justus Kleberg home at Cat Spring, Texas, 1960.

See brand number 664.

Nº 695   Dash B Dash
Beetle Ranch

The **Dash B Dash** brand was recorded in Matagorda, Brazoria, and Fort Bend counties by the Beetle Ranch near Buckeye, Texas, owned by Clive Runnels. Runnels is a part owner of the Pierce Estate.

Nº 696   C Cross
Cobb Cattle Company

The **C Cross** brand was recorded in 1940 in Fort Bend County by the Cobb Cattle Company of Needville, Texas. The brand is placed on the left thigh.

Source: 1961.

Nº 697   H T Bar
Owner unknown

There is no information on the **H T Bar** brand.

Nº 698   Pitchfork
Pitchfork Land & Cattle Company

The **Pitchfork** brand was recorded in King and Dickens counties in 1883 by the Pitchfork Land & Cattle Company of Guthrie, Texas.

*(About May 1879, an Irishman, Jerry Savage, drove 2,300 head of cattle carrying the **Pitchfork** brand through Fort Griffin, Texas. He sold his cattle and his brand in 1881 to D. B. Gardner and Col. J. S. Godwin, and they acquired land in King and Dickens counties. In 1882, Godwin sold his interests to Eugene F. Williams, and one year later, A. P. Bush Jr. of St. Louis became a co-owner of the ranch. The current Pitchfork Land & Cattle Company was organized in St. Louis in 1883.*

D. B. Gardner was manager of the ranch for forty-seven years, followed by Virgil Parr, D. Burns, and Jim Humphreys. Each man made significant contributions to developing the Pitchfork into a modern ranching operation with cultivation of winter wheat and oats, cross fencing, water development, mill operations, improved feeding, and the establishment of swine, sheep, and horse programs. Since 1969, helicopters have been used during roundups, and in 1980, oil production greatly boosted ranch income.

Today, the Texas ranch of 165,000 acres is divided into eighty pastures. The ranch also has holdings near Topeka, Kansas. The Pitchfork Ranch currently runs registered Herefords plus Simbrah, Limousin, and Beefmaster cattle. Ranch operations are directed by Eugene F. Williams Jr., a grandson of one of the founders, and Bob Moorhouse has been manager since 1986.)

Nº 699   Double H
Harry Hudgins

The **Double H** brand was recorded in Grayson County by Harry Hudgins of Sherman, Texas.

Source: Lee and Harry Hudgins, while in Sherman with Sheriff Tiny Gaston of Fort Bend County.

See brand numbers 680 and 685.

Nº 700   Pitcher
Ed Raymond

The **Pitcher** brand was recorded in Willacy County by Ed Raymond of Raymondville, Texas. The brand is also called **La Jarra**. E. B. Raymond first recorded it in Cameron County in 1882.

Source: Ed Raymond, Raymondville, Texas, 1961.

Nº 701   O O
Roscoe Seago

The **O O** brand was originally recorded in Duval County in 1895 by Francis Smith. It was then recorded by Smith and Ed Corkill of the Solidad Ranch in 1916 in Freer, Texas, and placed on the right side. A rock house over 100 years old still stands on the Solidad Ranch. Roscoe Seagoe recorded the brand in Duval County in 1949 and places it on the left rib.

Source: I received the original iron from Roscoe Seago.

Nº 702   Brand name unknown
Sartartia Plantation

This brand was recorded in Fort Bend County by the Sartartia Plantation of Sugarland, Texas.

Nº 703   Backward R
Bob Raley

The **Backward R** brand on the right hip is recorded by Bob Raley of Garwood, Texas, and is used on the Cedar Post Ranch. Raley is Bill Frnka's son-in-law.

Nº 704   Brand name unknown
Sinencio and Cinencio Guitierrez

This Mexican-style brand was recorded in Webb and Duval counties in 1900 by Sinencio and Cinencio Guitierrez. The iron is over 100 years old and was found near the Dobe house-store on the Solidad Ranch. This old place is made with square nails and is about four miles from the present house.

Source: ranch foreman Roscoe Seago, 1961.

Nº 705   Half Moon
Armstrong Ranch

The **Half Moon** brand was recorded in Kenedy and Willacy counties by the Armstrong Ranch of Armstrong, Texas, forty-two miles south of Kingsville.

See brand numbers 706, 728, and 805.

(The Armstrong Ranch was founded by Major James H. Durst, Collector of Customs for the District of Brazos Santiago. In 1852, he bought 92,000 acres, ⅕ of the La Barreta grant, located forty miles south of Captain Richard King's Santa Gertrudis grant. He was at one time a partner of Mifflin Kenedy and Richard King in a transport business. After Durst died, his widow sold the land but received little for it. John B. Armstrong, who married Durst's daughter, later regained the land for the family.

Armstrong made his mark as a Texas Ranger before he did as a rancher. He was Captain Leander McNelly's sergeant and Captain Lee Hall's lieutenant. The history of the family and the ranch is told in the Armstrong Chronicles, published in 1986.

When John Armstrong died, his brother Tom took over management of the ranch and continued to improve and upgrade the operation. Management of the ranch next passed to Tom's nephew, Tobin Armstrong, whose wife Anne was named Ambassador to Great Britain. Armstrong continued to stock the ranches in Jim Hogg, Willacy, and Kenedy counties and in Louisiana with both registered and commercial Santa Gertrudis cattle. The Armstrong family is well known in ranching circles and continues its rich South Texas heritage.)

Nº 706   Circle 7 6
Armstrong Ranch

The **Circle 7 6** brand was recorded in Kenedy and Willacy counties by the Armstrong Ranch of Armstrong, Texas. Tobin Armstrong's foreman, Augustine Cavazos, remembers riding **Circle 7 6** horses for army buyers during remount days.

Source: Augustine Cavazos, 1961.
See brand numbers 705, 728, and 805.

Nº 707   O
Vernon L. Chambliss

The **O** brand on the left shoulder was recorded in Brazoria County by Vernon L. Chambliss of Sweeny, Texas.

Nº 708   H Seven Bar
Alex F. Hood

The **H Seven Bar** brand was recorded in Brazoria County by Alex F. Hood of Sweeny, Texas.

Nº 709   Four H Connected Bar
Owner unknown

There is no information on the **Four H Connected Bar** brand.

Nº 710   S U
Willard Johnston

The **S U** brand was recorded in Austin and Fort Bend counties by Willard Johnston of Wallis, Texas.

Nº 711   9 6
Roscoe Seago

The **9 6** brand, recorded in Duval County by Roscoe Seago of San Diego, Texas, was first recorded by J. D. "Doss" Seago in 1922 and again in 1945. It was transferred to Roscoe Seago in 1951. The brand is placed on the left side.

See brand number 712.

(One iron is used to make both the 9 and the 6. It is the same iron as used to make brand number 712—the 9.)

Nº 712   9
Roscoe Seago

The **9** brand, recorded in Duval, Webb, and Medina counties by Roscoe Seago of Freer, Texas, was originally recorded in Duval County by J. D. "Doss" Seago of San Diego in 1945. It was transferred to Roscoe Seago in 1951. This is the same iron used to brand the **9 6** (brand number 711).

Source: 1961.
See brand number 711.

Nº 713   A W H
Heath Brothers

The **A W H** brand was recorded in 1935 in Cameron County by Aubrey and Wayne Heath of Rio Hondo, Texas. It is placed on the left hip or left loin.

Source: 1961.

Nº 714   J F Connected
W. A. Furber & Albert Johnson

The **J F Connected** brand was recorded in Matagorda County from 1914 to 1946 by W. A. Furber and Albert Johnson of Markham, Texas.

Source: A. H. Johnson at his ranch.

Nº 715   Bar H
Bill Huvar

The **Bar H** brand was recorded in Colorado County by Bill Huvar of Garwood, Texas.

Nº 716   L F C
Lauro F. Cavazos

The **L F C** brand was recorded in Kleberg and Willacy counties in 1940 by Lauro F. Cavazos of Kingsville, Texas. This iron was lost in route from Germany after a portion of the collection had been on tour in Europe.

(Lauro Cavazos went to work for the King Ranch in 1912 when he was eighteen years old. When Sam Ragland retired in 1926, Cavazos replaced him as foreman of the Santa Gertrudis Division, a position he held until his death in 1958.)

Nº 717   E Lazy E
Dr. C. M. Corbett

The **E Lazy E** brand was recorded in Willacy County by Dr. C. M. Corbett of Raymondville, Texas. It is placed anywhere on either side of cattle. This brand is put on with the same iron used on brand number 718.

See brand number 718.

Nº 718   Upside Down E Backward E
Dr. C. M. Corbett

The **Upside Down E Backward E** brand was recorded in Hidalgo County by Dr. C. M. Corbett of Raymondville, Texas. It is put on with the same iron used on brand number 717.

See brand number 717.

Nº 719   V D Connected Bar
V. N. "Dick" Dawson

The **V D Connected Bar** brand was recorded in Victoria County in 1907 by V. N. "Dick" Dawson of Alvin, Texas, who recorded it in Jackson County in 1912; in Brazoria County in 1917; and in Galveston County in 1938. The **D** and **Bar** are separate irons.

Source: 1961.

Nº 720   T I X
B. J. Resoft

The **T I X** brand was recorded in Brazoria County in 1927 by B. J. Resoft of Alvin, Texas. The brand is made with a bar iron.

Source: 1961.

Nº 721   6 2
Sherwood Cook

The **6 2** brand was recorded in Anderson County by Sherwood Cook in Palestine, Texas. The iron is first used to make the **6** part of the brand and then reversed and a tail is added to form the **2**. Cook's grandfather originally used this brand in 1862, and Cook runs cattle in the same pasture his grandfather did.

Source: Tom H. Carothers, Palestine, Texas.

Nº 722   Seven H C Connected
R. H. Clark

The **Seven H C Connected** brand was recorded in Brazoria County in 1948 by R. H. Clark of Kingsville, Texas.

Nº 723   3 3
Owner unknown

There is no information on the **3 3** brand.

Nº 724   Half Circle Dot
R. S. Muil

The **Half Circle Dot** brand was recorded in Kleberg County in 1947 by R. S. Muil.

Source: Stan McFarland, Kingsville, Texas, 1964.

Nº 725   A V
J. A. Matthews Ranch Company

The **A V** brand of the Lambshead Ranch was recorded in Throckmorton and Shackelford counties in 1885 by the J. A. Matthews Ranch Company of Albany, Texas. It is one iron stamped twice.

Source: Watt Matthews, 1962.

(The 45,000-acre Lambshead Ranch near Albany, Texas, was established by J. A. Matthews and named for Thomas Lambshead of Devon, England, an early settler of the area.

The Matthews family came to Throckmorton and Shackelford counties in 1858, and after the Civil War, they established ranching operations in the bend of the Clear Fork of the Brazos River. They became friends with their neighbors, the Reynolds, who arrived in 1859. The merging of these two great ranching families through marriage is told in the 1936 book, Interwoven by Sallie Ann Reynolds Matthews.

J. A. Matthews and Sallie Ann Reynolds married in 1876 and together, they established what has become one of Texas' most historic ranches. They had nine children. The youngest was a son, Watkins Reynolds Matthews, born in 1899. Watt lived his whole life on the ranch except for his years at Princeton University in the early 1920s.

When J. A. Matthews died in 1941, Watt and his brother, Joe B. Matthews, assumed joint control of the ranch. Joe, a TSCRA director, died in 1977.

Lambshead Ranch was the center of Watt Matthews' life, and he devoted all of his time and energies into holding the vast ranch together. Over the years, he worked the land and constantly improved the herds of their prize-winning Herefords. Since 1920, Watt kept a diary of daily events including such things as the price of cattle, rainfall, direction of the wind, pasture conditions, fence mending, and other factors pertaining to ranching business.

Matthews not only preserved the history of his family ranch, but he was involved in the activities of Albany and of the Fort Griffin Fandangle each June. Watt Matthews died at the age of ninety-eight in 1997.)

№ 726   J K Connected Bar
Dr. J. K. Northway

The **J K Connected Bar** brand was recorded in Kleberg County in 1917 by Dr. J. K. Northway of Kingsville, Texas, and is placed on the left hip or the left shoulder of horses.

Source: Dr. J. K. Northway, 1964.

See brand numbers 811 and 813.

(J. K. Northway, Doctor of Veterinary Medicine, arrived at the King Ranch in 1916 when he was just out of college and was the head veterinarian there until his death. Dr. Northway was gifted in the knowledge of livestock conformation and genetics, and he was instrumental in the ranch's development of its outstanding Quarter Horses and Thoroughbreds and the creation of a new breed of cattle, the Santa Gertrudis.)

№ 727   Diamond
Tom East

The **Diamond** brand was recorded in Jim Hogg, Starr, Zapata, Frio, and Webb counties by Tom East of Hebbronville, Texas.

Source: Tom East, April 21, 1964.

(Tom T. East married Alice Gertrudis Kleberg, Captain Richard King's granddaughter, on January 30, 1915, in the newly finished "big house" on the King Ranch. They lived on the San Antonio Viejo Ranch in Jim Hogg and Starr counties to the southwest of the Santa Gertrudis Division.)

№ 728   Star
John B. Armstrong

The **Star** brand was recorded in Duval County, Texas, and in Autauga County, Alabama, by John B. Armstrong of Armstrong, Texas.

(John B. Armstrong is a descendant of the founder of the Armstrong Ranch who in 1944 married a member of the King Ranch family and later served as president of the ranch. He has long been active in the cattle and ranching business and was president of the TSCRA from 1978–1980.)

№ 729   Lazy Y T
Yturria Ranch

The **Lazy Y T** brand was recorded in Kenedy and Willacy counties by the Yturria Ranch of Brownsville, Texas. The **Y** is for Yturria, and the **T** is for Trevino.

(The Yturria Ranch was founded by Francisco Yturria during the 1850s. Yturria ranched in Mexico and in five counties in Texas. He was in the banking business and worked closely with other well-known South Texas ranchers including Mifflin Kenedy and Captain Richard King. The Yturria Ranch became known for its fine Santa Gertrudis cattle. Today, the ranch continues operation directed by Frank Yturria, great-grandson of its founder.)

№ 730   C
R. A. Coughran

The **C** brand was recorded in Harris and Brazoria counties.

Source: 1964.

№ 731   Running W
King Ranch

The **Running W** brand is recorded in Kleberg County by the King Ranch, Kingsville, Texas.

See brand numbers 45, 93, 584, and 980.

№ 732   Bow Tie or Corbota
Callaghan Land and Cattle and Pastoral Company

The **Bow Tie** or **Corbota** brand was recorded in La Salle and Webb counties in 1909 by the Callaghan Land and Cattle and Pastoral Company of Encinal, Texas.

Source: Travis Peeler, 1964.

See brand numbers 29, 737, and 765.

(The Callaghan Land and Cattle and Pastoral Company was founded as a sheep ranch soon after the Civil War by Charles Callaghan, who had served in the war and was a younger brother of one of the early mayors of San Antonio. He died of pneumonia in 1874, and the 70,000-acre ranch went to his heirs. In 1909, they sold it to Thomas A. Coleman, David Beals, and George Ford, who converted it to a cattle ranch once they could drill wells and water became more plentiful. Coleman managed the ranch, and when he retired, Joe B. Finley Sr. was named manager. The ranch grew to more than 200,000 acres and prospered under Finley's able management during the next forty-seven years. Then he became joint-owner when he and his son, Joe Finley Jr., purchased the Callaghan Ranch.)

№ 733   F M J Connected
Joseph F. Meyers

The **F M J Connected** brand was recorded in Harris County by Joseph F. Meyers of Houston, Texas.

№ 734   S G
Sally Gregory

The **S G** brand was recorded in Matagorda County by Sally Gregory of Bay City, Texas.

№ 735   7 1 1
Lucky 7 1 1 Ranch

The **7 1 1** brand was recorded in Bexar County by the Lucky 7 1 1 Ranch of San Antonio, Texas.

№ 736   E L
Elsinore Cattle Company

The **E L** brand was started in 1886 in Pecos County by J. S. Lockwood and is the first two letters in the name of his Elsinore Cattle Company. The **E** is placed on the left side and the **L** on the left hip.

Lockwood sold the Elsinore Cattle Company in 1900 to E. W. Giddings and William Lennox, the present owners. The 186,000-acre ranch runs from 4,000 to 5,000 Hereford cattle in this brand.

№ 737   Brand name unknown
Callaghan Land and Cattle and
Pastoral Company

This brand was recorded in South Texas, probably in La Salle and Webb counties, and in Mexico by the Callaghan Land and Cattle and Pastoral Company of Encinal, Texas.

See brand numbers 29, 732, and 765.

№ 738   T D Connected
Tom Browner

The **T D Connected** brand was recorded in Fort Bend County by Tom Browner of Houston, Texas. He was lost in Alaska in 1965.

Source: Tom Browner in Dr. Northway's office on the King Ranch, 1964.

№ 739   J H E Connected
Joe B. Finley Jr.

The **J H E Connected** brand is recorded in Webb County by Joe B. Finley Jr. of the Callaghan Land and Cattle Company, Encinal, Texas.

See brand numbers 743, 771, and 773.

№ 740   Stirrup
Dr. Tom Fagan

The **Stirrup** brand was recorded by Dr. Tom Fagan of Tivoli, Texas.

Source: Dr. Tom Fagan, 1964, in Dr. Northway's office, the King Ranch.

№ 741   Lazy S
Jim Beggs

The **Lazy S** brand on the left rib was recorded in Cameron County by Jim Beggs of the Herbert Buesing Estate of San Benito, Texas.

Source: Texas Ranger Jerome H. Preiss, Harlingen, Texas.

№ 742   Z A
Mrs. Corinne Cecilia Byrne

The **Z A** brand was recorded in 1881 in McMullen County by Mrs. Corinne Cecilia Byrne. It is believed she used this brand on the coast prior to that time. Her late husband, Charles Byrne, was one of the founders of Lamar, Texas. Her children use variations of the brand as their own brands.

Source: Raymond Block, her granddaughter's husband, 1964.

№ 743   F Cross
Joe B. Finley Jr.

The **F Cross** brand belongs to Joe B. Finley of Encinal, Texas. It is used in Mexico as well as in Texas.

№ 744   Three
W. B. Clark

The **Three** brand on the left side was recorded in 1926 in Limestone County, Texas, and in Oklahoma by W. B. Clark. J. J. Beckham had recorded it in 1900 in Limestone County.

Source: W. B. Clark during a TSCRA convention in Dallas.

№ 745   Arrowhead
George Echols

The **Arrowhead** brand was recorded in Harris and McMullen counties by George Echols of Houston, Texas, and used on the Arrowhead Ranch at Tilden. Harry Brown is the present owner of the ranch.

Source: foreman Pryor Reagan at the ranch, 1964.

№ 746   D E E
G. F. Plummer

The **D E E** brand was recorded in 1923 in Galveston and Brazoria counties. This is the first iron Plummer had when he started in the cattle business. The brand was purchased by Doug Latimer.

See brand number 620.

№ 747   Lazy S
James A. Seymour

The **Lazy S** brand was recorded in 1885 in Columbus, Texas, in Colorado County by James A. Seymour.

№ 748   S P
L. L. Rhodes

The **S P** brand was recorded in Matagorda County by L. L. Rhodes of Blessing, Texas.

Source: 1963.

№ 749   Half Circle L
Les Geddes

The **Half Circle L** brand was recorded by Les Geddes of Rockford, Illinois, owner of Greenlee Machinery and Tools.

№ 750   J T
J. T. Whisenhutt

The **J T** brand was recorded in Jim Wells County by J. T. Whisenhutt of Alice, Texas.

Source: Travis Peeler, 1964.

№ 751   W R Connected
Winthrop Rockefeller

The **W R Connected** brand is recorded in Arkansas by Win-rock Farms, owned by Winthrop Rockefeller.

See brand number 873.

(Winthrop Rockefeller, a member of the famed Rockefeller family, was a well-known Santa Gertrudis and Hereford breeder. He was Governor of Arkansas from 1967–1971.)

№ 752 O L F Connected
Ursual Broussard

The **O L F Connected** brand was recorded in 1875 in Jefferson County, Texas, by Ursual Broussard of Taylor's Bayou. Her father, Tayo Broussard, came from Louisiana and settled near Port Acres, Texas. At his death, the ranch was abandoned, and T. F. Parish purchased it in 1903.

Parish story continues with brand number 754. See brand number 761 for earlier brands.

(From a 1963 letter from H. E. Parish of Menard, Texas, to his son, Norman Parish of Brownsville, concerning the branding irons given to Leonard Stiles: "The O L F brand was recorded in 1875 by Ursual Broussard, a sister of your Grandmother in Jefferson County. The father of the owner of this brand came to Texas from Louisiana in an ox cart and settled near Port Arthur on Taylor's Bayou. The old headquarters ranch consisted of approximately seven leagues of land which is partly covered by the town of Port Acres near Port Arthur. This ranch was abandoned after the death of Tayo Broussard who contracted pneumonia as a result of swimming cattle across the Neches River near Port Arthur to winter pasturage in the marshes on the coast near Orange.

"With the discovery of oil (1900), an active interest was again taken in this property, however it was too late for the heirs to do much about a clear title since much of the land was acquired by trading horses, cattle, etc., for the land which probably never had a clear title to start with. Tayo Broussard was one of Dick Dowling's men that defended Sabine Pass during the Civil War and captured a few Yankee ships that got stuck on the sand bars.

"The O L F brand and cattle were purchased by T. F. Parish in 1903, and this brand was used on cattle that were confined to pastures near Beaumont, Texas.")

№ 753 Arrowhead
Arrowhead Ranch

This brand could be a simplified version of the Arrowhead brand of the previous owner of the Arrowhead Ranch of Tilden, Texas. This brand was recorded in McMullen County by Harry Brown and used on his Arrowhead Ranch.

See brand number 745.

№ 754 Little h R
Clariece Broussard

The **Little h R** brand was recorded by Clariece Broussard in 1879 in Jefferson and Chambers counties. T. F. Parish purchased the brand and cattle carrying it in 1924. Perry DuBois and T. F. Parish used it as a company brand until 1945.

See brand numbers 752 and 761 for more of the Parish brands story.

(Continued from a 1963 letter written by H. E. Parish of Menard, Texas, to his son, Norman Parish of Brownsville, concerning the history of the branding irons given to Leonard Stiles:

". . . h R—This brand was recorded in Jefferson County, Texas, in 1879 by Clairece Broussard, a sister of your grandmother Parish and the daughter of Tayo Broussard who established the Broussard ranch referred to in an earlier paragraph in discussing the O L F brand.

"This brand and cattle were purchased by T. F. Parish in 1924. The brand was used rather extensively by Perry DuBois and T. F. Parish as a company brand until about 1945. Most of the cattle were maintained on holdings in Chambers County but were moved to summer pastures in Jefferson County when pastures got short.")

№ 755 Crown
Davila Family

The **Crown** (with **M C** placed under it) is part of the brand of the Davila family of Santa Marta, Colombia, in South America.

Source: Francisco Solano of the Davila family, 1959, Edgar Hudgins's office in Hungerford, Texas.

See brand number 756.

№ 756 M C
Davila Family

The **M C** brand is placed beneath the **Crown** brand by the Davila family of Santa Marta, Colombia, in South America.

Source: Francisco Solano of the Davila family, 1959, Edgar Hudgins's office in Hungerford, Texas.

See brand number 755.

№ 757 Pitcher
Button Evans

The **Pitcher** brand was recorded in 1877 by a Negro, Button Evans, who lived near Groesbeck in Limestone County. His horses were branded on the left shoulder and cattle were branded on the left hip. Evans had been a slave and was once owned by a man named Stroud who had land in that area. Evans was born in Vicksburg, Mississippi, in 1822, and died in 1935 at the age of 112.

Source: Norton Fox purchased this iron in 1963 from Button Evans's son, Arthur Evans, and gave it to me in 1964.

№ 758 C D
Norton Fox

History of the **C D** iron unknown.

Source: Norton Fox of Groesbeck, Texas, 1964.

№ 759 T E Connected N
Mrs. Elizabeth Dawdy

The **T E Connected N** brand was recorded in 1875 by Mrs. Elizabeth Dawdy. J. R. Rowles of Blessing, Texas, uses it in Matagorda County.

See brand number 287.

Nº 760   Four W
Wharton Weems

The **Four W** brand was recorded in Harris and Fort Bend counties of Texas and also in California by Wharton Weems of Houston, Texas.

Nº 761   Z H R Connected
T. F. Parish

The **Z H R Connected** brand was recorded in 1888 in Jefferson County, Texas, by T. F. "Tom" Parish. It was used by the Parish family until 1943, when all cattle wearing the Parish brands were sold. See excerpt from letter below.

Source: Norman Parish of Kingsville, Texas, 1963.

See brand numbers 752 and 754 for more Parish brand history.

(Excerpt from letter from H. E. Parish of Menard, Texas, to his son, Norman Parish of Kingsville, Texas, with history of the Parish branding irons given to Leonard Stiles in 1963: "The Z H R Connected brand was one that was used by George Parish in Georgia before the Civil War. It was inherited from George Parish by T. F. "Tom" Parish and recorded in Jefferson County, Texas, in 1888. It is not known if the brand was recorded in Georgia.

"This Z H R Connected brand was used by T. F. Parish on cattle known as outside cattle—in other words, cattle that were run on the open range which extended from Beaumont to Port Arthur, down the coast to Bolivar, Anahuac, and Devers, back to the Neches River.

"When the open range was fenced, this brand of cattle were moved to pastures in the vicinity of Beaumont. I helped gather the remainder of the outside cattle during 1919 and put them in confinement. I was unable to get an estimate to the number of cattle that were branded with the Z H R Connected brand since dad is ninety-four and his hearing is not so sharp. All cattle and horses were sold about 1943, but the brands were retained by the Parish family.")

Nº 762   D 7 Bar
T. F. Parish

The **D 7 Bar** brand was a Parish brand that was used very little. There is no history on it.

Source: Norman Parish, 1963.

See brand numbers 752, 754, and 761.

Nº 763   3 Half Circle
Raymond Black

The **3 Half Circle** brand was recorded in McMullen County, Texas, by Raymond Black.

Nº 764   A Half Circle
A. Hooge & Company

The **A Half Circle** brand was recorded in Atascosa County in 1926 and is used by A. Hooge & Company of Poteet, Texas. William Hickey, a blacksmith in Poteet, made this iron in 1917. The brand was canceled in 1961.

Source: L. A. Hooge.

Nº 765   Bosal
Callaghan Land & Cattle Company

The **Bosal** brand was recorded in Webb County by the Callaghan Land & Cattle Company of Encinal, Texas.

See brand numbers 29, 732, and 737.

Nº 766   Brand name unknown
Tom Browner

This brand was recorded in Harris County by Tom Browner of Houston, Texas. He was lost in Alaska in 1965.

See brand number 738 and 767.

Nº 767   Circle A
Tom Browner

The **Circle A** brand was recorded in Harris County by Tom Browner of Houston, Texas.

Source: Tom Browner.

See brand number 738 and 766.

Nº 768   4 E
Lonnie Stewart

The **4 E** brand was received from Lonnie Stewart of Three Rivers, Texas, in Live Oak County.

Nº 769   T A Connected
Francisco Armendiaz

The **T A Connected** brand was recorded by Francisco Armendiaz of Brownsville, Texas, in Cameron and Willacy counties.

Source: Mr. Gooch at Raymondville, 1966, through J. L. McDougald.

Nº 770   Dash J Dash
Lyndon Baines Johnson

The **Dash J Dash** brand on the left hip was recorded in 1952 in Gillespie County by Lyndon Baines Johnson.

Source: 1965, with the help of Ben Glusing. J. M. Dillinger of Corpus Christi made contact with President Johnson and his ranch manager, who sent the iron.

(Lyndon B. Johnson also recorded the J O brand in Blanco County in 1960. He served in the U.S. House of Representatives, the U.S. Senate as Majority Leader, as Vice-President of the United States, and as the 38th President of the United States from 1963–1968. LBJ raised Hereford cattle on his ranch near Johnson City in Blanco County.)

Nº 771   U S
Joe B. Finley

I received the **U S** branding iron from Joe B. Finley of Encinal, Texas, in 1964. He uses the brand in the United States and in Mexico.

See brand numbers 29, 732, 737, 739, 743, 765, 772, and 773.

O

№ 772   O
Callaghan Land & Cattle Company
The **O** brand was recorded in Webb County by the Callaghan Land & Cattle Company of Encinal, Texas.

See brand numbers 29, 732, 737, 739, 743, 765, 771, and 773.

SB

№ 773   S B
Joe B. Finley Jr.
The **S B** branding iron came from Joe B. Finley Jr. of Encinal, Texas, in Webb County through Travis Peeler, 1964.

See brand numbers 29, 732, 737, 739, 743, 765, 771, and 772.

FC

№ 774   F C
Felipe Guerra
The **F C** brand was purchased by the King Ranch in 1874 from Felipe Guerra of Las Viboras Ranch of northern Starr County.

Source: Texas Ranger Jerome Priess.

R

№ 775   R
Atwood Trust
The **R** brand is used by the Edwin, Alice, and Richard Atwood Trust of Raymondville, Texas, in Willacy and Kenedy Counties. The brand is placed on the left hip on cattle and on the left shoulder of horses. It is used on the part of the ranch north of Ranch Road 497.

Source: Beto Durham, Kingsville, Texas, 1965.

See brand number 776.

(*Henrietta M. King, called Nettie, was Captain and Mrs. Richard King's oldest child. She married Colonel E. B. Atwood. She and her mother were estranged, and the Atwoods lived in Chicago and had little to do with the ranch or their Texas kin. Nettie died in 1918 and was survived by three children—Edwin, Alice, and Richard. When Henrietta King died in 1925 at the age of ninety-two, her Atwood heirs inherited the Sauz Ranch, south of the Norias Division. While the legal matters were being settled, the Sauz Ranch was held in trust and managed for twenty-five years by Trustees of the estate.*)

∩

№ 776   Open A
Atwood Trust
The **Open A** brand is used by the Edwin, Alice, and Richard Atwood Trust of Raymondville, Texas, in Willacy and Kenedy counties. It is used on the Sauz Ranch south of Ranch Road 497. It is placed on the left hip on cattle and on the left shoulder on horses.

Source: Beto Durham, Kingsville, Texas, 1965.

See brand number 775.

S

№ 777   S
Santa Gertrudis Breeders International
The **S** is a brand of Santa Gertrudis Breeders International of Kingsville, Texas, and was first used on Santa Gertrudis cattle in 1951.

See brand number 778.

S̲

№ 778   S Bar
Santa Gertrudis Breeders International
The **S Bar** brand is the "International Certified" brand of the Santa Gertrudis Breeders International of Kingsville, Texas. The first classification of the breed was done by A. O. Rhodes, assisted by Walter M. Cardwell Sr., first president of the SGBI. This event took place on October 12, 1951, at the J. T. Maltsburger Jr. Ranch near Cotulla, Texas. At that time, 310 females and 14 bulls were branded. The irons in the collection were the actual irons used to brand the first of the Santa Gertrudis breed of cattle. These irons had been made into andirons for the fireplace in the Rhodes home.

Source: Mrs. Albert Rhodes at a polo game at John Armstrong's, 1964.

See brand number 777.

(*A great, red, prepotent bull named Monkey, born in 1920, was the foundation sire from whose progeny came the Santa Gertrudis breed developed by the King Ranch. The ranch held its first annual auction sale of Santa Gertrudis bulls at the ranch on November 10, 1950.*)

E

№ 779   T E Connected
Owner unknown
There is no information on the **T E Connected** brand.

JH

№ 780   J H H Connected
J. H. Harrison
The **J H H Connected** brand was recorded in Kleberg County by J. H. Harrison of Riviera, Texas.

Source: Orvil Heathcoat and J. L. McDougald, 1966.

‡

№ 781   Lorraine Cross
Ruthel McMahon
The **Lorraine Cross** brand is recorded in Lampasas and Mills counties by Mrs. F. H. (Ruthel) McMahon of Temple, Texas. Her daughter, Mrs. Calvin Barker of Fort Worth, named the brand. Ruthel McMahon has leased the Baugh Ranch, which is owned by her mother, since 1946. The ranch has been in the family since about 1870.

The McMahons are descendents of Marie Edme Patrice de McMahon, who was Marshall of France when Lorraine was a province of eastern France. During the Thirty Years War, a series of European wars from 1618–1648, Germany adopted the cross and named it after the Kingdom of Lotharingia Lorraine. Lorraine was under German control from 1871–1919 and 1940–1944. Since 1945, Lorraine has been divided into three departments of France.

Nº 782   Double Heart
Matthew Cartwright

The **Double Heart** brand is recorded in Kaufman and La Salle counties and has been used by the Cartwright family since 1870. Two irons are used to make the brand—a heart and a half heart. Matthew and Lon Cartwright's sister designed the brand when they ran cattle together. After a short time, Matthew bought his brother's part and continued in the cattle business alone. He registered the **Double Heart** brand in his name in 1870 in Kaufman and La Salle counties and again in 1902. He used it on the most cattle from 1895 to 1912 when he branded from 5,000 to 7,000 steers each year.

In later years, Matthew Cartwright Jr. used the brand in La Salle County for range cattle from 1940 to 1962 and on his ranch in Kaufman County for his certified Santa Gertrudis. Virginia DeWitt Cartwright, the daughter of James I. Cartwright Jr., continues to use the brand.

Source: Holman Cartwright of Dinero, Texas, at his Twin Oaks Ranch. An oak tree in Cartwright's front yard is said to be 700 years old.

See brand numbers 807, 808, and 810.

Nº 783   J P Connected
Jack and Polly Love

The **J P Connected** brand originated by using the **J** for Jack Love and the **P** for Polly Love. It was recorded in Llano County in 1938 and has since been recorded in Bastrop, Williamson, Atascosa, and Brewster counties, Texas. It is also recorded with the Registrar of Brands in South Dakota. Jack Love places it on the left side of cattle. Kathleen (now Mrs. James Orr) and Ben Love recorded it in Llano and Brewster counties and turned it sixty degrees to make a lazy brand on the left hip of steer cattle. Originally used on fifteen head of good Hereford heifers, today it is on about 800 cows and heifers.

Source: Ben Love at a polo game, 1965.

Nº 784   Bar C
D. N. Chambers Estate

The **Bar C** brand is used by the Bar C Ranches of the D. N. Chambers Estate of Houston, Texas. C. M. Morgan is the manager. The brand was originally recorded by Dunbor Chambers in Real, Houston, Waller, Harris, and Fort Bend counties and in Louisiana. At the time of his death in 1956, Chambers was president of Farnsworth & Chambers Company Incorporated of Houston, the world's third largest contracting company.

Source: Charlie Morgan, 1965.

No 785   C F
Mrs. C. A. Ford

The **C F** brand was recorded by Mrs. C. A. Ford in 1921. It is placed on the left butt or left hip.

Source: Mrs. C. A. Ford through Pat Hubert, 1964.

Nº 786   Dash H B Connected
Howard B. Gafford

The **Dash H B Connected** brand was recorded in Kleberg County by Howard B. Gafford of Kingsville, Texas, in 1951. Howard and Bob Gafford of Kingsville used it in Jim Wells and Kleberg counties.

Source: Brown Ranch at Riviera, Texas, 1965.

Nº 787   Flying B
W. B. Brown Jr.

The **Flying B** brand on the left side was recorded in Kleberg County in 1942 by W. B. Brown Jr. of Riviera, Texas.

Nº 788   L Half Circle
Randy Lee Brown

The **L Half Circle** was recorded in Kleberg County by Randy Lee Brown of Riviera, Texas.

Source: W. B. Brown, 1965.

Nº 789   W V Connected
Brown and Hubert

The **W V Connected** is a partnership brand recorded in 1950 in Kleberg County by W. B. Brown and Vernie Hubert of Riviera, Texas.

Source: W. B. Brown, 1965.

Nº 790   S M
Charlie Whall

I received the **S M** branding iron from Charlie Whall in 1965 at his home north of San Antonio, Texas. I also received an iron with a small **S M** brand.

See brand numbers 796 and 797.

Nº 791   A Bar
Amado Garza

The **A Bar** brand was recorded in 1920 in Starr County by Amado Garza of Santa Elena, Texas.

Source: John Armstrong, 1965.

Nº 792   W H Connected
W. E. Hopkins

The **W H Connected** brand on the left hip was recorded in Kleberg County in 1938 by W. E. Hopkins of Kingsville, Texas.

Source: W. B. Brown at the Brown Ranch, 1965.

Nº 793   A
Captain Bill McMurray

The **A** brand is recorded by retired Texas Ranger Captain Bill McMurray of Hebronville, Texas, and is used on one of his ranches.

Source: John Armstrong, 1965.

(Texas Ranger Captain Bill McMurray retired from law enforcement and became a full time rancher. In 1969, he owned and

operated three ranches: the Santa Anita in La Salle County, the Santa Niño in Zapata County, and the Palo Blanco in Dimmit County. Captain Bill, as he was known, died May 31, 1980.)

№ 794 Track J
Cleve and Jay Kerr

The **Track J** brand is recorded by Cleve and Jay Kerr of El Paso, Texas. Their Angus heifers are branded on the left hip.

Source: Cleve and Jay Kerr, 1965, in El Paso, Texas, during the TSCRA convention.

See brand numbers 795 and 798.

№ 795 2 Lazy 2
Cleve and Jay Kerr

The **2 Lazy 2** is a New Mexico brand of Cleve and Jay Kerr. The brand is made with a **2** iron.

Source: Cleve and Jay Kerr, 1965, at the Kerr Ranch near El Paso, Texas.

See brand numbers 794 and 798.

(Cleve and Jay Kerr come from a longtime Texas ranching family. Both were involved in stockyards and commission company activities. They have had operations in New Mexico and El Paso, Texas.)

№ 796 T J F Connected
Charlie Whall

The **T J F Connected** branding iron was received from Charlie Whall of San Antonio, Texas, in 1965.

See brands 790 and 797.

№ 797 7 H L Connected
Charlie Whall

This **7 H L Connected** branding iron was received from Charlie Whall of San Antonio, Texas.

See brands 790 and 796.

№ 798 Sun Dog
Cleve and Jay Kerr

The **Sun Dog** is a Wyoming brand.

Source: Cleve and Jay Kerr of El Paso, Texas, 1965 during the TSCRA convention, El Paso, Texas.

See brand numbers 794 and 795.

№ 799 Double H
Frank and Dick Hopper

The **Double H** brand was recorded in Brooks County by the Hopper brothers, Frank Hopper of Encino and Dick Hopper of Falfurrias, Texas. It is placed on the left loin.

Source: Encino Ranch, 1966.

№ 800 Horse Shoe
Frank S. Rachal

The **Horse Shoe** brand on the left loin was recorded in 1900 in Brooks and San Patricio counties by

Frank S. Rachal of Rachal, Texas. Mrs. Frank Rachal brands the **Horse Shoe** upside down.

Source: Frank Hopper, 1966, at the Encino Ranch.

№ 801 T Up T Down
Rocky Reagan

The **T Up T Down** was recorded in 1909 by Rocky Reagan of George West, Texas. This is an extra long iron.

Source: Rocky Reagan, 1965.

(Reagan was a well-known South Texas rancher and author of three books, including Rocky's Chuckwagon Stories. *He was born August 7, 1883, in Oakville, Texas, to a pioneer Live Oak County family. He lived in Live Oak and Bee counties all his life. He produced Beeville rodeos and was associated with the South Texas Hereford Association.)*

№ 802 Walking Cane
T. J. "Jeff" Martin

The **Walking Cane** brand was recorded in Duval, Live Oak, and McMullen counties by T. J. "Jeff" Martin of George West, Texas. It is placed on the right hip of cattle on the El Campono Ranch (Bell Ranch).

Source: Gene Jones, 1965.

See brand number 809.

(T. J. Martin ran a large commercial cattle operation and also had a herd of purebred Santa Gertrudis. He was a charter member of S.G.B.I. He was eighty-eight when he died in 1985. The **Walking Cane** *brand is also used by T. J. "Tom" Martin Jr. and is placed on the left hip or left loin.)*

№ 803 C A F Connected
C. A. Ford

The **C A F Connected** brand was recorded in Kleberg County by C. A. Ford of Riviera, Texas. The brand is placed on the left hip or left butt. This iron was found in an old barn at Riviera in 1964.

Source: Mrs. C. A. Ford through Pat Hubert, 1964.

See brand number 785.

№ 804 Brand name unknown
Cheshire & Brookshire

This is a partnership brand recorded in Waller and Fort Bend counties and used by Cheshire & Brookshire.

Source: Cheshire, 1965.

№ 805 A
Owner unknown

I received the **A** branding iron from John Armstrong.

Nº 806   L
Pryor Lucas

The **L** brand was recorded from 1850 until 1872 in Bee, Goliad, and Live Oak counties, Texas, and in Greenwood County, Kansas, by Pryor Lucas of Berclair, Texas. It was placed on the left side or left hip of cattle.

Nº 807   H C Connected
Holman Cartwright and Lon Cartwright

The **H C Connected** brand was recorded in 1917 in Live Oak County by Holman Cartwright and his cousin, Lon Cartwright of Dinero, Texas.

Source: Lon Cartwright at the ranch, 1966.

See brand numbers 782, 808, and 810.

(Holman Cartwright was widely known in the cattle business. He was president of TSCRA from 1944–1946 and was active in his participation in many research projects concerning livestock and range management. He owned and operated Fort Bend County Plantation, established in 1910, and the 18,000-acre Twin Oaks Cattle Ranch, established 1915. He died at Twin Oaks Ranch at the age of ninety in 1980.)

Nº 808   L Up L Down
Mrs. Holman Cartwright

The **L Up L Down** brand was recorded in Live Oak County by Mrs. Holman Cartwright of Dinero, Texas, in 1915. It is placed on the left hip or right hip.

Source: Lon Cartwright at the ranch, 1966.

See brand numbers 782, 807, and 810.

(Claire Lucas Cartwright died in 1961. She and Holman were married in 1914.)

Nº 809   Walking Cane
John Martin Jr.

The **Walking Cane** brand is recorded in Duval, Live Oak, Atascosa, and McMullen counties by T. J. Martin Jr. of George West, Texas. He places it on the left hip or left loin. His father, T. J. Martin Sr., brands the **Walking Cane** on the right hip.

Source: El Campono Ranch, 1965. It is the same iron as branding iron number 802, but it is placed in a different location.

(This brand was recorded in Duval and McMullen counties in 1910 by John Martin. He moved to Alice, Texas, and started his own Santa Gertrudis herd and operated under the name, John Martin & Son. At the time of his death in 1970, he grazed 1,000 purebred cows.)

Nº 810   L Dash
Holman Cartwright

The **L Dash** brand was recorded in Live Oak County in 1915 by Holman Cartwright of Dinero, Texas. It is placed on cattle's left loin and on a horse's left shoulder.

Source: Lon Cartwright, 1966.

See brand numbers 807 and 808.

(Holman Cartwright's great grandfather, John Cartwright, was among the first U. S. citizens to immigrate to the Mexican-owned territory of Texas. John's son, Matthew, fought for Texas independence.)

Nº 811   N Crescent
Hiram K. Northway

The **N Crescent** brand was registered in Bexar County by Hiram K. Northway. Dr. J. K. Northway, grandson of Hiram K. Northway, was veterinarian for the King Ranch from 1916 until his death in 1973.

Source: Dr. J. K. Northway, 1964.

(Brand numbers 726, 811, 812 and 813 are brands that belonged to the members of the Northway family.)

Nº 812   7 O
Marshal M. Seay

The **7 O** brand was registered in Bexar County Book 456 by Marshal M. Seay, maternal grandfather of Dr. J. K. Northway. Seay lived in the Berg's Mill area on the San Antonio River and the iron is of the Civil War era.

Source: Dr. J. K. Northway, 1964.

(In a letter dated November 5, 1964, Dr. Northway wrote to Richard Santos, Bexar County Archivist, the following: "My maternal grandfather, Marshal M. Seay, settled below the Berg's Mill on the San Antonio River. This property was, I am told, obtained through homesteading several years prior to the Civil War. Family information implies that he and my grandmother plowed a furrow around the premises and set up the metes and bounds using a yoke of oxen to do the plowing. This property was sold during the early part of the century around 1912.")

Nº 813   Crescent N
Hugh P. Northway

The **Crescent N** brand was registered in Bexar County, Texas, by Hugh P. Northway of San Antonio, Texas, uncle of Dr. J. K. Northway, King Ranch veterinarian.

Nº 814   C C
Carl C. Black

The **C C** Brand was recorded in Milam County in 1925 by Carl C. Black, longtime sheriff of Milam County. This brand is known as a "string out brand." A **C** is placed on the right hip and a **C** is placed on the right rib. Black's son, W. C. Black, is the county Judge in Temple, Texas, and his brand is **C** on the right shoulder

Source: Sheriff Carl Black, 1966, while working on a case in Cameron, Texas.

Nº 815   J N Connected
John and Nellie Connally

The **J N Connected** brand was recorded in Wilson County, Texas, by John and Nellie Connally.

The iron was included in an exhibit of my collection at Six Flags Over Texas in Arlington.

Source: Governor John Connally through Ben Glusing at the King Ranch, 1965.

(John Connally served as Secretary of the Navy during the Kennedy administration from 1961–1962. While Texas Governor from 1963–1969, he was wounded during the assassination of President John F. Kennedy in Dallas in 1963. Connally later was Secretary of the Treasury from 1971–1972 during the Nixon administration.)

Nº 816   C Cross Bar
J. Tom Flournoy

The **C Cross Bar** brand was recorded in 1880 in Colorado County by J. Tom Flournoy, an early-day Texas Ranger and lifetime peace officer. The brand is a "string out brand."

Source: Tom Flournoy's son, Jim Flournoy, sheriff of Fayette County in 1966 in La Grange, Texas. Sheriff Jim was a law enforcement officer in Central Texas for half a century and is the sheriff who took a stand against the closing of the celebrated "Chicken Ranch," made popular in the Broadway play, *The Best Little Whorehouse in Texas.*

Nº 817   O H
W. E Holthouse

The **O H** brand was registered in San Jose and Coyote, California, by W. E. Holthouse, who sold a ranch near San Francisco to B. K. Johnson, oldest son of Sarah Kleberg. Holthouse and a group of men visited the King Ranch in 1966. One of the men was a brand inspector for the state of California.

Source: W. E. Holthouse at King Ranch, 1966.

Nº 818   L Bar
Ed C. Lasater

The **L Bar** brand was recorded in 1893 in Brooks County, Texas, by Ed C. Lasater.

Source: Garland Lasater, 1967, during a polo game at John Armstrong's ranch.

See brand number 820.

(Ed Lasater had extensive land holdings in South Texas in the late 1880s. He founded the town of Falfurrias in 1883. When the 1893 drouth hit, he began buying land and fencing and drilling deeper water wells. He contracted for 30,000 head of cattle, and by 1900, he owned 380,000 acres. His ranch was known as La Mota. He introduced Brahman cattle to that area of South Texas in 1908 and served as president of TSCRA in 1911. He established the Falfurrias area as a dairy farming community and had one of the leading Jersey herds in the country. He helped establish the farm credit system and the U.S. Packers and Stockyards Administration. He was Chief of the Department of Livestock and Food Production during the Hoover administration.

When Ed Lasater died in 1930, his son, Tom, managed the ranch, while his brother, Garland, handled the Jersey herd and Falfurrias Creamery and other businesses. In 1931, the ranch ran 20,000 head of cattle.

The development of the Beefmaster cattle breed began in 1931 from a three-way cross of Hereford, Shorthorn, and Brahman cattle. Tom Lasater is the founder of the Beefmaster breed which was recognized by the U. S. Department of Agriculture in 1954.

Lasater Ranch ads first appeared in The Cattleman magazine in 1916 and since 1945, the ranch as advertised in every issue, making it the second-oldest continuous advertiser, preceded only by J. D. Hudgins.

When Tom Lasater retired, the Lasater ranching operations continued under his sons, Laurie, of San Angelo, and Dale, who manages the family's purebred Beefmaster operation in Matheson, Colorado.)

Nº 819   D T
Harl Thomas

The **D T** brand was recorded in Raymondville, Willacy County, Texas, by Harl Thomas and is used as a partnership brand by Thomas & Daughtry, Charolais breeders.

Source: 1966.

See brand number 822.

Nº 820   Bar L
Ed C. Lasater

The **Bar L** brand was registered in 1893 in Brooks County, Texas, by Ed C. Lasater as his horse brand.

Source: Garland Lasater, 1967 during a polo game at John Armstrong's ranch.

See brand number 818.

Nº 821   Double J Connected
Janss Cattle Industries

The **Double J Connected** brand was registered in Thermal, California, by the Janss Cattle Industries. James H. Daughtry is Vice-President of Janss and a friend of B. K. Johnson's. Daughtry attended an auction sale at the King Ranch in 1967.

Source: James Daughtry, 1967.

Nº 822   Flying U
Harl Thomas

The **Flying U** brand was recorded in Willacy County, Texas, by Harl Thomas. The Thomas ranch is nine miles north of Raymondville, and the brand is used on top Charolais and Charbray cattle that are raised there.

Source: Harl Thomas, 1966.

See brand number 819.

Nº 823   J R Connected
Los Jaboncillas Ranch

The **J R Connected** brand was recorded in Jim Wells County by Los Jaboncillas Ranch, owned by Mrs. Jed Roe. The ranch, near Premont, Texas, raises Santa Gertrudis cattle and Quarter Horses.

Source: ranch foreman John Kiker, 1967.

Nº 824   G J G
Federico Guerra

The **G J G** brand was recorded in 1898 in Starr County by Federico Guerra of San Carlos, Texas. It had previously been registered in 1750 by Juan de Diaz Guerra and in 1880 by Juan's son, Guellermo Guerra.

Source: Charlie Carter of TSCRA, 1967.

Nº 825   Backward C E Dot
Mr. and Mrs. Leonard Cornelius

The **Backward C E Dot** brand was registered for Molabulabaum Station of Queensland, Australia, by Mr. and Mrs. Leonard Cornelius.

Nº 826   Quarter Circle J A
John Almond

The **Quarter Circle J A** brand on the left shoulder is recorded in Jim Wells County by John Almond of Alice, Texas. Almond was a top RCA calf roper and raises outstanding rope horses and Thoroughbred race horses. His ranch is north of Alice.

Source: John Almond, 1966 at the King Ranch.

Nº 827   C L Connected Dot
Clifford Brothers and Athol Flynn

The **C L Connected Dot** brand was registered in Brisbane, Australia to Clifford Brothers and Athol Flynn. This is on old ranching family in Queensland.

Source: Leonard Cornelius, 1967 while he was visiting the King Ranch.

Nº 828   J B Dot
Thomas Boekwicks

The **J B Dot** brand is registered in Queensland, Australia to Thomas Boekwicks, a longtime rancher there.

Source: John Clifford, 1966.

Nº 829   Flying C Dot
Mr. and Mrs. John Clifford

The **Flying C Dot** brand was registered in Lowmead, Queensland, Australia by Mr. and Mrs. John Clifford, Chornwood Station.

Source: John Clifford, 1966.

Nº 830   7 l L
J. D. Hudgins Ranch

The **7 1 L** brand was recorded in Wharton County by the J. D. Hudgins Ranch of Hungerford, Texas. This is a very old iron used in the early days of the ranch.

Source: Bubba Hudgins, 1967.

See brand number 831.

(J. D. Hudgins and his descendants are a prominent South Texas ranching family known for their prize-winning Brahman cattle. Hudgins, along with other South Texas cattlemen such as J. D. Sartwelle and Al McFaddin, developed the Brahman breed and was a guiding force in the formation of the American Brahman Breeders Association.

The Hudgins Ranch began advertising its cattle in The Cattleman magazine in 1929 and have been in every issue since. All of J. D. Hudgins's children and grandchildren have continued in the ranching tradition.)

Nº 831   Horseshoe
Edgar Hudgins

The **Horseshoe** brand was recorded in Wharton County by Edgar Hudgins of the Hudgins Ranch of Hungerford, Texas.

Source: Edgar Hudgins, 1967.

See brand number 830.

(Edgar Hudgins, grandson of J. D. Hudgins, carried on the Brahman tradition until his death in 1986. He served as both first and second vice-president of the TSCRA from 1957–1958 but was unable to assume the presidency because of poor health. He was made an honorary vice-president in 1958.)

Nº 832   Half Circle L
Loyd Jinkens

The **Half Circle L** brand on the left butt was recorded in Tarrant County, Texas, by Loyd Jinkens of Fort Worth, known as "Mr. Quarter Horse." Many of the King Ranch horses went to the Jinkens Ranch northwest of Fort Worth during the 1950s to be conditioned and then exhibited at horse shows.

Source: Loyd Jinkens, 1966.

Nº 833   Half Circle P
Thomas Pugh

The **Half Circle P** brand was first recorded in 1836 in San Patricio and Nueces counties by Thomas Pugh, who came to Texas from Ireland.

Source: Charlie C. Campbell, foreman of West Wand Ranch near George West, Texas, 1967.

Nº 834   C F P
Coleman Fulton Pasture Company

The **C F P** brand was recorded in 1896 in San Patricio County by the Coleman Fulton Pasture Company, which had been the Taft Ranch. This is a horn brand.

Source: 1966, John W. Hunt Jr., the grandson of Joseph F. Green, manager of the Taft Ranch.

(G. W. Fulton was born in 1810 in Philadelphia. Beginning at the age of 18, he worked as a watchmaker, bookkeeper, sign painter, and school teacher. He traveled to Texas in 1836 to join the fight for independence. In Texas he worked as a surveyor and draftsman and

planned the town of Aransas City, which was incorporated in 1839. He married Harriet Smith, and they moved to Baltimore where he worked as a reporter and used his engineering skills in bridge building and railroad work.

The Fultons returned to Texas in 1867, where Fulton managed large land holdings inherited by his wife from her father. Fulton organized a meat packing company, and he entered into the ranching business in a partnership with Tom Coleman. The Coleman Fulton Pasture Company bought the Taft Ranch near Catarina, Texas. They built up their holdings to 115,000 acres and managed 273 brands. Fulton also established a turtle farm in the Gulf where he raised sea turtles to furnish fresh meat aboard ship for sailors on their long sea journeys. G. W. Fulton made a significant impact on the development of the Coastal Bend area. His magnificent home near Rockport has been restored and is open to the public.)

Nº 835   Bar Bell
Dunn Ranches
The **Bar Bell** brand was recorded in Nueces County at Corpus Christi, Texas, by the Dunn Ranches of Padre Island.
Source: Jack Tunnel or Fred Tolar.
See brand number 836.

Nº 836   Brand name unknown
Dunn Ranches
This brand was recorded in Nueces County and Padre Island in Jim Wells County by the Dunn Ranches. Dunn worked with the Civil Defense in Corpus Christi.
Source: Dunn
See brand number 835.

Nº 837   Y Cross Connected
Owner unknown
The **Y Cross Connected** brand was recorded in Fayette County, Texas, and is a broken iron.
Source: Sheriff Jim Flournoy of La Grange, Texas, 1966.

Nº 838   N
Carl Neuman Ranch
The **N** brand was registered in 1937 in Cottonwood, South Dakota, by the Carl Neuman Ranch. It was branded on the left rib, hip, or shoulder.
Source: 1966, Bob McConkey, a barbed wire collector in Sioux Falls, South Dakota.

Nº 839   Lazy S J E Connected
Owner unknown
The **Lazy S J E Connected** branding iron came from the Austin, Texas, area.
Source: Robert R. Shelton of the King Ranch, 1965.

Nº 840   M B Connected
Captain Wallace Reed Sr.
The **M B Connected** brand was recorded in Cameron County by Captain Wallace Reed Sr., Brownsville, Texas.
Source: Charlie Carter of TSCRA, 1967.
See brand numbers 841 and 844.

Nº 841   U P Connected
Captain Wallace Reed Sr.
The **U P Connected** brand was recorded in Cameron County by Captain Wallace Reed Sr., Brownsville, Texas.
Source: Charlie Carter of TSCRA, 1967.
See brand numbers 840 and 844.

Nº 842   7 1 1
Charlie Solitary
The **7 1 1** brand was recorded in Cameron County, Brownsville, Texas, by Charlie Solitary.
Source: Charlie Carter of TSCRA, 1967.

Nº 843   L Bar
Roy, Wallace III, and Howard Reed
The **L Bar** brand was recorded in Cameron County, Brownsville, Texas, by Roy, Wallace III, and Howard Reed.
Source: Charlie Carter of TSCRA, 1967.

Nº 844   Brand name unknown
Wallace Reed
This brand was recorded in Cameron County, Brownsville, Texas, by Wallace Reed.
Source: Charlie Carter, TSCRA.
See brand numbers 840, 841, and 843.

Nº 845   Running M
John J. Maca
The **Running M** brand on the right rib was recorded in Kingsville, Kleberg County, in 1923 and 1943 by John J. Maca. Maca was the state game warden at Kingsville.
Source: Maca and J. L. McDougald, 1966.

Nº 846   J K Connected
J. H. Keepers Jr.
The **J K Connected** brand on the left hip was recorded in 1922 in Kleberg County, Texas, by J. H. Keepers Jr. The iron was found in John Maca's barn.
Source: Mrs. J. K. Keepers, 1966.

Nº 847   E P
Earl T. Prade
The **E P** brand was recorded in 1920 in Real County by Earl T. Prade. The Prade Ranch, located in Frio Canyon on the West Frio River, is both a guest ranch and a

working ranch of 10,000 acres. Robert R. Shelton, a great grandson of Captain Richard King, is part owner of the ranch.

Source: Les and Betty Stapelton at Prade Ranch, 1968.

Nº 848   Pitchfork
Wilbourn S. Gibbs

The **Pitchfork** brand is recorded in Walker County at Huntsville, Texas, by Wilbourn S. Gibbs. It was first recorded in 1841 by Gibbs Brothers & Company and in 1890, by W. S. Gibbs. The brand is made with two bar irons. Wilbourn S. Gibbs is a TSCRA director.

Source: Wilbourn Gibbs, 1968 at a TSCRA convention in San Antonio, Texas.

(Wilbourn Gibbs died in 1982. He raised purebred Brahmans and Brahman-cross cattle on his W S Ranch and supervised the Gibbs Brothers & Company ranches in Walker County. He was well known for his soil conservation work.)

Nº 849   T Little h
J. L. Matthews

The **T Little h** brand on the left rib was recorded in 1870 in Uvalde County at Sabinal, Texas, by J. L. Matthews. Harold H. Matthews (grandson of J. L. Matthews and son of Peeler Matthews) was the longtime sheriff of Uvalde County.

Source: Harold H. Matthews, 1968 TSCRA convention.
See brand numbers 850 and 854.

Nº 850   1 4 1
J. L. Matthews

The **141** brand was recorded in 1870 in Uvalde County by J. L. Matthews. The brand is made with the same bar iron as brand number 854.

Source: Harold H. Matthews (grandson of J. L. Matthews), 1968 TSCRA convention in San Antonio.
See brand numbers 849 and 854.

Nº 851   J 3
Belton K. Johnson

The **J 3** brand was recorded in Zavala and Nueces counties by Belton Kleberg Johnson, owner of the Chaparrosa Ranch southwest of La Pryor, Texas. Jack Youngblood and Wayne Hamilton were managers of the Chaparrosa, and later, Pete Emmert was general manager.

Source: B. K. Johnson at the King Ranch, 1967.

(B. K. Johnson was a great grandson of Captain and Mrs. Richard King. His father and mother both died when he was small, and he and his half-brother, Bobby Shelton, were reared on the King Ranch by their uncle, Bob Kleberg and his wife, Helen. Johnson left the King Ranch in 1960 and bought the 68,000-acre Chaparrosa Ranch. He developed it into an excellent operation well known for its fine Quarter Horses and purebred Santa Gertrudis cattle as well as commercial Brahmans and crossbred cows.)

Nº 852   C
Gus T. Canales Jr.

The **C** brand was recorded in Jim Wells County at Premont, Texas, by Gus T. Canales Jr. This is a very old iron.

Source: Gus Canales Jr. at Robert R. Shelton's office, 1968.

Nº 853   Bar P
U. T. Pearson Sr.

The **Bar P** brand was recorded in Milam County in 1937 by U. T. Pearson Sr. and was used by Pearson and his son, J. C. Pearson of Rockdale, Texas.

Source: Dr. Travis C. Green, Rockdale, Texas.

Nº 854   Two Rails
J. L. Matthews

The **Two Rails** brand, also known as the **Panther Scratch** or **Lazy 11** brand, was recorded in 1870 in Uvalde County at Sabinal, Texas, by J. L. Matthews. It was a Kansas road brand and was placed on the left shoulder of cattle.

Source: Harold H. Matthews, grandson of J. L. Matthews.
See brand numbers 849 and 850.

Nº 855   Circle J
T. Harold Jambers

The **Circle J** brand on the right hip was recorded in McMullen County, Texas, in 1950 by T. Harold Jambers.

Source: Jambers Ranch, 1968.
See brand numbers 856.

(Harold Jambers and his twin brother, George, operated their family ranch of approximately 8,000 acres in McMullen County and were known for their work with native grasses and for their fine Beefmaster cattle and their commercial cattle of similar breeding.)

Nº 856   Quarter Circle Bar
George T. Jambers Jr.

The **Quarter Circle Bar** brand on the right hip was recorded in McMullen County by George T. Jambers, Jr.

Source: Jambers Ranch, 1968.
See brand numbers 855.

Nº 857   Quarter Circle J
George T. Jambers Sr.

The **Quarter Circle J** brand was recorded in McMullen County in 1933 by George T. Jambers Sr. and Tobie N. Jambers.

Source: Jambers Ranch, Whissett, Texas, 1968.

Nº 858   7 P L
Tom M. Peeler

The **7 P L** brand on the left hip was recorded in 1882 in Atascosa County at Campbellton, Texas, by

Tom M. Peeler and used on his Basin Hill Ranch. It was also used by his son, Graves Peeler, in McMullen County and placed on the right hip.

Source: Graves Peeler at his ranch, 1968.

See brand number 499.

(Tom Peeler was one of the first brand inspectors hired by the ranchers after they met in Graham, Texas, in 1877, to discuss forming the organization that was the forerunner of the Texas & Southwestern Cattle Raisers Association. Peeler was killed in Campbellton in 1897. Two sons, Travis and Graves Peeler, were both Inspectors for the TSCRA during the 1930s.)

Nº 859   O R Connected
Owner unknown

The **O R Connected** branding iron came from El Paso, Texas.

Source: Graves Peeler, 1968.

Nº 860   T V
Owner unknown

The **T V** branding iron came from El Paso, Texas.

Source: Graves Peeler in 1968.

Nº 861   Backward D H Connected
Charles W. Hellen

The **Backward D H Connected** brand was recorded in 1895 in El Sordo, Texas, Zapata County; in 1905 in Starr County; and in 1913 in Jim Hogg County by Charles W. Hellen. The brand is placed on the left side of cattle and horses.

Source: iron and the certificate of registration, C. W. Hellen Jr. of Hebbronville, Texas, 1967.

See brand number 895.

Nº 862   brand name unknown
Nicolas Cavazos

This brand, placed on the right leg of cattle, was recorded in 1880 in Cameron County, Texas, by Nicolas Cavazos of the El Mesquite Ranch. A similar brand, turned the opposite direcron, was recorded in Cameron County in 1851 and again in 1872 by Anastacio Cavazos. Steve Cavazos gave me the iron and a copy of the registration at his home on the King Ranch. I loaned the iron to another member of the Cavazos family, and he never returned it.

Source: Steve Cavazos, 1967.

Nº 863   Dollar Sign
Vernon and James Smith

The **Dollar Sign** brand was recorded in 1964 in Bosque County and used on El Colina Ranch at Walnut Springs, Texas, by Vernon and James Smith. The ranch is a 10,000-acre operation and is the home of the Santa Gertrudis bull, Apache 42. Bill Western is ranch foreman.

Source: James Smith, while at his ranch for a 1968 field day. I displayed irons from my collection.

Nº 864   Lead Ladle or Dipper
Leonard Traylor

The **Lead Ladle** or **Dipper** brand on the left shoulder was recorded in 1938 in Webb County, Texas, by Leonard Traylor. Traylor and Ed Lorance placed it on the right shoulder as a partnership brand. It was also recorded in Potter, Randall, Moore, Hartley, Oldham, Maverick, Kenny, Burnett, Uvalde, La Salle, and Zapata counties in Texas and in Chase County, Kansas. The King Ranch bought 7,000 head of two-year-old crossbred and Santa Gertrudis heifers from Traylor in 1968, 1969, and 1970.

Source: Leonard Traylor at the Monte Cortado Ranch, Webb County, 1968.

See brand number 868.

Nº 865   Cross J Connected
George H. Driskill

The **Cross J Connected** brand on the left rib was recorded in Webb County by George H. Driskill of Sabinal, Texas. Driskill died in 1970.

Source: 1968, George Driskill at the Monte Cortado Ranch twenty miles east of Encinal, Texas, while picking up heifers bought by the King Ranch.

See branding iron 866.

Nº 866   Brand name unknown
Driskill Estate

This brand was recorded in Duval County by the Driskill Estate. The ranch, known as the Sweden Ranch or the El Raya Ranch, was twelve miles west of Benavides, Texas. I received cattle there for King Ranch. Martin Perry was foreman. The place was operated by the Welder Ranch at the time.

Source: George Driskill, 1968.

See branding iron 865.

Nº 867   E H Connected
R. H. Welder Estate

The **E H Connected** brand was recorded in Refugio, Victoria, Bee, Duval, and San Patricio counties by the R. H. Welder Estate of Sinton, Texas. It was branded on the left hip, loin, or rib.

Source: George Driskill, 1968.

See brand number 880.

Nº 868   T Quarter Circle or
T Eye Lash
Leonard Traylor

The **T Quarter Circle** or **T Eye Lash** brand on the left rib of cattle was recorded in Bexar County at San Antonio, Texas, by Leonard Traylor, who operated in several Texas and New

Mexico counties. The brand was used in Duval County on the ranch west of Benavides, Texas, and most heifers bought by the King Ranch from Traylor carried this brand.

Source: Leonard Traylor and George Driskill.

See brand number 864.

**Nº 869   S Dash S
Phillip J. Swett**

The **S Dash S** brand was registered in 1943 by Phillip J. Swett in Covington, St. Tammany Parish with the Louisiana Brand Commission in Baton Rouge. I worked there recovering a truckload of cattle turned over in the swamps west of Covington. We used planes and dogs, and we recovered all but one.

Source: Phillip Swett, 1968.

**Nº 870   D I
Dave Addison**

The **D I** brand was registered in 1935 with the Louisiana Brand Commission in Baton Rouge by Dave Addison of Folsom, St. Tammany Parish, Louisiana.

Source: Mrs. Crockett of Folsom, Louisiana, where I helped to recover some cattle in the swamps on her place.

**Nº 871   Brand name unknown
Charles Yarborough**

This brand was registered in 1837 in DeWitt County by Charles Yarborough who ranched and owned a general store south of Yoakum, Texas. Yarborough moved to San Saba County in 1883 and helped found the town of San Saba. In 1968, the brand had been in continuous use for 131 years.

Source: Dalton F. Neill, Yarborough's great great grandson, 1968.

**Nº 872   D Bar
A. J. Loustlout**

The **D Bar** brand was registered in Abita Springs, Louisiana, by A. J. Loustlout. He was a typical Louisiana cowhand who roped with a hemp rope and raised good cattle in the marshes along Lake Pontchartrain. He rode a stud and had good dogs. The iron has a wooden handle.

Source: A. J. Loustlout, Covington, Louisiana, 1968.

**Nº 873   W R Connected
Winthrop Rockefeller**

The **W R Connected** brand was registered by Winthrop Rockefeller, Win-Rock Farms, Morrilton, Arkansas. Rockefeller purchased a bull from the King Ranch and named him Win-Rock. This iron was made by Mr. Hall, an employee of King Ranch, and Bill Bronax of Texas A&I College, branded the bull for Rockefeller. Later, Bob Childs of the Rockefeller Ranch had a new iron made like they were using at that time and sent it to me in 1968, so there are two Win-Rock irons in the collection.

Source: Bill Bronax, Kingsville, Texas.

See brand number 751.

**Nº 874   Guatemalan brand
Similiano Garcia**

This Guatemalan brand was registered at the office of Branding Rights in Santa Lucia, Cotzumalguapa, Guatemala, by Similiano Garcia, Maria Lucrecia Garcia de Minondo, and Ana Maria Garcia de Cottone. A certification of registration authorized them to brand their cattle and horses with this brand.

Source: Similiano Garcia, Guatemala, 1968.

**Nº 875   Bar L R
Leon Rakowitz**

The **Bar L R** brand was recorded in Atascosa County by Leon Rakowitz at Leming, Texas. It was also recorded in Wilson and Bexar counties. The brand was made with three irons.

Source: 1969.

**Nº 876   unknown name
D. R. Daniel**

This brand was registered in Dubois, Fremont County, Wyoming, to D. R. Daniel of WindRock Ranch. It is branded on the right rib. The Daniels worked for Santa Gertrudis Breeders International in Kingsville, Texas.

Source: D. R. and Edwina Daniel, 1969.

**Nº 877   Brand name unknown
Esten E. Denny**

This brand was recorded in 1913 in Fort Bend, Waller, and Harris counties by Esten E. Denny. It is placed on the right hip or right side of cattle.

Source: Esten Denny of Katy, Texas, 1969.

**Nº 878   O K Bar
Oscar Arneson**

The **O K Bar** brand was recorded in Harris and Fort Bend counties by Oscar Arneson.

Source: Esten Denny of Katy, Texas, 1969.

**Nº 879   J T
J. T. White**

The **J T** brand was recorded in 1909 in Robertson County, Texas, by J. T. White. It was placed on the left side or left rib. White was a breeder of gentle Brahmans and was present when every calf was born. He never missed a TSCRA convention and often addressed the convention on the problems of small operators.

Source: Mrs. J. T. White, 1970 TSCRA convention.

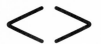

Nº 880   Lazy Open
R. H. Welder Estate

The **Lazy Open** brand was recorded in Refugio, Bee, Victoria, Duval, and San Patricio counties by the R. H. Welder Estate, Sinton, Texas. I received six irons in 1970 from Martin Perez, foreman for Leonard Traylor at the Sweden or El Raya Ranch west of Benavides. This ranch was owned by the Welder Estate.

See brand number 867.

(R. H. "Bob" Welder was a member of a pioneer South Texas ranching family. His great-grandfather built a ranch that one time covered San Patricio, Refugio, Victoria, and Goliad counties.)

Nº 881   Quarter Circle J
Josey Ranches

The **Quarter Circle J** brand was recorded in Harris and Fort Bend counties by Josey Ranches of Cypress, Texas. Buddy Smith was foreman, and they raised Santa Gertrudis cattle and Quarter Horses.

Source: Buddy Smith, 1970.

Nº 882   J C Dash
L. M. Josey

The **J C Dash** was recorded in Harris County by L. M. Josey of Houston, Texas.

Source: Josey Ranch.

See brand number 883.

Nº 883   Backward K 4
L. M. Josey

The **Backward K 4** brand on the right hip of cattle was recorded in Harris County by L. M. Josey of Houston, Texas.

Source: Josey Ranch.

See brand number 882.

Nº 884   U S and R
U. S. Army

This brand, **U S** and **R**, was used by the U. S. Cavalry. The iron was plowed up in a field in Oklahoma near Fort Reno, a Remount Station. The iron has no handle. The man who found it gave it to Leonard Milligan of Aurora, Colorado, who gave it to writer Jane Pattie of Fort Worth, Texas.

Source: Jane Pattie, at my home on the King Ranch.

Nº 885   Lazy S
C. E. "Babe" Glaze

The **Lazy S** brand on the left hip was recorded in Wharton County at El Campo, Texas, by C. E. "Babe" Glaze. Glaze often leased Kiddo Tacquard's land in Galveston County. He was a good horseman and raised Brangus cattle.

Source: Babe Glaze, 1961.

Nº 886   Bar Cross
Dr. Z. T. Scott

The **Bar Cross** brand on the left thigh was recorded in Travis County by Dr. Z. T. Scott of Austin, Texas. Dr. Scott was the father of Mary Lewis Kleberg, wife of Richard Kleberg II. The brand is made with a bar iron stamped two times.

Source: Mary Lewis Kleberg, 1967.

(Scott was part of the R. B. Masterson family, well-known ranchers in west Texas.)

Nº 887   F Cross (?)
Mallory Franklin

The **F Cross** (?) brand was recorded in 1920 in Atascosa and Hays counties, Texas, by Mallory Franklin. It was placed on the left thigh or anywhere on the left side. This is a small iron.

Source: Helen and Sammy Franklin, 1965.

Nº 888   7 hi
Frank G. Cobb

The **7 hi** brand was first recorded in 1917 in Matagorda County by L. G. Cobb of Citrus Grove, Texas. It is placed on the left hip of cattle and on the left shoulder of horses. The **7 h** and **7 h laying down** brands were recorded by Quincy Davidson in Matagorda County prior to 1900, and by Horace Yeamans of Palacios from about 1902–1917 and used on range cattle and dairy cattle. Yeamans sold his range cattle and the brands to L. G. Cobb of Citrus Grove, and he branded the **7 h i** from 1917–1920. His son, Frank G. Cobb of Blessing then branded the **7 h i** from 1920–1959, when he and his son, Charles L. Cobb, moved their cattle and the brand to Frank Cobb's 2,000-acre stock farm formerly known as "Cook's Island." There, north of Bay City in Matagorda County, they continued to use the brand on beef-type cattle.

Nº 889   C
Mrs. Jackie Henderson

The **C** brand was recorded in Jack County at Jacksboro, Texas, by Mrs. Jackie Henderson.

Source: J. G. "Jack" Phillips, 1965.

Nº 890   O 2
Lykes Brothers, Inc.

The **O2** brand was recorded in Webb, Duval, Brewster, and Presidio counties in Texas and also in Florida by Lykes Brothers, Inc. of Houston, Texas. It was placed on the left side of cattle.

Source: Carol Adams, 1970.

Nº 891   H K Connected
Richard King II

The **H K Connected** brand was recorded in Nueces County, Texas, in 1859 by Richard King in the name of "Mistress Henrietta M. King, wife of Richard King." It was placed on the left hip of cattle. The Kings gave the brand and the Agua Dulce Ranch to their son, Richard King II, and the brand was recorded in Jim Wells County in 1883. It continued to be used by his descendants. Mrs. Minerva Patch, the then eighty-nine-year-old granddaughter of Captain and Mrs. King and daughter of Richard King II, gave me the iron in 1970 at the Big House on the King Ranch.

Source: Mrs. Minerva Patch, 1970.

See brand number 601 and 892.

Nº 892　D
Richard King
The **D** brand was registered in 1857 in Nueces County by Richard King, La Puerta Ranch, Agua Dulce, Texas. It was placed on the left jaw with the **H K Connected** brand on the left hip.

See brand number 891.

*(The **D** brand is not included in the "List of Brands belonging to the Rancho Santa Gertrudes and its several Dependent Ranchos, Nueces County, Texas" dated March 26th, 1874, as reprinted in The King Ranch, Vol. 1, by Tom Lea. The **H K Connected** is listed as a cattle and horse brand.)*

Nº 893　Brand name unknown
Alexander Hamilton Reed
This brand on the left rib was recorded possibly as early as 1835 in Bee County by Alexander Hamilton Reed, who came to Texas from Mississippi and settled in Bee County. Reed was killed in 1871, and at the time of his death, he had 18,000 cattle.

Source: Tom Stotts who received it from D. M. Reed of Goliad, grandson of Alexander Hamilton Reed.

Nº 894　W H Connected
William C. Hoysradt
The **W H Connected** brand was registered in Manchester, Massachusetts, by William C. Hoysradt, a licensed lobster and crab fisherman. It is their practice to brand lobster traps.

Nº 895　Backward D H Connected
Charles W. Hellen
The **Backward D H Connected** was recorded in 1895 in Zapata, Starr, and Jim Hogg counties by Charles W. Hellen of El Sordo, Texas. It was placed on the left hip, left loin, or left side.

See brand number 861.

Nº 896　Nine Bar
Sterling Evans and Gus Wortham
The **Nine Bar** brand on the left hip was recorded in Harris County by Sterling Evans and Gus Wortham of Houston, Texas, who were Santa Gertrudis breeders.

Source: Evans and Wortham at a Nine Bar sale.

(Gus Wortham was a major figure in the development of Houston, Texas. He founded the multi-billion dollar American General Life Insurance Company and was one of Houston's leading philanthropists. Wortham began in the cattle business by "punching cows" in the Texas panhandle in 1911 for $25 a month. For many years, he owned a 146,000-acre crossbred operation near Santa Fe, New Mexico, and the 6,500-acre Nine Bar Ranch, northwest of Houston near Cypress. He and his partner, Sterling Evans, were well-known Santa Gertrudis cattle breeders. Wortham sold his cattle and ranch properties in 1975, only a year before he died at the age of eighty-five.)

Nº 897　H
Sheriff Halsey Wright
The **H** brand on the left hip was recorded in Jim Wells County by Sheriff Halsey Wright of Alice, Texas. It was also recorded in Live Oak County in 1928.

Source: Halsey Wright, 1970 at the sheriff's office.

Nº 898　Lazy Clover Leaf (?)
J. K. "Speck" New
This brand was recorded in Live Oak County by J. K. "Speck" New of the Live Oak Company, Whitsett, Texas.

See brand numbers 899 and 900.

Nº 899　N U
J. K. "Speck" New
The **N U** brand was recorded in Live Oak County, Texas, by J. K. "Speck" New.

See brand numbers 898 and 900.

Nº 900　1 3
J. K. "Speck" New
The **13** brand was recorded in Live Oak County, Texas, by J. K. "Speck" New.

See brand numbers 898 and 899.

Nº 901　Bar A R
Anton J. Ripps
The **Bar A R** brand was recorded about 1907 in San Antonio, Bexar County, Texas, by Anton J. Ripps. His son, August Ripps of San Antonio, gave me the iron and a dehorner in 1970.

(The old Ripps homestead was in the western part of San Antonio on the property where the noted trail driver, George W. Saunders, fed cattle for many years. August Ripps's uncle, Mike Ripps, was born at the Ripps place in 1858. He was a trail driver and went up the trail to Kansas with Joe Shiner's cattle in 1876 and 1878. In 1880 and 1881, he was a member of the party that surveyed the route of the Southern Pacific Railway west from San Antonio.)

Nº 902   Upside Down Heart Bar or Valentine Bar
Hart Mussey

The **Upside Down Heart Bar** or **Valentine Bar** brand was recorded in 1933 in Jim Wells and Duval counties by Hart Mussey of Kingsville, Texas. Mussey first used the **Heart** brand up-right, but after being advised by George Clegg and others that there were many Heart brands, he turned it upside down on cattle and up-right on horses. The family also called it a **Valentine**, because a little girl asked, "Who put all the valentines on the cattle?" The iron was made by a blacksmith in Alice, Texas.

Source: 1971, from Hart Mussey's daughter, Louise Mussey Moore.

2D

Nº 903   2 D
Ben Davis

The **2 D** brand was recorded by Ben Davis in Nueces, Kleberg, and Jim Wells counties in Texas and also in South Carolina. It is placed on the left shoulder. G. B. "Dick" Davis Jr. of Bishop, Texas, also used the brand in Nueces County.

Source: Dick Davis Jr., 1971, when my son, Joe Stiles, bought cattle from him.

JO

Nº 904   J O
Owner unknown

There is no information on the **J O** brand.

J9

Nº 905   J 9
A. T. Richardson

The **J 9** brand was recorded in 1870 in Limestone County and later in Jim Wells County by John Richardson of Hebbronville, Texas. In 1971, A. T. Richardson used the brand in Jim Hogg County and Jack Richardson branded it in Jim Wells County. It was chosen because of the **J** for John and the **9** for R, which is the ninth letter from the end of the alphabet.

Source: 1971, from Mrs. Jimmie Picquet, registrar at the Conner Museum at Texas A & I University and granddaughter of John Richardson.

Nº 906   Diamond K
Perry Kallison

The **Diamond K** brand was recorded by Perry Kallison of San Antonio, Texas, owner of Kallison's Saddle Shop, started in 1899 by his father, Nathan Kallison.

Source: 1971.

(Kallison was the owner of Kallison's Farm and Ranch Store and Kallison's Western Wear in San Antonio. He was well-known as the announcer on the longtime farm and ranch program, "Cow Country News." He is noted for his numerous civic accomplishments and his service to the South Texas livestock industry.)

Nº 907   Door Key
King Ranch España

The **Door Key** is a large brand from Spain that probably represents the keys used for the doors of the huge homes and buildings on King Ranch España's Finca Los Millares near Huelva.

Source: 1971 when I took cattle to the ranch in Spain from Texas.

(Stiles accompanied cattle and horses to the King Ranch's property in Spain in 1971.)

Nº 908   Concha Y Sierra
King Ranch España

The **Concha Y Sierra** is the brand of the largest fighting bull ranch in Spain, Finca Los Millares near Huelva.

Source: 1971 when I delivered Santa Gertrudis cattle from Texas to the King Ranch España, where the Concha Y Sierra cattle are bred.

Nº 909   Brand name unknown
King Ranch, Inc.

This brand was registered to the King Ranch, Inc. in Morroco. I accompanied Santa Gertrudis cattle and Quarter Horses from Texas by ship to Morroco in 1970. I brought the iron back in my suitcase.

Source: King Ranch, Inc. in Morroco, 1970.

Nº 910   Mashed O
Captain A. Y. Allee

The **Mashed O** brand was recorded in Dimmit County by Texas Ranger Captain Alfred Y. Allee of Carrizo Springs, Texas. Allee was captain of Ranger Company D and was known as the "Iron Captain." He was a Texas Ranger from 1931–1970, when he retired. He died in 1981.

Source: 1971 from his nephew, R. W. "Leroy" Williams.
See brand number 912.

C

Nº 911   C
A. Y. Allee

The **C** brand was recorded at Carrizo Springs in Dimmit County, Texas, by A. Y. Allee, grandfather of Texas Ranger Captain Alfred Y. Allee and of TSCRA Inspector Warren Allee. A. Y. Allee was a lawman and had a large ranch in Frio County during the 1880s. He was killed in Laredo in 1896.

UN

Nº 912   U Up U Down
Captain Alfred Y. Allee

The **U Up U Down** brand was recorded at in Dimmit County by Texas Ranger Captain Alfred Y. Allee. Captain Allee died in 1981 and his wife, Pearl, in 1989.

Source: Alfred Y. Allee, 1971, at a law enforcement meeting.
See brand number 910.

Nº 913   Brand name unknown
Leslie Vivian

This brand was recorded in Dimmit County by Leslie Vivian.

Source: Captain Alfred Y. Allee at his Carrizo Springs ranch, 1971.

Nº 914   Backward L E Connected
Lank and Eva Creacy

The **Backward L E Connected** brand on the left rib was recorded in Hutchinson County by Lank and Eva Creacy. Creacy was a horse trainer at the King Ranch.

Source: Lank Creacy, 1976.

Nº 915   Solis
King Ranch

The **Solis** brand was recorded in Kleberg County by the King Ranch. The iron was found at the Calora Pens on the ranch in 1971. It was made about 1920 and is thought to have been used on the well-known ranch stud, Solis. Valentin Quintinella, a ranch hand, remembered the horse being branded with the iron low on the right thigh in the early 1920s.

(Old Sorrel was bought in 1916 by Caesar Kleberg of the King Ranch as a colt from George Clegg of Alice, Texas. When the time came, he was bred to fifty of the best mares on the ranch, all Thoroughbreds or of Thoroughbred breeding. From that first colt crop, a young stallion named Solis was chosen. The first effort to concentrate and perpetuate the bloodlines and ability of Old Sorrel was when Solis was mated to Old Sorrel's daughters from this same colt crop. At the same time, six other sons of Old Sorrel were also bred to bands of selected mares. From this beginning came the King Ranch's famous sorrel family of Quarter Horses.

Wimpy by Solis was named the Grand Champion Stallion at the 1941 Fort Worth Stock Show and was awarded the first number in the registry of the American Quarter Horse Association.)

Nº 916   T Half h
T. A. Kincaid Sr.

The **T Half h** brand was recorded in 1887 in Tom Green County by T. A. Kincaid Sr. He later recorded it in Crockett County in 1902 and then in Val Verde County and in Upton County when he bought land there in 1930. T. A. Kincaid Jr. of El Sombrero Ranch of Ozona used the brand in the above named counties and in Wilson County since 1962. This iron was used during the 1890s.

Source: Charlie Haralson and Tommy Triplett at the King Ranch, 1974.

Nº 917   Brand name unknown
Owner unknown

This is an Arizona brand.

Source: Jack Phillips, 1972.

Nº 918   L N T
Ivor Paine

The **L N T** is an Australian brand in the Lake Nash Territory and was registered in 1890 by Ivor Paine with the Dept. of Agriculture, Darwin, Northern Territory. The brand is placed on the left thigh. In the Northern Territory, a brand must have three letters and one must be a **T**.

Source: Tio Kleberg, 1975.

Nº 919   J D Connected B
Dr. J. D. Beakley

The **J D Connected B** brand was recorded at La Vernia, Texas, in Wilson County by Dr. J. D. Beakley, a doctor who ranched there about 1900. T. A. Kincaid Jr. found the iron on his ranch in Wilson County in 1963. C. E. Scull Jr. and Mrs. C. E. Scull Sr., who remembered Dr. Beakley, gave him information about the iron.

Source: T. A. Kincaid Jr.

Nº 920   3 B Bar
Johnny Nix

The **3 B Bar** brand was recorded in Wilson County by Johnny Nix of the L & H Packing Company.

Source: Johnny Nix at the King Ranch, 1972.

Nº 921   Brand name unknown
iron found at King Ranch

No information on this brand.

Nº 922   P
Longfellow Ranch

The **P** branding iron is brass and was sent by Lewis Hill, manager of the Longfellow Ranch, thirteen miles northwest of Sanderson, Texas, in Pecos County. The ranch is owned by TSCRA director, W. B. Blakemore.

Source: 1975.

(The Longfellow Ranch was at one time owned by Buck Pyle.)

Nº 923   Brand name unknown
Owner unknown

The name of this brand is unknown. This is one of two irons sent by Louis Hill, manager of the Longfellow Ranch in Pecos County near Sanderson, Texas, and owned by W. B. Blakemore.

See brand numbers 922, 924, and 925 all sent by Longfellow Ranch.

Nº 924   Cross
Longfellow Ranch

The **Cross** brand is recorded by the Longfellow Ranch near Sanderson, Texas, in Pecos County.

Source: ranch foreman Lewis Hill, 1974.

See brand numbers 922, 923, and 925, all sent by Longfellow Ranch.

№ 925   Upside Down 2
Owner unknown
The **Upside Down 2** (or **7 6**) iron was found at the branding ground where it is thought a trail drive route began, possibly about 1876.

Source: R. P. Marshall of the Longfellow Ranch in Pecos County in the Big Bend.

See brand numbers 922, 923 and 924, all sent by Longfellow Ranch.

№ 926   U
U Ranch
The **U Ranch** brand was recorded in Reeves County at Balmorhea, Texas. It is placed behind the left shoulder. This hand forged iron was sold to the King Ranch by Gus Wortham of Houston, Texas.

Source: Rodney Lynch, 1975.

№ 927   Wine Cup
F. W. Neuhaus
The **Wine Cup** brand was recorded in 1848 in Fort Bend, Lavaca, Harris, and Brazoria counties by F. W. Neuhaus of Sugarland, Texas.

Source: Mrs. Picquet at the Conner Museum in Kingsville, Texas, 1975.

№ 928   Diamond Tail
Diamond Tail Ranch
The **Diamond Tail** brand is registered in Greybull, Wyoming, by the Diamond Tail Ranch in the Big Horn Mountains, owned by Stan and Mary Flitner. The original brand belonged to Mary Flitner's father, who had ranched since 1906.

Source: Stan and Mary Flitner of Flitner Herefords, 1972.

№ 929   O O
Robert May Ranch
The **O O** brand was recorded in Atascosa County by the Robert May Ranch, east of Campbellton, Texas.

Source: John Nix, an L & H Packing Company buyer, 1972.

№ 930   T Quarter Circle
Troy Woodward
The **T Quarter Circle** brand was recorded in Atascosa County at Campbellton, Texas, by Troy Woodward.

Source: John Nix, an L & H Packing Company buyer, 1972.

№ 931   Alabama
Alabama Department of Corrections
This brand, in the shape of the state of Alabama, is branded on cattle owned by the Alabama Department of Corrections. The state used Santa Gertrudis bulls on their cows.

Source: Ralph S. Eagle, breeder of registered Quarter Horses, 1972.

№ 932   Brand name unknown
Robert R. Shelton
This brand was recorded in Kleberg County at Kingsville, Texas, by Robert R. Shelton, great grandson of Captain Richard King.

№ 933   Brand name unknown
Spanish Creek Ranch
This brand is registered in Bozeman, Montana, by the Spanish Creek Ranch, owned by Robert R. Shelton and Jo Moran.

№ 934   A N B
Alice National Bank
The **A N B** brand is recorded in Jim Wells County by the Alice National Bank. The bank displayed a portion of Stiles's branding iron collection for a time.

№ 935   Brand name unknown
W. A. Maltsberger
This brand is recorded in LaSalle County by W. A. Maltsberger of the Maltsberger Ranch.

Source: Bill Maltsberger, 1975.

№ 936   Brand name unknown
Owner unknown
No name or information on this iron.

№ 937   Brand name unknown
Owner unknown
No name or information on this iron.

№ 938   Triangle Lazy S (?)
George Brian Clements
The **Triangle Lazy S** (?) brand is registered in Alberta, Canada, by George Brian Clements of Tofield. It is placed on the left rib.

Source: Clements Ranch, while on a trip with King Ranch people, 1974.

(It is not compulsory to brand livestock in Alberta, Canada, but it is unlawful to use an unregistered or expired brand. Cattle brands are registered in six positions: shoulder, rib, and hip on either side. Horse brands are registered in six positions: jaw, shoulder, and thigh on either side.)

№ 939   Brand name unknown
C. E. "Jack" Boyd
This brand is registered by C. E. "Jack" Boyd. No other information.

Source: Buster Welch.

№ 940   L S
Lynch and Stiles

The **L S** brand was recorded in 1970 in McMullen County by Rodney Lynch and Joe Stiles (son of Leonard and Mary Stiles), the L & S Cattle Company. It is also recorded in Reeves, Nueces, San Patricio, Duval, Live Oak, and Kleberg counties.

Source: Lynch and Stiles, 1979.

№ 941   Brand name unknown
Keatings Ranch

This brand was registered in Flagstaff, Arizona, by the Keatings Ranch. I met Keatings at a King Ranch auction in 1978.

Source: Keatings with the help of Larry and Ann Claflin of Flagstaff, 1980.

№ 942   C Dash L
Emert and Lucille Crocker

The **C Dash L** brand on the left hip was recorded in 1955 in Kleberg County by Emert and Lucille Crocker. Crocker was the cattle foreman of the Santa Gertrudis Division of the King Ranch for thirty years. The Crockers are pioneer breeders of Santa Gertrudis cattle, having SGBI Herd Number 69, established in 1945.

Source: Lucille Crocker.

№ 943   C
Filippini family

The **C** brand was first registered in Nevada in 1854 and is the oldest registered brand in the state. The Filippini family got the brand about 1889, possibly when they bought the ranch. Billie Filippini brought a mare to the King Ranch to be bred to Mr. San Peppy in 1980.

Source: Billie Filippini, Elko, Nevada, 1980.

№ 944   Umbrella
Jack Johnson

The **Umbrella** brand was recorded in 1965 in Hall County by Jack Johnson of the Umbrella Ranch, Estelline, Texas.

Source: Jack Johnson, 1979, while in Amarillo at the first American-Texas Longhorn Bull Sale.

№ 945   Double D
Danny Davidson

The **Double D** brand was recorded in Hall County by Texas Longhorn breeder Danny Davidson of the Double D Ranch, Estelline, Texas.

Source: 1979 while in Amarillo for a Longhorn bull sale.

№ 946   Brand name unknown
J. F. Marshall

This brand was recorded in Brazoria, Fort Bend, Wharton, and Matagorda counties by J. F. Marshall, father of J. W. "Jack" Marshall, longtime sheriff in Brazoria County. It was placed on the left hip.

Source: 1978, at the Marshall home east of Retrieve Prison Farm, Angleton, Texas.

№ 947   Tender Loving Care
Spooks Stream

The **T L C Connected** brand, called **Tender Loving Care**, was registered in 1914 in Opelousas, Louisiana, by Henry Gray who had bought it from J. L. Perry. Gray's widow, Mrs. Matilda Gray, registered the brand in 1944, and she transferred it in 1974 to the M-Heart Corporation. Spooks Stream, owner of M-Heart, came to the King Ranch in 1977 with entertainer Lynn Anderson to purchase Quarter Horses.

Source: Spooks Stream, 1977.

№ 948   T Up T Down
Gene Chase

The **T Up T Down** brand was recorded during the 1950s in Zavala County, Texas, by Eugene Chase of Council Grove, Kansas. The brand originated in and was registered in Chase County, Kansas. It was used in Texas on cattle Chase purchased in Mexico and wintered on 100,000 acres of leased land near Crystal City. Each spring, the cattle were shipped to blue stem and Lespedeza grass pastures on the Kansas ranch owned by Chase and his two brothers. They were fattened there and then shipped to market. Gene Chase's wife, Tate Rhea Chase, was Jane Pattie's cousin, and Chase gave Jane the iron. She brought it to me at the King Ranch.

Source: Jane Pattie, Aledo, Texas, 1977.

№ 949   Quarter Circle E
Owner unknown

There is no information on the Quarter Circle E brand.

Source: Charlie Shives of Midland, Texas, a farrier for the King Ranch, 1977.

№ 950   2 J
Owner unknown

There is no information on the **2 J** brand.

Source: John Gillett, Kingsville, Texas, 1969.

№ 951   V P Connected
Vernon Smith

There is no information on the **V P Connected** brand.

Source: 1978, Vernon Smith of North Texas. He and his foreman came to the King Ranch and bought colts.

№ 952   Quarter Circle j h
Edward Sadler

The **Quarter Circle j h** brand was recorded in 1900 in Atascosa and Frio counties by a man named Davidson, Edward Sadler's great grandfather.

№ 953   H V Bar
Dr. George H. Vincent

The **H V Bar** was registered in 1944 in Sulphur, Louisiana, by Dr. George Hardy Vincent's grandfather.

Source: Dr. G. H. Vincent, 1982, at a King Ranch cutting event.

№ 954   Backward C
Cage Cattle Company

The **Backward C** was recorded in Webb, Maverick, and adjacent counties by Cage Cattle Company of San Antonio, Texas. It is placed on the left hip, shoulder, or loin.

Source: Mr. Wakefield, 1967, at the King Ranch Saddle Shop in Kingsville.

(Richard Cage, a member of a prominent pioneer ranching family, operated the Cage Ranch near Falfurrias for more than fifty years. The ranch was known for its fine Beefmaster and Hereford cattle.)

№ 955   Running W Diamond
W. D. "Bill" Clark

The **Running W Diamond** brand was recorded in 1973 in Nacogdoches County by W. D. "Bill" Clark. It was placed on the left rib of registered Longhorns.

Source: Bill Clark, 1984 while at a sale.

№ 956   V
H. C. Lewis

The V Ranch was established about 1904 in Crosby, Garza, Lynn, and Lubbock counties by A. B. Robertson who acquired 36,000 acres from the St Louis Land Company. He recorded the **V** brand sometime later and used it until his death in 1921. The brand was then used by his son, A. L. Robertson, and his heirs who operated the ranch until 1969. At that time, they sold the cattle to H. C. Lewis and he leased the ranch. Lewis continued to use the brand. The **V** brand was also used on cattle on 32,000 acres of additional ranch lands owned and operated by Lewis.

Source: Larry Bounds of Chimney Creek Ranch, Spur, Texas, 1983 at a sale.

№ 957   Las Viboras
Calvin Bentsen

The **Las Viboras** brand was recorded by Calvin Bentsen of McAllen, Texas, in Hidalgo County and used on his La Coma Ranch near Linn on registered Red and Grey Brahman cattle. Bentsen is a cousin of Senator Lloyd Bentsen, who was Secretary of the Treasury in the Clinton administration.

Source: Ray Hernandez, 1984.

(In the 1980s and 1990s, Calvin Bentsen's La Coma Ranch also successfully bred and raised endangered Black Rhinos imported from Africa by Game Conservation International of which he is a founding member.)

№ 958   3 3
Esequiel Hernandez

The **3 3** brand on the right hip was recorded in 1933 in Cameron County by Esequiel Hernandez.

Source: Ray Hernandez, 1984.

№ 959   Wineglass
Graves Peeler

The **Wineglass** brand on either hip was recorded in 1943 in Atascosa County by Graves Peeler of Christine, Texas, long time TSCRA Inspector who raised Longhorn cattle.

Source: Lawrence Wallace, Graves Peeler's nephew, 1985.

(Peeler was a TSCRA Inspector from 1920–1930. Then he was manager of the Nash Ranch. With the financial backing of Fort Worth oil man, Sid Richardson in the 1930s, Peeler and J. Frank Dobie selected animals that best represented the fast-disappearing old-time Longhorn cattle and established the foundation of the State's herd that is now at Fort Griffin, Texas.)

№ 960   Quarter Circle L
Billy Lamb

The **Quarter Circle L** brand on the left rib was recorded in Harris and Burleson counties in 1937 by Mr. Lamb, the father of Billy Lamb of Somerville, Texas.

Source: Billy Lamb, 1986.

№ 961   Six Dukes
Ernest Duke

The **Six Dukes** brand was recorded in 1950 in Swisher and Tarrant counties, Texas, by Ernest Duke, a longtime employee of TSCRA.

Source: Ernest Duke during the 1981 opening of the new TSCRA headquarters in Fort Worth.

(Ernest Duke was assistant secretary-general manager of the TSCRA from 1947–1967. He was acting secretary for one year prior to the appointment of Joe Fletcher. Duke laid much of the groundwork for the modern brand recording system used by the Association.)

№ 962   Brand name unknown
Elmo Jones

This brand was recorded in Live Oak County, Texas, by Alex Coker (1860–1930), the first sheriff of that county. Elmo Jones then recorded the brand in Uvalde and Zavala counties.

Source: 1981 at the new TSCRA headquarters in Fort Worth.

Nº 963   U U
Double U Cattle Company

The **U** brand was recorded in 1906 in Garza County by C. W. Post, the Post Toastie King of Battle Creek, Michigan, founder of the Post Cereal Company. The brand later changed to **Double U** and was recorded by the Double U Cattle Company. Kenneth Marts is foreman of the Double U Hereford Ranch of Post, Texas.

Source: 1981 at the new TSCRA headquarters in Fort Worth.

(The first ranchers in Garza County, north of the later town of Post, were Young and Galbraith who arrived from the Fort Worth area in 1879 with a small herd of **Y G**-*branded cattle. The next year, they formed the Llano Live Stock Company and through stock sales, they expanded their ranch holdings with a $400,000 capitalization. They acquired more land along Yellowhouse Canyon and on the waterless plains to its west and continued to do business as one of the large ranches in the area. The* **Y G** *brand was soon replaced by the* **Currycomb** *brand, and in 1907 C. W. Post purchased the ranch. His interest was farming, and he enticed 100 farmers to the area and sold them tracks of flat land to farm on the plains west of the canyon. He also founded the town of Post as a supply center for the farmers. The good ranch land was off of the caprock, and the* U-*branded cattle grazed down in the sheltered areas along Yellowhouse Canyon.)*

Nº 964   Brand name unknown
W. C. Askew

This brand, placed on the right hip, was recorded in 1863 in Coolidge and Limestone counties, Texas, by W. C. Askew.

Source: 1981 at new TSCRA headquarters, Fort Worth.

Nº 965   Circle S
Walter Sandifer

The **Circle S** brand on the left rib of cattle was recorded in Kleberg County by Walter Sandifer of Kingsville, Texas, a longtime employee of the King Ranch who handled their hunting dogs. When Sandifer retired in 1987 and moved to East Texas, he bought a Longhorn bull from the ranch.

Source: Walter Sandifer, 1980.

Nº 966   7 F
R. T. Huebner

The **7 F** brand was recorded 1940–1955 in Bandera County by R. T. Huebner and then in Leon County in 1951 when Huebner moved to Buffalo, Texas.

Source: R. T. Huebner in Buffalo, 1977.

See brand number 1001.

Nº 967   Brand name unknown
Mrs. Roy Hindes

This brand was recorded in 1914 or 1915 by Mrs. Roy Hindes's parents.

Source: the Hindes Ranch near Fowlerton, Texas, 1978.

Nº 968   Dot Quarter Circle
Mrs. R. S. Muil

The **Dot Quarter Circle** brand on the left hip was recorded in Kleberg County by Mrs. R. S. Muil of Kingsville, Texas.

Nº 969   Bar 3
John Lacey

The **Bar 3** brand was recorded in 1929 in Jim Wells County by James D. Adams, brother of noted horse breeder, Ott Adams of Alice, Texas. John Lacey now uses the brand.

Source: 1984.

Nº 970   Y O
Charles Schreiner

The **Y O** Brand was recorded in Kerr County in 1880 by Captain Charles Schreiner. The Schreiner family still operates the ranch as both a cattle ranch and an exotic wildlife ranch.

Source: Charles Schreiner III, 1980, at the Schreiner Ranch Centennial Celebration.

See brand number 1025.

(The Y O Ranch near Kerrville, Texas, was established by Charles Schreiner who came to this country during the 1840s with his parents from Alsace-Lorraine. Schreiner was orphaned early and in 1854 when he was sixteen, he joined the Texas Rangers although he was below the legal age. In his travels with the Rangers, he saw the beauty of the Guadalupe River and the Texas Hill Country and decided this would be his future home.

By 1858, Schreiner had bought a small ranch on Turtle Creek in Kerr County and opened a general store in Kerrville that served the settlers and the nearby army post, Camp Verde. After serving in the Civil War, he bought more land and established himself in the cattle business. It is said that Schreiner and various partners trailed as many as 300,000 cattle to Kansas railheads. He was successful in the mercantile business, the cattle business, and with the Schreiner Wool & Mohair Company. He also established a band and a college in Kerrville.

In 1880, he bought the James River Ranch south of Mason, Texas, from James Clements and J. W. Taylor, survivors of the infamous Taylor-Sutton feud. Schreiner bought the cattle on the ranch, and with them, their **Y O** *brand.*

By 1919, Schreiner's holdings were approximately 500,000 acres in Kerr, Real, Bandera, Gillespie, Edwards, Mason, Sutton, and Kimble counties. Unlike some of the other Texas ranches, the Y O never had oil income, and the ranch often suffered hard times, but thanks to the mercantile business and the sheep and goat enterprise, it survived. Another source of more recent income was the stocking of exotic game for preservation and hunting. The Y O Ranch's wildlife refuge has 15,000 to 20,000 visitors a year.

The late Charles Schreiner III was the founder of the Texas Longhorn Breeders Association in the mid-1960s. To advertise the breed, he re-created two trail drives—one in 1966 from San Antonio to Dodge City, and one in 1976 from San Antonio to Lubbock.

Today's ranch is 50,000 acres, and Charles Schreiner III's three sons continue to operate it.)

Nº 971   Brand name unknown
Alton and Dorothy Rugh

This brand is recorded in Atascosa County.

Source: Alton and Dorothy Rugh, Christine, Texas.

Nº 972   Paintbrush D
Darol Dickinson

The **Paintbrush D** brand is registered by Longhorn breeder Darol Dickinson, owner of the Paintbrush D Ranch near Ellicott, Colorado. The brand is made with two irons and is placed on the right rib. Dickinson borrowed the iron in 1988 and has not returned it.

(Dickinson is a well-known Western artist and Longhorn breeder.)

Nº 973   Hairpin
Jim Leachman

The **Hairpin** brand is recorded by Jim Leachman of Billings, Montana.

Source: Joe Heather who was at the Leachman Ranch, 1987.

Nº 974   Rocking R
Walter Russell

The **Rocking R** brand was recorded in Kleberg County by Texas Ranger Walter Russell of Kingsville, Texas. Walter had owned that brand for more than forty years when he died in 1986. He was eighty-three years old.

Source: Mrs. Walter Russell (Beth Baker), Kingsville.

Nº 975   Bar Circle
Will D. Smith

The **Bar Circle** brand was recorded in 1935 in Grimes County by Will D. Smith of Bedias, Texas. He was a steer man from the old days. The brand was a bar back of the left shoulder and a circle on left hip.

Source: Will Smith, at a King Ranch sale in 1987.

Nº 976   Colt pistol
From G. O. Stoner

This is not a branding iron but an engraved silver .45 caliber Colt Single Action Pistol with a 4¾-inch barrel, Serial #345320, given to Leonard Stiles by retired TSCRA Inspector G. O. Stoner of Houston, Texas. Stoner was an inspector from 1910–1957.

Nº 977   Brand name unknown
Johnnie W. Hoffman

This brand was registered in Folsom, Louisiana, by Johnnie W. Hoffman of Metarie, a breeder of good Longhorn cattle. Hoffman's grandfather, Thomas McVea, first recorded the brand in 1895 in Gonzales County, Texas. It is placed on the right hip.

Source: Johnnie Hoffman at his ranch near Folsom, Louisiana.

Nº 978   T R Connected
Eligio Ruelos and Telesfero Trevino

The **T R Connected** brand was recorded in 1871 in Cameron County by Eligio Ruelos and Telesfero Trevino. A worker who was root plowing found this iron on the Norias Division of the King Ranch in 1987. Captain King bought the Norias in 1873.

Nº 979   Laurel Leaf
Mifflin Kenedy

The **Laurel Leaf** brand was recorded in Nueces and Cameron counties in 1868 by Captain Mifflin Kenedy, and it was used on his Laureles Ranch, which is now the Laureles Division of the King Ranch. Rogenigo Silva found this iron there about 1960 and gave it to Tio Kleberg.

Source: Tio Kleberg, 1988.
See brand number 590.

Nº 980   Running W
King Ranch, Inc.

The **Running W** brand is recorded in Kleberg County by the King Ranch, Inc. This iron was used to brand the wall at Texas A & M University and at the TSCRA office in Fort Worth. It hung in my office at the King Ranch for many years beside a photo of Richard Kleberg.

See brand numbers 45, 93, 584, and 731.

*(According to the List of Brands Belonging to the Rancho Santa Gertrudes in 1874, the **Running W** was "a cattle and horse brand. All animals are also branded with **K** on left cheek.")*

Nº 981   Big B
Big "B" Ranch

The **Big B** brand is registered in Belle Glade, Florida, to Big "B" Ranch, a division of the King Ranch.

Source: Don Archer of King Ranch, 1983.

Nº 982   Brand name unknown
Kleberg County Savings & Loan Assn.

This brand is registered in Kleberg County by Kleberg County Savings & Loan Association, Kingsville, Texas.

Source: 1986 from Susan Cude, an employee there who had previously worked in the King Ranch's Quarter Horse Department.

Nº 983   Brand name unknown
Russell Smith and Doug White
This brand is registered by Russell Smith and Doug White of the San Benito Ranch in California who bought Santa Gertrudis bulls from the King Ranch.
Source: the manager of the ranch, 1983.

 Nº 984   Mashed O
California Land and Cattle Company
This is the **Mashed O** brand of California Land and Cattle Company, owner of the Mee Ranch, King City, California.

 Nº 985   h
Haythorn Land & Cattle Company
The **h** brand is registered in Arthur, Nebraska, by the Haythorn Land & Cattle Company.
Source: Jerry Gillispi while at a sale there.

 Nº 986   Brand name unknown
Frank Schuster Sr.
This brand was recorded in 1952 in Hidalgo County by Frank Schuster Sr.
Source: ranch foreman Bobbie E. Brown.

 Nº 987   Lazy B
Lazy B Cattle Company
The **Lazy B** brand was registered in 1880 by H. C. Day. The ranch is located partly in Arizona and partly in New Mexico, so it is registered in both states. It is operated by the Day family as the Lazy B Cattle Company of Lordsburg, New Mexico. H. C. Day's daughter is Supreme Court Justice Sandra Day O'Connor.

 Nº 988   Brand name unknown
Oscar Beyers
This brand was recorded in Menard County by Oscar Beyers, who was born in 1894. The handle is cut off.
Source: Norman Parish who worked for the King Ranch, 1981.

Nº 989   Golden Arches
McDonald's Hamburgers
The **Golden Arches** brand was used by the King Ranch to signify cattle in the Eslavon Feedyards sold to the McDonald (Hamburgers) company. Jokiem Arredondo, blacksmith at the King Ranch, made these two irons in 1986 or 1987. The ranch had a contract with McDonald's to furnish them with all the ranch cattle—bulls, cows, and weaned calves—fed at the feedyards.

 Nº 990   2 K A
Arthur Thomas and George Holding
The **2KA** brand was registered in 1970 in Queensland, Australia, by Arthur Thomas and George Holding of Brisbane.
Source: iron received at King Ranch, 1984.

Nº 991   Brand name unknown
No information
This iron was given to me by Leonard Cornelius who owned Gin-Gin, a station in southern Australia, before he moved back to Texas.

Nº 992   Z Bar Dot
Owner unknown
The **Z Bar Dot** branding iron from Australia was given to me by Leonard Cornelius when he moved back to Texas. He had owned Gin-Gin Station in Southern Australia.

 Nº 993   3 h
F. M. "Blackie" Graves
The **3 h** brand was recorded in Liberty County by F. M. "Blackie" Graves of Dayton, Texas. Graves is the owner of "Classic," the first Longhorn bull to be syndicated for one million dollars.
Source: Blackie Graves at his ranch, 1989.

 Nº 994   Bar T Bar
Charlie Griffith
The **Bar T Bar** brand was recorded in 1935 in Liberty County by Charlie Griffith of Dayton, Texas.
Source: Blackie Graves, 1989.

Nº 995   Brand name unknown
Marcus Brothers
This brand was recorded in Harris and Liberty counties in 1910 by the Marcus Brothers of Houston, Texas. They were cattle buyers and steer men in the early days.
Source: Blackie Graves, 1989.

 Nº 996   H 4 Connected
L. C. and J. W. Trousdale
The **H 4 Connected** brand was recorded in Liberty County by L. C. and J. W. Trousdale of Dayton, Texas.
Source: Blackie Graves, 1989.

 Nº 997   Brand name unknown
No information on this brand.
Source: Blackie Graves, 1989.

Nº 998   I T
No information on this brand.
Source: Blackie Graves, 1989.

V̲

№ 999   H V Bar
Dr. George Hardy Vincent
The **H V Bar** brand was recorded by Hardy Vincent in 1944 in Sulphur, Louisiana.

V P

№ 1000   V P Connected
Owner unknown
No information on the **V P Connected** brand.

₸

№ 1001   T F Connected
R. T. Huebner
The **T F Connected** brand was recorded in Leon County by R. T. "Bob" Huebner of Buffalo, Texas.

KRC

№ 1002   K R C
King Ranch
The **K R C** brand was registered by the King Ranch in Canada. King Ranch's Bob Kleberg selected a group of cows with outstanding bloodlines and sent them to Canada to raise a top Santa Gertrudis bull that could be proven by producing a high percent of bull and heifer calves that could be classified. Then this Canadian bull could be collected and semen sent to Australia.

The irons were made by Joaquim Arradando in the blacksmith shop on the King Ranch in Texas. Bobby Shelton and I flew with the ranch's pilot, Sam Hare, to the Clement Ranch near Calgary, and I branded the calf crop that year with this brand. The **K R C**, separate letters, were placed on the left rib.

$

№ 1003   Dollar Sign
Ivan R. Arnett &
A. C. "Sonny" Arnett
The **Dollar Sign** brand is recorded in Coleman County by Ivan R. Arnett & A. C. "Sonny" Arnett of Coleman, Texas. The 1,840-acre ranch is twenty-one miles west of Coleman.

T̲

№ 1004   T Bar
Ivan R. Arnett
The **T Bar** brand is recorded in Coleman County by Ivan R. Arnett.

Note: The remaining branding irons were added after Leonard and Mary Stiles had delivered the collection to the Cattle Raisers Museum in 1988. Stiles continued to collect irons and send them to the museum and others came directly to the museum through the staff's efforts. It is hoped that the collection will continue to grow and when ranchers donate their irons, they will send their histories. In the following list, the irons collected by the museum have (CRM)— Cattle Raisers Museum —following the numbers.

G

№ 1005   G
Granada Cattle Company
The **G** brand was recorded in Brazos County by the Granada Cattle Company of Bryan, Texas.
Source: Mr. Eller.

W

№ 1006   Loop Heart Loop
Spooks Stream
The **Loop Heart Loop** brand was recorded by Spooks Stream of Opelousas, Louisana, who came to the King Ranch with Lynn Anderson to buy horses.

N-R

№ 1007 (CRM)   N Bar R
Nolan Ryan
The **N Bar R** brand was recorded in Brazoria County by Nolan Ryan of Angleton, Texas, famed pitcher for the Texas Rangers baseball team from 1989 to 1993. He was the all-time strike-out leader.

L̲J

№ 1008 (CRM)   L Bar J
Leroy Jordan
The **L Bar J** brand belongs to Leroy Jordan, a former member of the Dallas Cowboy football team.

ⵛH

№ 1009 (CRM)   C H Connected
Chuck Howley
The **C H Connected** brand was recorded in 1986 in Van Zandt County by Chuck Howley, a former Dallas Cowboys football player.

№ 1010   A horseshoe tool
Not a brand
A cowboy carries this tool on his saddle. It is a horseshoe with a handle and is put in the mouth of a cow that has swallowed a bone and has it hung in her throat. You force this into her mouth, turn it sideways, and stick your hand through the horseshoe to get the bone and pull it out. You work carefully, because a cut from a cow's tooth is very hard to cure. I carried this tool when I worked horseback on the Laureles Division of the King Ranch in 1955.

∏

№ 1011 (CRM)   Hat
Bill Wittliff
The **Hat** brand is recorded in Gonzales County by Bill Wittliff, noted screenwriter and producer of the CBS mini-series, *Lonesome Dove.*

TLJ

№ 1012 (CRM)   T L J
Tommy Lee Jones
The **T L J** brand is recorded in San Saba County by Tommy Lee Jones, rancher and actor who has starred in numerous motion pictures including the TV mini-series *Lonesome Dove* and *The Good Old Boys,* adapted from Elmer Kelton's novel by the same name.

U

№ 1013 (CRM)   U
Edward Willoughby

The **U** brand was recorded in Schleicher County in 1911 by Edward Willoughby.

JB

№ 1014 (CRM)   J B Connected
J. S. Bridwell

The **J B Connected** brand was recorded in 1932 in Wichita County by J. S. Bridwell.

(Well-known Wichita Falls, Texas, rancher J. S. Bridwell, the originator of the Larry Domino bloodline of Hereford cattle, was known as "Mr. Hereford" and served as a director of the TSCRA. He owned a large independent oil company and was instrumental in locating Sheppard Air Force base in Wichita Falls. He was a noted philanthropist recognized for his work with the Texas 4-H Youth Foundation. J. B Bridwell died in 1966.)

/S/

№ 1015 (CRM)   Slash S Slash
Bryant Edwards

The **Slash S Slash** brand was recorded in Clay County of North Texas in 1926 by Bryant Edwards.

T̄

№ 1016 (CRM)   Bar Coat Hanger
Jay Novacek

The **Bar Coat Hanger** brand is recorded by Jay Novacek, tight end for the Dallas Cowboys football team.

W

№ 1017   W
Wilber Webb Jr.

The **W** was branded on commercial cattle and registered Brahmans in Wharton County by Wilber Webb Jr. of Danevang, Texas, beginning in 1937. The most cattle to carry the **W** brand at one time were 300 commercial and 300 registered Brahmans. Mrs. Marentze Webb's niece, Doris Gray, delivered this iron and the **A** iron to Leonard Stiles at the Cattle Raisers Museum in Fort Worth in 1989.

See brand number 1018.

(When Wilber and Marentze Webb married in 1937, he was in the commercial cattle business, and they started a registered Brahman herd. They sold and shipped registered Brahmans all over the United States, Canada, Cuba, Central and South America, as well as Africa. Wilber Webb died in 1976, and Marentze Webb continued in the Brahman business until she retired in 1982. Mrs. Webb died in 1991.)

AA

№ 1018   Double A
Wilber Webb Jr.

The **Double A** brand, stamped twice with an **A** iron, was used by Wilber Webb Jr. and Marentze Webb in Wharton County on registered Brahman cattle beginning in 1937.

Source: Marentze Webb's niece, Doris Gray, left for Stiles at the museum.

See brand numbers 1017.

(The Webbs won many awards with their registered Brahman cattle, which were shown in many livestock shows, including Houston, San Antonio, Dallas, Fort Worth, Los Angeles, and Laredo.)

T

№ 1019   T
Bryant Edwards

The **T** brand was recorded in 1926 in Clay County, Texas, by Bryant Edwards of Henrietta, Texas, who was recognized as having one of the foremost herds of commercial Hereford cattle in the country.

See brand number 1015.

5

№ 1020   5
Scharbauer Cattle Company

The **5** brand was recorded in Martin, Midland, Oldham, Ector, and Andrews counties, Texas, and in Chavez County, New Mexico by the Scharbauer Cattle Company and Scharbauer Bros. & Co. of Midland, Texas. George Crosson, who used the **5** brand in 1866 in Bexar County, brought it from Ireland, where his father had branded sheep with the number **5** in the early 1800s. Other versions of the **5** brand were used by Bailey Daugherty in Kaufman County in 1860 and by Capt. L. W. Burrell in Medina County in 1880.

(Clarence Scharbauer is a leading rancher in West Texas. He has played a significant role in the development of Midland where he owned a radio station, built a hotel, and was president of the First National Bank of Midland. He has vast ranch lands, where he raises cattle, horses, and sheep.)

12̲

№ 1021   Twelve Bar
J. W. McAdams

The **Twelve Bar** brand on the left shoulder was recorded in 1899 in Walker County by J. W. McAdams. It is now used by Doyle F. McAdams and son, Jim McAdams of the McAdams Cattle Company, Huntsville, Texas.

Source: left at TSCRA, 1991.

JE

№ 1022   Brand name unknown
B. T. Pipkin

This brand was recorded in 1885 by B. T. Pipkin.

OS

№ 1023 (CRM)   O S
G. O. Stoner

The **O S** brand belonged to G. O. Stoner.
See number 976.

*(The **Quarter Circle O S brand** was recorded in 1877 in Victoria County, Texas, by George Overton Stoner (1845–1920), who successfully managed the Stoner Pasture Company Ranch near Kemper City. He was the son of wealthy pioneer stockman, Michael L. Stoner and his wife, Zilpa Rose Stoner. G. O. Stoner was born in Tennessee, and both he and his father fought for the Confederacy during the Civil War. His son, the late G. O. Stoner of Houston, was a longtime TSCRA Inspector.)*

№ 1024 (CRM) Cross Bar
Pete Darter
The **Cross Bar** brand was recorded in Grayson County, Texas, by Pete Darter.

№ 1025   Y O Ranch
Schreiner Family
The **Y O** brand is recordeded in Kerr County by the Schreiner family of the Y O Ranch.

See brand number 970.

*(After Capt. Charles Schreiner left the Texas Rangers, he made a fortune in the mercantile business in Kerrville, Texas. By 1900, this money enabled him to purchase more than 600,000 acres between Kerrville and Menard, Texas. He first registered the **Y** brand in 1887 in Kerr, Kimball, Mason, Bandera, Edwards, Gillespie, and Kendall counties. In 1919, the ranch was divided and the brand went to Gus F. Schreiner. TSCRA Director Charles Schreiner III, who managed 60,000 acres of the original ranch from 1949 to 1976, began using the **Y O** brand in 1949, and the ranch, near Mountain Home, became known as the Y O Ranch. Today's ranch is famous for its Texas Longhorns, crossbred cattle, Angora goats, Rambouillet sheep, Quarter Horses, and exotic animals.)*

№ 1026   Brand name unknown
Don and Paula Stiles Jr.
This brand is the initials of its owners, Don and Paula Stiles Jr. of Cuero, Texas. It was recorded in 1970 in DeWitt County and is placed on the right hip or left hip.

Source: Don and Paula Stiles Jr., 1991.

№ 1027   Pitchfork
Jack and Lili Turnell
The **Pitchfork** brand was registered in Wyoming in 1878.

Source: Jack and Lili Turnell of the Pitchfork Ranch, Meeteetse, Wyoming.

№ 1028   H S
Harvey Stiles
The **H S** brand on the right hip was recorded in DeWitt County in 1971 by Harvey Stiles.

Source: Harvey Stiles, 1991.

№ 1029   C S
Clint Stiles
The **C S** brand was recorded in 1971 in Dewitt County by Clint Stiles and is placed on the right hip.

Source: Clint Stiles, 1991.

№ 1030   Brand name unknown
Sheri King
This brand came from Canada, but it was recorded in 1989 in Brazoria County by Sheri King of Angleton, Texas. She is Sheriff Joe King's daughter.

Source: 1991.

№ 1031   0 6
Lee M. Kokernot
The **0 6** is the oldest recorded brand in the Big Bend section of Texas. It was first registered in the early 1850s in Gonzales County, Texas, by Captain W. E. Jones. He sold the brand to Levi "Lee" M. Kokernot in 1873, and he recorded it in several south Texas counties. He moved it to West Texas in 1883 and established the 0 6 Ranch before Alpine was founded.

In 1897, Lee sold his interest to his only brother, John W. Kokernot, and his eldest son, Herbert L. Kokernot Sr. They ran the brand in West and South Texas. Then Herbert Sr. bought John Kokernot's interest, and he used the brand until 1949. His son, H. L. Kokernot Jr., also used the brand until 1987.

The **0 6** is still recorded by Kokernot heirs in Brewster, Jeff Davis, and Pecos counties. A member of the F. D. Kokernot Jr. family has recorded it in Gonzales County. —information from Fred D. Kokernot Jr., Cuero, Texas.

The most cattle to carry the **0 6** brand at one time were 35,000 head. In 1935, there were 25,000 Kokernot cattle on 400,000 acres. The ranch lies between Alpine and Fort Davis, Texas, and is managed by H. L. Kokernot Jr.'s grandson, Chris Lacy Jr., a TSCRA director.

This is one of three new irons of Kokernot brands in the collection. F. D. Kokernot Jr. furnished the information about the brands.

Source: Fred Kokernot, 1991.
See brand numbers 1032 and 1033.

№ 1032   1 O 1
Lee M. Kokernot
Fred D. Kokernot Jr. writes, "The **1 O 1** was one of several trail brands used by my grandfather, Lee M. Kokernot (1836–1914). Lee Kokernot and Colonel Miller formed a partnership in the 1880s, taking the **1 O 1** as a holding brand. My grandfather and two Indians used moldboard plows and laid the land off that was later to become the 101 Ranch in Oklahoma. The last herd they trailed north from South Texas was in 1888. In time, they dissolved their partnership, and Miller bought Kokernot out and took the brand." Fred Kokernot Jr. was born in 1917 and lives in Cuero, Texas.

Source: Fred D. Kokernot Jr., 1991.
See brand numbers 1031 and 1033.

№ 1033   L K
Captain David L. Kokernot
The **L K** brand was first recorded by Captain David L. Kokernot (1805–1892) in Anahuac, while Texas was still "under the flag of Mexico and registered later in the Republic of Texas," as his great grandson, Fred Kokernot relates.

"This brand was moved to Gonzales County, Texas, in 1854 and recorded by David's son, Levi "Lee" M. Kokernot

(1836–1914). It was also registered in the 1850s in Matagorda, Jackson, Victoria, Lavaca, and DeWitt counties. Lee Kokernut lived near Big Hill in Gonzales County.

"In 1916, my father, Fred D. Kokernot Sr., the youngest son of Lee Kokernot, took this brand and ran it until his death in 1976. He was born in 1882. My father was a brother of Walter H. Kokernot Sr. of Alpine, Texas, and Herbert L. Kokernot Sr. of San Antonio.

"The **L K** brand is now recorded in Gonzales County in my name, Fred D. Kokernot Jr., the fourth generation to own the brand. Flesh marks are a swallow fork in the right ear and crop and under half bit in the left ear." —Fred D Kokernot, great-grandson of David L. Kokernot.

See brand numbers 1031 and 1032.

(David Kokernot came to this country in 1817 from Amsterdam. He worked as a riverboat pilot for a while and fought for Texas independence. He opened a mercantile store in Gonzales and went into the cattle business. His sons, Lee and John, formed a partnership in the land and cattle business. Lee took care of the South Texas cattle business and John ran the West Texas O 6 Ranch in the Davis Mountains. Lee sent his eldest son, Herbert L. Kokernot (born in 1867), to help John, and in 1897, Lee sold his interest in the O 6 Ranch to his brother and son. Lee and his son, Fred, continued to use the L K brand in south Texas.)

№ 1034   E K Heart
Dr. Kleberg Eckhardt

The **E K Heart** brand was recorded in 1873 in DeWitt County, Texas, by Robert C. Eckhardt and used on cattle on his Yorktown ranch. Eckhardt also recorded the Heart brand in 1875 as a sheep brand. His wife, Caroline Kleberg Eckhardt, was the daughter of neighbor, Judge Robert J. Kleberg, a hero of the Battle of San Jacinto. She was the sister of Robert J. Kleberg Jr., husband of Alice King Kleberg of the King Ranch. Judge Kleberg came to Texas in 1834 from Westphalia. He and other early Klebergs are buried in the old Eckhardt Ranch's cemetery.

The **E K Heart** brand was transferred to Dr. Eckhardt in 1952 who used it on Hereford cattle on his Yorktown ranch.

Source: Dr. Kleberg Eckhardt, Corpus Christi, 1991.

№ 1035   4 9
Otto Kriegel

The **4 9** brand was recorded in 1930 in Kleberg County by Otto Kriegel. It was chosen because of Otto's birthday—April 1889. The **4** for April, the fourth month—**9** for the last number of the year 1889. This is a hand-forged iron made by Otto's son, Melvin Kriegel, a Kingsville, Texas, blacksmith who makes branding irons for the public.

Source: Melvin Kriegel, Kingsville, Texas.

№ 1036   Bootjack
John & Nancy Kendall

The **Bootjack** brand was registered in 1990 in Arizona by John and Nancy Kendall of the Lone Mountain Ranch of Hereford, Arizona. This 64,000-acre property is also known as the d'Albini Ranch.

Source: John and Nancy Kendall, Lone Mountain Ranch, 1991.

See brand number 1037.

№ 1037   Mill Iron Rafter
Collins Canyon Land & Cattle Company

The **Mill Iron Rafter** brand was registered in Arizona by the Collins Canyon Land & Cattle Company, Patagonia, Arizona.

Source: received in 1991 at Lone Mountain Ranch, Arizona.

See brand number 1036.

№ 1038   Circle T
Daniel Boone Friar

The **Circle T** brand was recorded in DeWitt County, Texas, by Daniel Boone Friar in 1847. This brand is still in use today by his descendant, Jean Ann Friar Sheppard and Henry F. Sheppard.

Source: Jean Ann Friar and Henry Sheppard.

(Friar came to Texas with Stephen F. Austin's second colony. He was a grandson of Daniel Boone. Friar was in command of Rangers between the Brazos and Colorado rivers in 1835. Friar participated in the Texas fight for independence from Mexico in 1836 and was a scout at the Battle of San Jacinto. He fought against the Indians on the frontier and took part in the Battle of Plum Creek near Lockhart. He was also a member of the historic Mier Expedition. He was later instrumental in the development of DeWitt County as a postmaster, local businessman, schoolteacher, and rancher.)

№ 1039   Oak Tree
Bob & Myrna Davis

The **Oak Tree** brand was recorded in DeWitt County in 1981 by Bob & Myrna Davis of the Thousand Oaks Ranch, Cuero, Texas.

Source: Don Stiles while on a nilgai hunt on the Norias Division of the King Ranch.

№ 1040   Y Cross
Mannie & Edwin Fowlkes

The **Y Cross** brand on the left side of cattle was recorded in Presidio County in 1935 by Mannie & Edwin Fowlkes of Marfa, Texas. The Fowlkes sold the ranch to Robert O. Anderson, who sold it to the Texas Parks & Wildlife Department in 1988. It is now known as Big Bend Ranch. There are sixty sections (300,000 acres) in the ranch. They brand a **Diamond A** on the left rib. A lodge was built in 1955 at Sauceda

Camp. The Rancho Viejo has rock pens and cattle are pastured nearby. John Gulderman was Superintendent for a time, but he left the ranch in 1992 and moved to Marfa where he ran Longhorn cattle of the Jinglebob bloodline.

Source: John Gulderman at Sauceda Ranch Headquarters, 1991.

№ 1041   Brand name unknown
Raymond Holstein

This brand was recorded in Pecos, Brewster, and Jeff Davis counties in 1950 by Raymond Holstein of Fort Stockton, Texas. His ranch is in the Glass Mountains, ten miles north of Marathon.

Source: Raymond Holstein, 1991.

№ 1042   Cannon
Cannonade Ranch

The **Cannon** brand was recorded in Gonzalas County by Josephine Abercrombie of the Cannonade Ranch. The King Ranch purchased the Cannonade Ranch, which has feedyards and irrigated pastures, in the fall of 1991.

Source: Jay Evans, Cannonade Ranch, 1992.

№ 1043   C Cross
Marcia & Reimer Calhoun Jr.

The **C Cross** brand is registered by Marcia & Reimer Calhoun Jr. of Mansfield, Louisiana. Calhoun was president of the Texas Longhorn Breeders Association of America.

Source: Reimer Calhoun, 1992.

(Calhoun writes: "The **C** brand has been the Calhoun brand for generations. Fifteen years ago when I was running steers in heavy woods, we added the **+**, making the brand more visible as **C+**.

"An amusing story about my brand came about when we first branded 200 steers with the **C+**. I told my foreman to brand on both sides so we could identify our steers coming and going (meaning from either side.) The foreman was confused about what I meant. I am sure it was puzzling to the feed lot folks in California to see steers branded **C+** on the left (or coming) side and a mirror image, **+Ɔ**, on the right (or going) side!")

№ 1044   Brand from Paraguay
Phil Kent

This brand in registered in Paraguay by Phil Kent of the Palo Blanco Ranch in the western part of the Chaco region of Paraguay. Kent is a Paraguayan citizen of British decent. He runs Hereford cattle on 25,000 acres.

Source: Rhett Butler and Dennis Murphy, King Ranch visitors, 1992.

№ 1045   Brand name unknown
Rhett Butler

This brand is recorded in Fort Bend County by Rhett Butler of Richmond, Texas, and in Paraguay where it is used on his Estancia El Tejano, located in the western part of the country. The estancia is a steer fattening operation. His cattle in Paraguay are descendants of Brahmans from J. D. Hudgins's V 8 Ranch of Hungerford, Texas.

Source: Rhett Butler and Dennis Murphy at the King Ranch, 1992.

№ 1046   Brand name unknown
Robert J. Eaton

This brand in registered in Paraguay by Robert J. Eaton, an American from Vermont who has lived in Paraguay since 1929. His ranch, the Estancia Zacazar, is in the Chaco Region of western Paraguay and covers 272,000 acres. This brand is not used often.

Source: Rhett Butler and Dennis Murphy at the King Ranch, 1992.

See brand numbers 1047 and 1048.

№ 1047   Brand name unknown
Eaton & Company

This brand was registered in Paraguay in 1929 by Eaton & Company for use on Estancia Zacazar. The brand is not used often now.

Source: Rhett Butler and Dennis Murphy at the King Ranch, 1992.

See brand numbers 1046 and 1048.

№ 1048   Brand name unknown
Robert J. Eaton & Company

This brand was registered in Paraguay in 1929 by Robert J. Eaton & Company for use on the Estancia Zacazar. This is the main brand used on both cattle and horses. The estancia covers 272,000 acres and carries 20,000 head of Hereford cattle. It takes 13.6 acres per head.

Source: Rhett Butler and Dennis Murphy, 1992.

See brand numbers 1046 and 1047.

№ 1049   Brand name unknown
W. J. Loops

This brand, placed on the left shoulder, was recorded in Brazoria County in 1953 by W. J. Loops of Freeport, Texas. His ranch is near Stringfellow, west of Freeport.

Source: Sheriff Joe King, Angleton, Texas.

№ 1050   M P Connected
C. P. "Matt" Matheson

The **M P Connected** brand on the right hip was recorded in Brazoria County by C. P. "Matt"

Matheson of Danbury, Texas, in 1964. His ranch was the old Hudeck Ranch north of Angleton. A Detention Center is now on the property.

Source: Sheriff Joe King, 1992.

Nº 1051   J H D Connected
Jim and Janie McDaniel Ranch

The **J H D Connected** brand was recorded in Wilson County in 1861 by James "Jim" Harrison McDaniel. He used the brand on the left hip and a crop and under bit in the left ear on straight Hereford cattle until 1935. At that time, James Hunter "Hunter" McDaniel took over the cattle operation and used the same brand and ear mark. In 1959, James "Jim" Hunter McDaniel Jr. took charge of the ranch and began phasing out the straight Herefords in favor of a Hereford-Brahman cross. The ear mark on crossbred cattle changed to a swallow fork and under bit in the left ear. The brand remained the same and is now recorded by Jim and Janie McDaniel and used on their ranch near McCoy, Texas.

Source: Jim and Janie McDaniel, 1992.

Nº 1052   T Anchor
W. C. Tiller

The **T Anchor** brand was recorded in Nueces County in 1939 by W. C. Tiller of Peternilla and Robstown, Texas. The brand was placed on the right hip of Hereford cattle. W. C. was the father of Jimmy Tiller, who bought several Longhorns from the King Ranch. The Tillers—Jimmy, Lee, Jim, Travis, and Richard—are pilots and own several helicopters that they use to spray and work cattle.

Source: 1993 at Tiller's ranch near Alice, Texas.
See brand number 1053.

Nº 1053   Quarter Circle J
Jimmy and Martha Tiller.

This brand was recorded in 1949 in Nueces County by Jimmy and Martha Tiller. They now live on a ranch near Alice, Texas, in Jim Wells County where the brand is recorded. Tiller is a rancher, minister, pilot, and farmer. He works a lot of cattle in South Texas by helicopter. This brand is used on his Longhorn herd and on Brahman cattle in the feed yard.

Source: 1993.
See brand number 1052.

Nº 1054   Half Circle Top J
Guy L. Jeanes II

The **Half Circle Top J** brand was recorded in 1939 in Liberty County and is used by Guy L. Jeanes II of Dayton, Texas. He and his two sons operate 2,500 acres with 250 registered Brahman cows.

Source: Guy L. Jeanes II, Dayton, Texas, 1993, with the help of Delores Parker of Decatur, who learned of my collection on a VIP tour of the King Ranch.

Nº 1055   Brand name unknown
Lenus Radford

This brand was recorded in 1928 in Kleberg County by Lenus Radford of Ricardo, Texas. This is a hand-forged iron.

Source: Fred Radford in Kingsville, 1993.

Nº 1056   T Five Connected
Cecil Burney

The **T Five Connected** brand was recorded in Nueces County, Texas, by Cecil Burney of Corpus Christi.

Source: Mrs. Inez True, Bishop, Texas, 1993.

Nº 1057   C U
Charles Underbrink

The **C U** brand was recorded in 1974 in Kleberg County by Cornelius Underbrink of Kingsville, Texas. The Underbrinks were early settlers in the county. Charles Underbrink records a stylized **C U** brand in Kleberg County. It represents his initials, and he uses it on his Limousin cattle.

Source: Charles Underbrink, 1996.

Nº 1058   8 0
Lester & Mary Alyce Stiles

The **8 0** brand was registered in Taylor, Williamson County, Texas, in 1876. It was placed on the left side of cattle and on the left shoulder of horses.

Source: Lester & Mary Alyce Stiles, 1995.

Nº 1059   Insignia of
Third Army Corp.
U. S. Army

This brand, the insignia of the Third U. S. Army Corps at Fort Hood, Texas, was given to my collection by General Paul Funk, Garrison Commander, and Colonel Roger L. Mumby, after a ranch tour in 1995. Larry Jobe, Corpus Christi Army Depot, delivered the iron to me at the King Ranch Visitor Center.

Nº 1060   I V
Owner unknown

The **I V** iron was given to me in 1996 by Ruth Wimberly and her husband, whose grandfather used this brand in North Texas.

Nº 1061   Diamond Dot
Wesley E. Signs

The **Diamond Dot** brand was registered in 1933 in Hayden, Colorado, by E. C. Signs.

Nº 1062   Rocking Chair
William L. "Bill" Arrington

I received the Rocking Chair branding iron from William L. "Bill" Arrington of Pampa, Texas, in 1997.

(The Rocking Chair brand was first recorded in Collingsworth County in the Texas Panhandle in 1877 by John T. Lytle and A.

akle. In 1882, it passed to Earl Spencer and J. John Drew, both of New York, who represented moneyed investors in England and Scotland and formed the Rocking Chair Ranche Company of London. The cowboys called it "Nobility's Ranch." Poor management led to the ousting of ranch management, and in 1893, the British owners appointed ex-Texas Ranger Captain G. W. Arrington as manager with directions to sell the ranch.

In December 1896, Continental Land and Cattle Company that branded the **Mill Iron** brand, bought the Rocking Chair Ranche. The new owners did not want the brand, so Cap. Arrington bought the brand and 1,200 head of cattle and drove them to the headwaters of the Washita River in Hemphill County where he established his own ranch. Cap Arrington died in 1923. His grandson, Bill Arrington, now operates the ranch and has offices in Pampa, Texas.)

Nº 1063   Y O
Charles Schreiner

The **Y O** brand was recorded by Charles Schreiner III in 1949 in Kerr County.

Source: 1997.

See brand 1025.

Nº 1064   N Bar
Norman Moser

The **N Bar** brand is recorded in Bowie County by Norman Moser of De Kalb, Texas. Moser is a commercial cattleman and operates as Norman Moser Land and Cattle Company.

See brand number 384.

Nº 1065   Turkey Track
J. A. Whittenburg

The **Turkey Track** brand is recorded in Hutchinson and Hansford counties by J. A. Whittenberg of Amarillo, Texas, and used on the Turkey Track Ranch.

Source: Mickey Richardson, Turkey Track Ranch, 1997.

(The **Turkey Track** brand originally came into the Texas Panhandle on a herd of cattle driven by Richard E. McAnulty in 1879. It is said that the brand was sometimes called the Rafter I. The **Turkey Track** brand has been passed down through other owners— C. S. Word & Jack Snider in 1881; and Hansford Land & Cattle Co. in 1882, of which J. M. Colburn of Kansas City was the founder. Colburn bought several herds in the Panhandle, and he used the **Turkey Track** brand on the combined herds. He hired the noted cowman, Cape Willingham, to manage his ranch, which he did for twenty years. Willingham and Colburn established a New Mexico ranch on a portion of the old John Chisum ranch, and the **Turkey Track** brand went to New Mexico.

In 1903, Willingham retired and went into the cattle commission business in El Paso. Price, Patton & Hyde acquired the Turkey Track Panhandle range, and soon Patton bought his partners out. By 1916, the **Turkey Track** brand had been closed out.

W. T. Coble began business in the Panhandle as a small operator in 1899, but he began buying ranches and soon had put together thirty-two pastures of the old Turkey Track Ranch, so he registered the brand in his name. He had one child and heir, Kathrine Coble Whittenburg. It is her descendants who now own the ranch and cattle carrying the **Turkey Track** brand.)

XIT   Nº 1066   X I T
Capitol Freehold Land and Investment Company, Ltd.

TSCRA Inspector Kelly Rushing left this **X I T** stamp iron at the Fort Worth office for me in 1997.

(The X I T Ranch covered 3,000,000 acres of land in ten Texas counties in the Panhandle and a half mile wide strip 350 miles long along the state line in New Mexico. It was established in 1884 on state land that was swapped to John V. Farwell, C. B. Farwell, Colonel A. C. Babcock, and Abner Taylor in exchange for building the Texas State Capitol in Austin, Texas. Their firm became known as the Capitol Syndicate.

They needed a great amount of money to fence the land, build headquarters, barns, pens, furnish water, buy stock, and hire men, so Farwell went to Britain in search of financial backers. He was successful, and The Capitol Freehold Land and Investment Company, Ltd. was formed. In the spring of 1885 when fencing was completed, 6,000 miles of wire fence had been built, and the famed trail driver, Ab Blocker, delivered the first cattle to the ranch—2,500 Longhorns. Blocker, who later became a TSCRA Inspector, designed the now famous X I T brand.

In addition to their Texas ranch, for eleven years the X I T owned and operated grazing land in Montana and South Dakota where they matured their cattle. The ranch had been in business for twenty-seven years when the syndicate members voted to sell. In 1912, the dispersal of the stock was completed and all of the X I T holdings had been sold or leased. It was the end of the largest ranch in Texas and the end of an era.)

Nº 1067   J
John M. Shelton III

The **J** brand is recorded in Hartley and Oldham counties by John M. Shelton III of Amarillo, Texas. The brand is used on commercial Hereford/Angus crossbred cattle. Shelton's grandfather, John M. Shelton, first used the brand as a **Lazy J** in 1900. John M. Shelton III was TSCRA President from 1984–1986.

Source: John Shelton at the 1997 TSCRA convention.

Nº 1068   Beehive
Deseret Ranch

The **Beehive** brand is registered in Florida by the Deseret Ranch, one of the state's largest cow-calf operations. Paul Genho, manager of all King Ranch cattle in the United States, came to the ranch from Florida.

Source: Paul Genho, 1998.

Nº 1069   M
L. C. Link Ranch

The **M** brand is recorded in Stephens County by the L. C. Link Ranch of Caddo, Texas.

Source: Gene Brandenberger, 1998.

Nº 1070 (CRM)   T Heart
Mary Virginia Todd Henson

The **T Heart** brand was recorded in Hemphill County in the Texas Panhandle by Mary Virginia Todd Henson. The Todd Ranch was founded in Hemphill County in 1895 by William J. Todd and his wife, Laura Virginia DeBusk Todd. They branded a **Circle and a Half**. After William Todd's death in 1921, his wife continued to operate the ranch with their son, William J. Todd Jr., who branded a **Heart A**. His sister, Mary Virginia Todd Henson, branded the **T Heart**, and her sister, Annie Laura Todd Nix branded a **Circle T**. Annie's son, William Dale Nix, succeeded his uncle in operating the ranch, and he branded a **Running N**. He and his son, William D. Nix Jr., now operate the Nix Cattle Company and Nix Ranch, Ltd. and continue to use the **Running N** brand.

Nº 1071 (CRM)   brand name unknown
Donnell Ranch

This brand is recorded in McMullen, LaSalle, and Duval counties by the Donnell Ranch, operated by James L. Donnell and his son, Jamie Donnell, fifth and sixth generation South Texas ranchers. James Lowe came to Texas from North Carolina in 1850 and settled in Atascosa County. Then in 1856, he moved to Rio Frio, the town later known as Dogtown and now called Tilden.

Jim Lowe's son, Boy Lowe, established the nucleus of the Dull Ranch, which his son-in-law, J. W. Donnell, later continued to increase in size and still operates. The Donnell Ranch runs crossbred cows and a yearling operation.

Nº 1072   Two J O
James B. Owen

The **Two J O** brand is recorded in Smith County, Texas, by James B. Owen of Tyler, Texas. Owen's original brand was a **Ram's Horn**, two Js (one reversed) joined together. When Owen formed a partnership with his son, John, he turned the brand over and added an **O** at the top.

James B. Owen was TSCRA President from 1990–1992.

Nº 1073   3 C
Ben H. Carpenter

The **3 C** brand is recorded in Dallas, Navarro, Anderson, Kaufman, Ellis, Freestone, and Henderson counties by Ben H. Carpenter of Irving, Texas. It is used on commercial crossbred cattle. Ben Carpenter was TSCRA President from 1966–1968.

Nº 1074   T L
T. L. Roach Jr.

The **T L** brand was recorded in Donley County by T. L. Roach Jr. of Amarillo, Texas, TSCRA President from 1968–1970. The brand was first used by Roach's father, T. L. "Jack" Roach, about 1930 on "keeper cattle." Jack Roach was also a TSCRA president from 1952–1954. T. L. Roach Jr.'s widow, Rosemary, her son, Tom L. Roach III, and daughters, Susan Higgins and Sheri Brosier, continue to use the brand on the Allen Creek Ranch in Donley County.

Nº 1075   Lightning
William C. Donnell

The **Lightning** brand is recorded in Brewster, Presidio, and Culberson counties by William C. Donnell of Marathon, Texas. Alfred S. Gage first registered the **Lightning** brand in 1886 and again in 1890. Donnell uses the brand on commercial and registered Santa Gertrudis cattle. William Donnell was TSCRA President from 1972–1974.

Nº 1076   J S
John S. Cargile

The **J S** brand is recorded by John S. Cargile of San Angelo, Texas, TSCRA President from 1980–1982. Cargile runs Beefmaster and Brangus cattle on the Cargile Ranch, Turner Ranch, and S Ranch, all in the San Angelo area, and on the A T A Ranch near Big Lake, Texas.

Nº 1077   J P
James L. Powell

The **J P** brand is recorded in Schleicher, Sutton, and Edwards counties, Texas, and also in Nebraska by James L. Powell of Fort McKavett, Texas. Powell raises commercial Hereford and Angus cattle and began using this brand in 1988.

Nº 1078 (CRM)   2 6 Bar
John Wayne and Louis Johnson

The **26 Bar** brand was recorded in Arizona in 1963 by Western movie legend John Wayne and partner, Louis Johnson of Stanfield, Arizona. It was used on registered Hereford cattle on their 26 Bar Ranch near Springerville, Arizona, after they purchased the old Milky Way Hereford Ranch and brand, the 99th brand registered in the state of Arizona. The 26 Bar Ranch consisted of 50,000 acres owned in fee and Forest Service leases. Their annual bull sale held at Louis and Alice Johnson's place near Stanfield, Arizona, brought buyers from around the country, and many **26 Bar** bulls went to new pastures in Texas. Following Wayne's death in 1979, Johnson and the Wayne Estate sold their holdings, including the ranch and the brand, to Karl Eller of Phoenix. The ranch is now owned and operated by the Hopi Indian tribe.

Source: replica of **26 Bar** branding iron donated to Cattle Raisers Museum by TSCRA Secretary-General Manager Don King, who was a buyer at a **26 Bar** sale.

Nº 1079 (CRM)   Unknown
Iena Seay

This brand belonged to a ranch woman, Iena Seay, in the Texas Panhandle during the early 1900s.

Nº 1080 (CRM)   Circle Dot
Quanah Parker

The **Circle Dot** was one of two brands used by Quanah Parker, the Comanche war chief-turned-cattleman on the Kiowa-Comanche reservation in what is now southwestern Oklahoma. During the 1880s and until his death in 1911, he had long-standing friendships with several Texas cattlemen, including Charles Goodnight. Burk Burnett, Tom Waggoner, and E. C. Sugg had half million-acre grazing leases on part of the Kiowa-Comanche reservation where they ran cattle during the 1880s and 1890s. Quanah was on Waggoner's payroll and often rode the fence lines in his wagon.

In recognition of Quanah's friendship with the Texas cattlemen, his **Circle Dot** was branded on one of the Longhorn steers in *The Herd*, belonging to the City of Fort Worth.

Source: Quanah's descendant, Ben Tahmahkera, had a **Circle Dot** iron made to brand the steer, and it was presented to the museum by Councilman Jim Lane on behalf of the City of Fort Worth.

Circle Within a Circle
Quanah Parker

The **Circle Within a Circle** brand was also used by Quanah.

Source: Tawana Spivey, Director of Fort Sill Museum, Lawton, Oklahoma.

Nº 1081   Half Circle 10
Saunders Ranch

The **Half Circle 10** brand is recorded in Parker, Palo Pinto, and Jack counties by the Saunders Ranch of Weatherford, Texas. It was first used in 1850 by Tom B. Saunders who came from Mississippi to Gonzales County, Texas, with his family in a covered wagon. They brought a small herd of cattle with them. In 1864, Saunders gave this brand to his son, George W. Saunders, on his tenth birthday. George Saunders started ranching as a teen when his father and brother left to fight in the Civil War. In 1871, he made his first of nine trips in fifteen years, trailing cattle from Texas to Kansas. He established the George Saunders Commission Company in 1888 and later founded Union Stockyards, both in San Antonio. He was also the founder of the Trail Drivers Association. He used this brand until 1933. It is now recorded by Tom B. Saunders V, the great-great-great-nephew of George W. Saunders.

Nº 1082   Hip O
J. E. Birdwell II

The **Hip O** brand, placed on the left hip, was recorded by J. E. Birdwell II of Lubbock, Texas, TSCRA President from 1986–1988. He began using the brand in the 1940s on cattle throughout West Texas and the Panhandle. His widow, Genene Birdwell, and son, John E. Birdwell III, a TSCRA director, recorded the brand in Bailey and Lubbock counties.

Nº 1083   K Bar
Robert R. King

The **K Bar** brand was recorded in Guadalupe County by Robert R. King of Seguin, Texas, who purchased a King Ranch Longhorn bull in 1989.

Nº 1084   F S
Fred Schuster

The **F S** brand was recorded in Hidalgo County by Fred Schuster of San Juan, Texas.

Source: Fred Schuster, manager of the Carl Schuster Ranch, 1989.

See brand number 1088.

No 1085   S C
Carl Schuster

The **S C** brand was recorded in Hidalgo County by Carl Schuster of San Juan, Texas. The Schuster Ranch raises polled and horned Santa Gertrudis cattle.

Source: ranch manager Fred Schuster, 1989.

See brand number 1088.

Nº 1086   Running W
King Ranch Inc.

This large **Running W** brand is a steer brand used at the King Ranch's Buck & Doe Ranch in Coatsville, Pennsylvania. Helen Kleberg Groves, Bob and Helen Kleberg's daughter, used it on bought steers or cattle raised on the Buck & Doe Ranch. It was also used on the Kingsville, Texas, ranch on Longhorn steers.

Nº 1087   3 Triangle
Buckeye Ranch

The **3 Triangle** brand was recorded in Matagorda County by the Buckeye Ranch.

Nº 1088   C S
Carl Schuster

The **C S** brand was recorded in Hidalgo County, Texas, by Carl Schuster.

Source: Schuster Ranch manager, Fred Schuster, 1989.

See brand number 1085.

№ 1089   Horseshoe J
Jimmy Jones

The **Horseshoe J** brand is recorded by Jimmy Jones of Greenville, Alabama. Jones bought several Longhorn bull calves, heifers, and cows from the King Ranch. He is a partner with Randy Hoke of San Antonio, Texas.

Source: 1988.

 № 1090 (CRM)   Bell A
John MacLoughlin

The **Bell A** brand was recorded by John MacLoughlin of the Bell A Ranch of Burns, Oregon.

*(Michael F. Hanley IV writes: "My great-grandfather, Michael Hanley, who had a ranch at Jacksonville, Oregon, first used the **Bell A** on his cattle in 1852. In 1857, he purchased "thoroughbred" Hereford cattle from the estate of former chief factor of the Hudson Bay Company, John MacLoughlin. Before he returned home with his cattle from the territorial capital at Oregon City where the auction was held, he recorded the **Bell A**. The **Bell A** brand is believed to be the second oldest recorded brand in Oregon. It has been in continuous use on Hanley cattle since that time and the famous Bell A Ranch at Burns, Oregon, is named for the brand. This particular branding iron is a calf iron and was made by me and has branded hundreds of cattle on our Jordan Valley Ranch in southeastern Oregon.")*

 № 1091 (CRM)   9
William Bryant

The **9** brand was recorded in Midland County, Texas, by William Bryant. Bryant bought his first land in Midland County from T. W. and J. S. Lanier in 1905. He recorded the **9** brand on the left hip at that time and used it until his death in 1921. When his ranch land was partitioned, his six children drew lots for the location where each would place the **9** brand on cattle. When this iron was added to the museum's collection in 1991, second, third, and fourth-generation family members still used the brand in Midland County.

 № 1092   Brand name unknown
Juan Maria Mailhos

This brand was registered in 1890 in Colonia, Uraguay, and now belongs to Juan Maria Mailhos, who sent this iron and another to me at the King Ranch after seeing my branding iron collection at the Cattle Raisers Museum.

See brand number 1093.

№ 1093   X W
Juan Maria Mailhos

The **X W** brand is used by Juan Maria Mailhos of Colonia, Uraguay, and was first registered in 1890. The handle of this iron had been cut off when it arrived at the King Ranch with iron number 1092.

Source: Juan Maria Mailhos.
See brand number 1092.

 № 1094   Brand name unknown
Dan Mitchell

This brand was recorded in Wharton County at El Campo, Texas, by Dan Mitchell.

Source: Wharton County Deputy Sheriff Peewee Mitchell and his wife, 1991.

 № 1095   J K Connected
Sheriff Joe King

The **J K Connected** brand was recorded in 1953 in Chambers and Liberty counties by Sheriff Joe King of Brazoria County.

Source: Sheriff Joe King, Angleton, Texas, 1991.

№ 1096   M
E. J. King

This brand was recorded in Chambers and Liberty counties in 1953 by E. J. King, father of Sheriff Joe King.

Source: Sheriff Joe King, Angleton, Texas, 1991.

Bibliography

It has been more than thirty years since I interviewed Leonard Stiles for the first time at the King Ranch west of Kingsville, Texas. His branding iron collection was in full swing at that time, and I wrote articles about it in several magazines, including *The Cattleman* and *The Quarter Horse Journal*. I returned many times after that and enjoyed Leonard and Mary's hospitality, as well as that of Tio Kleberg and his staff. In the years before and since, I have also written stories about many of the ranchers and ranches represented by the "ironclad signatures" collected by Stiles. And I wrote of Leonard's life and work with both the TSCRA and the King Ranch. Those articles appeared in several issues of *The Cattleman* and are repeated here. This book evolved from all those interviews and stories and from Leonard's hard work as the collector.

Much of the information included here came from his files and from *The Cattleman* magazine whose many issues have recorded the history of the industry in Texas and the West since 1914. Each article has been invaluable. Two in particular helped to lay the foundation for the story of the development of the cattle business — "Texas Cattle Origins" by Dan Kilgore and "In Search of the Origins of the Texas Cattle Industry," by Doug Perkins. Another good source was the *Southwestern Historical Quarterly* in which Ray August wrote "Cowboys v. Rancheros: The Origins of Western American Livestock Law."

I also gleaned many facts from booklets, newspaper clippings, obituaries, and personal letters and notebooks full of notes. Leonard must have envisioned the possibility of this book from the very beginning.

Jane Pattie

Books

Adams, Ramon F. *Western Words: A Dictionary of the American West*. University of Oklahoma Press, Norman, 1968.

Alba, Victor. *The Horizon Concise History of Mexico*. American Heritage Publishing Co., Inc., New York, 1973.

Baldridge, Melissa, editor. *Visions of the West*. Gibbs-Smith Company, Salt Lake City, 1999.

Barrett, Neal Jr. *Long Days and Short Nights*. Y-O Press, Mountain Home, Texas, 1980.

Brenner, Anita. *The Wind That Swept Mexico*. University of Texas Press, Austin & London, 1943.

Brown, Dee and Martin F. Schmitt. *Trail Driving Days*. Charles Scribner's and Sons, New York, 1952.

The Cattle Industry of Texas and Adjacent Territories, 1895. Antiquarian Press, Ltd., New York, 1959.

Clark, Mary Whatley. *A Century of Cow Business*. Texas and Southwestern Cattle Raisers Association, Fort Worth, 1976.

Clayton, Lawrence. *Historic Ranches of Texas*. University of Texas Press, Austin. 1993.

Dobie, J. Frank. *Cow People*. Little Brown & Company, Boston and Toronto, 1964.

_____. *The Longhorns*. Little Brown & Company, Boston, 1941.

_____. *The Mustangs*. Little Brown & Company, Boston, 1934.

_____. *The Vaquero of the Brush Country*. Southwest Press, Dallas, 1929.

Douglas, C. L. *Cattle Kings of Texas*. Branch Smith, Inc., Fort Worth, 1939.

Emmett, Chris. *Shanghai Pierce: A Fair Likeness*. University of Oklahoma Press, Norman, 1953.

Ford, Gus L. *Texas Cattle Brands*. Clyde L. Cockrell Co., Dallas, 1936.

Foster-Harris. *The Look of the Old West*. Viking Press, New York, 1955.

Gard, Wayne. *The Chisholm Trail*. University of Oklahoma, Norman, 1954.

Gressley, Gene M. *Bankers and Cattlemen*. Alfred A. Knopf, New York, 1966.

Haley, J. Evetts. *Charles Goodnight: Cowman and Plainsman*. Houghton Mifflin Co., Boston, 1936.

_____. *The XIT Ranch of Texas and the Early Days of the Llano Estacado*. University of Oklahoma Press, Norman, 1929.

_____. *George W. Littlefield, Texan*. University of Oklahoma Press, Norman, 1943.

The Handbook of Texas. Texas State Historical Association, Austin, 1952.

History of the Cattlemen of Texas. Texas State Historical Association, Austin, 1991.

Hunter, Marvin J., ed. *The Trail Drivers of Texas*. Cokesbury Press, Nashville, Tenn., 1925.

Jordan, Terry G. *North American Cattle-Ranching Frontiers*. University of New Mexico Press, Albuquerque, 1993.

Lea, Tom. *The King Ranch*. Little, Brown and Co., Boston, 1957.

Malouf, Dian. *Cattle Kings of Texas*. Beyond Words Publishing, Inc. 1991.

Matthews, Sallie Reynolds. *Interwoven*. Texas A&M University Press, College Station, 1936.

Mora, Jo. *Trail Dust and Saddle Leather*. Charles Scribner's and Sons, New York, 1946.

_____. *Californios*. R. R. Donnelley & Sons, Crawfordsville, Ind., 1986.

Murrah, David J. *The Pitchfork Land and Cattle Company—The First Century*. Texas Tech University Press, Lubbock, 1983.

Nixon, Jay. *Stewards of a Vision—A History of the King Ranch*. King Ranch, Inc. 1986.

Nordyke, Lewis. *Great Roundup—The Story of Texas and Southwestern Cowmen*. William Morrow & Co., New York, 1955.

Nye, Nelson C. *The Complete Book of the Quarter Horse*. A. S. Barnes & Co., South Brunswick and New York, 1964.

O'Connor, Kathryn Stoner. *Presidio La Bahia*. printed by Von Boeckmann-Jones Co., Austin, TX, 1966.

Pearce, W. M. *The Matador Land and Cattle Company*. University of Oklahoma Press, Norman, 1964.

Robertson, Pauline Durrett, and R. L. Robertson. *Cowman's Country—Fifty Frontier Ranches in the Texas Panhandle 1876–1887*. Paramount Publishing Co., 1981.

Saunders, Tom B. IV. *The Texas Cowboys*. Dober Hill Ltd., an Imprint of Stoecklein Publishing, Ketchum, Idaho, 1997.

Schreiner, Charles III, compiled by. *A Pictorial History of the Texas Rangers*. Y-O Press, Mountain Home, TX, 1969.

Share the Legend of the West. Compiled and written by Carol Williams and Doug Perkins. Texas and Southwestern Cattle Raisers Foundation, Fort Worth, Texas.

Sinise, Jerry. *George Washington Arrington—Civil War Spy, Texas Ranger, Sheriff, and Rancher*. Eakin Press, 1979.

Sonnichsen, C. L. *Colonel Greene and the Copper Skyrocket*. University of Arizona Press, Tucson, 1974.

Stephens, A. Ray. *The Taft Ranch. A Texas Principality*. University of Texas Press, Austin, 1964.

The Stock Manual. George B. Loving, Publisher. Fort Worth, Texas, 1881.

Texas Almanac and State Industrial Guide. The Dallas Morning News, 1978–1979.

Vernam, Glenn R. *Man on Horseback*. Harper & Row, Publishers, New York, Evanston & London, 1964.

Wallis, George A. *Cattle Kings of the Staked Plains*. Wallis Publications, Melbourne, Florida, 1957.

Ward, Faye E. *The Cowboy at Work*. Hastings House, New York, 1958.

Whitlock, V. H. (Ol' Waddy). *Cowboy Life on the Llano Estacado*. University of Oklahoma Press, Norman, 1970.

Williams, J. W. *The Big Ranch Country*. Terry Brothers Printers, Wichita Falls, TX, 1954.

Wolfenstine, Manfred R. *The Manual of Brands and Marks*. University of Oklahoma Press, Norman, 1970.

Worcester, Don. *The Chisholm Trail*. Published for Amon Carter Museum of Western Art: Fort Worth, by University of Nebraska Press, Lincoln and London, 1980.

Index

Brands are indicated by bolding.

Lone Mountain Ranch, 147
Long, James, 63
Long, Jane H., 63
Long X, 111
Longfellow Ranch, 110, 137
Longhorn cattle, 6, 7, 8
Loop Heart Loop, 144
Loops, W. J., 148
Lorance, Ed, 132
Lorraine Cross, 124
Los Jaboncillas Ranch, 128
Louisville Land & Cattle Company, 66
Loustlout, A. J., 133
Love, Ben, 125
Love, Jack, 125
Love, Polly, 125
Loving, George B., 7
Lowe, Boy, 151
Lowe, James, 151
Lucas, Pryor, 127
Lucky 7 1 1 Ranch, 120
Luman, Jim, 106
Lundquist, Dave, 100
Lundquist Ranch, 100
Lundy, P. A., 54
Lykes Brothers Inc., 67, 134
Lynch and Stiles, 139
Lynch, Rodney, 139
Lytle, John T., 149

M, 50, 56, 96, 98, 114, 151, 153
M A Connected Half Circle, 98
M B Connected, 130
M C, 122
M H Connected, 114
M J, 89
M J Connected, 67
M K Connected, 111
M L Connected, 64, 66
M O R, 72
M P Connected, 148
M.R., 50
M Six, 104
M Y Connected, 111
Maca, John J., 130
MacLoughlin, John, 153
Maddy family, 9
Maddy, Harvey, 10
Magee, A. L., 111
Magee, I. D., 110
Maher, John, 104
Mailhos, Juan Maria, 153
Maltsburger, J. T., Jr., Ranch, 124
Maltsberger Ranch, 138
Maltsberger, W. A., 138
Mangum, Ted, 100, 103
Mann, William, 60, 108
Manzanet, Father Damian, 4
Maraposa Cattle Company, 104
Marcus Brothers, 94, 143
Marcus, Max, 95
Marion, Anne W., 66
Markham, Texas, 14
Marks, August Texas, 53
Marks, Emil H., 53, 108
Marks, Gothilf, 53, 108
Marks, Milo, 53, 108
Marshall, J. F., 139
Marshall, Sheriff Jack, 13, 15, 96
Marshall, M. W., 105
Marshall, Monte, 95
Marshall, R. P., 138
Martin, J. A. "Archie," 94
Martin, John & Son, 127
Martin, John, Jr., 127
Martin, John R., 97
Martin, Lee, 81, 82
Martin, Roy, 60
Martin, T., 58
Martin, T. J. "Jeff," 126
Martin, T. J., Jr., 127
Martin, T. J., Sr., 127
Martinique, 33
Marts, Kenneth, 141
Mascot Land & Cattle Company, 89
Mashed O, 60, 136, 143
Masterson, Harris, 105
Masterson, R. B., 134

Matheson, C. P. "Matt," 148
Mathis, Gary, 116
Mathis, J. M., 67
Mathis, T. H., 67
Matthews, Harold H., 131
Matthews, J. A., 119
Matthews, J. A., Ranch Company, 119
Matthews, J. L., 131
Matthews, Joe B., 19
Matthews, John, 85
Matthews, Peeler, 131
Matthews, Sallie Ann Reynolds, 111, 119
Matthews, Watkins Reynolds, 119
May, Albert J., 94
May, Grover, 94
May, Robert, Ranch, 138
McAdams, Warden C. L., 64
McAdams Cattle Company, 145
McAdams, Doyle F., 145
McAdams, J. W., 145
McAdams, Jim, 145
McAnulty, Richard E., 150
McBride and Stiles, 73
McBride, Peter, 39, 40
McCan, Claude K., 104
McCauley, Ralph B., 71
McCloy, Bert, 80
McCloy, J. B. "Bert," 95
McConkey, Bob, 130
McCoy Ranch, 65
McCrosky, Voss, 88
McCulloch, Mrs. Artillery, 105, 106
McCulloch, John, 105, 106
McCulloch, W. I., 106
McCulloch, William Irvin, 105, 106
McDaniel, Jim & Janie, Ranch, 149
McDonald, E. L., 77
McDonald, R. D., 113
McDonald's Hamburgers, 143
McDougald, J. L., 123, 124, 130
McElroy, Morris, 109
McFaddin, Al, 104, 129
McFaddin, J. A., Estate, 104
McFaddin, James, 104
McFaddin Ranch, 104
McFarland, Robert, 59, 62
McFarland, Stan, 119
McGaw, Samuel, 60
McGill Brothers, 92
McGill, Frank, 92
McGill, Frank, Jr., 92
McGill, J. C. "Claude," 92
McMahon, Marie Edme Patrice de, 124
McMahon, Ruthel, 124
McMullen County Ranch, 8
McMurray, Captain Bill, 125
McMurrey, Captain W. C. "Bill," 98, 99
McNeal, George, 104
McNeal, John, 104
McNeil, Philip, 81
McNeill, Jordie, 61, 99
McNeill, Jordie, Sr., 55
McNeill, Mary E., 99
McNeill, Perry, 86
McNeill, Philip, 85, 86
McVea, Thomas, 142
Means, John A., 85
Meatblock, 77
Medford, Oklahoma, 9
Mee Ranch, 143
Melbourn, W. C., 88
Melgaard, Andrew, 94
Meninkie, C. H. 113
Mesopotamia, 1
mestizos, 3
Mewis, C. A., 100
Mewis, Colbert A. "Boody," 100
Mexican brand, 99
Mexico, 2, 3, 57
Meyer, Leonard, 95
Meyers, Joseph F., 120
Middlebrook, R. O., 79
Middle East, 1
Middleton, Archie, 81
Middleton, David, 80, 81

Middleton, Mayes, 80, 81, 87
Middleton, R. M., 79, 81
Middleton Ranch, 81
Milk Way Hereford Ranch, 151
Mill Iron, 102
Mill Iron Rafter, 147
Mill Iron Ranches, 102
Miller, J. P., 110
Milligan Brothers, 55
Milligan, Cecil, 55
Milligan, Leonard, 134
Minondo, Maria Lucrecia Garcia de, 133
Mission Espìritu Santo, 4, 5
Mission Santìsimo Nomber de Marìa, 4
Mississippi River, 4, 28, 29, 30
Missouri, 6
Mitchell, Mrs. C. S., 99
Mitchell, Dan, 153
Mitchell, Mrs. I. N., 99
Mitchell, Deputy Sheriff Peewee, 153
Moller, Adrian, 83
Moller, Andrew, 83
Moller, C. A., & Son, 84
Moller, Gottfreidt, 83
Moller, L. J., 83
Monclova, Mexico 3
Moncrief, Monte, 40
Monkey, Santa Gertrudis sire, 27
Monte Cortado Ranch, 132
Moody, W. L., 97
Moore Brothers, 77
Moore, Dyer, 57, 98
Moore, H. H., 106
Moore, H. H., & Son, 106
Moore, Hilmar, 57, 59, 62, 77
Moore, J. F. D., 98
Moore, John, 77
Moore, John M., 98
Moore, John M., Jr., 77
Moore, John M., Sr., 77, 98
Moore, Junior, 103, 104
Moore, Lottie Dyer, 77
Moore, Mrs. Lottie Dyer, 98
Moore, Louise Mussey, 136
Moore Ranch, 72, 98, 106
Moore, W. N., 72
Moore, Warren, 72
Moorhouse, Bob, 117
Moran, Jo, 138
Morgan, C. M., 125
Morgan City, Louisiana, 28
Morgan, Rand, 111
Morgan, Sam, 93
Morocco, 33, 40
Morrison and Briscoe, 55
Moser, C. O., 91
Moser, Chris, 91
Moser, Norman, 91, 150
Moser, Norman, Land and cattle Company, 91
Moss, Charlie, 85
Mount Albin Ranch, 116
Moyle, John C., 69
Muil, R. S., 119
Muil, Mrs. R. S., 141
Mumby, Colonel Roger L., 149
Munson, Armour, 83, 112
Munson, Bascom, 73
Munson, Houston, 54
Munson, Houston, Jr., 54
Munson, Houston, Ranch, 55
Munson, J. W., 54
Munson, Joe, 112
Munson, Mrs. Joe, 112
Munson M, 73
Munson Ranch, 54
Murphy, Dennis, 148
Murray, Lee, 10
Muske, Hub, 106
Muske, Mrs. Hub, 105, 106
Muske, John Frederick, 106
Muske, Roy, 106
Muske, Rufe, 53
Mussey, Hart, 136
Myatt, J. L., 73
Myatt, Jesse Lee, 73

N, 130
N A Connected, 85
N Bar, 150
N Bar R, 144
N Connected A L, 96
N Crescent, 127
N H B Connected, 101
N N, 78
N Seven Connected, 75
N U, 135
N U Connected, 83
Nash Groce Ranch, 62
Nash Ranch, 59, 64, 67, 69, 101, 140
Nave, Mr. & Mrs. Buster O., 88
Nebraska, 6
Neches River, 4
Needville, Texas, 49
Netherlands, 1
Neuhaus, F. W., 138
Neuman, Carl, Ranch, 130
New, J. K. "Speck," 135
New Mexico, 3, 5, 7
New Spain, 2, 4
Nile River, 1
Nine, 57, 61
Nine Bar, 135
Nine Bar Ranch, 135
Nineteen Half Circle, 103
Ninety Bar, 81
Nix, Annie Laura Todd, 151
Nix Cattle Company, 151
Nix, John, 138
Nix, Johnny, 137
Nix Ranch, Ltd, 151
Nix, William D, Jr., 151
Nix, William Dale, 151
Nixon, Jay, 28
Norman Moser Land and Cattle Company, 150
Norris, Harry Allen, 77
North Africa, 12
North America, 2
Northern (tug), 28
Northern Headquarters Ranch, 61, 69, 86
Northington, Andrew, 78
Northington, G. H., Sr., 78, 79, 91
Northington, George, 80
Northington, George, Jr., 78
Northington, Mentor, 78
Northington, Mentor, & Sons, 78
Northington, W. A., 78
Northway, Hiram K., 127
Northway, Hugh P., 127
Northway, Dr. J. K., 40, 120, 127
Novacek, Jay, 145
Novak, Adolph, 100
Nunley, R. J. "Red," 53, 55
Nunley Ranch, 53

O, 78, 109, 118, 124
O 2, 134
O Bar, 69
O Cross Connected, 61
O H, 128
O H L Connected, 76
O J F Connected, 95
O K Bar, 133
O L F Connected, 122
O N, 75
O O, 117, 138
O O Bar, 70
O R Connected, 132
O S, 67, 145
O T with a Tail, 56
O U, 58
O Y Connected, 59
O'Conner Brothers, 92
O'Conner, Dennis, 92
O'Conner, Martin, 92
O'Conner, Tom, 92
O'Connor, Mrs. Blanche, 74, 75
O'Connor Ranch, 67
O'Connor, Sandra Day, 143
Oak Tree, 147
Oberhoff, T. W., 63
Odem, Dave, 110
Ogle, Clay, 93